This is a work of fiction. All the characters and events portrayed in this book are fictitious or used fictitiously.

RELIC OF WAR

Copyright © 2025 by Daniel Hatch

All rights reserved, including the right to reproduce this book, or portions thereof, in any form.

ISBN: 979-8-9920397-8-8

A portion of this book appeared in Analog Science Fiction:

Siege Perilous, November 2012

Cover Design by Jay O'Connell

Previous books:

Den of Thieves, Slow Space Series 1
The Long Game, Slow Space Series 2

Relic of War

Daniel Hatch

Timmy's War

I found the jar of green supercomputing nanotech goo first. Then I found Dave's body.

The goo was in a peanut butter jar on a long table in the middle of the dark loft. The loft was lit only by the flickering of fresh fire from the night's artillery bombardment, reflected off low clouds of smoke and dust.

I'd spent more than an hour digging my way through the rubble that blocked the entrance to the building and another hour clearing enough of the stairwell to get to the top floor. It chewed up most of my favorite little plastic shovel, but I had a feeling it would be worth it.

I didn't know the half of it.

The little peanut butter jar was the kind my mother kept in her cupboard, and that made it hard to resist. I'd been hungry ever since the day the last refugee buses left the city and things shut down.

I unscrewed the top and shined my little penlight inside. I was afraid I'd find nothing but mold.

Instead I found about two tablespoons of viscous green stuff that glowed with a flickering greenish light. The light revealed layers and layers of hidden depths. I didn't panic – I'd spent too much time scavenging through the ruins of the shelled city for that. But this was something strange and new and frightening.

And it did not look like peanut butter.

More frightening was Dave's body – but only because I didn't see it at first.

When I put the jar down on the table and stepped back, I bumped into it. I turned and saw something large and movable – a dark figure in a big desk chair with wheels. All my insides turned to water.

But that's the kind of thing that happens whenever you are surprised by the dead, no matter how well-prepared you are. It's involuntary. It happens. You learn to get a quick grip on yourself, calm your breathing, and move on.

"Hey, man," I said. "You don't look too good."

I ran my light over him. He was big and he had long dark curls, a thick beard, a round nose, and rolls of fat.

And pinned to his jacket was a note that said: "Read me."

A yellow flash of light filled the loft, pouring in from four high windows on one side of the space. I ducked down below the table and started counting.

"One Mississippi ... two Mississippi ... three Mississippi ..." It was a reflex now, after weeks of artillery shelling. Two Mississippis was enough to mean safety – almost half a mile of distance from the blast. Three meant it wasn't even directed at my neighborhood.

KA-KA-KA-BOOM!!!!

The windows rattled, the floor vibrated.

"That was a big one," I said. "Someone isn't sleeping well tonight." I tried to drive away the image of civilians caught under the barrage, but I couldn't.

It was a 150mm howitzer. I'd learned the differences among them all since the general started smashing the city – the 150mm howitzer, the 100mm rail gun, the 90mm rocket, the 81mm mortar, and most small arms.

The light had illuminated the body with ghoulish intensity. And the note.

I shivered and stood up. "OK, I'll bite."

I grabbed the note and tore it from the pin.

"To the Little Guy," it read inside.

A chill ran up my back. I'm just 160 centimeters tall in my bare feet. It gave me an advantage scavenging wrecked buildings of the city – I could get in and out of places larger scavengers couldn't.

"Looks like I had a stalker," I said.

The light trembled in my hand as I read on.

"I hope you are the one reading this note. Barney and I have been watching you with my drone cameras as you went through the buildings this week. I was hoping you would get here before it was too late. But I'm out of insulin now and I've been peeing like crazy all day."

That would explain why the loft smelled like a men's room at the train station.

"So I may never get to meet you and you may never get to save my sorry butt. That stuff in the jar on the table is what they're calling cog oil. It's nanotech that thinks – information processing is embedded in its microchemistry. I managed to get it out of the labs before the war came through. I was in too much of a hurry to sync it up, so it's just raw cogs. No database. And no cloud connection since they took down all the satellites."

I reached over and grabbed the peanut butter jar and looked inside again. The flickering glow continued.

What was going on in there?

"But it's still good stuff," the note said. "You'll find it very useful. I don't know if I still have any family left, so everything I have here is yours now. That is, if you're the Little Guy. If you're just another loser looter, watch out for the booby traps. And if you work for that son of a bitch who's blowing up my city, I hope you miss the big one.

"But Little Guy, I'm betting on you. You've got real spirit. I'm starting to feel like crap now, so I'll just say good luck to you. Because all mine has finally run out. Diabetes is a bitch.

"Best wishes, Dave."

I looked at Dave's face, relaxed in the long sleep of death.

And there it was, this awful war in person.

Dave was no soldier – not for the general and not for the rebels. He wasn't killed by an artillery bombardment or a drone or a sniper or a machine gun.

He was an ordinary person like me and the other survivors, struggling to stay alive in the wreckage of a civilization that was tearing itself to tiny pieces. And he had died because one of the fragile threads that held people together and kept us all alive had broken.

Nothing more. Nothing less.

And I knew that it could just as easily have been me in that chair, despite everything I was trying to do to prevent it.

**

They invented nanotech on a Tuesday and the war broke out on a Thursday.

That's what everyone said – in that way everyone says things whether they're exactly true or not. It was close, though. I barely thought about it now, but a few things still stood out. The stories on the newsbooks before and the things people said afterward.

We had it. The people who didn't have it wanted it. And they were willing to fight us to get it. That was the main thing. Then they started blowing up the cities. After that, there wasn't much of anyone left to say things.

My mother and I made it from day to day here in Springfield as the war progressed. News from outside was scarce once they took out the satellites. The New Wireless World of the '90s wasn't so exciting after that.

Then the rebels came through, truckloads of them. The drones came after them, buzzing and coughing and spitting, firing missiles and shooting guns. City officials organized the evacuation. I got my mother and my sister seats on the bus and promised her I'd be on the next one. There never was a next one.

Then the general had come.

The first thing he did was to fire his big guns into the tall buildings in the city center – the bank, the hotel, the insurance company. People said there was no military purpose to it – he just wanted to show us who was the boss. They said he had taken some National Guard units and everything he could find in an armory and was trying to take over this part of the state.

No one from any other part of the state was in a position to stop him. And the rebels just hid.

And I spent the weeks that followed trying to stay alive.

* * *

The loft was like falling into heaven.

"Dave, you've got a lot of good stuff here," Timmy said.

I ignored the jar full of goo for now and went to work. I had learned to be systematic in my search through the abandoned living spaces of this neighborhood. The Wireless World meant solar cells on the rooftop and Walter batteries in the walls. And refrigeration in the loft.

"You have ice cream!"

And frozen steaks and chicken and pork chops and those irradiated mili-meals in the foil bags.

I almost cried. I'd never found a cache of food like this before. "They're going to love this when I get back home."

I dug two scoops of ice cream out and plopped them into a bowl. Then I found a spoon and scarfed it down like it was the last ice cream in the world – and it might just have been that. Butter pecan!

I opened a mili-meal. The self-heating stew gave off an aroma that masked the men's room smell that Dave had left. I used the spoon to fill my belly, opened the pack of biscuits and smeared them with butter and honey, and swallowed them almost whole.

When I was finished with the apple cobbler, I carefully placed the coffee in my jacket pocket and clasped it shut. Coffee was good for trading. Then I exercised all my discipline to turn away from the next mili-meal and save it and all the other food for another day – even though hunger still clawed at me from inside.

"Time to make an inventory," I said.

I worked my way methodically around the loft. There were treasures galore. Books – ink-on-paper books. A video tablet with gamer controls. A 3-D printer – an old one, big and clunky enough to require some planning and engineering to get out the loft window and down to the street if we were to carry it to the house. Clothes – Dave's oversized coats and a pair of well-worn boots.

Another flash. Another count. Another KA-KA-KA-BOOM! This one slightly closer. The dark business of the night – random shellings to keep people frightened.

I returned to Dave, resting timelessly in his chair.

After a while the dead become familiar and unremarkable. Still deserving of respect, of course.

"Let's see what you've got here," I said.

I went through Dave's pockets. I found a security badge with his photo on it and the name David Berringer stamped across it in big letters and Panda Tech in smaller letters. There was a wallet that flickered to life at my touch, then went dark when it realized it wasn't Dave's touch. And there was a plastic device with the name "Gluvax" embossed in one face – I figured it had something to do with Dave's diabetes.

Then I tapped on the jar.

"Anyone there?" I asked.

"Hello!" said a voice.

I almost jumped a foot.

* * *

"My name is Barney. You must be The Little Guy. I see you."

I looked over the peanut butter jar and saw two jointed metal eyestalks, poking out of the top, pointing at me.

"My name is Timmy and you can drop the 'Little Guy' thing," I said. "It's annoying. And how did you get a name like Barney?"

"I have a number of recorded messages from Dave to answer your questions. Would you like to hear one?"

"Sure. I'll bite."

"Take a note," he said – the voice in my ear dropped an octave and fell into an obvious local accent. "Why Barney? It's an old tech joke. It's my dog's name."

"OK. I'm not sure why that's a joke."

"Dave told me it has to do with password protocols," Barney said.

"Sure," I said. "So what about those booby traps?"

"There are no booby traps. I have a number of recorded messages from Dave to answer your questions. Would you like to hear one?"

I frowned, but I don't think Barney noticed. Talking to this thing was going to get tedious.

"Take a note," said a husky, raspy voice. Dave's voice, I assumed. "There are no booby traps. If I made any, I'd keep setting them off myself. It's just a bluff, so don't worry. Help yourself to the goodies."

So I did. I pulled a big canvass bag out of my backpack and unfolded it. Then I began filling it. Mili-meals. Produce. The most important tech gadgets.

And clean socks! I stopped to pull my boots off and make a swap. There's nothing like clean socks when you haven't had any for two weeks.

When the canvas bag was full, I went back and took another close look at the peanut butter jar.

"I have an announcement," Barney said suddenly, almost making drop the jar. "I have determined that there is a 70 percent chance of rain in the next two hours."

I stuffed Barney and his jar into my backpack, strapped everything together, and headed back down the stairs to the street.

* * *

The air was sharp and chilly and smelled of gunpowder and dust. If it weren't so depressing, I would have loved it. I did like the intense joy of being alone in the dark in the night in a city that was empty and shattered. It was like nothing else in the world and no one else but me and a few others had ever seen or felt it.

A brand new world. Dangerous and full of shadows.

And sharply bounded. To the west was the interstate, sunk below street level, wide open to snipers and drone fire, a no-man's land filled with certain death in and out of downtown. To the east was the river, with the park along its banks at one end and the big expensive houses that used to belong to city fathers at the other. To the north was downtown – and the general with his army. To the south, in the narrow space between the convergence of the interstate and the river, was an obstacle too frightening to think about.

About couple square miles all told. Three wide boulevards ran north and south, a half dozen smaller avenues crossed them, and a couple diagonals broke up the monotony, forming little triangular parks where they intersected the grid.

Dave's loft was off one of the avenues. It had gone unnoticed and untouched because the block was obstructed at both ends by fallen apartment buildings. The general loved those big targets for his guns. I knew my way around, though, like how to get through between the row houses.

I'd found a few hidden jackpots that way. A car park filled with tools and equipment and smashed selfie-cars. A bodega still running on rooftop panels with food still in the coolers. Some nice homes with good stuff. Only a few dead bodies. Dave was my fifth.

Sixth, if you counted that guy with the phone in his hand and his head blown off by a drone over on Centennial Boulevard. But he was lying in the street, not waiting for me in the dark in a room with big windows.

"So what about those drones Dave mentioned?" I asked Barney as we came out onto East Boulevard from a narrow alley. "Any chance I can scout ahead?"

"All our drones have expired," Barney said. "I do not currently have sufficient capacity to maintain their operation."

"Too bad."

"I do detect several drones operating in the immediate area, however."

"What?"

"There are three to your north and two on the far side of the street. They are communicating by VHF using encoded data transmissions."

I leaned against the wall of a big brownstone building from another century with elaborate carvings in the corners and along the roof line. I looked up, but couldn't see a thing.

"Would you like me to hack into their communications? I have a 25 percent chance of doing so without detection."

"NO!" I said, then in a whisper: "Don't do that. Please don't do that. Is 25 percent the best you can do? I thought you were something new and special."

"I do not currently have sufficient capacity to accomplish that task with a higher chance of success."

"Let's just keep it chill until they find something else to do."

"Very well," Barney said. "I also detect a number of individuals moving up the street to your south."

"How many?"

"Seventeen. In two groups. One on each side of the street. Moving north."

Damn! Moving north meant they were probably rebels. Just my luck. I moved back into the darkness of the alleyway. Maybe they would just pass me by.

The street was not totally dark. Three streetlights powered by solar cells flickered erratically and gave me a view of the storefront on the far side. In front of the store was a selfie-car, abandoned by its rider weeks ago. And as I waited tensely to see what the rebels and the drones did next, the car suddenly came to life.

They do that from time to time. They build up a charge in the daylight. Their drivers suddenly reboot. The next thing you know, they start moving – and in less than a minute or so a drone comes along to put a rocket through the engine compartment.

The headlights came on first. Then the car pulled away from the curb in a sharp, short circle, casting garish blue light down the length of the alley and into my eyes.

The next thing I knew, eight guys with armor vests and helmets and really big guns were crowding into the alley, looking up at the sky, looking around in my direction.

And I was suddenly afraid they might shoot me.

* * *

I may be short, but I'm not stupid. I crouched down as low as I could, back against the wall, and began to whistle "St. James Infirmary."

It was hard. My lips were dry and I licked them quick. But I kept on going until someone hissed loudly and all the rebels stopped moving.

"Who's back there?" asked one of them in a harsh whisper.

"Just me," I said. "I'm not armed. Please don't shoot me."

"You some kind of a wise guy, whistling like that?" the rebel asked.

"No – just a musician."

"Come forward slowly and show your hands."

I did.

"You're just a kid! What are doing out at night? You trying to get killed?"

I'm 21 years old, not a kid any more, but I didn't disabuse him of the notion. "Just looking for useful stuff," I said. Then I added: "Hey, did you know there's a bunch of drones flying overhead around here?"

"Drones? How do you know?"

"I saw them earlier," I said, lying. "Three towards downtown, two across the street."

"Damn! Someone tell O'Brien –"

I heard a WHOOOOOOSSSSHHH and a BANG! We'd found the drones. Or rather, the drones had found us. And popped off a missile to see what it could do.

"Back – back – back!"

The rebels pushed me towards the far end of the alley. I just barely grabbed my bag of loot.

Then the mortar shells began to rain on the street in front of us.

Hot flashes of fire, chest-pounding-ear-blocking waves of sound, marched up the boulevard. I pushed past the rebels. Because I knew where the alley came out.

"Follow me," I said as I passed the leader. "If you want to live …"

I didn't care if they followed at me. At the moment, I was kind of angry with them. Because they were coming close to getting me killed.

A minute later, we were out the other end of the alley into the space behind Dave's loft. The mortar explosions were muffled. The smoke rose in thick clouds illuminated by orange flames over the triple-decker apartment buildings. Porches sagged in the shadows. Windows rattled. Pieces of metal roof flashing clattered to the ground.

The top floor of one of the buildings erupted in flame.

It was Dave's loft.

My heart sank at the treasure I had left behind. Dave's funeral pyre blazed brightly, illuminating the alley and casting dancing shadows along its length.

"Which way are you guys heading?" I asked the leader.

"Into the city. If we keep up the patrols, we own the turf. My name's Zack, by the way. Do you know your way around here?"

"Actually you're on my turf," I bragged. "I know every street. Every alley. Every house."

"You want to tag along and help guide us?"

"And see if I can catch some more mortar shells? I don't think so. Besides – I've got to get my loot back home before the sun comes up and the snipers come out."

"Then how about we talk for a few minutes about what's up ahead?"

"Maybe we can make a deal," I said. "Got anything good to eat?"

About twenty minutes later, I had a couple containers of self-cooking beef stew and Zack had a detailed map of the city between here and the trolley line that marked the outer edge of downtown.

He gave me a salute as we parted ways.

But I was still pissed at them. They'd almost gotten me killed. And they'd gotten Dave's loft blown to smithereens.

As I slipped from shadow to shadow, Barney's voice spoke from my backpack: "I have an announcement. Using recent observations of the impact of military ordinance on permanent structures, I have calculated the explosive force and tensile strength of several modes of construction and ordinance size."

* * *

I heard three more mortar attacks as I made my way south, away from downtown and away from the rebels. At least I hoped I was moving away from them.

There were obviously more squads out there tonight. That was why the mortars were still thumping around.

They called themselves the Kung Fu Pandas.

"I'm not just a big fat panda," Zack had said. "I'm the big fat panda!"

I had no idea what he was talking about, but he said it with enough confidence to make even me feel good. They said the general didn't have much manpower, just the big guns. They were sure if they could get enough fighters in close enough, they could take the guns out. Some day. Maybe in a week or two.

I was somewhere a few blocks away from Dave's loft and quite a few more from home when I felt the hot yellow flash on my ears and the back of my head.

"One Mississ – "

The blast lifted me up and threw me a half dozen feet. The bag of loot stayed put. Tiny rocks lifted off the ground stung my face and hands. I looked over my shoulder and saw the stone front of an old building lean out over the street, then collapse straight down into a pile of rubble with dust blowing out in every direction.

I grabbed the loot and ran.

"Barney, are there any more drones around?" I asked.

"There is one drone," he said. "Directly overhead."

Another hot yellow flash bloomed to my right, in one of those pocket parks. It illuminated what was left of the leaves and branches of the trees. Then the splinters blew out in every direction. I put the loot bag up on end and hid behind it.

Then I ran some more.

Three more blasts came after me. Each one missed by just enough to avoid killing me.

We talked about this from time to time. It was one of those morbid things that come up in a war. The general's gunners had perfect maps of the city and computer fire control that would let them dial up any target they wanted to hit. And yet their bombardment seemed so random. What were they shooting at? What were they up to? Were they on drugs or drunk on wood alcohol? It didn't make sense. But it was war ... and nothing made sense.

Then they stopped.

The silence was not really silent. My ears screamed a high-pitch whine, like little motors were spinning away inside my head. I felt it, though. Like a down comforter – weightless and enfolding.

I looked around. I'd reached the end of the block and a wide cross avenue opened before me. The kind of empty space that always gave me the creeps because there was no place to hide from the drones or the snipers.

But this was just any open space. On the far side of the avenue was a large complex building of poured concrete and hanging glass walls, a marbled plaza, and a broad parking lot where a handful of selfie-cars sat silently.

I knew what this place was. The obstacle that was so frightening that no one spoke about it.

Inside the plaza in sunken courtyards, beneath the building in an empty parking garage, in the drainage swales, in every barren depression that would hold them, churned a horror that carried a dread name we never said aloud.

Gray goo.

***

The three of us sat under the marquee of an upscale apartment building, contemplating the problem of runaway nanotech – me, Barney, and Dave's ghost.

"Warning," Barney announced loudly in my ear. "My signal monitoring systems detect a large mass of undifferentiated nanotech assemblers in close proximity to the south. We are currently within the minimum approach range for such technology."

"A little late in the game, isn't it?" I said. "And everyone in town knows there's gray goo over there. It's how we knew the war had arrived."

"I recommend withdrawal to a safer range," Barney said. "At least 100 meters to the north."

"You mean back where the artillery drone has me sighted in?"

"That drone has withdrawn to a safe range," Barney said.

"I'm sure he has, but I'm not taking any chances. If the goo was going to get me here, there wouldn't be weeds in the planters along the sidewalk. So what can you tell me about that stuff?"

"I have a number of recorded messages from Dave to answer your questions. Would you like to hear one?"

"What are my choices?"

Barney went through a brief list and I picked what sounded like the most useful one.

"Take a note to the Little Guy," said Dave's ghost. "Stay away from that gray goo. It's nasty. As soon as it hit, we started to shut down the lab and get the hell out of Dodge. No one knows who used it on us. Reports said it was hitting all over the country – from Maine to Texas to Seattle. Someone is getting serious about the next stage of the game. And they don't want the U.S. to be in a position to stop them."

"How about another one?" I said.

Barney queued it up.

"This stuff is incredibly primitive compared to cog oil," Dave's ghost said. "Cog oil is a generation or two beyond it. The goo is just raw assemblers. Cog oil has the whole information processing system built in. It doesn't just replicate and make stuff. It's the computers that control everything. All in one integrated package. Of course, that means the cognitive side slows down when it's making stuff. And vice versa. Life is all about choices."

"Very useful," I said. "Didn't he tell you some way to turn it off?"

As I watched, a shadow came scurrying up the street. At first I thought it was a rat, but when it got closer I could see it was a muskrat from the river.

The muskrat crossed over to the wrong side of the street – the one with the gray goo. It continued on up to the plaza, then did one of those stupid things that animals do because they don't know things. It got within reach of the goo.

A tendril about two feet long reached out of the pool of goo around the fountain in front of the main building. It swung around, lashed out at the muskrat, doubled its length, and snagged him.

It separated itself from the goo in the pool, surrounded the animal, and shivered for a moment. Then it set about the work of disassembling its prey.

It made my skin crawl, but I couldn't stop watching it.

Barney found another message.

"When they first started thinking about nanotech, they scared themselves silly over gray goo. Runaway assemblers could devour the earth and turn the entire planet into copies of itself. Like a bacterial plague, only faster, more powerful, more destructive. But as they got into the details, they realized that it wasn't that simple.

"Assemblers need to self-repair. They need energy sources. They need complex molecules as feedstock. They need metallic crystals for structural engineering. There's a limit to what a mass of goo can do. And without programming, it isn't very effective at finding the resources it needs. So it's just scary. Don't step in it. Don't fall into it. Don't get too close to it. But don't get hysterical about it. It's a terror weapon – and if you aren't terrified, it doesn't work."

"It works just fine on me," I said. "There isn't something that would activate it and make it expand its limits from where it, is there?"

"I do not have that information," Barney said. "And I do not have a recording from Dave that addresses it."

"Is there some way to turn those things off?"

"I do not have that information. Further investigation would be required."

"Have you ever gotten a close look at the stuff?"

"I have not," the cog brain in the jar said. "Dave's mobility was limited. So was mine."

"What could you do if you got close up to it?"

"I could analyze its internal informational organization," he said. "But I would recommend against moving closer to the gray goo than we are already."

I pulled the jar out of my backpack and opened it up. The glowing green and yellow light reflected off the marquee above us.

"So you're sort of the same as the goo, only smarter," I said.

"Exponentially so," Barney said.

"Lots of tiny little machines all working together. Why that green goop? What's up with that?"

"It provides a secure medium for operation of my nanoprocessors. Materials flow through a circulatory system. Individual nanoprocessors are unlikely to escape into the environment. Gray goo is its own medium – nanoprocessors bound together, exposed to the environment, the environment exposed to them."

"So if I got a spoonful of cog oil out of the jar, it would be as smart as you are?"

"Not entirely," Barney said. "But it would have its own information processing technology. It would communicate with the larger whole. It would still be a part of my functional unit – up to an undetermined range where communications would break down."

"So I've got a slingshot and some one-centimeter hex nuts that Tony gave me to hunt rats. Suppose I dripped some of your cog oil onto the hex nut and shot it over there into the plaza. Would that give you a better look at the goo?"

"I have a number of recorded messages from Dave to answer your questions. Would you like to hear one?"

"Sure," I said. "What Dave's ghost got to say about this one?"

"Whatever you do, Little Guy, don't try mixing cog oil and gray goo. No one knows what would happen. The big guys at the lab are worried that the goo would absorb the cog oil, duplicate its information structures, and acquire its capacities. They were working on anti-virus and anti-malware systems and when the war broke out, they started putting in overtime. No one told me what they'd come up with. Or how much of it they packed into our batch of the stuff. But don't take any chances.

"Steer clear of the goo and stay safe."

I frowned and sighed.

"You don't seem to be good for a whole lot of things," I said.

"My current capacities are limited," Barney said.

"Too bad."

After a while, I decided that the artillery fire was a safer bet than the goo.

I went through the ground floor of the upscale apartment building and out the back.

"Any drones?" I asked.

"I do not detect any," Barney said.

I stepped out into the alley and a buzzing and whirring device came flying down its length.

"Well I'm detecting one!" I shouted.

I pulled my slingshot out of my pocket and grabbed a hex nut. I pulled back, took aim, waited for the drone to line up on me and stopped drifting off its path. Then ...

WHAM!

Bits and parts of drone when flying in every direction. The main body continued on a flat trajectory and hit the wall. I grabbed my crowbar and smacked it a few times to make sure it was dead. Then I grabbed the pieces that were left and started running.

Just in time too – BOOM! BOOM! BOOM!

… and with a slow rumbling crescendo the upscale apartment building became a pile of rubble and a cloud of dust.

When the shelling stopped and the dust settled, I stepped out from the store entrance where I'd taken shelter and looked up and around for more drones. There weren't any.

"Bite me, you son of a bitch!" I shouted at the sky and at the distant gunner who'd blown up the apartment building. "I'm still alive!"

* * *

I came home as the low clouds of dust and smoke from the shattered city began to turn faint brown and yellow from the dawn light.

Tony met me at the door.

"Back off!" he said. "I have a gun!"

"Tony, it's me, Timmy," I called back.

"Hey, Tim, I'm sorry," he said as he slid back the locking bars that held the door in place. "I was nodding off and you woke me up. I didn't have time to look to see who it was. I'm still jumpy from Monday night – those guys were serious."

Not serious enough to keep you from nodding off, I thought without saying out loud.

Mr. Skorch's house was old. Nearly two centuries old. The whole neighborhood was like that. Big houses with big porches. Three stories high with gables at the top. No front yards, but they ran so far back from the street that you could easily get lost trying to find the back door if you came in the front. Block after block of the behemoths filled the spaces between the big boulevards, standing shoulder to shoulder on narrow lots. People walked everywhere or took the trolley when these places were built. Now they walked everywhere again.

Mr. Skorch was lucky. Half the places on this street had been hit by artillery fire in that first week, when the general was letting us know who was boss.

The big door rolled aside and Tony let me in. It was a garage door he'd salvaged from down the street and hung across the entrance to the house – a barrier against raiders.

Tony was a mechanic in a selfie-car barn – or had been before the war brought down the roof and set fire to the cars. He was one of Mr. Skorch's neighbors – or had been before the war brought down the trees in his backyard, which tore through the walls of his house.

He stuck an unlit little black cigar in his mouth. He'd been nursing it without smoking for at least a week now.

"We had a problem tonight. I'll tell you about it later. What did you get?"

He grabbed my duffel bag and carried it into the kitchen, where a camping lantern sat on the counter casting long shadows into the corners.

"Lots of stuff," I said. "Strange stuff."

"Look at all the mili-meals!" Tony said. "We'll be fat by the end of the week. And are those books?"

"Real ones. I'd have brought more, but they were too heavy.

There's two game tablets for the Hungarian brothers." Besides Tony and me and Mr. Skorch's family, living in the big old house were two of Mr. Skorch's neighbors and Carol, who used to work at the school.

"How much more stuff did you leave behind?" Tony asked.

"You don't want to know," I said. "The general blew it all up?"

"He did? That sucks."

I told him about the rebels and the mortar attack and Dave's loft getting lit up.

And he told me about the problem they'd had.

"These two guys came pounding on the door about midnight," he said. "Lazlo watched the door while I went up to the window upstairs to see who was there. They were all: 'Let us talk to the old man' and everything. So Mr. Skorch came up and they were all: 'You need to talk to us about making hooch.'"

"Hooch?"

"They must have found about his still," Tony said. "We've been trading that stuff down at the food mart for vegetables and cooking oil. You get some of the survivors like us down there every night. They were all: 'You look fat and comfortable and still in one piece – time to do your share.'"

"None of that sounds good."

"They said they worked for some guy – Paul Danton – who used to own real estate all over the place. He's got a big house by the park and a bunch of big guys working for him. They were all: 'We're here for the long haul' and said he was getting things organized."

"Is he now?"

"Final page was they want Mr. Skorch to crank out a couple liters of alcohol every day. They'll provide some of the raw materials – they had a big bag of sugar. But we have to come up with the rest. In return, they say they've got some way to keep us safe from raiders. And from the general."

"Did Mr. Skorch believe that?"

"I don't know. He went off to the basement talking to himself, cussing out this Paul Danton guy, cussing out the general. I guess he took them seriously."

"Just what we need," I said. "If the guns don't kill us, guys like this are going to nickel and dime us to death."

* * *

"I'd like to make a toast to the late great United States of America," Mr. Skorch said, lifting a tiny glass with a tiny amount of clear liquid at the bottom. "And make an elegy to the concept of the nation-state itself, which died along with it."

He threw the liquid into his mouth, swallowed hard, then wheezed and coughed.

"It's alcohol," he said.

The still bubbled and clicked and emitted strange smells as Mr. Skorch played with the valves and dials. When I was in school, his hair and beard were starting to turn gray. Now they were mostly white.

"It'll get better with time," he said. "But the U.S.A. won't, I'm afraid. The general is just one more sign of that. We have witnessed the end of what has been known as the Modern Era. Perhaps even of Western civilization itself."

Julie – Mr. Skorch's teenage daughter – and I sat on a lumpy couch on the other side of the basement from the still. Neither of us were much impressed with her father's oratory, but it didn't seem to restrain him.

Back after my mother left on the bus with my sister, Julie had found me scavenging a convenience store at the corner and recognized me from school. Mr. Skorch was a science teacher. His real name wasn't Skorch – just something with too many consonants that the kids shortened to a simpler form. He'd retired while I was finishing my classes. The war was not part of his retirement plan.

"Of course, the nation-state has been on the skids for a long time," Mr. Skorch said as he lifted a 20-pound bag of sugar off a shelf and lugged it over to the still. "They've been losing power for decades. First to the global corporations, then to the squillionaires, and then to the social-media movements."

"Don't mind my father," Julie said to me. "He just lectures like this to keep his mind off the war. My mother just cries."

"I heard that," Mr. Skorch said.

Julie was right, of course. All of us had different ways of coping with the collapse of the entire world we had known.

When I came in that morning, Marta – Mrs. Skorch – had fixed me a mug of stew and a cup of tea with a teabag that had already been used at least twice. She smiled, gave me a hug, then went up to her room. If you were still and the shelling paused, you could hear her crying most of the day and sometimes at night.

Julie and I had our own way of coping – we spent a lot of time in the sack together. It was purely a physical, last-boy-and-girl-on-Earth kind of thing, but it beat sitting around getting bored all day while waiting for an artillery shell to come through the ceiling.

"What nobody seemed to realize was that even though they didn't have much power to do things, nation-states had tremendous power to destroy things."

Julie grabbed my hand, pulled me up off the couch, and down

into the laundry room. She pulled at my belt buckle and undid it quickly while her father kept talking at the other end of the basement.

"And when they announced they'd solved the nanotech problems and made a working design, people's fears got the better of them. The weak and twisted men who found their way into positions of power realized their moment had arrived. And the rest is history ... or possibly the end of history."

We exercised the better part of passion for a while, as Mr. Skorch droned on.

"Most of this century has been an elaborate conspiracy by smart people to keep power out of the hands of stupid people. But sometimes, stupid wins," he said.

When Julie and I were through with our intense business, we wandered back down to the still. The amount of alcohol in the jar at the far end of the plumbing was pitifully small.

I pulled Barney's jar out of my backpack and unscrewed the lid. I looked inside – the green goo looked unchanged, flickering with artificial life.

"It hardly looks like the kind of stuff that would destroy the world," I said.

"What's that?" Mr. Skorch asked.

"Cog oil," I said. "The stuff that dreams are made of. It doesn't look like much. And it doesn't seem to do much."

Mr. Skorch came over and peered into the jar.

I told him about the loft. He sighed, shook his head, and sat down on a wooden stool.

* * *

"It's supposed to make stuff," Tony said. He had come in from the garage where he had set up his workshop. He chewed on the end of his unlit cigar.

"It's supposed to be a computer," said Mr. Skorch.

"It is," I said.

"Say hello, Barney."

"Hello, Mr. Skorch," the cogbrain said. "Hello, Julie. Hello, Tony. Hello, Timmy."

"Well I'll be damned," Tony said.

"They built this stuff with the voice embedded deep in the programming," Mr. Skorch said.

"That's what Dave says too," I said.

"Dave?"

I told him about Dave. "It was one of the notes Dave recorded," I said. "Barney learned to talk before he learned much of anything else."

"Tell him to make something," Tony said.

"Something like what?"

"I don't know. A knife?"

"Can you do that, Barney?"

"I do not have access to a database," he declared. "I would need a sample."

Tony pulled a worknife out of a scabbard on his belt. "How's this?"

I stuck the knife into Barney's jar. The cog oil flowed quickly up the blade and over the hilt, then surrounded the handle.

"Analyzing," Barney said. "Analysis complete. I would require two hundred grams of metal and an equal amount of plastic."

"I've got that," Tony said.

"And twelve hours," Barney added.

"Twelve hours?"

"My capacity is currently limited," Barney said.

"That's kind of a pain," Tony said.

"They started a war over this?" Julie quipped.

"What about alcohol?" Mr. Skorch asked.

"I can make alcohol," Barney said. "It requires water and sugar or other simple carbohydrates. Would you prefer pure alcohol, brandy, bourbon, or rum?"

"That's quite an assortment for someone without access to a database," Mr. Skorch said.

"Dave and I conducted several experiments into this matter," Barney said.

"Brandy would be a nice place to start," Mr. Skorch said. He fetched the ingredients, a funnel and a small hopper and a discharge tube that ran into an empty jar.

He filled hopper with sugar, poured water into the funnel, and stood back while Barney sent a tendril of cog oil into the hopper.

Then we waited. And waited. And waited.

After about ten minutes, the first drops of amber fluid came out of the discharge tube.

After another ten minutes, we had a dozen drops.

"How long to fill the jar?" I asked.

"Twelve hours," Barney said.

Everyone else moaned. I just sighed.

***

The dust was everywhere – in the air, on the ground, on the

furniture and the floors and the counters – and it got into everything. All that shelling, all those buildings, all pounded into dust, all the dust blown into the air. It got into your clothes and your food and your water. It got into the wrinkles in Mr. Skorch's face and made him look a hundred years old.

"This is the stuff that started the war," he said. "Nanotech combined with information technology in one toxic stew. The nanoprocessors form their own operating system and memory storage. If you use them to make stuff, they lose information capacity."

"That's what Dave's ghost said."

"So how do we increase its capacity?" he asked.

He was looking at me. He thought I knew the answer. I felt like an idiot – because I didn't.

"Dave recorded a number of notes on that subject," Barney said. "Would you like to hear them?"

"Thanks," Mr. Skorch said. "I'd love to hear them."

Dave's ghost explained that the way to control nanotech and keeping it from turning into gray goo was to limit its ability to replicate itself. With cog oil, the trick was platinum.

"Platinum?" Mr. Skorch asked.

"They included it in the molecular design," Dave's ghost said, ignoring Mr. Skorch. "In order to make more cog processors, you need platinum. It's not the kind of thing you find laying around, so they're not going to run away with themselves. But you can usually get your hands on some if you need it."

"Where do we find platinum?" Julie asked.

"A jeweler," I said. "There's a half dozen jewelry shops around here. But every one of them I've seen has been looted clean. As if anyone was going to need necklaces and earrings any more."

"Car fuel cells," Tony said. "There's some platinum inside those things. It's not easy to get out, though."

"Excellent," Mr. Skorch said. "We have a plan for the night. Or the beginnings of one."

"I can see if I can get some platinum out of a fuel cell," Tony said. "The Hungarian brothers can watch the doors."

"I can check out the jewelry shops," I said. "Someone may have missed something."

"And I can go with you," Julie said, defiantly. That was a surprise. Julie never went out at night.

Mr. Skorch didn't say a word, but gave her a look.

"I just don't want to listen to Momma weep any more," she said.

"Very well," her father replied. "But there's one more place I want you to go …"

* * *

The library was old and small and made of stone, with fluted columns on either side of the door. One of the columns had been knocked down – probably by the blast that had knocked over the apartment building next door.

The rain was coming down hard by the time Julie and I got there. My poncho was barely enough to keep me dry and only around my shoulders. We ran up the steps and squeezed through a door that someone else had already pried open.

Our expedition to the jewelry shops had come up empty. Professional looters – such as there were now – had picked them clean. Every drawer, every box, every cabinet. Everything was gone.

I pulled out my penlight and swept it around the library, mainly looking for squatters. Something skittered across the floor.

"What was that?" Julie gasped.

"A cat," I said. "I hope."

The rain ran through cracks in the ceiling, streaming down the walls, dripping into puddles in the middle of the single large room in the front of the building. In the rear were bookcases, empty now. A few piles of soggy books remained. The rest had probably been taken for tinder to help start fires. Dave would have been pissed.

Then, for no particular reason that I could figure out, Julie grabbed my hand and said: "Did you ever wonder what happened to your mother and your sister? Did you ever wonder where those buses were going or if they got there?"

"I try not to worry about those things," I said. "Because there's nothing I can do about them."

"Are you afraid they're dead?"

"Not afraid," I said. "But the thought has crossed my mind."

"Sometimes I think we're all dead," Julie said, letting go of my hand as she looked up at the domed ceiling. "That this is just the nightmare that comes afterward. That we're all waiting for lights to go out and the sound to fade away."

"I know that I'm alive," I said. "I'm breathing and moving and I can see things and I can think about what I'm doing. That's all it takes for me to know I'm alive. And I plan on staying that way as long as I possibly can."

"We all die, Tim. We're all already dead. The world is over. We're just waiting for our turn to check out."

"Yes, we all die," I said. "But we're not dead yet. And I don't plan on checking out. I want to see what comes next. I'm going to see what comes next." Then I felt a chill. All those were words, just words. Empty words.

She sighed, let her shoulders slump, and leaned back against a dusty bookshelf. "There is no next." she said.

"So why did my father think we should come here?" I asked.

"Because this place might have a database Barney could tap into," I said. "Anything that might boost his capacity."

"Right," she said dubiously.

I pulled the peanut butter jar out of my back pack. "All right, Barney, what do you hear in here?"

His answer was immediate. "Mr. Skorch was correct. There is a database in here and it appears to still be active."

"Wow," Julie said. "Sometimes my dad is right."

I tried to restrain a sudden rush of optimism. War is a game of disappointments. And it turned out I was right.

"There is a problem," Barney said.

"What kind of problem?" I asked.

"There's a problem?" Julie asked.

"One at a time," I said.

Barney spoke first. "The catalog system contains errors. 'Pride and Prejudice' was not written by H.G. Wells. 'Moby-Dick' was not written by Nathaniel Hawthorne. And 'I Robot' was not written by Alfred Bester. I know, because Dave owned hard copies of those books and he had me catalog them for him. This library has been hit by a dumb bomb."

"What's a dumb bomb?"

"Dave has recorded a note on that subject. Would you like to hear it?"

"Sure," I said.

Dave spoke. "Those dumb bombs are nasty. They go through a database and mix everything up. They don't erase anything, but they swap values, swap texts, swap amounts. All your accounting is false. All your scientific data is ruined. All your research sources are worse than wrong – they're corrupt. You might as well wipe the core and start over."

"Damn!" I said. "I was hoping this would be worth walking ten blocks in the rain."

"Twenty," Julie said.

"That's not good enough," I said. "There must be something else I can do. Didn't Dave leave any messages on how to make you do something useful?"

"Dave has recorded a note on that subject. Would you like to hear it?"

I frowned and told him to go ahead.

"The thing about artificial intelligence is that it doesn't work so good on its own," Dave's ghost said. "It really needs adult guidance. It won't think up solutions to your problems. It won't tell you why it isn't giving you what you want. It won't explain things unless you ask it the right questions – in the right order. It's a challenge. A big challenge. You really have to outsmart it if you want to get the best use out of it. You have to be smarter than the machine."

"Oh great," I said. "Now I feel really dumb."

"That's not much help," Julie said.

"Of course it's all my fault," I said. "Because who am I? Just a guy who couldn't make it all the way through college because the world blew up before I was finished. A guy who's small enough to fit in places in wrecked buildings and smashed houses to get the things other people left behind. A guy who isn't big enough to carry a gun and fight with the rebels."

"Stop, Timmy. Stop. Let's just do it. Right here on the books. Right here in the dust."

I looked at her – and suddenly I felt different. Something had changed. I knew what it was. We never had any real feelings for each other. We were just the last boy and girl alive in a dying city in a dying world and until the end came for us, we were going to squeeze out every last possibility.

But that was before. Now, thanks to Barney and Dave, we were no longer dying. There was a chance, however slight, that the world might go on. That life might find a way to pull us back from the grave we were living in.

And those weren't just words, they were real feelings. If I could just figure out a way to make the cog-oil do it.

And once there was a chance that there might be a future, the thing that pulled Julie and me together was gone.

I looked into her eyes. And almost as if she had some kind of telepathy, she knew. She looked away.

"We should go," she said.

"Right," I said. I stuck Barney's jar into my backpack. "Because there's nothing I can do to make the most dangerous machine ever made do what it's supposed to do. And because some dead guy says it's all my fault."

I kicked aside a shelf and sent a pile of books flying.

"Let's go," I said, "and see if I can find my way back home without any help."

"I have an announcement," Barney said. "I have determined the structure of another amino acid."

* * *

When we got home, trouble was already waiting for us.

Trouble wore a sharkskin jacket with a fur collar and fur lining that spilled out onto the lapels. Trouble had a double-swirled hairdo with sparkling lights embedded in the gel. Trouble had a name that I'd seen on big yellow "For Sale" signs slapped on the big empty buildings all over the city for the last five years.

"Tim, this is Paul Danton," Mr. Skorch said. Danton glared at Mr. Skorch, then at me. We had dared to interrupt him.

Everyone was sitting around the living room. The big house had a big living room with three big couches facing a big fireplace. The fireplace was cold and empty. Five guys with big guns stood in the corners. Danton stood in the middle of the floor.

Julie and I had come back from the library with wet feet and wet faces, but no one had let us take off our boots or dry ourselves off. They just shoved us onto one of the couches.

"As I was saying," Danton declared with straining emphasis, "this is how things will be from now on. There is no county. There is no state. There is no nation. No one will be coming to give us federal aid. Money is next to worthless and useless. This is the way life will be for all of us."

Mr. Skorch looked older than I'd ever seen him. Mrs. Skorch's eyes were red and she sniffled, but she had the good sense to stop crying. Tony and the Hungarian brothers were under the watchful eyes of two of the guys with the big guns.

"Without money, we are going to have to come up with something else to exchange value," Danton said. He strutted back and forth on the oriental rug, leaving bits of drying mud on the fabric.

"One of those things is alcohol. I know about you – you're a smart man, an educated man. You should be able to produce what we told you we needed. When we need it. I don't understand why you couldn't do what you were told."

Tony and the Hungarians seethed. You could see they didn't like the way Danton was talking to Mr. Skorch.

I felt the same way. But I had a different reason. Because I knew that Danton was wrong.

In my backpack, inside that peanut butter jar, was something that made him wrong. Something that changed everything. Barney was a pain. I had no idea how to use him right. I know I was doing everything wrong. But I knew what that green goo with the lights meant. The world had not ended and the story was not over and Danton was just wrong.

But I had the sense to keep my mouth shut. I didn't think he was in the mood for an argument.

"So we're going to give you more of an incentive," Danton said. He looked over at one of the tough guys with the guns, who strapped his weapon onto his shoulder and stepped forward.

"Is this your daughter?" he asked. Mr. Skorch nodded. Mrs. Skorch sobbed. "Good. She's going to come with us. And if she's nice, we'll even feed her. When we come back in a couple days, we'll see how you do with the alcohol. Then we might bring her back."

The tough guy stepped forward and grabbed Julie's wrist, lifting her up onto her feet. She looked at me with a silent plea for help in her eyes.

I jumped to my feet beside her –

– and WHAM! Someone behind me hit me in the back of the head with something hard, knocking me to the floor, where I lay stunned and immobile while Danton and his crew marched out of the room, down the hall, and out the front door.

* * *

An hour later, my head had stopped spinning, but there was still a spot on the back of my skull where it met my neck that hurt because the skin was broken. Mrs. Skorch had fussed around cleaning the blood off it for a while, but the bleeding had stopped and I didn't really need a bandage.

"Now what do we do?" Tony asked.

"Now I go get her," I said.

"Don't be foolish, Tim," Mr. Skorch said. He looked old and sad and tired.

"I'm not foolish," I said. "I'm not going to leave her there. And I've got the only thing we can use to help her right here in my backpack."

I pulled the jar out of my bag, and opened the lid.

"Barney, I don't know if you can do what I want, but the time has come to show your stuff."

I'd been thinking. I had a few ideas. I knew where Danton lived – in a big house on the edge of the park. And I knew I'd need something to find Julie when I got there.

I fished around in my pack for the pieces of the drone I'd shot down back by the gray goo the night before.

"Can you put this thing back together and make it fly? Make it into a drone I could use?" I asked the cog-brain.

"Place the pieces near the jar and I can analyze them," Barney said. I did as he said and waited a minute.

"I can fabricate a device similar in function to the original design," Barney said. "If you wish, I can fabricate several, depending on the size you wish them to be."

"Several? That would be great. How long would it take? And please don't say 12 hours."

"It would take 27 minutes to make one device with a mass of 12 grams," Barney said. "And 43 minutes to make several. Is that sufficient?"

"Does a dog have four legs?" I asked. "You bet it's sufficient. Get started. You can make them while we're on the move."

* * *

I couldn't take my eyes off the image on the screen that Barney was projecting inside the peanut butter jar.

Two men stood talking in a large hall with a huge fireplace and a roaring fire in it.

One was Paul Danton, with a glass in one hand and a bottle of brandy in the other.

One was a smaller man, wider in the shoulders, wearing military camouflage and a helmet with a star on the front – the general himself.

"You realize, don't you, that a good portion of those buildings are what's left of my real estate holdings?"

"Do you really think anyone is going to care whose name is on the deeds for those properties – assuming anyone ever finds them? They're certainly not going to trust the electronic records now that they've been dumb-bombed."

"I know what's mine," Danton said. "And I have it on paper, on maps, and with paper originals of the deeds and bills of sale and everything."

"You're putting a lot of faith in the restoration of some kind of civil order," the general said.

"I'm putting a lot of faith in you," Danton replied.

They went on like that endlessly. I'm not sure if there was a point to the argument. I'm not even sure it was an argument. It was just two strong men with big egos trying bully one another with creepy dominance games.

I'd made it to Danton's mansion by the park in less than an hour. Barney spent the time disassembling the optics and control circuits of the drone and reconfiguring them into a half dozen mechanical bugs with long legs, little black eyes, and whip antennas on their backs – one the size of my hand, two half that size, and three a quarter that size.

We got through the gate pretty easily. Barney extended a shaft of hardened green cog oil into the control panel and opened it up. I ran through the high grass of what had once been a manicured lawn, found a recessed entrance to a basement, and had Barney pull the same trick on the lock that he had at the gate.

I went through the door, then sat down on the floor and let loose the bugs.

Within a few minutes, I'd found the guards, the storerooms full of food and alcohol and supplies, the big hall with fireplace … and Julie.

She wasn't alone. A half dozen girls were all in one big room with a half dozen sleeping bags and floor mats and a padlock. The padlock meant nothing at this point. Barney poked around inside it and in a few minutes, Julie was making a loud whispering scream: "Timmy!"

"Everyone stay quiet and follow us," I said. The other girls looked at me like I was crazy, then ran out the door like I'd been speaking to them in Chinese.

"Doesn't anyone listen to me?" I said. "If only I were taller."

"I'm listening," Julie said.

"There are guards all over the place," I told. "We have to be careful."

We'd gotten as far as the door out into the yard when Barney's insect-drone started feeding me the conversation between Danton and the general.

We had to stop. I couldn't ignore them. What if they said something important? Julie was all jumpy and jittery and didn't want to wait, but I wasn't about to move just yet. So we stood there in the dim light of the door marker listening to the two men go on and on.

That was the mistake.

Two guards came out of a dark hallway and grabbed Julie by the arms.

"Who are you?" asked one of them.

"What have you got?" demanded the other.

He grabbed the peanut-butter jar out of my hand before I could react. My blood turn to ice water.

"Barney," I cried. "Make needles. Lots of needles. Sticking out of the jar."

Two seconds later, the guard started screaming: "Ahhhhhhh!" He swung his arm out and opened his hand, but the jar was stuck to it and he couldn't let go.

"Pull the needles in!" I shouted and the jar dropped to the floor.

Julie was quicker than I though she could be. She put a knee to the groin of the other guard. He doubled over and I kicked at his head, hitting him somewhere in the shoulder instead and knocking him down.

"Quick," I said. "Let's go."

Julie was right behind me as we ran through the tall grass. The crumpled thump of artillery fire echoed across the sky.

"I have an announcement," Barney said. "Using echo-location, I have determined the positions of all the active artillery batteries within 20 kilometers."

A minute later, we were at the gate. Lights were on all over the house. I could hear shouting.

I looked into the jar and Barney put on the display screen. In the hall with the big fireplace, Danton was pouring brandy into his glass from the bottle.

Suddenly the field of view was filled with a big military boot. It came crashing down and filled the screen. The image died, but the sound continued.

"Hey," a voice said. "I know what this green stuff is."

Before we knew it, a loud engine came to life in the front of the house and an armored car rolled into view.

Julie and I began to run.

* * *

We raced through the dark city, our path lit by flashes of yellow light as artillery rounds exploded nearby. The hulking shadows of trees and houses danced and jumped. The shock waves pounded our faces and chests. We clung to the narrow residential streets, keeping away from where the targeting drones could see us.

At one point, we had to get to the other side of a wide cross street. Julie hung back while I scouted around the corner. Barney whispered on the phone: "No drones are detected here."

We scurried through the open space and down an alley, then around a store, then up a driveway, then across a pocket park, then through a schoolyard.

We could see houses burning as we neared home.

Our house!

I gasped. Julie sobbed.

We started to run towards it when another artillery round exploded across the street. Splinters and cinders and smoke filled the air.

"Julie! Tim!"

I heard Tony calling out to us from the street corner. He was there with Mr. and Mrs. Skorch and the Hungarian brothers. Julie rushed to her father. He looked dazed – and then I saw that his arm was limp and bloody and more blood dripped down onto the ground.

"Where's Carol?" I asked, looking around for the woman who used to work at the school.

"She didn't make it," Tony said. "We need to help Mr. Skorch. He's hurt pretty bad."

"Bandage him up!" Julie cried. "Stop the bleeding!"

One of the Hungarian brothers pulled off his shirt and started tearing it into strips. Julie tied them around his arm. Mr. Skorch grimaced in pain, but bit back the screams.

"Where do we go?" Tony asked.

"We can't go back the way we came," I said. "The general is after us."

"That's bad," he said. "Only one direction we can go. And you know what's down there."

"Gray goo can't be as bad as the general," I said.

"Then let's go." The Hungarian brothers put one arm each around Mr. Skorch, Julie took her mother by the arm, and Tony and I led the way.

* * *

We ended up across the street from the plaza full of gray goo, huddled against a big apartment building. The steady barrage of artillery fire had followed us here, but stopped on the back side of the building. No one wanted to disturb the goo.

Julie's mother cried. Mr. Skorch breathed hard and heavy. I didn't know what to do.

I heard the rattle of small arms fire not far away. Then mortar rounds began to fall somewhere down the street in the same direction as the gunfire. I saw a handful of dark shapes moving against the flashes of red fire – rebel soldiers. They were moving our way.

Then an armored car emerged from the smoke and fire and rolled to a stop about five blocks away.

We were trapped. There was nowhere left to go. There was nothing to go back to. Gray goo sat ahead of us. And the general and the war were coming up the street.

And then Barney spoke up.

"I have an important announcement," he said.

"What is it?" I asked.

"I have completed my analysis of the structure of insulin. I am now capable of producing therapeutic quantities. And all my capacities are now free to complete other assignments."

"What other capacities?"

"I have been carrying out Dave's final orders to dedicate most of my capacity to solving the problem of insulin," Barney said. "Insulin is a complicated organic compound. It consists of two peptide chains of 21 amino acids in one and 30 amino acids in the other. Without access to an existing database, I had to analyze and calculate the chemical structure of all the amino acids and the structure of both chains. This took much longer than Dave expected."

"I don't think it's going to help him now," I said.

"And now all my capacities are free to employ on other projects," Barney said.

"All your capacities? What other projects?"

"Ask me anything," the cog-brain said. "Anything at all."

* * *

Tony was busy under the hood of the selfie-car while I kept watch down the street. The rebels were keeping busy – first with small arms fire, then with a couple of explosives of their own. Mortars continued to pepper the woods in an attempt to suppress the rebels. As long as the armored car was occupied with them, we were safe.

"I've almost got it," Tony said. "Wish I had some better tools."

Then he growled and pulled out the power cell for the car in both hands and stepped back from the curb.

"We've got the power cell," I told Barney.

"Yes," he said. "The next steps must be executed as close to simultaneously as possible. I've run several thousand iterations of how this proceeds and providing the nanoassemblers with a power source for too long can lead to a catastrophic failure."

"How catastrophic?"

"Everyone dies."

"All right. But are you sure you really want me to throw you into the gray goo?"

"It is the quickest way to make contact and infiltrate the matrix," Barney said. "They provide massive mechanical power, but they need the control of my nanoprocessors to be of any use."

"Do you remember what Dave said letting you get into the goo?" Tony asked.

"Dave was misinformed."

I looked down the street at the firefight. The armored car was starting to pull away from the rebels – and toward us.

"We're out of time anyway," I said. "Let's go."

We crept low across the broad avenue to the edge of the concrete plaza. The gray goo quivered in a pool just beyond the parking lot. It was as close as I wanted to get. I just hoped it was close enough to toss our payloads.

Tony went first, swinging the heavy power cell from behind his back, up into the air, releasing it, and then watching it fly the short distance to the goo.

Then I flung the peanut butter jar of cog oil after it. It splashed in the silvery fluid-like puddle – but the substance that flew up and away froze in midflight, catching the sparkle of distant mortar fire.

We ran back to the apartment building where the others huddled against the wall and waited.

The armored car didn't.

The firefight with the rebels was over. It was rolling towards us, faster and faster, and the gun in its turret was swinging our way.

* * *

Dave's Ghost had apologized almost immediately after Barney's message.

"Sorry, kid, but I can't tell him to stop working on the insulin," the recorded message said. "What if he suddenly unravels it? I keep telling myself that if I get really bad, I'll have him stop so you get the full cog-brain effect. But I don't' know if I'm strong enough for that. Because to tell you the truth, this dying thing is scaring the hell out of me."

And so the little cog-brain without access to any outside database, without any grounding in biochemistry, used every bit of computing power it could spare to save the guy who had stolen it from the lab and kept it free. I just hoped it was going to do as much for me.

"I want it to be big," I told him. "And I want it to fly."

"I have the design specifications for a drone," Barney said. "Shall I use that as a model?"

"As long as it flies. And it's got to shoot."

"What shall I use for projectiles?"

"I don't know," I said. "Rocks. Nails. Gray goo."

"I will attempt to accommodate all three."

***

The armored car kept accelerating. I knew it was the general and I knew he was coming for me. My and my peanut butter jar full of cog oil. Because that was the stuff that this war was all about. And that was the stuff he could use to win it.

But he didn't have it. I did. Or rather, I had before I threw into the goo.

The surface of the pool of gray goo quivered and rippled around the spot where Barney had landed.

I kept looking from the goo to the armored car and the time slipped away. I expected the car to start shooting at us, but the gun remained silent. Maybe the general was afraid of hurting the cog oil. I didn't know. My heart was pounding and I was too scared to think much about it.

Then the surface of the goo erupted and a great shape about ten meters wide rose up.

"I want it to be big," I'd said.

There was a central pillar and four outriggers. Spinning propellers at the end of each outrigger provided the lift.

As I watched, I could see the propellers flex and pulse and grow as Barney adjusted the mass and structure. The whole thing was made of gray goo, stringing itself together in great strands of nanotech assemblers.

And at the top of the pillar was a glowing green eye – Barney the cog-brain.

The assemblage rose into the air.

"And I want it to fly."

It wobbled, advanced uncertainly, then swooped up above the trees and the buildings that ran the length of the street across from the plaza.

"Yea, though I walk through the valley of the shadow of death, I will fear no evil," said Tony.

"Get the armored car!" I shouted. "Open it up and pull them out of there!"

No one inside the car seemed to realize what was happening around them.

Barney flew his giant drone down the avenue towards it, then flared and halted and dropped long tendrils of gray goo assemblers down from the central pillar.

The tendrils engulfed the armored car. They penetrated the engine compartment. Smoke poured out. The car skidded to a halt, spinning from the momentum and tipping onto its side.

The tendrils dissolved the hull of the car. Pieces of armor fell to the ground, peeled apart by the assemblers. Suddenly two bodies were yanked skywards, twisting and writhing in a vain attempt to escape.

Barney set them down on the pavement in front of the rebels. Then he brought the oversized drone to a soft landing astride the street.

There was no more artillery fire. No mortar shells exploding. No small arms fire.

Everything was silent.

I went over to rebels and the two figures lying prone on the pavement. Danton and the general. I strode up to them, then kicked Danton – hard. Danton moaned.

"You son of a bitch," I said.

Then it was the general's turn. He flinched and pulled away.

It was over.

I didn't know it yet, but it was all over. My war was over. It had ended forever.

No one would ever try to kill me again.

***

After that night, I never saw Julie again. The Kung Fu Pandas took me and Barney and Dave's Ghost away from the city. A few days later, we were on our way to Seattle, where we would spend the rest of the war.

When it was over – over for everyone and not just for me – we tried our best to see who was still alive and bury those who weren't.

They helped Barney grow, but he remained the feckless, friendly persona that Dave had impressed on him. Dave's Ghost became a living thing inside him, a simulated copy of the original hero who had rescued a bit of cog-oil from the end of the world.

I never found my mother and sister. I never found out what happened to them.

But like the half of humanity who had survived the Last War, I mourned them for the rest of my life.

And like that half of humanity, I always had sense of guilt. A sense that never went away. A sense that I had been able to do what they had not.

I had lived through it all to tell the tale.

Siege Perilous

When the warship appeared in the space around our asteroid, Declan Kyle was tending his garden and I was having my breakfast.

It was the third year of the Last War and everyone was used to the routine. You got through each day by taking care of the day's work – and you tried not to think about all the horrors that had already come and the horrors that might be in store.

For Declan, the day's work consisted of tending to a garden of thousands of flowers strung through the vacuum that wrapped our piece of rock and metal and carbonaceous chondrite.

Each flower was several centimeters long. The leaves soaked up sunlight and turned it into electrical power. The petals focused light and other forms of electromagnetic radiation and monitored the flower's surroundings near and far. The seeds contained the processors – little sacs of cog oil capable of reading the data the flower received and reconfiguring its parts to meet changing conditions.

On average, they were spaced 200 meters apart. But they bunched up and dispersed as they drifted and danced in elaborate pseudorandom patterns so that an outside observer would conclude they were bits of dust from the asteroid's surface thrown up by collisions with space debris.

It was still nearly impossible to drive a sizable spacecraft through them without smacking a few and setting off the alarms.

Declan heard the alarms while he and his girlfriend, Krissie Dahlquist, were weeding a tangle of vegetables in a micrograv planter.

"Gardener online," he said, bringing up the AI persona that ran his array of sensors.

"Gardener here," said the persona.

"What's got your flowers in an uproar?" he asked, his Irish brogue lifting his voice at the end.

"I don't know for sure, but it's about 200 meters long, space black, all stealthed up, and moving slow relative to us."

"We'll be moving some assets around then. Open our eyes a bit and see what we can see of it."

"Aye aye," said Gardener.

Declan returned to his weeding, while Gardener attended to the flowers. Gardener also sent an alarm to me, even though Declan hadn't told him to. Declan was still young and from Dublin and was prone to overlooking things like that. Gardener wasn't.

As I said, I was eating my breakfast. Pancakes, to be precise, with coffee and orange juice. On my veranda, overlooking the farm that takes up much of the Big Spin Ring at the heart of the asteroid we called Castle Anthrax. (It had a numerical identifier, but it's hard to feel an attachment to a string of digits.)

Nanotech can do a lot of great things, but cogs are wasted trying to cobble together complex carbohydrates from dirt and water and air when nature does such a good job itself. The farm stretched for only a couple of acres, with a wheat field at one end and a corn field at the other and some veggies in between. Above it ran a few rows of high-intensity sun-yellow lighting tubes that cycled through the 24-hour diurnal pattern that plants (and people) like most.

I was attending to my simple daily duties as I ate. Specifically, I was reviewing the Question of the Day on the Castle Anthrax intranet.

"Today's question involves the fictional city of Alexandria again," the text read. Oh good, I thought, Alexandria was interesting. "The city contains a large library of paper books, scientific documents, and research materials."

In the early days of the war, everyone was throwing around Dumb Bombs – malware that went through databases, libraries, text files, and anything resembling an official record and rearranged things. Banking and credit records disappeared, newspaper archives were erased or rewritten, history textbooks were altered, and much, much more. It didn't take many of them to make people doubt all electronic data. And the printed stuff was harder to find after the first few exchanges of fire laid waste to the cities.

"Alexandria sits at the edge of political control of Paris, a metropolitan state-like entity run by Achilles, a political leader who has been designated as narcissistic, obstinate, short-tempered, and unrealistic – a leader previously designated as highly likely to engage in military conflict to achieve his goals."

I was familiar with the type. Achilles had been selected for this exercise because of his flaws, not in spite of them.

"Yesterday's scenario involved Chicago, an adjacent metropolitan state-like entity that wants to use the resources at Alexandria. Yesterday's survey indicates that the crew of Castle Anthrax believes there is a 90 percent chance of military conflict arising over this scenario. Such conflict has a high probability of destroying the resources contained in Alexandria. Today, we are soliciting possible responses by the residents of Paris aimed at preserving those resources."

Of course we were. The question of the day was a program aimed at teaching the AI constructs of our resident cog technology how to analyze political problems. Cogs could do wonders with multiple parallel processing of trial-and-error models. But they couldn't originate concepts or make value judgments. Not yet, anyway. By asking us, the local human population, to offer our analysis and our judgments, they were creating a base of knowledge that would guide their modeling and provide nuance to their evaluations.

Or so we hoped. It was a gamble. But after three years of war, everything was a gamble. From planting wheat in the heart of an asteroid to scattering flowers through space to spot your enemies when they arrived.

"Please enter any options you believe the residents of Paris can take in this situation," the Question continued. "Options already proposed include the following:

"Encourage Alexandria to declare its independence from Paris and negotiate its own terms with Chicago.

"Work to overthrow the regime of Achilles.

"Work to overthrow the regime of Chicago and bring it under the control of Paris.

"Destroy Alexandria to deny Chicago its resources."

I frowned at that last one, but it had to come up. And I knew a few of the people on the Castle who might have suggested it. War makes some people bitter.

"Please endorse one of the options or propose one of your own. Complete polling will continue tomorrow."

When everyone had a chance to vote, the cogs would tally it up and publish the results. Of course, you weren't supposed to vote for the option you supported. You were supposed to vote for the option you thought the people of Paris were most likely to choose for themselves. Subtle difference.

And whatever the outcome, the cogs would log it as an event, add it to the history of the state-like entity of Paris, and go to work on the next scenario. Such was the slow work of making artificial intelligence less artificial and more intelligent.

I added my own option: "Work with Alexandria to use its resources to overthrow the regime of Achilles." I didn't get to be boss of Castle Anthrax by thinking inside of the box.

I was about to look over the daily reports when the message from Declan Kyle's Gardener made it to my attention.

"Boss, you there?" It was Mike, my AI executive officer and my interface with the Castle's cogs.

"I'm here, Mike."

"Looks like trouble," Mike said. He described what Declan's flowers had detected.

"A 200-meter stealthed up vessel sneaking into our local space," I said. "Sounds unfriendly. No signals from it, I take it."

"Complete electromagnetic silence," Gardener said.

"We've had scouts pass by before, but nothing big like this. And there's too many rocks in the sky for them to be checking them all in turn. They know we're in here."

"Most likely," Mike said. I assumed that was an official assessment from the cogs.

"I've been waiting for this," I said. "Sooner or later, we knew someone would come our way. Let's just hope we're ready for them. Sound General Quarters. Batten down the Castle. Seal up everything, pull in the sensors and receivers. Get everyone up to full alert. We're about to come under siege."

* * *

The first order of business was to take a walk.

I had to make my rounds of Castle Anthrax. Show myself to the thousand or so inhabitants and crew members. It is not enough to care, you must also be seen to care. At least you must be seen.

From the collection of bamboo shacks that made up my quarters to the edge of the Big Spin Ring was a short distance along a narrow path lined with 4-billion-year-old stones, across an irrigation ditch disguised as a pleasantly babbling brook, and up a short slope to the ring edge and the sure-grip walkway that ran its circumference. Across a tiny gap, a similar walkway ran along Spin Ring Amber, moving at about five meters a second slower than the big ring. Just slow enough to make the jump safe instead of uncomfortable.

Ring Amber was filled with bamboo patches. It was the perfect building material for interior structures in both spin-gravity and microgravity – fast-growing, lightweight, sturdy, and heir to several thousand years of design enhancements.

Amber rolled along as I waited for a path to line up. A handful of young girls planting new shoots in mud on the edge of the central creek rolled by. I waved to them and they waved back. I'm not hard to recognize at a distance – it's the scruffy white beard and the shiny high forehead (features I forget I bear unless I'm looking the mirror in the morning).

Next step was Ring Gold, coffee and hops, barley and sugar, followed by Ring Emerald and Ring Umber, the complex cog-assisted microbiologies that managed our life support systems.

It's a nice little walk, not much more than 250 meters, with each ring taking a little more weight off your feet. Except that when you step off the last of the spin rings, you find yourself adrift in microgravity unless you pay attention and grab one of the nets at the entrance to the tunnels.

Off the rings, the best way to get around was a hand-trac – you clipped it onto a cable that ran the length of the tunnel and the cogs spun up the wheels until you were moving along at an exhilarating clip.

My first stop was The Brewery, the heart of Castle Anthrax and our reason for existence, to talk to Willie Hamilton, our brewmaster.

* * *

There were guards on the gates to The Brewery. That made me smile. Someone was thinking. Or something.

Beyond the gates was a large void a few dozen meters across, its surface lined with elaborate bamboo and plastic frameworks containing dozens of glass vessels, all filled with the glowing green fluid that was cog oil.

"Mike, you there?"

"Right here, boss." And for once, that's where he was, I realized. Right here in jars that held most of our cog capacity.

"Let Mr. Hamilton know I'm here, would you?"

"Sure, boss."

Almost immediately, Willie came swinging over a heavy railing that ringed a well into the wall of the void. He grabbed a stanchion and pulled himself up short in front of me.

"So it's come?" he asked me.

"That's what it looks like," I said. "They may be here because there are people here. Or they may be here because they know what we're doing. A lot of people know there are people here. Not many know what we're doing."

"How could they know what we're doing here when I don't know what we're doing here?"

"I was hoping you could do a better job than that of reassuring me. Tell me you've been doing something in here for the past year besides talking to cog AIs."

"There's not that much more to it than that," Willie replied. "We just sit around and talk about stuff. There isn't much else for me to do. Sometimes I connect one jar with another for them. Sometimes I dump some carbon or sand into the jars for them. The rest is just talk."

I looked around. The jars of cog oil were thickest around us here. Glass globes of random sizes from a handspan up to a couple of meters were held tightly by polyhedral cradles of bamboo, joined at the intersections with twine.

The oil itself was just a medium for the cogs, to hold them safe from the environment and the environment safe from them. The glow came from photonic leakage in their internal processing.

Working nanites in the oil could form the hulls of spacecraft, fabricate complex molecular structures of precise engineering characteristics, convert sugar into alcohol, and paint a barn.

But the cogs in these jars were concentrated CPUs for a powerful collection of artificial intelligences. Some of them were more than simple personas like Mike. Some were trying to figure out something about human nature. Some were trying to figure out how to reprogram themselves into something they were not yet (those were the ones that scared me). And some were trying to solve simpler, more approachable problems (those were the ones I liked).

"Are we ready for this?" I asked Willie.

He just shook his head and snorted. He pulled himself up to the rail around the well. "Come here, there's someone you should talk to."

I swung around the rail and pulled myself along behind him to its end. Here, instead of bamboo structure, was a copper mesh box. "A Faraday cage?"

"Two points for the boss," Willie said.

"What do you keep in there?"

"Monsters."

We transited a short tunnel, also lined with copper mesh, closed a mesh hatch cover behind us, and entered the cage. A single jar sat in the corner, cradled in a dodecahedron of bamboo. A couple of hardwired cables connected it to an ordinary video screen.

"We don't do a lot of video with our personas," Willie said. "But this is different. Boss, meet the Black Knight. Black Knight, you there?"

"I'm here, as are we all." A face faded into view on the video screen, scarred, broken, wearing a dented helmet with the visor up. "Ready to do service against you once more."

"We?" I asked, looking at Willie. "Is anyone else in there with him?"

"A lot of the more aggressive malware wants to create a persona right away," Willie said. "It works better if we just let them do it. Then the Knight keeps them under control."

"So far," the Knight said. "Some day you may find one more powerful than I."

"In that case, he'll be the next Black Knight," Willie said.

"So be it," said the Knight.

"What kinds of personas are we keeping?" I asked.

"Knight, introduce him to Magicar."

"As you will." The Knight faded to black.

Then the screen exploded in fiery red and orange, black smoke roiling at its edges. A roar – half animal, half tortured human – filled my ears. A face drawn in fire appeared, heavy brows, pointed ears, dagger teeth in a hungry smile.

"Magicar, I presume," I said.

"I'm coming for you!" he roared back. "Don't look at me too long! I can put a worm inside your brain and turn you into my slave with nothing more than blinking lights!"

I smiled.

There are two myths about AIs that refuse to die.

One is that they are self-conscious, like humans only faster and smarter. This is false. They process information faster than we can, sure. And they have access to large databases. But they are just machines. You put a copy of "Hamlet" in a box and it doesn't turn the box into Shakespeare. You put information into an AI, it doesn't make it Einstein. Any appearance to the contrary is the result of a century of trying to make computers sound like humans. Well-designed fakery. Even Magicar. Especially Magicar.

The other is that you can put a computer virus into the human brain – by blinking lights or injected cogs or designer pheromones.

No one knows enough about how the brain works yet to be able to pull that one off. Not even an AI.

"So tell me, Knight, are we ready for an attack?"

"I am still here in my cage, despite the best I can muster from all the worms, viruses, agents, poison personas, Trojan horses, and adolescent Belgian malware that I've been fed. If the attackers have anything I haven't tried, then it must be very new and very powerful."

"He's telling the truth," Willie said. "I'm not afraid of them."

"Of course, there's nothing I can do to help you against brute force," the Knight said. "Who knows? I might get free after all."

I felt an uncontrollable shiver. I wondered who had written in the ability to plant doubts and fears when they created that persona. I didn't want to meet whoever it was.

Willie led me back through the tunnel to exit the Faraday cage. We hung there in the microgravity, surrounded by the big tanks of glowing green cog oil. One of the really big ones sat behind him.

"Who's this?" I asked.

Simpler personas like my assistant Mike were distributed throughout the cog oil network, accessible at any node. But the big tanks here in The Brewery were dedicated containment for high-functioning AIs. The shorter distance for internal communication was necessary for them to run at high speeds. In the depths of the tanks, the cogs created dynamic structures that shifted as processing needs changed. They threw up massive multiple processors to crunch huge problems, running endless trial-and-error simulations in search of the right answers.

"Moses," Willie said. "Because he's older than dirt. Do you want to talk to him?"

"Not necessary," I said, with another uncontrollable shiver. "Do you talk to him?"

"Yes," Willie said.

"A lot?"

"Yes."

"Does it ever scare you?"

"Sometimes. Not often, but sometimes."

"What do you talk about?"

"Justice," Willie said.

"Justice?"

"My great-grandfather marched with Dr. King back in the day. My grandfather worked to rebuild Detroit. So yes, boss, we talk about justice. Quite a bit. So you don't have much to worry about from Moses and his gang."

"And you're confident that the cog oil you brew up will work the way it's supposed to?"

"It does so far. You heard what the Black Knight said."

"Then I will put my fears and doubts aside and carry on," I said. I nodded, and pulled my way back to the rail at the top of well, then over it and on out the gate.

***

They perfected cog technology on a Tuesday and the war broke out on a Wednesday. At least that's the way I remember it.

It wasn't like no one saw it coming. Those who didn't have cogs were warning those who did long before they went live.

The advantages of cog technology were just too great. And it would only push the gap between the haves and the have-nots wider and wider as time went on. So the response was to start fighting on Day One.

Conventional weapons and armies went first. Cities were attacked with missiles and tank armies and special forces and bombers.

Then cog technology began producing new weapons and new armies. Cities were attacked with dumb bombs and gray goo and nukes and kinetic weapons from space.

Finally, the cogs themselves became weapons. Malware and viruses and rootkits and worse.

Nation-states collapsed under the weight of Armageddon. Big ones first, because they were most vulnerable to the breaking links of commerce and communications. The little ones next, because they had no reserves of strength or resources.

But the war went on.

Now it was waged by ad hoc alliances of cities, corporate entities, NGOs, space colonies, and other organizations that had survived the wreckage so far.

Castle Anthrax was part of the Kung Fu Pandas, with links to Tycho Base, some of the Lagrange settlements, and universities in the Pacific Northwest, New Zealand, and Italy.

Our research work could hold the key to peace. If we survived long enough to bring it home.

And that was a matter now in doubt.

Back in the '50s, when I was young and foolish, I was a Spiritual Realist – yes, a silly rilly. I ran an anti-bank for a few years, lending out fiat money to neighborhood projects.

Then all of us Reallys grew up and got lives. I went to work for a bunch of NGOs, moving up over the years to executive director positions. I jumped around a lot, from one group to another, using my management expertise to straighten things out, get them running smoothly, then pointing them on down the road under their own power.

A year before things fell apart, my wife died – one of those things medical science hasn't conquered yet. We'd had thirty good years together, and it was the end of the world for me. So when the world ended for real, I was already used to it.

It was no surprise when the Kung Fu Pandas asked me to take over Castle Anthrax. Maybe my wife's passing was a good thing. At least I wasn't overcome by the shock of losing all that had mattered to me. Not anymore.

I guess the Pandas were just lucky with that. And maybe the rest of humanity too.

* * *

Meanwhile, on the other side of the hill ...

The Divine Sword belonged to the International Healthdata Network – a diversified alliance that included health care and mercenary services. This was the third assault mission for the vessel since its commissioning a year earlier. They were beginning to get good at it.

The captain of the Divine Sword was an Egyptian, Omar Zadran. He was from Cairo. He'd lost his family early on in the war. Never an emotional man before that, he'd become hardened since. A rocket jock risen to command in a private militia that had hijacked its own medical unit.

The First Officer was from Chicago. Her name was Courtney Olson and she was 33 years old. It was her job on the Divine Sword to handle the cogware end of the attack on the asteroid before them.

She'd been in Amsterdam, working in the IT division of International Healthdata, when the war reached Europe. When the first malware attack hit, the computers that ran the dikes broke down. Courtney fled the country just ahead of the flood waters. She ended up in Hamburg as they were evacuating the city. International Healthdata had clinics in southern Germany and after a long month on the road she'd found refuge in Munich.

The Divine Sword had paid a visit to two asteroids in the year since Courtney joined its crew. The first was a supply base. They didn't know that going in, so it was a big surprise and a good one. The bounty would be enough to keep the alliance's two warships going for a couple years.

The second assault mission had been a scientific base – physics experiments, the crew said. The place lacked logistical support and was pretty close to collapse when the Divine Sword arrived.

Courtney didn't look forward to the coming assault. The violence bothered her.

The operational side of the alliance was running a bit too high on testosterone – too many people just wanted to smash things. Some of them were even important people.

But Courtney had some idea what weaponized cogs could do to flesh and blood. She was afraid that sooner or later, they were going to run into some of that and she wasn't going to be able to neutralize it before it was too late.

So she worked doubly hard to prepare her own weaponized cogware for what could be a long siege.

* * *

The opening salvo in the siege was a round of heavy fire from the warship.

BOOM! BOOM! BOOM! BOOM! BOOM!

You could hear them all when they hit, one after another, in quick succession. You felt it in your bones and your chest and your face. Somehow they had managed to target the right spots to make the entire stony-iron keel of Castle Anthrax resonate.

It had to be high explosives, but enhanced somehow by cog-tech and employed with smart targeting. In an atmosphere, explosives do their damage with overpressure spikes that compress the atmosphere. Here in the vacuum of space on a tiny little rock, it was the physical shock of impact and chemical detonation.

And immediately afterwards came the shouts and screams of the crew. I heard them all on the sound-net.

"What was that?!" "Holy cow!" "Jesus, Jesus, Jesus … help me Jesus!"

People called out the names of their partners and mates and a large number of them called out for me.

"Make it stop, boss!" "Moriarty! I need help down here!" "Have we got something to shoot back with, boss?"

I ignored them for a while. No one expected an answer. There were regular channels, a chain of command, Mike and his cohorts keeping things under control.

But then came a second round of BOOM! BOOM! BOOM! And a third. BOOM! BOOM! BOOM!

If I wasn't going to say something to the crew, then there wasn't much need for me at all. So I lit up the net and made my speech.

"This is Mr. Moriarty. Settle down, everyone," I said. "This is just the beginning. No one's dead, are they? Check yourselves to make sure, and if you are, let me know. The key to withstanding a siege is to stay calm and don't panic. We're sitting under meters of rock and iron. Little explosives like that make noise, but they don't do much damage. And what damage they do can be fixed by the cogs. So keep on doing your jobs, follow Mike's orders and mine, and we'll get through this together. There are worse things than explosives. And we're probably going to get some of them thrown at us before this is all through. Mr. Moriarty out."

I hoped I had eased their fears. And I wished someone would come along to ease mine.

* * *

The shelling continued for the next 32 hours. After a while, it was less intense. But something hit us every ten minutes or so, sometimes a big barrage, sometimes just a singleton to keep us on our toes. Most of them hit just the right place to make the entire asteroid ring like a bell. And we were the clapper.

The cogs worked overtime to ensure the explosions weren't cracking the biosphere. When they weren't checking for leaks, they were compartmentalizing all the living spaces with airtight seals. Flexible seals that would be breached by shock waves or overpressure (on the off chance that one of the blasts penetrated into the atmosphere).

Meanwhile, the real attack was taking place elsewhere.

Willie was keeping an eye on it.

High-energy signal traffic poured out of the warship without interruption. Willie had the cogs build receivers that were completely isolated from the rest of Castle Anthrax's IT systems and then distilled what they received.

By distilling it, I mean disarming the malware, deactivating the worms and agents, quarantining the viruses. He turned it all into passive lines of code, available without risk for the next level of receivers, which were also isolated from our IT systems.

They analyzed the code, identified its pedigree and usually its authors, and on the rare occasion when something new and creative came through, they passed pieces of it along. Moses and his cohort worked on those pieces.

The big cog engines digested them, disassembling them into component parts, then reassembled them into new configurations. And, because we are talking about the quantum chemistry that makes cogs work, that is only partly a metaphorical description of what the cog AIs were doing. In many ways, it is quite literal. In addition to digital signals running through the viscous green goop we called cog oil, there were long atomic chains embedded with the code. Breaking up the chains and putting them back together again was something cogs did as a matter of reflex. Now it was a matter of survival.

"What do you see, Willie?" I asked after the first day.

"Nothing terrible," he said. "Pretty basic microware. The kind of thing we went through early on. Nothing original or creative or unexpected. Our basic firewall would keep most of it out. Anything else would get chewed up by our phagocytes."

"And yet you don't sound excited about that," I pointed out.

"It just makes me wonder where the big stuff is," Willie said. "That's a pretty big warship out there. They wouldn't send something like that our way if they were just going to throw whipped cream pies at us."

"So we're just going to let them throw this stuff at us without throwing anything back?"

"For now," Willie said. "That's what Moses and the others tell me."

"I know. Like Beowulf waiting for Grendel."

"Exactly," Willie said.

"I hope they're right."

"If they're not, then we've been wasting our time out here with them."

It wasn't much, but it was all I had to keep me happy between explosions.

Then, after 32 hours, things fell silent. The blasts stopped. The malware attack ended. And the naive could easily have come to the conclusion that the warship had given up and gone on its way.

I was not one of the naïve. And the first thing I did was head for the little garden where Declan Kyle continued to tend his larger "garden" in space around us.

* * *

Whenever I'd been in the big plenum chamber at the airlocks before, it was full of people, cargo, and equipment, all moving and full of energy. Now it was empty and dimly lit and somewhat creepy.

Big fans behind grills at one end kept the air circulating. Anyone who came unanchored in the microgravity would be blown into the plastic netting at the other end. Now the fans just made a mournful noise.

Big pipes that ran into the depths of Castle Anthrax lined the "top" of the chamber. The opening to the lock might have had a huge metal door if this base had been built a decade earlier. But a thin screen of cog-engineered material served the same purpose for us. (The outer door, of course, was still a huge chunk of steel – we weren't entirely dimwitted even if we did rely on cog AIs a lot.)

A network of green-veined cog-lines filled the empty surfaces of the chamber, casting a ghostly pallor over everything.

But I wasn't about to let the place get the better of me.

"Mike, you there?" I asked, looking for company to banish the lonelies.

"I'm here, boss."

"What's the latest?"

"They're feeding the folks in the hardened shelters," Mike said. "Cold sandwiches, reheated rice, iced tea and hot coffee."

"Don't save me any," I said. "I've got something stashed in my icebox for later."

At the far end of the plenum chamber, opposite the main passage, was a narrower tunnel that lead towards the south pole of Castle Anthrax. I clipped my hand-trac onto the wire and let it pull me along for a couple hundred meters to the tunnel's end.

From there I had to negotiate a smaller passage somewhat bigger than a chimney, lined with bamboo ladderworks and lit by green veins of cog oil.

But the effort was worth it. I pushed back the flimsy air shield at the end of the chimney and pulled myself over the lip into a fifty-meter void filled with rich vegetation, fragrant and alive, a vibrant world of authentic green, compared to the artificial cog-light.

A skylight at one end sparkled with sunshine. Patches of planters lashed together, anchored to pylons, covered the inner surface of the void. I could identify sweet corn and coffee and mangoes and bananas, but most of it was a leafy conflagration mixed with plastic tubes of irrigation water. Also lashed to the pylons were filter fans wrapped in absorbent pads designed to take water droplets out of the air and keep the gardeners from contracting pneumonia.

A bamboo lattice ran from the entrance to a sprawling series of shacks with thatched-leaf roofs – and to Declan and Krissie.

What called my attention to them was the shouting. Krissie's shouting. At Declan.

As I got closer, I could make out some of the words.

"My mother always told me that men only have half a chromosome and you know what? She was right!"

When she looked up at me, surprised by my sudden and unannounced appearance, she stopped.

"I know you," she said. "You're the boss. Can you kick some sense into this boy? Just because he's Irish doesn't mean he hasn't got a brain. It's time to get out of this place and down to one of the hard spots. Everyone else left this morning. Everyone but him. And me."

I knew Krissie. She was one of the kids from Seattle.

About nine months ago, we'd taken them aboard the Castle. Seattle was still mostly intact. No big attacks while they were still throwing nukes and rocks around. But most of the population had moved to western Washington to be closer to the food supply. Those who remained behind lived on the shadowy battlefield of the twilight war that raged on after the armies had spent themselves and the nations had fallen.

Krissie had cute features – a button nose, a perky smile, sparkly eyes – which could turn fierce without warning. She wore her long blond hair in a braided pigtail that snapped in the microgravity when she spun her head. A long blue snake writhed across her back – animated cog-ink tattoos were all the rage (mine was small and nondescript – a clock tower on my wrist in place of a watch).

Her story was simple.

"My phone taught the toaster to make the microwave oven into a death ray, and it killed my mom."

This was a war fought on a battleground of morale and fear was the primary weapon.

We evacuated five hundred kids from sixteen to twenty. It took ten heavy lifters out of Puget Sound to get them into orbit – we raised the money for the launch costs by selling access to the Seattle Public Library (still safe, secure, and guaranteed reliable after all these years by double-checking against printed books).

Since they came aboard, they'd helped support the Castle's small economy – skilled and semi-skilled labor, eager to be trained and happy to be safe. Until now.

I could tell by the way Krissie's lip trembled that the siege was getting to her.

"I came to see if Declan could help me," I said. "The warship that's been pounding on us has gone to ground, so to speak. We need to find it and figure out what it's up to."

"It's trying to kill us," Krissie said. "What more do you need to know?"

"Enough to stop it," I said. "We will stop it, you know," I added, with some extra moral force in my voice aimed at putting her fear at some distance.

She looked at me, then launched herself into my arms and hugged me tightly. Then she let go and apologized. "Look at me, all girlie and afraid. And in front of the boss."

"It's not a matter of being unafraid," I said. "It's just a matter of not letting it stop you from doing what needs to be done."

Then Declan appeared, pulling himself along the bamboo lattice.

"Hello, boss," he said. "What can I do for you this fine afternoon?"

Declan was true Irish – not Boston Irish like me. He still had a brogue and an attitude and was still a bit wild and untameable, as Krissie was discovering. He was smart, too.

"Where's the guy that's been trying to blow up my asteroid?" I asked.

"I was wondering the exact same thing myself," Declan said. "I put Gardener onto it a wee bit ago and I was just coming in to see what it had found."

"Let's look together," I said.

* * *

The biggest problem we had was trying to use the cog-based AIs to their best ability. One of the major advances of cog technology was the giant leap in artificial intelligence. It was one of the things that precipitated the war. Cog AI s were so much more like intelligence than anything that came before them – partly because they incorporated everything that came before them and partly because of the tremendous increase in calculating power.

But you had to know how to talk to them. They weren't imaginative. They didn't get ideas. They were never inspired. They could know all the answers, and if you didn't ask the right questions they'd never tell them to you. And we'd only been talking to them for a couple years now.

So it took us a few minutes to get Gardener to provide what we needed.

"We want a real-time position of the warship," Declan said.

"It is beyond their current position distribution," Gardener said.

"Then we need an indirect method of detection," I said.

"Except that the warship is pretty stealthed up. No heat signature. No radiation since they stopped shooting at us," Declan said. "They're tight as tick in dog's ear."

"It doesn't reflect any sunlight at all?" I asked.

"A small amount," Gardener said. "But they were keeping the sun behind them as much as possible to degrade any visual tracking."

"Too bad they're not blocking it," I said.

"Too bad," said Declan. "But now that ya mention it, they might be blocking some others. Gardener, check star occultations. Have all the flowers on it."

After a long moment of silence, Gardener responded. "I'm integrating data from the array. I have three observations ... four ... seven ... I have a real-time position."

"Huzzah!" I shouted.

"I owe you a drink," Declan said, and he began to hoot.

Gardener spewed out a string of numbers and technical terms until I stopped him.

"Never mind all that," I said. "I need to know what those numbers mean. Where is it? Where is it going? What is it doing?"

Gardener paused. Perhaps he was consulting with larger and wiser cog-heads. Then he said: "It's five minutes away from us at its current speed. And it's headed almost directly towards us. Wait ... wait ... The warship appear to be launching projectiles."

All three of us fell silent.

"Projectiles?" Declan asked.

"Four separate objects in addition to the warship, the integrations say," Gardener said. "Approximately 30 meters in length. Heading towards us at the same speed. Impact in about four minutes."

"Four minutes?" Krissie said. "What do we do?"

"One impact likely within 50 meters of your position," Gardener said.

I looked at Krissie and said: "Run!"

* * *

Running in microgravity is a figure of speech. But we managed to put some speed on.

I found myself dragging along a mesh bag that Krissie had handed me as he left their shack – she had produced three of them from somewhere almost as if by magic.

And I made the effort to alert the rest of Castle Anthrax. "Mike, you there?"

"Right here, boss."

"Projectiles incoming. Impact in less than four minutes. Sound the alarm."

"Gardener told me what he found. We're making preparations. Alarms are going off now."

As we approached the tunnel out of the chamber, a red circle began flashing around its perimeter and a "General Quarters" bell began to clang. "Impact in 90 seconds," Mike announced. "Brace for impact in 90 seconds."

If you pull yourself hand over hand along a bamboo ladder, you can get yourself up to five or six meters a second fairly quickly. Unless you snag a mesh bag on the bamboo ... which explained why Krissie wasn't coming along as quickly as Declan and I. We waited for her to catch up with us at the end of the tube. She was crying when she got there.

Five or six meters a second is a good running speed. Ten meters per second is about the speed you hit the ground at when you fall off the roof of a two-story house, so you don't want to get going quite that fast. Nevertheless, once a week or so, someone on Castle Anthrax shows up at the infirmary with broken bones from hitting the tunnel walls at that speed or faster. Foolish kids.

All you have to do is boost yourself a bit every time you make contact with the tunnel walls.

Faster and faster. Each time.

Nothing to slow you down but air resistance, and that doesn't kick in until you're up past fifty meters a second.

Even Krissie was flying through the tunnel with us at literally breakneck speed.

We were almost to the big plenum chamber at the locks when the roof caved in.

* * *

Obviously, without gravity, it's hard for a roof to cave in. In this case, it had a push ... from a 30-meter long chunk of olivine, one of the projectiles launched by the warship.

Declan, Krissie and I were engulfed in a roiling cloud of dust, and all of us, dust clouds included, burst out into the plenum chamber. The green light of the cog oil and the red telltales of the control panels faded as the dust filled the chamber.

I shot across the void and knew that somewhere ahead of me was a large wall. One that I could not see. I pulled the mesh bag that Krissie had given me around in the direction I was moving – just in time to hit that wall.

I caromed off, much of my kinetic energy absorbed by Krissie's bag and by my shoulders and back in a somewhat less than elastic collision. I caromed off another wall before I found myself within reach of cargo netting, which I grabbed and held myself in place.

I was still shrouded in darkness, but I could tell where Declan and Krissie were by the sound of their ragged coughs (when I wasn't hacking my own lungs out). Krissie's were higher pitched and they both had stopped moving.

Our lungs cleared of dust about the same time as the atmosphere. Big fans rattled loudly at both ends of the plenum.

"What happened?" Krissie asked.

"We've been hit," I said. "By something big. Come on with me, I want to get a closer look at it."

"Back there?" Krissie said. "Aren't you afraid?"

"Afraid of what?"

"I don't know. Grey goo or something."

"Darling, gray goo was the very first problem we solved here. I need to see what that thing is."

As I got closer, I could see that it wasn't a monolith, but a series of nested pyramids that resembled a large arrowhead. The first few appeared to have broken off, but the remainder had sufficient momentum to break through the crust of Castle Anthrax and into the passageway.

I notice the sharp wheezing whistle of air escaping around the edges of the thing. They diminished as the cogs worked on sealing the leaks.

A quick examination of the gap made by the projectile showed a break in the cog line – a tube about the thickness of a garden hose that ran along the outboard side of the tunnel.

"Mike, you still there?"

"Right here, boss."

"We've got an impact just south of the plenum chamber. Anyplace else hit?"

"One of them penetrated to Ring Umber and stopped it in its tracks. A lot of damage from flying objects when it happened. Another broke through a greenhouse and vacuum-fried the contents."

"Send damage control crews down here and Ring Umber. Don't worry about the greenhouse for now," I said.

"Aye aye, boss," Mike said.

"It looks frightening big." I turned and saw Declan Kyle beside me. Krissie was right behind him, swallowing her fear of gray goo.

"See?" I said. "Nothing to worry about."

"Unless it explodes," Krissie said. "I think we need to get out of here."

"In a minute. First, I want to –"

"What's that?" Krissie screeched.

"What's what?"

"Running down the side of that thing," she said, bringing her voice down an octave and pointing emphatically.

I looked at the source of her fears and saw a viscous fluid emerging from one of the joints where the pyramids were joined. "It's just cog oil," I said.

"Is it supposed to be yellow like that?"

I looked again. It was not supposed to be yellow like that.

"Mike, we've got a problem here," I said. "Exotic cog technology.

They've found a way to get it on board. We're going to need more volume down here for our own cog oil, so get that started."

In a few minutes, the garden hose tubing filled with glowing green cog oil should swell to firehouse size. And in an hour, it could be as thick as a tree trunk. The more volume, the more cogs would be available to fight the invading cogtech.

At least that was the theory.

* * *

Grey goo – the nightmare spawned by nanotech.

Runaway disassemblers breaking everything down. Turning trees and rocks and houses and cars and Grandma and Grandpa into an undifferentiated mass of molecules. Spreading everywhere, lurking in shadows, in caves, in the ruins of bombed out buildings. Falling from the sky.

The fear was so great that cities had been nuked and hit by orbital kinetic energy weapons – smart rocks – in an attempt to stop its spread.

And as I'd told Krissie, it was the first problem we had solved here on Castle Anthrax.

Cog oil was only part of the solution. Creating a medium to contain the nanotech went a long way to keeping it from getting out of control, but there was nothing inherent in cog oil that would prevent the cogs from outstripping their instructions. Or from launching themselves on an endless von Neumann loop of infinite replication (though incorporating platinum into the replication process was supposed to limit that nightmare).

No, the solution had to be built into the operating system itself.

And it had to be replicated with every single cog unit that would ever be built. Nothing less could stop it.

So we'd designed the operating system. Willie and his team had worked for months to get it right, with Moses and the other newly spawned AIs doing the heavy lifting to test each bit of code.

And once we had it, we started on the next problem – how to spread that protection to all the other nanotech that had been hacked together since its inception.

How could we make our operating system not just the dominant one, but the only one. The only one that could be allowed to exist, because anything less would be incompatible with the survival of the human race. No wonder Willie got cranky sometimes.

So for more than two years, we'd been working on that part of the problem. Breeding a super operating system that would allow humanity to coexist with cog technology. Doing it here in the isolation of a remote asteroid base posed certain problems. How could we test it? How could we be sure we had the right stuff? We'd tried to do our best with the resources at hand. The AIs ran endless scenarios to game out the possibilities. Willie sat up sleepless and bleary-eyed, waiting for the next inspiration. We polled the crew for ideas, polled them some more to search the depths of those ideas. And now it seemed as if we'd done all that we could.

Would it be enough?

Would it survive first contact with a truly hostile operating system?

Would it defeat that system and convert it into a copy of itself?

According to Mike, not right away.

"I recommend getting some distance between you and that yellow cog oil," he said.

"You would?"

"It's hostile and it's taking over our cogs."

"That's not supposed to happen, is it?"

"We're at a disadvantage at the moment," Mike said. "It's attacking the segments that are cut off from the main cog oil network. And it's winning them over."

"Tell Willie I'm coming down to talk to him," I said.

"Aye aye, boss."

I took Declan and Krissie by their arms. "Come on kids, time to start running again."

* * *

We made one more stop before going down the The Brewery to meet Willie.

The tunnel was secured at the entrance by a pair of well-muscled damage control team members wearing hardhats and hazard vests. They ushered us through and we were greeted by the chief of the team. He led us – all three of us, even Krissie, despite her fears, making me admire her strength a bit more – up to the greenhouse door.

"I've never seen anything like this before," he said. "It's scary."

He opened the door and we leaned into the fifty-meter void, looking through a cog-extruded air-sealed dome.

The first thing I noticed was the gray leaves on the dead branches, lining the entire surface of the chamber. The next thing was the big arrowhead harpoon lodged against one wall, covered in glowing yellow slime.

The slime had extended itself through the lifeless remains of the farm, creeping up the branches here and there and extruding antennae and eyestalks.

On our side of the chamber, glowing green cog oil oozed across the chamber walls. I could see it advancing on a salient a few meters away, trying to outflank the yellow slime. It stopped, crystallized into sharp-edged structures, and stood fast as the yellow slime spread toward it.

Then the yellow stuff gathered itself together, pulled away from the surface, and pounced on the green cog oil rampart. Nothing moved for a moment, then the crystallized green cog oil dissolved under the yellow slime.

Further away, the cog oil raised up small towers and embankments. Across the void, the cog structures seemed to drain the yellow slime from its lodgement. But in other places, they looked ready to go down before the onslaught.

"We are so screwed," Krissie said. "It's all over, isn't it?"

"When I was a silly rilly, I learned an important lesson," I said. "In reality, 'one,' 'some,' 'many,' 'most,' and 'all' are not interchangeable terms."

"Yeah?" she said. "What's that mean?"

"They're only interchangeable in your mind. That's where one setback becomes a total defeat. Come on, let's see what Willie wants to do."

We left quickly, and a chill ran up my spine. Even if I knew better, I couldn't help but share Krissie's doubts and fears.

* * *

"What you got is your core and your peripherals," Willie said.

Little beads of sweat covered his hairless skull, and without gravity to pull them down they just stayed in place.

"The yellow stuff is fighting to take over our peripherals. And where they've got an advantage in processors, they're winning. There's no way they could take over the core, of course."

"No way?"

"None. I don't have any doubts. My guys have done an analysis of what they're running in the yellow stuff. Nothing we can't beat ... given enough time and enough oil."

"We have enough oil," I said, wiping the sweat from my own brow. It was hot in The Brewery. The cog-brains were cranking at full capacity, and that meant borrowing some from the processors needed to manage environmental systems. They could make it cooler, but that would mean thinking slower. "But do we have enough time?"

"I don't know," Willie said. "But we've got something better. We have a plan."

"And what's the plan?"

"We're going to let Black Knight loose upon them."

My jaw swiveled and one eyebrow scrunched up as I shook my head. "Are you out of your mind?"

"Just in the peripherals," Willie said. "We know we can defeat the Knight. And I'm pretty sure the Knight can beat the yellow stuff. If it can't, it can slow it down enough that our regular oil will do it in."

"This is your best idea?"

"Moses backs me up on this," Willie said.

I sighed. I let my mind go clear, waiting to see if something else would rise up out of the dark place where my ideas usually come from. Nothing happened.

"All right," I said. "Go ahead. But if this doesn't work, I'm probably going to ask for your resignation or something."

Willie laughed. "If it doesn't work, we're cooked anyway."

A few minutes later, three of Willie's crew manhandled a globe full of cog oil out of the vault where the Black Knight and his cohort were kept. They pulled it over to a work station and lashed it into place. Then they plugged a firehose-thick pipe of cog oil into a socket on one end of the globe.

Nothing happened at first. Then Willie pulled up a screen with a remote view of the plenum chamber at the locks.

Lights began to flicker and the cog-plumbing shimmered at points along its length. What looked like flames appeared on the walls – and I felt a sudden flare of panic before realizing that stone didn't burn. A closer look made it clear that the "flames" were just projections from the cog-plumbing.

"Look upon me!" I heard the voice on the screen and its echo on the repeater in my ear from the crews in the chamber.

"Look upon me!" the voice commanded. "I'll show you the life of the mind! Arrrrgh! Arrrgh! I'll show you the life of the mind. I will show you the life of the mind."

"I'm thinking that's probably Magicar," I said.

"Sounds like his kind of thing," Willie said. "It's from an old movie."

"It certainly sets my skin crawling," I said.

Then the battle was joined. Willie warned me that it could take hours before it was settled. He wasn't kidding.

We turned the sound off so that Magicar stopped making us nervous, and Willie found something cold to drink.

Declan and Krissie stayed with us. There was no safer place in Castle Anthrax. Krissie saw to it that we ate something from time to time. All the while muttering something about "missing chromosomes" and asking us how long we'd go without eating if she weren't around.

"Where did you get the beer?" I asked.

"We make it here," he said. "We don't call this place The Brewery for nothing. The cogs cultivate the yeast and then crank up the processing. We can duplicate almost anything they make back home."

After a while, Declan and Krissie both fell into a ragged sleep while Willie and I kept talking. Talking about Detroit and Boston. About justice and peace. About poetry and history.

"When it comes to defending against a siege, the true masters were the Knights Hospitaller," Willie said. "Old crusaders who got kicked out of Jerusalem. They went Cyprus first, then they moved to Rhodes because they didn't like the local politics. They built a castle there from pieces of an old wonder of the world. Then Suleiman the Magnificent invaded the island with 200,000 men against 7,000 knights. They had a secret weapon – the hospital. They bound up the wounded and sent them back into battle. They held out against Suleiman for six months."

"That's pretty good," I said. "But I'm thinking they still lost."

"True, but the survivors were allowed to move to Sicily. A few years later, they were given the island of Malta. They fortified that from one end to the other, using it as a base to police the Mediterranean against pirates."

"You know, that sounds like a great racket. We should try and set up a business like that when the war is over. How long did they keep that up?"

"A couple of centuries," Willie said. "Until Napoleon came along and made them quit."

He went off for a while and found a couple more containers of beer.

"Ever read any poetry?" he asked.

"As little as possible," I replied. "I was interested in other things whenever I had spare time to read."

"When I first got here, I started reading stuff about King Arthur. Grail poetry. There's a lot of that."

"I think I knew that," I said.

"There's one by an American poet called the 'Siege Perilous,'" he said. "'Long warned of many terrors more severe, to scorch him than hell's engines could awaken, he scanned again, too far to be so near, the fearful seat no man had ever taken.'"

"That's pretty good," I said. "I can remember 'Jabberwocky' and 'Casey at the Bat,' but they're easy."

Willie smiled. "I cheated," he said. "I looked it up again today. You see, the Siege Perilous was a seat at the Round Table. It was reserved by Merlin for the knight who was going to find the Holy Grail. And anyone who sat in it who wasn't worthy would die."

"Merlin was pretty strict," I said.

"Sure was," Willie said. "But you get my point, don't you? The Holy Grail was supposed to cure all ills. Make you healthy and whole again. And what we've brewed up here could be the Holy Grail – at least for cogs."

"You've mentioned that before," I said. "After someone asked where the name 'Castle Anthrax' came from."

"I guess I did," Willie said. "But the point I'm making is that this could be the Siege Perilous for us. We're about to take that seat. And if we haven't really found the grail, it could be fatal. For all of us."

"You know what I think?" I asked him.

"What's that?"

"I think you've spent too much time talking to Moses," I said. "And I think you're right about this grail thing. And I think I need some more beer."

* * *

I woke up tethered to a crossbeam in a corner of Willie's workshop. It felt like someone had wrapped my tongue in a dirty woolen sock. I wasn't awake and moving more than a couple of minutes when Krissie appeared with a bulb of orange juice.

"It's the real thing," she said. "From the Emerald Ring. Not a cog-made substitute."

Krissie had changed her clothes, retrieving something from one of her mesh bags, no doubt. Her tattoo snake danced across her shoulders as she swung around the bamboo to bring a bulb of juice to Declan.

"You look less alive than usual," Willie said when he popped out of a tunnel at one end of the shop.

"I feel less alive than usual," I said.

"Well, I have some good news and some bad news," he said.

"Good news first. It's too early for bad news straight."

"The Black Knight has won the battle for control of the yellow slime peripherals."

"That's certainly good news," I said. "What's the rest of the story?"

"We think we know where the yellow core is. Theoretically, if not actually."

"And what's that mean?"

"There were four missiles. One hit the kids' place. One hit Ring Umber. One hit that greenhouse you looked at. And we think the core is in the fourth one. We just don't know exactly where that is yet."

"You think? How sure are you?"

"The cogs have analyzed the yellow slime signals. They're definitely in contact with a core somewhere close by. And the fourth missile is the only logical place it could be."

"We've got search parties looking for it, don't we?"

"Of course," Willie said. "Damage control kids in suits and external cog units backing them up. But it's going to take time."

"The one thing we are running out of," I said. "All right, we need to call a Council of War. You, me, Mike, the big AIs, if you think they'll help."

"Right here, boss," Mike said.

"Moses here, boss," said a voice with a deep timbre and resonance. I wondered who had come up with it.

"I've given this a lot of thought, and here's our dilemma. We've got the most powerful cog system in the world, ready to take down any other operating system and replace it with ours. But we don't have any way to deliver it."

"We agree," Moses said. "This was not the scenario that we anticipated when our work was ready to be deployed. This is a scientific base, not a war machine."

"Until now," I said. "So Moses, have you given any thought to what the other side is thinking? Do you think they know what they're up against?"

"If they knew what we were doing here, they would have destroyed us without wasting time on a preliminary attack. Most likely with nuclear weapons. That is how we have gamed it out – hundreds of times now."

"Even if they wanted to take over the base and use our technology themselves?" I asked.

"If that were the case, they would have started with more force. They would have deemed us worth the risk of a human boarding party."

"That's sort of what I've been thinking myself," I said. "They're not acting like they know how absolutely important we are. If they did, they wouldn't have sent one ship, they'd have sent three. And we'd already be their prisoners. So they're kind of clueless ... poking around in the dark, trying to figure out what kind of defense we can put up."

"Agreed," said Moses.

"And what's going to happen when they figure out that we can't put up any kind of defense? At least not one that would be effective."

"Then they will board us. People on Castle Anthrax will be killed. From 10 to 25 percent casualties, a fifth of them killed."

"That's as many as 50 dead and 200 wounded. Not a good outcome. How long before they figure this out and send in the storm troopers?"

"Soon," Moses said. "A matter of some hours. Probably not more than a day. It depends on how much imagination they have."

"Can we figure out some way to get our cogs onto that ship before then?"

"Perhaps. The best way would be to find the yellow core. If we could take it over and turn it into a Trojan horse, it would transmit our software through any firewalls before they could stop it."

"And how long before we find that core?"

"We have no way of knowing."

"That's what I was afraid of," I said. "Then it looks like we're going to have to do something radical. Something I've been hoping it wouldn't come to."

"What's that, boss?" Willie asked as he wiped the sweat from his brow with a kerchief.

"We're going to have to surrender."

* * *

Meanwhile, on the other side of the hill…

The war had not treated Courtney kindly. Some of the things that had happened in Germany while she was a refugee had turned her hard. She even carried a gun. She'd never used it, but she got it because when she was in Germany and had nothing but a knife, she wished she'd had a gun. The one time she'd had to use it, there was an element of closeness with the knife that repelled her. Which was why she got the gun.

International Healthdata was small enough of an organization that she was able to shine pretty quickly. She showed the mercenaries how to tap into the warehouse networks where medical supplies and other useful booty could be found. Then she learned about weaponizing cogtech. There were only a couple of steps up the ladder to the Divine Sword.

And beyond those steps…

What Courtney really wanted was something safe and secure to do, something that didn't involve sleeping with someone to get it. Actually or virtually. (In fact, the virtual option was more disgusting than the actual one.)

When the data came in from the asteroid base, she thought she might have found what she wanted. One purpose of the explosives barrage was to probe the asteroid's interior. They'd fired a few seismic sensors at the surface of the rock and the explosions gave them a good three-dimensional map of its insides.

It was big. There could be hundreds of people in there.

If they were smart and didn't repeat their mistakes with the science base, they could make serious use of this place. And that would require a prize crew with a reliable leader.

She could be that leader. She saw no downside to separating herself from Zadran. And this could be her own private empire within International Healthdata. If only Zadran would go along with it.

And with that thought, her hopes and dreams dimmed.

One bright light shined in the darkness – she was about to send the order that would beat the asteroid's cogware. In a few minutes, endless rows of dominoes would fall through the cog oil, flipping endless rows of switches and giving her the prize.

* * *

It seemed obvious to me.

The only way to buy enough time, the only way to get our cogware into their system, the only way to avoid senseless bloodshed and loss of life, was to invite them in closer. As long as they kept their distance, we couldn't use our advantage.

But it wasn't immediately obvious to anyone else.

Moses seemed to see it before Willie.

"You know you are completely out of your mind," Willie said. "This isn't a game of chess where you go out for a beer with the other guy after you resign."

The cog-AI took his time responding – I believe he was thinking it through, in his cog fashion of gaming the scenarios.

"It does appear to give us some leverage," Moses said after Willie and I went back and forth for a few minutes. "The boss is correct. It gives us time and increases our chance of access to their system."

Then, before we could discuss it further, things changed.

"Excuse me a moment," Moses said.

"Boss, you there?" Mike asked, and without waiting for an answer, he added: "The yellow cogs have switched off Magicar and are deleting the Black Knight from their peripherals."

"What in the nine blue hells of Triton is going on?" Willie asked.

"We have suffered an unforeseen reversal," Moses said.

"I thought you said we were almost done with the yellow stuff," I said.

"Apparently we were mistaken," Moses replied.

"Willie? What's up?"

Willie was talking to another cog persona and he didn't answer me for until he was done.

"They figured out how to defeat our malware," he said. "It took them a while, but once they had it analyzed and countermeasures written up, they filled their peripherals with the code and activated it all at once. Magicar just went dead. The Black Knight is losing contact with his cogs and they seem to be closing in on his core processors."

"Are they going to beat us?" I asked.

"Not likely," Willie said. "They didn't do anything that we didn't learn to do long ago. Turning off Magicar is easy when you know where the switches are. The Black Knight has a whole list of vulnerabilities – I keep them on my phone in case of an emergency. Once we had them safe in a can, I was going to do exactly what they just did."

"But we don't have them safe in a can."

"No," Willie said. "But if we find that stupid core, we can do to them what they did to Magicar. Isn't that right, Moses."

"We have analyzed their operating system," Moses said. "It can be defeated."

"What if it has more surprises in its bag of tricks?" I asked.

"Then we'll have to do it the hard way – rely on our superior computing power to outthink it," Willie said. "We've got fifteen tons of cog processing systems here in The Brewery. All central processing power. There's very little chance that they can match us if we go cog to cog."

"If we can find the core," I said. "If we can get at them. If we can't, it's just a Mexican standoff – except we don't have a gun, just bullets."

"Well yeah," Willie said. "If you're going to put it that way."

"It looks like we don't have much choice but to go with my original plan," I said. "Does anyone know if we have a white flag somewhere?"

* * *

We didn't have a white flag, but we did have a VHF-FM radio transmitter – simple voice comms, a low-bandwidth signal with little capacity for sending serious malware.

We set it up to transmit a simple message.

"This is KFP Research Station Alpha," it said. "I am David

Mulcahey, the station commander. We wish to surrender. We make no preconditions. We are not a military installation and have no defensive capabilities. Please contact us on this VHF channel. Please stop your attacks. We are not a hostile agency."

It was not an honest message, of course. No one with fifteen tons of cog AI could be considered to be without defensive capabilities. And we were certainly hostile towards anyone who attacked us. But those were the niceties of a surrender offer by a research station.

During the next few hours, in which no response came our way, I thought some more about what the guys on the other side of the wall must be thinking.

If their core was sending back signals from its hiding place, then they would know what it had experienced. Their peripherals had been attacked by our security system – Magicar. They were able to defeat Magicar and were shutting down The Black Knight – which they would consider to be our main core. After all, they had no reason to suspect that we had more than a dozen tanks full of cog central processors. They had no reason to suspect what our purpose was.

It should have reassured me. It did not. It only made me wonder what they were up to that I didn't suspect.

Then they replied.

The message came over on the same VHF channel we were using.

"This is the Divine Sword," the message said, in a woman's voice. "If you want to surrender, stop all attempts to block our operating system from accessing your central processor. Stop all attempts to block our microwave transmissions. Cease all defensive actions."

That made sense, I was thinking. Then they stopped making sense.

"And you must surrender your commander into our custody. A

transport container will be sent to your main lock in one hour. Have him board the container unarmed and without information systems technology. He will remain hostage to your good faith. Divine Sword out."

Willie looked at me with a puzzled expression. Declan, who was still with me, made an odd crowing sound.

"That's an odd idea," he said.

"It certainly is," I replied. "I've been trying for hours to figure out a way to get one of us aboard that ship. I never thought they'd make it a condition of surrender."

"It was not one of our likely scenarios," Moses said. "There are too many opportunities for catastrophic failure for the warship."

"I just figured that if I was them and they were us, the last thing in the world I'd want to do is let one of them onto my ship," I said.

"It's crazy," Willie added.

"Or stupid," Declan offered.

"Or both," I said. "Or maybe they have something planned that we just can't imagine. In any case, we've got an hour. Anyone have any ideas about how we can get cog tech onto that warship?"

"I have one ..." Declan said.

"Me too," Krissie said.

"I don't know how to get our cogs over there," Willie said. "But I've been thinking about how to take over their core here on the castle."

"Then let's get to work and see if we can turn this thing around," I said. "Because in a little while, I'm not going to be in much of a position to help anyone."

The awful prospect of becoming a hostage on board the warship was starting to sink in, and it made my blood feel like liquid hydrogen.

* * *

Meanwhile, on the other side of the hill ...

It was wrong, wrong, wrong for Zadran to bring someone aboard from the asteroid. There was no way to control them, no way to adequately scan them, no way to defeat their guile. Courtney tried to explain it to the captain, but explaining things generally was a one-way process with Zadran.

"You have no idea what could happen if we take the wrong risks," she told him. "If you must bring him aboard, you need to keep him in strict quarantine. There's no telling what he could have with him."

"I have my own ways of neutralizing a risk," Zadran said. "And they are based on strength, not fear."

His dark eyes locked with hers briefly, and in one terrifying moment she knew that all her hopes were dashed. Zadran would never give her control of the asteroid base. She was too weak. She had given herself away as too fearful. She would never be more than the men above her wanted her to be. She would never escape the Divine Sword or the hard men who ran International Healthdata.

* * *

The transport container wasn't much more than a spacebuoy with jetpack built in. It glided into the open lock, we shut the outer door, we opened the inner door, and I pulled myself through into the chamber.

There wasn't enough space in the container to straighten out, and

I was forced to tuck my legs under me into a buddha-like squat. One of my boys pulled the seal shut and the buoy pressurized.

The inner door closed and sealed, the chamber was evacuated, the outer door opened, and the jetpack hissed, pushing me out into space.

I was all alone with my increasingly despairing thoughts as I drifted slowly away from Castle Anthrax and towards the looming black silhouette of the Divine Sword.

When I arrived, they went through the reverse process at their lock. Doors closed, the chamber filled with air, a door opened, and a pair of large spacehands unsealed the buoy and pulled me out.

They handled me roughly. And it got worse.

They pulled me down a narrow passageway crowded with pipes and conduits and yellow veins of cog oil. They didn't seem to mind if they banged me against the bulkheads and the fittings.

They pushed me into a mostly featureless compartment a few meters wide, stripped my clothing off me, then left me naked, floating in midair. I'd been naked before, so it didn't bother me much. Someone else might have felt powerless and afraid. I felt powerless, because for the most part I was. And afraid, but not because of my nakedness – I was a prisoner of war.

So I spent the time admiring the new set of tattoos I wore. None of them moved like Krissie's snake, but they were elegant and elaborate. Maltese crosses, Maori scrollwork, Celtic runes. They covered much of my flesh. Maybe that was why I didn't feel as exposed in my nakedness.

One of the spacehands who entered the chamber after a long while commented on them.

"Nice ink," he said. "Too bad we're going to have to mess it up."

That made me afraid.

There were two of them. They had magnetic anchors to hold them in place against the metal walls of the compartment. And once they were anchored, their feet secured, they began to beat me.

The first few blows hurt the most – partly because they were so unexpected.

They were methodical in their work, aiming at muscles that would stay bruised for a long time, and the kidneys and the ribs. One of my ribs cracked during the process – it felt like it would hurt for days afterwards.

But all the while, I thanked Professor Newton and his Third Law. Every blow they landed forced them away from me. If we had all been grounded by gravity on Earth, the force of their efforts would have gone entirely into hurting me. But here in microgravity, even anchored the way they were, the punches were pulled and the impact more elastic.

The last punch landed in my face. It missed the nose, but smacked my cheek. It cut the inside of my mouth on my teeth and tasted blood.

The two spacehands unhooked their feet from their anchors, detached them from the walls, and sent them caroming out the door into the passageway. A third man tossed a package at me.

"Put this one," he said. It was a yellow paper coverall.

Then he threw me a towel. "And wipe your face," he said as he shut the door.

I floated there for a few minutes, one large ball of pain and ache with hands and feet and ears. Then I put on the coverall, wiped my face, and pushed myself into one of the corners, where the plumbing gave me enough purchase to hold myself in place.

Then I watched as the ink from my tattoos crawled down my

arms, onto the pipes, and out through the fittings in the wall.

* * *

"I wanted you to know that you have been defeated," said the dark man in the screen on the left.

The blonde woman in the screen on the right said nothing.

An hour had passed after my beating before someone returned to my compartment, brought in the two screens, attached them to the wall, and left.

The dark man was Omar Zadran, captain of the Divine Sword. He said he was from Cairo.

The woman was Courtney Olson, from Chicago. She was the ship's first officer.

"I want you to know that you have been beaten in body and soul, not just in some elaborate video game," he said, waving his fingers at the term. "Your base is now belong to us, as they say. We will be deciding how many of your personnel will be useful to us. And how many will not."

I noticed the slightest wince from First Officer Olson, as if she wasn't entirely comfortable with the idea that some of my personnel might not be useful. And with what that might mean.

"So you will start by telling me what research you are conducting and what facilities you have available," Captain Zadran said.

I took a deep breath, which hurt terribly and made tears well up in my eyes.

"Well here I am, hat in my hand, except I don't seem to have it in my hand anymore," I said. "I came to surrender, so I can't complain about the treatment." I coughed, which was sheer agony, and I had to wipe my eyes before I could see the two screens again.

"Let me start with a little history. The 21st century has not been humanity's finest hour. We've been trying since it began to avoid being dragged into the future with all our might. Insane wars fought for no useful purpose. Political movements that celebrated the most irrational parts of our past. Elites who insisted on doing the exact opposite of what any sensible elite would do – financially, economically, politically, militarily. It's been just one damned thing after another from start to finish. And here we are, at the end of the century and we're all carrying knives – what a bunch of barbarians we've turned into."

"You should be thinking about getting to the point," Zadran said. He didn't seem like a patient man, but I wasn't going to let that stop me. I was playing for time.

"The point. Yes. So in spite of all our efforts, we manage at the end of the century to invent the solution to all humanity's problems. Cog technology. The end of scarcity. The end of scraping around in the dirt trying to find enough to eat and stay warm and keep out of the rain. The end of a system controlled by people who lived by profiting from everyone else's need – and who sustained that need to sustain those profits.

"It's no wonder everyone went to war over it. And now here we are. The world is a broken, bleeding wreck. Nations are gone forever. Five billion people are dead. The survivors huddle in the rubble, clinging to the few secure networks that maintain their lives. And we go around fighting over who gets which scraps.

"Back when it started, the thing we all feared the most was uncontrolled cog technology. Gray goo. The end of the electronic nervous system that held the planet together. Something had to be done to attack that problem. Something radical. So the people in Seattle and elsewhere sent their top guys out here into space, somewhere safe and isolated from the chaos on the ground, to work on the problem."

"I hope this is your point," Zadran said, shifting uncomfortably in his impatience. I could understand now why he had blundered so badly, bringing me aboard his vessel. A patient man would not have done that.

"This is my point," I said. "For three years, we've been working on that problem. And we think we've solved it. In order for cog technology to be safe for humanity – and humanity to be safe for cog technology – we needed to create an operating system that would prevent the catastrophes we all feared. Something that would prevent runaway disassemblers at its very roots, by locking in code that would keep it from running away. Something that would defend itself against attacks, maintaining its integrity and security in a world of paranoid hysteria, thick with malware and viruses and worms. Something that could take over any other cogware and make it a part of itself."

I noticed First Officer Olson's eyes widen just a bit. She was quiet, but she seemed to be paying attention.

"Something that would bind the world together again and make it safe. Something that would cure the ills, banish the evils, and make this endless war of all against all ... well ... end. The head of my research team says he spends a lot of time talking to one of our AIs. He says they talk a lot about justice. I'm thinking that this operating system we've come up with is probably going to go a long ways to restoring justice to an unjust world. Perhaps by making it impossible for the unjust to use it. I don't know. They haven't gone into the details with me."

"And this is your point?" Zadran said. "You've done antivirus research to protect cog technology?"

"My point?" I said. "No. That's not my point. My point is that we've got the future in our hands. We've got the end of this war in our hands. And to make the war end, we've got to be generous and selfless. So my point is that we've got to invite everyone to take part. And I'm here to invite you. I'm inviting you to join us. Become a part of the world that will emerge from the madness."

I looked at First Officer Olson and hoped she would sense that my attention was directed at her.

"My research guy says we've got the Holy Grail of cog technology in our hands," I said. "I'm inviting you to come over to our side. Come drink from our grail."

"I think I need to have you beaten some more," Zadran said.

"Excuse me a moment," First Officer Olson said as she slid out of her micrograv chair and out of the picture. Zadran looked surprised, but said nothing.

In the silence, I thought about Declan's plan, doing the math in my head. Each of his "flowers" contained a gram of cogtech. Here in close to the Castle, there were a couple dozen flowers per cubic kilometer ... about sixteen hundred flowers within a few kilometers for a total of about a kilogram and a half of cogtech.

One by one, the flowers vented gases and veered toward the Divine Sword. One by one, they smacked silently against its hull, each in the same targeted spot. A few at first, then a steady stream. Undetected, because no one was crazy enough to light up a radar system in an environment of powerful malware. Undetected, because each flower was so small.

In the five hours since we'd started sending them in, most of the sixteen hundred flowers hit the spot, sending the cogtech on its way to find a path into the warship and into its heart and soul.

Willie had been terrified that we'd get the core on Castle Anthrax, but it wouldn't make a link back to the warship. But with our own cogware on board, the problems became drastically easier to solve.

Either Declan's flowers or the cogs in my new tattoos would find a way into the system and get our cogware over the wall.

Any minute now, I expected them to succeed. Hopefully before Zadran ordered his spacehands to work me over some more.

Suddenly, on the left-hand screen, Captain Zadran turned his head. For a brief moment, I saw First Officer Olson beside him.

Then I saw a flash of light and a loud BANG! Captain Zadran's face went slack. First Officer Olson pulled him from his micrograv chair and pushed him aside.

"Mr. Moriarty, Captain Zadran was an evil man. He would never appreciate what you have done here," she said. "Now tell me more about your plans. How are you going to bring your technology back to Earth?"

At that moment, the vein of yellow light above the doorway turned to a vein of green light.

"Boss, you there?" asked a familiar voice.

"Right here, Mike," I said. "Right here."

Relic of War

1

She felt her fingertips lose contact with the wall and for the first time in her life, Amy Hackenyos felt truly alone.

"That was a really dumb thing to do," she said aloud, her voice swallowed quickly by the dome of her spacesuit helmet and the empty vacuum beyond.

And the realization caught her completely unprepared.

It hit her as she drifted in the microgravity of the Grand Concourse – joined by the sudden panic of losing contact with the safety wire and the wall and any other solid anchor. It was layered upon the terrible embarrassment she felt at getting herself into such a predicament. And upon the anger she felt at being left behind by her shipmates as they went on to explore the labyrinthine depths of asteroid 12375 Burnham.

She hung in space, close to one wall of the shaft, but not close enough to reach it – and there was no one to help her.

"Now what do I do?" she asked. The spacesuit might have answered her, but it did not. Was it incapable of offering suggestions? Or was it designed to force her to use her own wits? That was just the kind of thing the Patrol would do to cadets like her.

Mud Month back on Mars had not included microgravity instruction. They'd taught her how to wear her uniform, how to march, how to salute, and little else. What little training she'd had in weightlessness had come back aboard the *Able Countryman* – occasional drills under the supervision of Mother Janus where the six cadets would practice moving about in the center of the gym. It had reminded her a bit of swimming, only you didn't have to hold your breath.

But none of it was much use now. The gym was only a few meters wide, and you were never out of reach of one wall or the other. The Grand Concourse was twenty meters across.

She tried to slow her breathing and suppress the panic reaction. Part of the panic was the insistence of her senses and her autonomic nervous system that she was about to fall down the deepest rabbit hole she had ever seen. She was close to the docks, but nearly a thousand meters from the entrance to Fort Apache at the other end of the tunnel. Bars of light illuminated the shaft, gathering the shadows up into bands of darkness that seemed to descend into the bottom of the asteroid.

"Don't look down," she told herself sternly. But it was too late. A wave of vertigo swept over her.

It took a moment for Amy to remind herself that she was not at the top of the shaft, but at one end. Closing her eyes seemed to help, and visualizing a cross-section of the big rock did even more. Some deep-breathing exercises brought her racing heart under control.

When she opened her eyes, Amy knew what she had to do to rescue herself. It was just a matter of Newton's third law of motion put into practice. For every action there was an equal and opposite reaction. The same principal made rockets work.

Except that she had no reaction mass to get her out of her predicament.

Her spacesuit was completely self-contained. Air-processing packs and other subsystems were little more than bulges under the suit's slick skin. The helmet was a big glass globe sealed to the suit's collar. She had pockets, but a quick check showed nothing in them.

She knew of no way to vent gases from the suit, which would have been a quick solution to the problem. A maneuvering gun that could have done that for her would have been useful, but the other cadets had taken those with them.

That was two foolish mistakes in one day: Letting go of the safety wire without grabbing hold of something else first – and not insisting that they leave a gasgun with her.

All right, she asked herself, if she couldn't move, what would happen to her?

She would fall after all, she decided. Microgravity wasn't zero-gravity. The asteroid was still massive enough to have some pull. She tried to remember what Ivan Blandings had said when they arrived two days earlier. Two millimeters per second every second – that was it.

She did some mental math, struggling to avoid confusion over the distance- time formulas. The result was nearly enough to send her back into a panic – a million seconds to fall the length of the Grand Concourse. That was nearly two weeks.

Then she remembered that the shaft did not pass through the asteroid's center of gravity. It was well up towards one end of the mass, and the center was somewhere on the far side of the opposite wall. Twenty meters, then. No, thirty to include the offset from being so close to the surface.

That was better – thirty thousand seconds. Only eight hours. She could survive eight hours. It might get boring, but she could survive it.

"I just need to be patient."

Once she resigned herself to her fate, though, she discovered that boredom was not the problem. Her sense of isolation and loneliness returned with a vengeance.

And it surprised her once again. She'd spent most of her seventeen years in virtual isolation. Or rather, in real isolation in a virtual community. She'd had her parents and five brothers and sisters around, of course, but in the Idaho valley where she'd grown up, it was easy to get away from the homestead and be by yourself. And all her virtual neighbors were little more than bits of light and color in the parlor or on her personal screen. They all could be whisked away with the touch of switch.

But now she was truly alone. There were only five other souls within a million of kilometers of her – and they had left her behind to go further into the asteroid.

She knew why she'd been chosen. She didn't get along well with the other cadets. They were always getting annoyed at her, and she never understood why.

Ivan in particular didn't like her. Maybe because she pointed out when he made mistakes of fact – one of her greatest personal failings – and refused to back down when he tried to bully his way out of the error.

It had been Ivan's idea to bring the ship to Burnham.

"It will make our reputations in the Patrol for the rest of our lives," he'd said.

Amy wasn't sure if she wanted that kind of reputation, but there was little she could do to talk the other cadets out of it. She didn't even try.

So when it came time to decide who would go on and who would stay to make contact with the follow-up team, they'd decided Amy could be spared.

The significance of their decision was not lost on her.

She was used to that, anyway. Even her virtual friends never let her get close to them. It was as if they knew her secret life on the virtual net. But no, that was too frightening and too unlikely. There was no reason for them to suspect and no way for them to learn the truth.

She tried to put it out of her mind. She would show everyone some day. When she became a full officer in the Solar Patrol, they would realize who she had always been inside. And they would ignore her no longer.

In the meantime, she was moving ever so slowly and imperceptibly towards the far wall of the shaft.

After a time, she was successful at pushing her feelings and fears away. She drifted in both internal and external silence, her eyes glazing over at the unchanging sight of the far wall of the Concourse.

And it was partly because of that state that she noticed the movement before her.

She dismissed it at first sight, but the motion continued. And when she came fully alert, focusing on its source, her heart begin to pound in her chest.

It looked like a tiny insect, passing between her and the far wall at a few centimeters per second. The thing was no more than a centimeter in length, and it looked like a large ladybug. There were no wings, of course, since there was no air in the concourse to make them useful.

And that thought set her blood racing even stronger.

If there was no air, then how could an insect live here? And since there was no way that she could imagine to allow such a thing, what was the tiny beast flying before her eyes?

* * *

Nathaniel Ybarro-Carson had been in his cabin on the *Evan Hill* reading a newscast about the signals from the Barnard's Star probe when the call to the captain's cabin came – the call that eventually sent him searching for the partridge ship *Able Countryman*.

And now, a day later, as he scanned the empty black volume before him, he wondered if the AI aboard that probe felt the same way he did.

It wasn't that he was all alone in vast space, wrapped in a few tons of metal and gas. It was that he couldn't find what he'd come looking for.

The Barnard's probe had had much the same problem. The pictures and the commentary on the video-net had been disappointing – no Earth-like planets. So Nat had gone looking for a written story to get a more optimistic review of the story.

Whoever said a picture was worth a thousand words had never seen the way the videonet told a story. The words were infinitely more informative. Certainly the probe had found nothing Earth-like

– that is, no planets with oxygen in the atmosphere or liquid water on the surface. But what it did find was so rich in treasure that Nat couldn't understand why they'd left it out of the videonet news.

Barnard's Star was a dim, red ember compared to the bright yellow pyres of Sol and Alpha Centauri A. It held its planets close – a couple of small tide-locked worlds with thick ice-shields and a swarm of asteroids with orbits that swung close to the star itself.

Earth-like planets were nothing but useless gravity wells. You had to pump tons of chemicals together to get up out of them with the kind of stuff you already had available in clear space. And the Barnard's Star system seemed to have more than an abundance of the stuff – all in dynamically convenient orbits. The author of the newstext had been much more excited than the videonet's computer-generated newsreaders could ever have been.

He remembered the Alpha Centauri Probe a few years earlier. The story had been similar then. No Earth-like planets, everyone said, and back home on Earth the disappointment was all anyone heard about. But there weren't any Earth-like planets here in the solar system once you got off Earth – and more than half a billion people had made their homes out here in space.

At Alpha, there had been small but volatile-rich versions of gas giants – like Uranus, only smaller. Ice-worlds the size of Mars and wrapped in glaciers circled both A, the G-class primary at Alpha Centauri, and B, its K-class mate. Clouds of asteroids and comets surrounded the two stars, their orbits stirred up and their distribution skewed so much that they were thick as fruit flies above a week-old orange.

They were both a spacer's dream – quick orbits, handy volatiles, and lots of rock and metal for building. Who cared about Earth-like planets when there was wealth like this to be had?

Nat, on the other hand, could report nothing nearly as tantalizing.

He'd been looking over this piece of space for nearly an hour and hadn't found a thing. And he should have spotted the *Able Countryman* easily by now. Commander Nkada had been right – the partridge ship had disappeared.

"Are you sure, sir?" Nat had asked when the captain of the *Evan Hill* told him of the situation. "I thought the Argos system watched everything in the inner system and most of the outer."

"It does," Nkada said. "It watched the *Countryman* disappear."

Nat felt embarrassed and slow-witted. He knew he shouldn't, but he couldn't help but be somewhat awe-struck by the man – he was a Survivor.

Nkada was eighty-two years old and had come out of retirement to ferry the cruiser out to Mars. His commissioning certificate from the old EDC cops – older than the Solar Patrol itself – hung on the wall of his cabin. He'd been on the Moon during the Last War and was one of the defenders of Clavius City. Nat was never sure how to act before him. What could you say to a man who'd lived through the end of the world and helped build a new one?

"Here are the images – one every five seconds. You can see the exhaust plume here. Then it goes out, and you can see the ship itself. Follow it for about eighty frames – more than six minutes – and the ship itself vanishes."

"Yes, sir," Nat replied. "Could there have been an explosion during the interval between images?"

"Not that wouldn't have left evidence of some kind. An expanding cloud of hot gas. Wreckage. No, that's the problem. It vanished without a trace. So we're sending you to go look for it.

They're budding off a hummingbird ship for you right now. You'll have orders downloaded by the time it's ready to go. You'll be given enough reaction mass to get you to the orbital parameters of the *Countryman's* last vector and then to Mars or Earth orbit when you're done."

"Yes, sir. What do you think happened to them?"

"Who knows, son?" Nkada said, a gray-white smile breaking across his dark face. "Maybe it's some smart-ass cadets who've found a way to make their vessel stealthy. Maybe it was an explosion so powerful that the residue was driven off too quickly to see. Or maybe it was an invisible ship-eating alien the size of Phobos. That's what you'll have to find out."

Nat had nodded and saluted before leaving the captain's cabin. But as he pulled himself along the main passageway a few minutes later, he began to grow suspicious. Nkada knew more than he was letting on. Those suggestions about the fate of the *Countryman* – Nat had the feeling he was being led on and that Commander Nkada had recited them too quickly. It was almost as if he'd rehearsed them too many times.

That was silly, he thought at the time. He couldn't possibly have been serious about an invisible alien the size of Phobos. But what other explanation was there for the disappearance of the *Countryman*?

And why else should it be so hard to find?

* * *

"Everyone ready?" Pham asked, her voice close by in Peter Salerno's spacesuit helmet. "We're going in."

Peter stood back as the others crowded around the heavy metal of the door, putting the hastily crafted equipment into place.

Pham Noc Do was carrying the cog oil. She drew a glass syringe out of her bag, drew a few cc's of the luminescent green stuff, then sealed the port on the lantern. Placing the syringe in the right spot was more difficult, however. Maneuvering in microgravity was an awkward and frustrating practice. Just when you thought you were OK, you put out a stray moment arm and began spinning.

And without any sense of balance, you could be hit with panic attacks. Like imagining that you were at the top of the Well looking down instead of at the bottom looking up. Peter kept his eyes on the great doorway that stretched forty meters from wall to wall to avoid such an attack.

Sure enough, Pham began to spin as she moved in close to the surface.

"Uh oh," she said. "Someone give me a hand."

Peter reached out to steady her while holding himself fast to a stanchion. She followed Cheng Li Hui's directions, and Peter could see her set the needle in the tiny gap beside one of the big wheels that turned the locks on the portal.

She pumped the syringe dry, sending little cogs into the works of the door. Then she put the syringe away and poked a stiff wire into the same gap. At the other end of the wire were leads connected to the flat data board that Cheng held in her hand.

Peter swallowed hard. Cogs still made him nervous. He knew it was a feeling he would have to overcome if he wanted to be a success in the Patrol. But he just didn't trust the stuff. He figured it was because he didn't know enough about it. That was why he'd signed up for the whole battery of nanotechnology courses from the

Institute.

Unfortunately, what he'd learned so far did not reassure him. The basic-level classes were heavy on the dangers of uncontrolled nanos – the old technology from the war – with pictures of gray goo and a lot of video scenes taken from popular melodramas intermixed with documentary imaging.

He was not one to admit to a squeamish stomach, but some of the real stuff was more disturbing than the special effects.

So he kept a healthy distance from the rest of the group while they waited for the cogs to do their job.

"I'm getting an image," Cheng said. "There – you can see the bolts and the turning mechanism. And there's the electronics. And here's the lock."

"Are you still in touch with them?" asked Ivan Blandings. Now there was a cool one. You knew he wasn't squeamish about the Wee Littles. Or anything else for that matter. Peter remember the remarks they made about Ivan during Mud Month – his father was an AI and his mother was a vat of cog oil. The truth, that one was a history professor at the University of America's Vladivostok campus and the other was a deputy of the state parliament, wasn't that far from the fiction. No one was sure if he'd gotten into the Patrol on the basis of test scores or politics, since either one would have ensured it. Staying in, however, would be another story.

You couldn't wash out in your first year – no one was going to come and bring you home from a partridge ship. But when you got back after that year, all kinds of things could happen to you. He'd seen the list of Patrol billets – some were in places so remote and isolated that Peter was sure the dumb-bombs had erased them from the rolls long ago. Places like the Plato Navigation Maintenance

Station, the Geographos Observatory, Venus Equilateral, and the L-5 Vessel Traffic Control Center. And there were always expeditions to the Oort Cloud, looking for "volunteers."

If this expedition backfired, for example, what would happen to the five cadets who'd let Ivan talk them into it?

Peter had reason to be nervous – more reasons than simple cog oil. One of them a big one. Ever since they arrived at Burnham, Peter had had a nagging suspicion that he was afraid to voice aloud.

What terrible reason did they have for making the asteroid invisible in the first place?

"Can't we just have the cogs cut through the wires and bolts and spin the wheel?" asked Ivan.

"Probably not," Cheng said. "There's got to be back-ups and safeguards in a door like this. Watch and you'll see. Pham, tell them to eat through the bolt at the top of the wheel."

The Vietnamese girl mumbled into the lantern, and Cheng swung the data board around so Ivan could see it too. "Watch what happens," he said.

Peter watched over Ivan's should and saw the image of the metal works inside the door. His eyes widened at the bit of red fire that appeared along the side of one bolt. The fire raced through the metal and extinguished itself on the far side.

"See, it cut through," Ivan said. "No problem."

"No, wait a minute. See what happens."

Peter didn't notice it, but Cheng pointed it out when it happened. "A new bolt has slipped in over there – at the edge of the doorway where the door is dogged down."

Ivan cursed. "What about picking the lock?" he asked.

"It would take forever," Pham said. "There just isn't enough computing power in this much cog oil to get through something that complex."

"I wish we could just cook up something that would blow a hole through the thing so we could get on our way," Howard Efi said. Peter looked over at the big Samoan, a wide grin settling across his face.

"I'd like to see you try. Even research-type information about explosives is harder to get out of Mother's Watcher than the answers to your final exams," Ivan said. "All right, we can't get through the machinery, what can we do?"

"Get a picture of the other side," Pham said. "I'll send the cogs all the way through."

A moment later the data board showed another broad tunnel – the Grand Concourse, continued.

"More Concourse," said Howie. "Just what we need."

"It's just another tunnel," Cheng said. "Just like this one – only without cadets."

"It's not just like this one," Ivan said. "The walls aren't smooth. And there's a row of doorways leading off the main shaft. The lighting systems are all different too – more random and haphazard."

"Great, but how do we get over there?" Howie asked.

"Don't force it," Cheng said. "Just get a bigger screwdriver. Why can't we just bore a hole through the thing? They couldn't have planned on that."

"It'll take some time," Pham said. "There's a lot of metal there."

"They don't have to eat the whole thing," Cheng said. "Just around the edges."

"That's right," Pham said. "I didn't think of that. What about it, Ivan? Do we try it?"

Ivan narrowed his eyes and looked at the data board. "Go ahead. But everyone clear back. We don't know if the other side is pressurized or what. We don't want to get hit by pieces of door if we get some blowback."

Peter was first to seek a more secure position, over by the juncture of the doorway and the wall of the Grand Concourse behind one of the meter-thick hinges. But the precautions were unnecessary. One by one, the layers of metal came out or fell aside. And with the last there was nothing but a few puffs of dust scattering dynamically in the vacuum.

"All right, let's go," Ivan said without hesitation. "Cheng and Howie first. Pham and I will leapfrog you. Peter – "

Peter felt his blood grow cold as Ivan looked at him – even from so far away. " – I want you to stay here. Just like Amy did up above. When the follow-up team gets here, you'll be able to tell them exactly what we did and where we went."

"Yes, Ivan," Peter said. At least he didn't give his nervousness away by stammering. In truth, he was relieved. He didn't want to go on with the rest of them. Maybe they would get all the glory. Or maybe just the blame. Peter didn't want to say what he was thinking, either. That there may not be a follow-up team. And that there must have been a reason for building a door with a lock that couldn't be broken.

One by one, the other cadets pulled themselves through the hole, until all were gone and Peter was alone. He waited for a while until he was sure they weren't coming right back, then he breathed his sigh of relief.

Now he could do what he'd wanted to do all along.

Back up the Grand Concourse were a series of side shafts, all marked prominently as access ways to surface weapons emplacements. They'd explored one together, then Ivan had sent individuals up each of them in turn. He wasn't interested in them once he'd decided they were from an earlier century. But Peter wanted to take a closer look at them – to see what was in the ones he had climbed himself.

So he opened the hatch and scooted up the nearest one. It was five hundred meters or so to the end of the shaft, but the clearance was wide, and Peter never had a claustrophobic side. The journey took long enough that he was more bored than nervous when he reached the end.

The emplacement had long been stripped of anything remotely dangerous or useful. The empty metal bins outside the clear bubble windows were a reminder of the big guns and launchers of a long-gone century. The only thing that might come in handy was the escape hatch that led to the surface. Peter made careful note of the fact that it was not locked and that opening instructions were printed on it in big letters.

He took a look at the sky. It was pitch black above, and the surface was barely visible. The only lighting came from the docks, their big frames poking above the horizon. Warning lights burned red and yellow and blinked at random intervals, giving the illusion of life on a cold and long-abandoned bit of rock and ice.

Before the mood got to him, Peter headed back down the shaft. He decided he wanted to get a better look at the docks.

But when he reached the Grand Concourse and looked over at the big door, he got a shock that was enough to send his skin buzzing with electricity.

The hole in the door – the one that had opened so quickly and swallowed up four of his shipmates – was gone!

2

"Well, Kit, this looks like a refried nightmare," Nat Ybarro-Carson said to his long lost identical twin brother. Kit, the invisible but immediate sibling, had been a constant companion through a long and sometimes lonely childhood, and the habits of a lifetime died hard. Harder than the real thing, anyway.

"I mean look at this mess. Billions of cubic kilometers of Big Empty. How accurate are those Argos sensors, anyway? How many seconds go between scans?"

"The Argos sensors are several orders of magnitude beyond 99 percent," said a voice that sounded similar to his own, though higher and thinner. It was the voice of the hummingbird's cog-intelligence, set to mimic Nat's voice – and by genetic connection, the voice of the late and absent Kit. "And in the case of the *Able Countryman*, the Argos system did a scan every six seconds."

"Better than 99 percent? Great. The nearest sensor with a solidly known position is at least 100 million kilometers away. And 99 percent accuracy there means an error of a million klicks. Enough space to lose the Earth and the Moon in together, with room left over to ride all night. Now that means an accuracy of ten thousand kilometers. Slightly smaller than the Earth. The *Countryman* could be in Singapore and we could be in San Francisco."

"The recommended procedure at this point is an expanding cube search," the hummingbird's impression of Kit-Nat said.

"I know. Commence the search. Full sensor arrays activated. Pay particularly close watch for an invisible alien the size of Phobos."

"Aye, aye."

"Now 99 percent accuracy of ten thousand klicks is one hundred klicks. If your meson detectors are working, they should be easy to find. Sort of like trying to hide a siren in a tube station while it's going off."

"And 99 percent accuracy again is one kilometer. Even you should be able to find the *Countryman* at that range."

"So which is it? What order of accuracy are we dealing with here? How close are we to the point the *Countryman* disappeared?"

"In theory, something less than one thousand kilometers and something more than ten kilometers."

Nat snorted, then laughed. "Great. That makes my life a lot easier."

The hours went by slowly as they traversed kilometer after kilometer of empty space. Nat had directed the hummingbird's cogs to create a substantial sensor array on the journey to this patch of space. Of course, he wasn't searching a fixed position. The *Countryman* had disappeared while maneuvering into a new orbit around the sun. And Nat had maneuvered himself into the same orbit – and in theory at the same point as the ship full of cadets.

Now his search centered on that point, which was itself moving towards Nu Leonis, a low-magnitude star near Regulus in Leo. If the numbers he'd been given were as accurate as Kit had said, then the *Countryman* should be shadowing the movement of that point – or what was left of it.

He had spent a lot of time thinking about his tactical problem. Specifically, he had considered ways to spot an invisible ship-eating alien the size of Phobos. There would be occluded stars, for example. So he had told the cogs to work out a method for spotting the occlusion. And invisibility was a relative thing. Something might not be visible in ordinary light but still be seen in infrared. There were limits to the physical universe, and one of these was the conservation of energy and matter. In simple terms, that meant that all the energy absorbed by an invisible ship-eating alien had to be reradiated. There was a formula for that, something called the Black Body Law. Nat had seen the formula and even used it, but he hadn't committed it to memory. But he did remember that it involved an inverse fourth-power exponent – the square of a square. And that meant that the wavelength of the energy reradiated would be a lot higher and a lot farther into the infrared than the energy absorbed.

Really good infrared sensors required supercooled elements. Liquid hydrogen was best for that. Liquid nitrogen would work almost as well. Unfortunately, he didn't have any of the first and only a little bit of the other. Nanotech had its limits, and the poor overworked cogs aboard the little hummingbird ship had been stretched to the theirs in processing some of the ship's atmosphere.

Now he waited for his devices to do their job. And waited. And waited. And slept, then waited some more.

When he was a kid back in El Paso-Chihuahua, Nat had built himself a telescope. It was a little thing with a mirror at one end and an eyepiece at the other. The eyepiece had been pretty high power, which meant a small field of view. And it had no viewfinder. So sighting on anything smaller than the moon meant bending down and looking up the tube at the night sky, then criss-crossing the heavens star by star as he looked in vain for the nebulas, galaxies, and other mysteries he had read so much about. And in the end, mostly what he found was fuzzy gray blobs.

This search was much like that. Tedious, boring, and a majestic pain in the neck.

He hoped the cadets aboard the *Countryman* were still alive. He wanted to thank them personally for putting him through the ordeal. And then he wanted to punish each and every one of them for their foolish impertinence.

He had conceived of several complex and interesting forms of punishment when the collision came.

* * *

SMASH!!!

That was the first thing to disturb Nat's silent reverie. A bone-jarring sound from outside the hull, where no sound at all could exist.

The glass bowl of the hummingbird's control deck was plunged into sudden darkness as a million blazing stars disappeared from view.

The collision alarm – a high-pitched beep – sounded off, counting the seconds after the impact one by one. Kit's voice echoed the alarm: "Collision ... collision ... brace for collision."

Nat shook his head in confusion. Brace for collision? Wasn't it a bit late for that?

The soft glow of the virtual instrument panel, distorted by the inner curve of the glass, illuminated the control deck. The light was just enough for Nat to see blisters rising from the surface of the compartment's bulkheads.

When the collision alarm counted the fifth second after the initial jolt, the blisters erupted. The air was suddenly filled with droplets of cog oil, green and faintly luminescent.

Nat barely had time to think about what was happening when the droplets themselves exploded, spreading streamers of white polymer throughout the cramped control deck.

He didn't even have time to take a breath, which was just as well considering the potential consequences of inhaling large amounts of nanotech. He only had time to wonder in amazement as the cogs filled the chamber with an intricate cloud of spiderwebs, which grew thick and bloated as they clung to his arms, his legs, his hands, and his face.

By the time the sixth second had passed, he was surrounded by foam. His eyes blinked shut before being clogged with the strange confection, and in the self-imposed dark he could hear the rough hiss of the hummingbird's verniers and feel the ship pivoting.

WHAM!!!

The first crash was a gentle love tap compared to this concussion. Nat felt himself driven sideways, restrained in his cocoon of cog-stuff. His eyeballs ached from the impact. His blood flooded toward one side of his body, then washed back. And his ears rang from the sound of the collision.

The collision alarm continued is steady beat, counting off additional seconds. But Kit's voice now issued new warnings: "Damage ... damage ... ship's engines damaged. Hull weakened. Cracks in load-bearing structures ... damage ... damage."

Another six seconds passed. To Nat they might have been hours. His body ached, his head hurt, and behind his tightly closed eyes, stars burst and sparkled.

SMASH!!!

This was the same noisy but essentially harmless impact as the first, muffled now by the cloud of polymers and cogs that covered his ears. Nat noticed immediately that the collision alarm finally fell silent, as he waited for the next beep that never came.

Then he felt the protective cocoon dissolve around him. He opened his eyes in time to see the milky white substance melt and congeal, then turn to dusty flakes that were sucked into the ventilation system. The cogs would recover the material and the assemblers that had produced it when they had time. First they had to attend to the damage to the hummingbird.

He looked around and saw that the stars had returned – too many of them. He was seeing double and his head was beginning to throb. Even inside the safety cocoon, his brain had been bounced around. And his ribs ached where they'd been compressed by the shock of impact.

"What was that?" he asked.

"I'm trying to find out," replied Kit's voice. "But my data-processing capacity is somewhat reduced at the moment, since we are working to repair the damage and prevent further structural weakening."

Nat nodded uncomfortably. He was reluctant to distract the cogs from the important task at hand. He wished, however, that the same microscopic machines that did the thinking for his ship didn't also have to do the physical work required to keep him safe.

"Maybe it was an invisible ship-eating alien the size of Phobos," he said with a sigh.

"First reports indicate that you may be correct," Kit's voice replied. "At least, the object we hit was on that order of magnitude in size."

Nat spun around quickly and pressed his face against the glass, trying to get a better look at the vast empty space surrounding him.

"Great," he said. "This is just what we needed."

* * *

The hummingbird drifted for nearly an hour before the cogs had things back under control. Nat had donned his spacesuit as a precaution against sudden leaks, while the cogs rushed needed materials to the damaged parts of the vessel and began shoring up the cracks and patching split seams.

Getting the suit on had been a challenge all its own. His muscles had stiffened where they'd been insulted by the crash. His neck ached and it was hard to turn his head. And his side burned where his ribs were bruised. He was still seeing double, and his headache had spread around to the rear of his skull.

He heard little from Kit for that hour and he demanded little from the artificial persona – despite the million questions that swarmed through his brain. He passed the time by trying to recreate the collision in his own mind.

It didn't make sense. What had they hit?

There were three separate impacts. The first and the last of them were light and inconsequential. No damage reports from them, nothing but noise. The one in the middle had been the bruiser. His neck was beginning to ache and the muscles in the left side of his chest throbbed almost subliminally.

So they had smashed through something light and thin, then hit the hard candy center. It must have been a glancing blow, since it didn't stop them cold. It barely slowed them down, now that he thought about it. The collision alarm sounded six seconds before the main impact and six seconds after it.

The stars had gone out with the first crash, he recalled now. They had plowed into something opaque. Was it some kind of alien exoskeleton? Had they collided with the invisible ship-eating alien? That would explain why they hadn't seen it coming – it was invisible!

The silence from the hummingbird's computer persona was all the more frustrating because he knew that whatever it was, they knew its location. After the collision they had continued in a straight line, following Newton's laws, for a fixed and measured interval along a steady and constant bearing – and that meant they could calculate the distance and bearing, reverse direction, and retrace their path to the object.

And Nat was not foolish enough to doubt that this strange object also was connected to the disappearance of the *Able Countryman* and six Solar Patrol cadets. Space was too vast and too deep for any such coincidence.

* * *

Of course, they did not actually turn about and run straight back at the point of impact. Both Nat and the cog-mind of the hummingbird were too well-trained for that. Space was as hostile a set of environments as any human being was likely to encounter. But not so hostile that those human beings couldn't find ways to improve on it. Every one of the combatants in the Last War had transacted some of its business out here, and every year an expanding population stumbled across new reminders of an old conflict – mines, derelict warships, hidden pockets of pestilence or contagion for humans and machines.

Records of the era weren't all corrupted by dumb-bombs – not physically. But it was impossible to erase the doubt that hung over any record or document forever after. As a result, no one ever was really sure what they were going up against, no one ever really felt safe, and every unplanned, unexpected, or unanticipated event had to be treated as if it could be the worst possibility imaginable. Because some of them were.

When the cogs had the hummingbird back in what the Kit-voice called "stable flight," they paused in their work to reconstitute the ship's AI. "The recommendation is to make a long looping approach, scanning the area of impact as we go to see what we can find. It's sunward of us, or we'd be trying an approach from that direction. We're 212 kilometers away from it right now, traveling at 103 kilometers an hour relative."

"A hundred klicks an hour?" Nat moaned. "No wonder I hurt so bad."

"We are lucky you only hit it with a glancing blow. A direct impact would have exceeded the ship's ability to protect you from serious or lethal injury."

"Have you figured out why we didn't see it coming?"

"No," Kit answered. "We had no echo from radar. No infrared indication. And the only indication of anything unusual was a series of tracking logic errors in the sensor algorithms."

Nat shook his head and groaned. "Say that again in English. You stopped making sense after the word 'logic.'"

"There were internal errors in the new sensors. Something didn't work quite right in the artificial intelligence processing."

"Something like what?"

"They use guide stars to orient the ship in space. In this error, the sensors tracking the guide stars in the direction of the impact zone lost sight of the guide star, then recovered it again and had to recalibrate."

Nat tried to visualize the process, then winced. "Show me a picture," he said.

A data screen flickered to life with a sparsely populated starfield centered on a bright star. It burned there for a few seconds, then blinked out, only to reappear immediately a few centimeters away on the screen. The starfield flickered – the recalibration, Kit noted.

"That's all that happened?" Nat asked.

"Well, it happened four times."

"Four times? And you didn't mention it?"

"Four times in eight minutes. The third and fourth events came in the last 90 seconds. I was about to say something when we hit."

"Weren't the sensors looking for an invisible alien? I mean, weren't they looking for occultations, eclipses, things like that?"

"Absolutely yes. But this didn't fit into any of those categories. The stars around the guide star didn't disappear. There was no consistent pattern of occultations – it takes more than just two or three to set off the indicators. And the pattern of data didn't fit any of the categories for searches."

"I guess if you've never encountered it before, you wouldn't know what you were looking at," Nat said. "Geez, if we hadn't hit it, we might still not know it was there."

"That's very likely," Kit replied.

Nat stretched back in his seat against the comfortable pressure of the hummingbird's engines. They were putting out almost half a gee of acceleration as they looped back towards their target.

"So what is it?"

Nat wasn't sure if heard Kit chuckle under his breath – since Kit had no breath and probably shouldn't know how to chuckle. "It's not an invisible ship-eating alien, if that's what you're afraid of."

"Good. I was getting worried for a moment," Nat said, hoping the irony would not be lost on the cog AI.

"It is a giant, though. We were in the dark for a good twelve seconds. That's 360 meters. And once we were in that close, we got full occultation from the thing long enough to make a call of a good kilometer long and something less than that wide. We retrieved samples from the hull at the point of impact – you dug a big piece out of the thing when you hit. Carbonaceous chondritic material. Asteroid regolith. Space dirt. We hit an invisible asteroid."

Nat felt a wide grin spread across his face, pushing his cheeks against his eyes. "An invisible ship-eating asteroid – I like it."

"I guess it didn't like us very much. It spit us back out," Kit said.

"So it would have appeared to an outside observer. But I felt three impacts. What were the little ones before and after the big one?"

"We got samples from the front end of the hull where we hit going in and the side where we hit coming out," Kit said. "That stuff was different. Processed material. Processed by atomic and molecular synthesis."

"Cogwork?"

"Maybe. Nanotech almost certainly."

"Nanotech, but not cogs?"

"This place is old, whatever it is. There's no record of an asteroid in this orbit. That probably means that the record is corrupted. But it may mean something else."

"That someone moved it since the record was made?"

"That's the consensus of the on-line experts. I've only been in touch with Mars, but I'll get an answer from Earth in a few minutes to see if they back me up."

Nat shook his head. "Nope. It hasn't been moved. I'd bet a Gold Star on that."

"What makes you so sure?"

"Because if it wasn't on a record somewhere, half a dozen cadets in a partridge ship wouldn't have been able to find it."

* * *

Nat watched silently while Kit displayed a synthetic image of the collision integrated from all the data they had collected or derived. A silhouette of the asteroid, longer than it was wide, appeared at the center of the screen, grew slowly at first, then quickly, until it swelled suddenly in the last few accelerated seconds of flight before it swallowed them up. He replaced it with the rear view, then chained the two together into a continuous loop that continued to unreel before Nat's unseeing eyes.

He stopped noticing the stars passing behind the asteroid, yet remaining visible to the hummingbird's sensors. He had long since attributed it to some currently unknown process that he would have to analyze when he had more data. He had even stopped watching the stars make their flickering little jumps from time to time as they passed behind the dark shadow. He still wondered how the asteroid did that, but other things weighed on his mind.

What were the cadets on the *Able Countryman* doing here? How did they know there would be an invisible asteroid here? Did they really know, or had their experience mirrored his – but with a more deadly result? Could they have smashed headlong into the object, leaving nothing behind but an expensive smear of metal, muscle, and cog oil?

That was unlikely, Nat thought. That would be too easy. He had learned long ago that the universe was not kind enough to offer only easy challenges – not to young officers with only a few short years more experience than the cadets themselves. No, he was going to be stuck with a shipload of smartass kay-dets who thought that flying around in a spaceship for a year wasn't enough adventure on its own and had to go looking for more.

He remembered his own cadet year – the losses and the suffering as well as the adventure and the excitement. Like that of the *Countryman's* crew, it had not been a standard tour. He hoped they would not have to repeat the lessons he had learned at such a high cost.

But he knew better.

Then he spun about in place and grabbed a stanchion as he was struck by a sudden intuition. "Say Kit, how long did the *Countryman* sit around out here before it disappeared from the scopes?"

"Good question," Kit replied. Nat shook his head. Cogs were not very good at intuition. This one obviously had neglected to mention important information until asked. "The last contact was a radar sweep, and they make those less often than the visual checks. The last burn of the partridge ship engines came at 1537 Zulu time. The last registered contact by radar was at 2017. The next sweep was at 2343. So anywhere from four and a half to six hours passed once they'd arrived in the area of this asteroid."

"I guess they had time to try out our search methods," Nat said. "I hope they had better luck than we did."

3

Amy Hackenyos had nothing but time on her hands. Lots of time. She had confirmed her original analysis and was indeed moving towards the wall of the Grand Concourse at about the speed she had calculated. And that meant hours before she could rescue herself from her predicament.

She occupied that time by thinking. First about home, her brothers and sisters, her mother and father, the horses, the dogs, the mountains, the sky full of towering clouds. But that started to make her homesick for the first time since she had been sworn into the Patrol.

So she began thinking about her shipmates.

Peter Salerno – now there was an odd mix of genes, with his blond hair imported from Normandy to Italy by the Crusaders and his British heritage passing through Buenos Aires back in the 20th century. There was something about him, some hidden quirk that she had yet to uncover. She would be relentless until she did. She told him she thought everyone from Baia del Plata spoke Spanish and he explained that Argentina was settled first by the Spanish, but later by the English and Italians.

And Pham Noc Do was another one with a secret of some sort. She was intense and sharp, too often cold and distant. But she could be sweet and open with surprising and unexpected suddenness. She'd brought the seeds for a rapidly growing plant collection with her when she came aboard the *Able Countryman* – and Amy was still trying to figure out how that fit in to her character.

Cheng Li Hui was still a mystery. She was so quiet, spending most of her time in front of a datapad. Her personal property consisted of elaborate machines that turned and cranked and slid and pushed, which she built from balsa wood kits.

Howard Efi, however, was nothing but himself – big, broad-faced, and unabashed. He seemed anchored in the world in a way that none of the others did. He was older than them and had spent a year as a seaman on a merchant ship in the Pacific. That seemed to have given him the experience with hard reality that the others were only seeking when they joined the Patrol.

And Ivan Blandings. There was a real piece of work. Why had they ever listened to him? How had they let him talk them into this? For personal property, he had brought with him a book – a single, crudely bound, thick, blue book with pages made of paper. Now Amy wished someone had declared it excess weight before he ever got it aboard. She shook her head. If someone had done that, Ivan would have just torn pages out of the back until it came in under the limit.

"It's an ephemeris. Do you know what an ephemeris is?" Ivan had asked when the subject first came up.

Amy couldn't forget that watch. They were at their first formal mess after the *Countryman* was launched into solar orbit – a ritual that Mother Janus said was one of their training requirements. Dress uniform, formal table manners, the whole nine meters. Howard Efi was in command of the partridge ship. He had the earliest date of service. He was sworn in while at sea in the Pacific, a thousand kilometers from land, in order to travel under orders to the nearest spaceport. That gave him a couple more weeks seniority over Pham, who made the long trek in from the Belt to Tharsis Academy.

Howie was from Samoa and was a strange conglomerate of ethnic traits. Asian, Polynesian, some African from the American influence of an earlier era. He boasted once that he could walk through almost any neighborhood in Tharsis City and be accepted as a local.

Mother Janus had ordered the formal mess as part of their regular instruction in Solar Patrol ceremonies, military courtesy, and social interaction. Without such get-togethers, she said, too many cadets would spend their year in space cooped up in their staterooms with their eyeballs jacked into the datascreens.

As part of the formality, they had introduced themselves and told their shipmates what they'd brought along. Ivan's question had a hint of condescension – as if he didn't expect her to know what an ephemeris was.

"Uh, gee, no," Amy replied. "I got into the Patrol on athletics, not brains."

She was disappointed to see her sarcasm lost on him. For a moment he almost took her seriously, then Peter Salerno laughed hard and Ivan smiled wanly.

"Of course I know what an ephemeris is. What did you bring it along for? Are you afraid the cogs will forget how to astrogate?"

"Not at all," Ivan answered, looking down at the table in an attempt at humility. "It's a research project of mine."

"I'm afraid I don't know what an ephemeris is," Pham said. "I recognize the word, but I forget just how it's different from an almanac."

"An almanac is a list of local observation times – sunset, sunrise, moonset, moonrise," Ivan said.

"And an ephemeris is the basic orbital data for planets and other objects that you can use to calculate orbits and positions," Amy said.

Ivan caught his breath at her interruption, and scowled slightly. "Yes. Exactly."

"It's a very thick book for something like that, isn't it?" Pham noted.

"It's an ephemeris for the asteroids," Ivan explained. "Several thousand of them."

"And your research project involves them?"

"Yes. I am trying to verify our current databases. The book was published just a few months before the Last War broke out, so it's the most up-to-date bombproof document we have. I plan to make observations from the *Countryman* over the next year and double-check them against the standard astronomical sources."

"I plan to spend the year learning how to play checkers with my toes," Amy said, trying hard to take the wind out Ivan's pompous sails.

* * *

"I still don't understand," Peter Salerno said.

"You do know how a dumb-bomb works, don't you?" Ivan said.

Amy still hadn't made up her mind up Peter. She had him pegged as something of a twerp – certainly not in the Patrol on an athletic qualifier. But the way Ivan treated him made her judgment of him turn. That and the eager way he brushed off that treatment.

"Sure. It wipes out the data in a memory bank and leaves the system dumb."

"That's an awfully general and unspecific description," Ivan said with more than faint disdain. "It's a lot more complicated process. They aren't bombs, you know. Nothing explodes."

"I knew that," Peter said.

"It's a code that infects a data system. And it doesn't wipe out the data, it changes it in subtle ways. Sometimes it erases it, but other times it replaces numbers. Or creates false entries."

"I've heard that some of the codes are so subtle that they stick around in the system forever, changing things even after they've been corrected," Amy said.

"That happens," Ivan said begrudgingly. "Not often, but it happens."

"And it's not just numbers," she added. "During the war they went after texts. False police reports. Stories about riots and dissent. And the history texts – well, my parents say never trust a text over 60."

"History texts?" Peter said. "They got into the history texts?"

Amy was surprised. Peter looked more than a little disturbed. Ivan noticed too, because he went right after him on it.

"Does that bother you?" he asked with a touch of delightful interest in his tone.

"Well, I just never thought about it. Why would they want to change the history texts?"

"My goodness, Mr. Salerno, what did they teach you in Baia del Plata?"

"History," Peter replied. "Simon Bolivar to the Malvinas to the Last War in two semesters. Three, if you want to know what's happened since then. They always ended the first year's class just when things get interesting."

"I suppose they taught you about the Buenos Aires strike?"

"Of course," Peter said proudly. "Our finest hour. We sacrificed our greatest city to prevent the gray goo from wiping out the world."

Ivan snorted and sneered. "That's what I thought."

"Why? What's wrong with that?"

"Nothing," Ivan said. "Nothing at all. Except that it isn't true."

Without warning, Peter slipped out of his zero-G seat, spun in place, then kicked against the wall, launching himself directly across the compartment at Ivan Blandings. At the last minute, he grabbed a stanchion with one hand and hooked an arm around another and stopped himself, their faces only centimeters apart.

"That's a dirty lie and I want you to take it back right now!"

* * *

Amy was the first to touch him, but she stopped short of grabbing at his arm. He had stopped where he wanted to stop and wasn't going to advance another centimeter. And at the same time, she had the immense satisfaction of watching Ivan's lips curl back in sheer terror at the sudden fury of Peter's advance.

Then Howard reached out and pulled Ivan away from the confrontation. Amy's touch was enough to bring Peter down from full alert. And to top it all off, they drew a swift reprimand from Mother Janus.

"Physical assault is not considered appropriate table manners at a formal mess, Cadet Salerno," said the stern mistress of the *Countryman*. "And neither are provocative statements, Cadet Blandings. This conduct has been noted on your records and if it does not cease at once, further notations will be made."

Ivan and Peter both looked stunned, then sheepish – in their own ways, Peter making the better of it than Ivan.

"And just so you are all aware of it, the entire ship's company gets a notation in their record in a case like this," Mother Janus added. "You live and die as a group, cadets."

Pham, Howie, Amy, and Cheng all groaned in unison at that announcement. But it only drew another rebuke from Mother Janus. "Group moaning is another behavior that is not acceptable at a formal mess."

Amy drew in a breath at the near occasion of punishment. No one wanted a black mark in their records – and now their ship had two. Howie tried to steer the conversation gamely back towards small talk and got Pham going on the social life of Nouvelle Hanoi. Ivan and Peter sulked, but kept silent. They escaped the remainder of the meal with their dignity and their records intact.

Peter came to Amy later and apologized.

"Thanks for backing me up in there," he said. "It was beginning to look like a long and lonely year aboard this ship for moment."

"Don't think anything of it," Amy said. "Really. Next time I may not be there."

"Just the same, I appreciate it. It's just that I never thought about it before. Do you really suppose the history instructors weren't telling us the truth?"

Amy took a deep breath, started to launch into a lecture that she knew would take up most of the watch, then thought twice about it and sighed. "Peter, you probably know the answer to that question as well as I do."

"I guess I do. That's why I was so angry with Ivan. But I just don't understand why."

"Why you're angry with Ivan?"

"No – why would anyone lie about history?"

"Look at it this way," Amy said. "The world if full of people like Ivan Blandings. People like him get put in charge of things. People who are in charge of things get to write the history. And if you were like him, wouldn't you lie about yourself?"

"When you put it like that, it all makes sense," he said, spinning head for heels in the middle of the gym until just watching it made Amy dizzy. "Anyway, I'm sorry I got everyone in trouble and I'll make sure it doesn't happen again."

"Sure," Amy said, as if she believed it.

* * *

But they didn't stay out of trouble, and it was all because of Ivan's book.

He was obsessed with it, from what she could see. First, he had the ship's cogs cook him up an optical tracking telescope and install it on the ship's control deck. Then he spent hours calibrating it on stars and planets. Finally, he organized a viewing schedule that kept him at the equipment for hours at a time.

He was on the equipment for at least an hour out of every eight-hour watch. By Solar Patrol custom, the *Countryman* maintained darkened ship during the nightwatch and most of the cadets would be asleep at once – but not Ivan Blandings. Amy had seen him at it on her way to bed and still there when she awoke.

His routine was always the same. She had watched him for a while – he didn't object. He looked up the asteroids in the book and then cross-checked them in the standard database. Once he was sure the entries agreed, he dialed them up in the telescope, filed notes, and went on to the next one.

"What are you looking for?" she finally asked after a few days of observing the process.

"I'm not sure," he replied. "But I will know it when I find it."

"And what have you found so far?"

"Nothing unusual. You can look at my notes." He looked over at the nearest data node and said: "Mother Janus, please take them off my password."

"Certainly, Cadet Blandings."

Amy had read through them all. He was right, there was nothing you wouldn't find in a basic astronomy tutorial. Surface brightness tracks, a couple of astrogational positions, and the characteristics of the resulting orbit. And always the notation: "Current databases concur with ephemeris."

All she could deduce was that he was checking the contents of the ephemeris against the standard Patrol astrogational database – and both against his own observations. But he had pretty much told them that already.

A few days later, she was struck by an inspiration. "How many asteroids are there, Mother Janus?"

"That's an open-ended question, Miss Hackenyos," the cog-brain replied. "It depends on how you define asteroid. Size is the critical factor. I can provide you with numbers based on a minimum size."

"How many big ones are there?"

"Define big," Mother Janus snapped back with a hint of condescension in her artificial voice.

"Larger than a kilometer in diameter."

"There are 24,156 known and identified asteroid bodies of at least one kilometer in diameter. These include only those bodies in orbits whose semimajor axis falls between those of Jupiter and Mars and excludes those with clearly cometary composition."

"More than twenty-four thousand. How many asteroids does Ivan check each day?"

"A maximum of forty-seven, a minimum of twenty, median of thirty-three."

"At that rate, it will take him – uh, three per hundred makes 720 days. He'll never finish."

"One might assume that."

"Except he isn't looking at all of them, is he? If I recall his notes properly, he's only going after small ones – a couple of kilometers across."

"That is correct. His parameters have an upper limit of four kilometers in the longest dimension."

"And how many asteroids is that?"

"About a third of the total," Mother Janus answered.

"And that makes it what? Nine months to go through his list?"

"That's correct," the cog-brain said.

"And why?"

"I'm afraid I don't know the reason for that."

Amy sighed and pounded the wall, recoiling across her cabin in faithful adherence to Newton's laws of motion. And there the question sat for fifty-seven days.

Then came the watch when Ivan entered the wardroom, pulling himself across the compartment with grim-faced seriousness, to announce his discovery.

Amy might not have been privy to the event, but she was there when Howie was there, as were Pham and Cheng. It was Howie he came after. Of course, since there was going to be more than simply an announcement of personal pride.

Ivan's expression was unnatural – for him and for anyone. His face was all pinched up and tight, as if he were holding everything in that he wanted to let out. He looked almost ready to burst when he came through the door. At first he said nothing, then a grin – as unnatural as his repressed excitement had been – crept across his face. He floated in midspace, gawking at the others, as if waiting for them to notice him and ask him what was new. Skinny odds on that, Amy thought, in a spaceship that in two months had grown as familiar and unexciting as an ingrown toenail.

When no one took the bait, he finally cleared his throat loudly and proclaimed: "I've done it."

The response from his shipmates was highly anti-climactic. "Done what?" Howie asked.

"I've found what I was looking for."

That drew everyone's attention, pulling Pham from her cineviewer and Cheng from her tutorial. Amy almost choked on her supper.

"And what is it?" she asked after working her food down.

"An asteroid that isn't there."

"It isn't there?" Howie asked.

"No – and it should be. The others were there. They stole them off the lists and erased the records, but they were there."

"There were others?" Amy shot back.

"Eight," Ivan said, beaming. "Eight asteroids that were in my ephemeris and not in the standard databases. Eight asteroids that some dumb-bomb erased from the records back in the Last War. And each one of them is still there, gliding effortlessly through space on its own perfect little orbit. All of them except the last one. Number Nine. That's the one. It isn't there. I looked and looked. We spent half the watch trying to find it. But it's not there."

Amy was still confused. There was something missing in his declaration. Like a point. But she wasn't about to provoke him by saying so.

The others weren't so reluctant.

"So what?" Howie said. He was good-natured about it, so Ivan didn't seem resentful. But his explanation was labored – and a bit fantastical.

"Why isn't it there?" he asked. "What happened to it?"

"Maybe your ephemeris is wrong," Amy said. "You must have considered that possibility."

"It's not my book that's wrong," he said, spinning on her suddenly. She almost expected him to attack her physically in all his excitement, but he was too worked up to take offense. "Not my ephemeris. It is the twenty-third edition. It's been verified and checked and re-checked. No, this is something bigger. Much bigger."

"Bigger?"

"Before the war it was there. After the war, it is gone. Was it moved? Of course not. We can't do that today, and sixty years ago we were even less capable. Was it eaten by runaway nanotech? If so, it would leave behind gray goo. Even broken down into primordial atoms, it would still be there. It would still orbit the sun and still reflect the light. Anything big enough to destroy an asteroid would be too big to hide – even with the kind of lies the dumb-bombs spread. I have searched the histories and the records and there is nothing there.

"No – there is something going on there. Something strange and unusual. And now we must go find out what it is."

That brought the reaction he had been seeking. Everyone talking at once. Everyone telling him he was crazy. Everyone trying to make him see how little sense he was making.

But in the end it would be futile. In the end, they went. And now Amy Hackenyos floated in midspace, too far from the bulkheads of the Grand Concourse, with too much time on her hands.

She hadn't seen any more of those vacuum-loving ladybugs, thank goodness. But being alone and helpless was beginning to get to her. She wished the others would come back early.

When the voice crackled in her ear, she expected it to be one of them. And when it was not, her blood suddenly turned to liquid nitrogen.

"Good lord, Cadet Hackenyos, what have you done to yourself?"

4

The approach to the invisible asteroid was long and slow – a couple of hours.

"As long as you're not otherwise occupied, we should spend some time on your calculus lessons," Kit said.

Nat groaned in protest, but the cog-AI had on its instructor persona and could not be deterred. "After all, you have to learn to exercise grace under pressure. As a leader, you must set a good example for your officers and crew. You must learn to pretend that you are not afraid, nervous, anxious, uneasy, or uncertain about the course of an action that will take some time to unfold. You must be patient, relaxed, and yet ready to respond instantly to whatever exigency arises."

"Exigency?"

"Necessity. Urgency. Should we work on your vocabulary instead of your math?"

"No, calculus is fine with me."

"Very good. The derivative of e to the x?"

"That's simple. E to the x."

"And the inverse …"

Kit kept it up right to the last possible minute, and Nat kept up with him every step of the way. Integral calculus required recognizing more than a hundred different patterns of equation, and Nat was good at pattern recognition. But he was relieved when the cog-AI relented and switched on the freshest image of the asteroid.

"I'm using a combination of microwave speckle interferometry and neutrino whisker-sensors. We're dealing with a surface that absorbs light like aerogel absorbs water and gives nothing up in return. Not even infrared. Whoever built this found a way around the black body law."

"Which is?" Nat said without thinking. He instantly regretted it.

"I ashamed of you, Lieutenant Carson. You should be able to explain it to me."

"I certainly should. Black body law. A black body is an object that gives off all the energy it receives from the sun. It radiates at a given electromagnetic frequency dependent on the fourth power of its temperature. So the black body law is ..."

" ... is that specific mathematical relationship. A black body at room temperature this far from the sun – about 250 Kelvins – should radiate well into the infrared. But I get nothing."

"Is that possible?"

"There are probably ways around it. Engineering solutions. If they have a radiator somewhere on the other side of the asteroid, they could get away with it. But we've made a complete circuit of the thing and there's no indication of such a thing. I don't think they could move something like that around very quickly."

"What if they put it opposite the sun? We'd lose it against the glare, wouldn't we?"

"Conceivably," Kit replied. "And if the asteroid stays oriented with the radiator facing out, they could pump all the heat into a safe sector of space without fear of discovery."

"Unless you get real close," Nat said. "At some point, this piece of rock has to become detectable."

"Yes, it does. We have reached that point. We're about 10 kilometers out and closing quickly. I am concerned about one thing."

"Don't keep me in suspense."

"I have reconstructed the collision with the object and superimposed it on the image I've assembled in the last few minutes. The initial impact point was here – " The image on the datascreen, a lumpy thing that looked like a burnt potato, grew a red star at one end. " – and the exit track runs through here." An orange line appeared a short distance away from the star.

"Very pretty," Nat said. "What's the problem?"

"There's no evidence of damage."

"That's a problem?"

"There's only way to make repairs on that scale so quickly – nanotech."

"That's what I assumed."

"It means that we're evenly matched for whoever put that stealth screen on this thing. Whoever that is."

"Whoever that is. That's the real problem, Kit, isn't it? We don't know why this asteroid is all stealthed up or who did it, do we?"

"That information is not contained in any records that I can access," Kit replied. "The short answer is: No, we don't know."

* * *

They found the radiator at the bottom of a deep well at the small end of the asteroid.

The well was only a few hundred meters wide and the floor was about that far down. The radiator consisted of a few dozen large cells pumping out prodigious amounts of infrared radiation – heat. Kit said the temperature was above 400 Kelvins, enough to boil water. But it radiated straight out into space along the ecliptic. The only way someone could see it was to put the asteroid between himself and the sun.

"What gets me is the way the stars seem to move with you," Nat said as they took a leisurely ride along the length of the asteroid towards the large end. "How do they do that?"

"It's got to be a closeup phenomenon," Kit replied. "The processing alone must be enormous, calculating our position and the line-of-sight bearings for hundreds of stars behind the asteroid."

"You mean they aim the lights at us?"

"They have to. The whole thing is observer-oriented. In order to maintain its camouflage, it has to identify all possible observers and present the proper face at all times to each one."

"How would you do that?" Nat asked the cog-AI. He didn't really expect an answer. That kind of question would keep it crunching bytes for hours as it considered all the alternatives and worked through the ramifications of each one. Then an image flashed in his mind's eye and answered his own question. "I'll bet it's like the radiators. Each light is embedded in its own well. They're aimed independently by the master controller."

"Possibly," Kit said. "Although you wouldn't need a well. You could aim the light electronically and accomplish the same effect."

The difference between what Nat saw outside the window of the hummingbird's control deck and the enhanced image Kit presented on the datascreen gave him a shiver. If he watched very carefully, he thought he could see the flicker of a star here and there as it shifted across the surface of the asteroid. But on the screen was the lumpy, irregular, well-cratered surface of a small-scale planetesimal – the kind of stony and carbon-rich debris that littered the solar system.

"Did you notice that this thing isn't spinning?" Nat said suddenly.

"Yes. None of this stealth equipment would work well if the asteroid spun. Is that important?"

Nat suppressed a nasty remark about the limitations of artificial intelligence. While cogs could process data as fast as electrons could change spin, they could not mimic the human imagination, with all its curiosity and inspiration. It would not occur to Kit's artificial mind that the lack of a spin was more significant than the length of the object.

"Kind of. Who would go to all the trouble of stopping an asteroid's spin. That's a whole lot of angular momentum. Immense amounts. More if there was any tumble to it at all – and little rocks like this can do that after a collision without a lot of provocation."

"More than seven hundred million tonnes times the rate of rotation," Kit volunteered.

"They must have had a big tugboat to do the job."

"Or a little one and lots of time," Kit replied. Nat looked askance at the speaker beside him from which Kit's voice issued, but again withheld any sharp reply. It wasn't worth the effort.

They came upon the entrance to the beast without warning.

The ship hugged the contour of the small body closely as they rounded the large end. They were passing directly over the apex of the curve of the butt end of the asteroid. Then all hell broke loose.

Several audible alarms went off, softly, but suddenly enough to give Nat a rush of adrenaline.

The communications monitor issued a loud chirping sound. And a laser-bright green light illuminated the control deck from the surface below.

*　*　*

The sight of the *Able Countryman*, nestled into the scaffolding of the asteroid's space dock, gave Nat his first genuine sigh of relief since leaving on this mission.

His first thought was that the worst possibilities could now be ruled out. His second thought was that he would now have to put on his officer's face and start acting like a leader. There was always a difficult moment of transition for spacefarers. They spent so many hours and days alone, out of touch with real humans. He was a good example – or a poor one, in another sense. Someone who talked to himself shouldn't make a practice of creating an artificial companion that mimicked him so completely, even if it hid behind the transparent fiction of a long-dead twin brother. Now he would have to put away the raw face that he wore when off on his own like this and return to some semblance of common humanity. Luckily he was not without resources. Much of the Solar Patrol's collection of customs, traditions, and ceremony was aimed at bolstering that transition. They gave you a quick and easy way of relating to your fellow officers and crew.

At one time, Nat had entertained the unusual notion that everyone else in the Patrol was just another incarnation of Nat Carson, all parceled out into separate individuals, but all sharing the original Nat spirit. After a while, though, he realized that this was just an illusion created by the shared creed of the service. Everyone seemed to share the same mind because they all shared the same mental framework, the same set of values, the same scale of human existence – vast and intimate all at once.

He would have to remind himself that the cadets who had brought him here were not reflections of himself. Not yet. They were still too raw themselves. Many months would have to pass before they learned what they needed to really belong. Many, many months.

"We're being painted by a commlaser from the *Countryman*," Kit announced. "Should I respond."

"Absolutely, Mr. Carson," Nat said enthusiastically. "It's about time we got a report. You know what they say about kids in the Patrol."

"I'm afraid there are no cadets aboard the vessel, Nat. The cog-AI Mother Janus says they've all gone inside the asteroid."

"Inside?"

"Yes. I'm still getting the download from Mother Janus, but apparently the entire thing is honeycombed with tunnels. There's a military base at this end. That's where they docked. But they've been in there for hours. Every one of them."

Nat felt his bright mood turn sour. Of course they were all gone. He was just about ready to deal with them, so it only made sense. The universe – and cadets – had an uncanny ability to anticipate his actions and then move one step beyond them.

"Well, you could introduce us any time you like."

"Certainly," Kit said. "Lieutenant Nathaniel Carson, may I present Mother Janus of the partridge ship *Able Countryman*. Mother, my human counterpart, Lieutenant Carson. You may call him Nat."

"Nice to meet you, Lieutenant. You've been told that my cadets have deserted me. I'm sorry I couldn't talk them out of it, but they were very determined."

"Cadets can be like that," Nat said. "It's part of being an adolescent."

"Tell me about it," Mother Janus said. "I could write a text."

"So what is this place?" Nat asked. "And what are we all doing here?"

* * *

Pham Noc Do ached from one end of her body to the other. Exercising in the tiny volume set aside on the partridge ship as a gymnasium had been no preparation at all for the strenuous workout of maneuvering across long distances in microgravity. It was like rock climbing and water polo rolled into one, and always with the feeling that you were clinging to the ceiling of whatever chamber you were in and about to fall off.

They had made their way about 500 meters down the central shaft of the asteroid, but every centimeter had to be pried from the rock by hand. A single piece of fiberglass line connected the four cadets to one another. In order to advance, the lead cadet – Cheng, because she was the lightest – waited until they were all clustered together and the line had the most slack, then half-leaped and half-swung out into the empty space of the shaft and forward. Each time she would reach the end of the tether and loop back towards the wall. And each time she would try to cling to its smooth surface before bouncing back into space. About half the time she was successful, even with the adhesive pads her suit cogs had synthesized for her.

Once Cheng had anchored herself securely, the others would

follow, either by pulling themselves along the rope or being pulled along by those ahead, depending on the precise topography of their passage. Pham's hands were cramped from clutching the line, which kept growing longer as the cogs worked on the lump of rock she had placed in the cache of the lantern. Her arms were sore, her calves and thighs burned, and small muscles all up and down her back made their presence known for the first time in her life.

This momentary pause in the exploration of the asteroid base only brought all the aches and pains to the surface of awareness.

What would Madame Zhang have done?

That was a silly question that was terribly out of place for the circumstances. She frowned at her own childish imagination for it. But she couldn't help what she considered her one small vice – an attachment to the odd genre of video-cinema known as samizdat noir. The dark dramas were produced right after the Last War. They were chock full of ironic commentary on life and dangerous realism – and they were all cynically apolitical. That meant they were banned in closed colonies like Nouvelle Hanoi and had to be smuggled in hypercompressed and disguised as other kinds of data transmission. The sound uncompressed well, but in order to conserve bandwidth and avoid detection, the video was edited sharply. The result was a flickering image that paced by at a frame or two a second. To complete the gritty thrill of watching the forbidden videos, one had to listen to them through a single hard-wired earphone.

There were three main kinds of stories – romances from before the war that always ended tragically, romances from after the war that always began in tragedy, and adventure stories about the war that always ended in betrayal. The stories about Madame Zhang, however, fell into all three categories and always cut against the formula. Her pre-war romances ended in betrayal, her war adventures began in tragedy, and her post-war affairs were always shattered by pre-war tragedies that returned to haunt her. Despite all, she was resolute and unbroken, a true Survivor.

But of course, she was just a character in a melodrama, and not a very realistic one. She probably never ached or suffered the way Pham did now. No task ever took her more than a moment or two to complete – and never encompassed the hours of relentless struggle that had brought the party of cadets this far. And her fear was always framed in brief moments of high emotion, instead of grinding away like the ache of a bad tooth.

Pham had brought along her entire collection of samizdat noir in her personal data cache. The whole thing only filled up a few megs. But she had pointedly left her viewer and earphone behind when suiting up for the expedition. It would have been nice to bring them along to kill time, but it also would have been a needless distraction when all her concentration was needed elsewhere. And she was no longer a childish adolescent who needed such distractions to occupy her time. She was a cadet in the Solar Patrol.

"Hey look!"

Howard Efi's voice rattled in her ear, but the figure that waved was several meters away, wedged in a crevice in the shaft wall. He pointed down the wall a few more meters.

"What is it?" Ivan asked.

"A door, I think," Howard replied as he dislodged himself from the crevice and began pulling on the fiberglass line. "Give me some slack and I'll get closer."

It was a door and a few moments of sweat and cursing brought them all around it. It was rectangular with rounded corners and sat in an airtight seal. But the locking lever moved easily and the door opened without resistance. Pham snuck a fiber through the crack and determined that the chamber beyond the door was empty and not particularly large.

"Howie, you go first," Ivan directed. "Then Cheng. Pham and I will follow up." They formed up, then Howie flung himself through the opening, the lights of his spacesuit suddenly blazing at their highest intensity. Cheng, the line wrapped around her waist, plunged afterward, her face contorted with some combination of pain and fear that made Pham cringe. She was only a few seconds behind Ivan in joining them.

Howie's lights made the walls seem to dance, but they were really necessary. The surfaces glowed with a dim light of their own where his high-beams did not fall. He turned them down a notch and they quickly took in their new surroundings. The walls were smooth, not like the organic smoothness of the main shaft, but like a well-manufactured interior bulkhead. There was another door in one wall, opposite the entrance they had used.

"Try it," Ivan said. Howie pushed off cautiously, drifted across the compartment, and caught the locking lever of the door. It swung up and the door came loose.

Pham floated up alongside Howie and poked her spy-fiber through again. The room beyond was identical to the one they were now in, except that the chamber's second door was in an adjacent wall and not the opposite one.

"Cheng, stay here," Ivan ordered. "Everyone else, let's go."

Behind the next door lay another chamber, beyond that lay another, and beyond that lay a third. And by then they had run out of cadets.

5

Amy Hackenyos swung her arm out sharply and held it there. The motion was enough to set her spinning. As she came around and faced back up the Grand Concourse towards the docks she caught sight of the stranger. He was floating next to the wall and gripping a guy wire.

Her heart pounded high inside her chest, faster than she had ever felt it beat before and stronger too. Relief broke over her like a sudden cloudburst when she recognized the standard Solar Patrol markings on the stranger's spacesuit. He was still a few hundred meters away, but the bright red and blue stripes were unmistakable. She realized in an instant, in a way more powerful than any lecture or discussion could convey, what it meant to be a member of a team. In this instance, it meant rescue and companionship. And perhaps even more. Perhaps it meant someone who could get Ivan Blandings under control and put an end to this insane adventure.

"Well Kit, it seems cadet Hackenyos is at a loss for words," the stranger said. "Or maybe she didn't hear me ... No, I think she heard.

There's a response ... You mean the hand signal? No, wait, she's spinning herself around ... That's right. She must have been startled ... Cadet Hackenyos, are you all right?"

The end of the long soliloquy and its abrupt question caught her by surprise, and she uttered a quick: "Uh, yeah."

Then she caught herself, realized the situation she was facing, and tried quickly to correct herself. "I mean, yes, sir. I'm in good shape. I just broke loose from the surface without any way to get back. I figured I'd be another five hours falling to the far wall."

"Is that right?" the stranger replied. Then he answered himself. "She's correct. At her current acceleration, she would continue to a soft impact on the far surface in about two hundred and fifty minutes ... Soft is probably a matter of interpretation ... Perhaps."

Amy shook her head in confusion. "Sir, would it be impertinent for the cadet to ask if you always talk to yourself like that or is this some kind of subtle psychological test?"

There was a moment of silence followed by a crash of static and a loud laugh. "My apologies, cadet. Lieutenant Nathaniel Carson, at your service. And my unseen companion is my AI counterpart, Kit. If it will help you any, I'll reset the pitch on his vocoder and make it easier for you to tell the two of us apart."

Amy felt her face grow warm in sudden embarrassment.

"Sorry, sir. But I've been hanging here for a few hours and I guess I'm a little disoriented."

"Three hours?" Carson asked with exaggerated astonishment. "What in space did you do that for?"

"I'm afraid I didn't have much choice."

"Did you think to ask your spacesuit cogs for help?"

For the second time in less than a minute Amy's face burned so hot that she was glad Carson was too far away to see her. She had thought of it, but never did more than make pointless and unfocused remark – and now she was afraid to admit it.

"Errp," she said, swallowing her shame and trying to shrink into the back of her spacesuit. It wasn't her fault, she protested silently. Until she was put inside the partridge ship with five other cadets and launched into solar orbit beyond Mars, she had never been given real access to the important parts of sensitive equipment like a spacesuit – up until a month before that, when she took the oath as a cadet and was shipped off to Mud Month on Mars, she had been just a kid. Kids weren't supposed to mess around with that kind of thing. And besides – in her whole life she had never used a help file for anything she could figure out herself.

But she couldn't tell this officer any of that. She had learned that much during Mud Month – when you do something wrong, don't make excuses.

"I'll take that as a negative," Carson said. She could see him shake his head inside the glass bowl of his helmet. "Typical cadet."

"Interrogative spacesuit," Amy said to get the attention of the cogs.

"Spacesuit aye," they replied.

"Help. I am stranded in freefall in a very slow trajectory. I need to move – increase my velocity vector – towards the nearest surface."

"Order the creation of nipples on the outer surface of your suit to release small amounts of pressurized gas to stabilize your motion in three dimensions and accelerate you towards the nearest surface – calculated to be nine meters distant. Estimated success rate is 99.9 percent. Command is 'exhale.'"

"Ask for more options. Command is 'more.'"

"Command: Execute exhale," Amy said.

"Well done, Cadet Hackenyos," Carson said. "Tell me – why didn't you ask for other options?"

"I figured the first one would work fine, I didn't see anything wrong with it, and I've been hanging here for a long time and I didn't want to listen to the entire list of choices. You know how AI's are."

"Yes, we do," came the reply. Amy cocked an ear to distinguish the voice. It was different from the Solar Patrol officer's, higher and with less resonance, and had to be his cog AI.

She heard a hissing sound, which produced a moment of involuntary panic as she realized it wasn't a suit leak, but the cogs following their orders. She felt herself drift, first like a spider web on a gentle draft, then like a balloon on a breeze. The surface came towards her with an exciting rush.

"It wouldn't hurt you to hear it, you know. The knowledge may come in handy sometime."

Her first thought was that she would prefer to have them unfold as they presented themselves – to increase the adventure. But her better reason kept her from voicing that thought.

The hissing stopped long before she clunked into the surface. She grabbed a stanchion and fended off the rest of the wall with one boot. Then she began working her way over to where Carson still hugged the rigging. It was hard work, with the handholds plentiful, but not always conveniently placed. It took her a few minutes to get there.

"Where is the rest of your crew?" Carson asked.

"They continued on inside. One of us will be staying behind at every major threshold to guide the follow-up party."

"Follow-up party? Are you sure you don't mean rescue party? As if the Patrol was going to notice you were even missing."

"We don't need to be rescued," Amy said, bristling suddenly. She calmed herself forcibly, then said: "With respect, sir, we are conducting a proper inspection of the facility."

"Proper inspection? Do you have any idea what you might have stumbled on here? Have you even begun to imagine what kinds of things might be floating around in space leftover from the war? Did any one of you ever consider the kinds of risks you might be running by charging in here without even contacting the Patrol and asking for help?"

Amy felt her face begin to burn again, but this time it was anger, not shame.

"Yes, sir," she said brusquely. "One of us did."

Carson was abruptly silent. She couldn't see his face closely yet, but she could hear his breathing on the commlink. After a moment, he said: "And I'll bet the others didn't listen to you."

"The cadet would rather not say, sir."

"Point taken," Carson said. "Whose idea was it to leave you behind like scattered bread crumbs?"

"Cadet Blandings, sir. The entire expedition was his idea."

"Does that mean you don't want any of the credit?"

Amy felt flustered and didn't know what to say. Carson relented and didn't press the question. "That was a good idea. Leaving you behind, that is. At least he's not a total fool."

She resented the idea that Ivan might not be all bad, but at the moment she wasn't being entirely objective.

When Amy reached Carson, she was surprised at what she found. Up close she could see that the officer was terribly young, not more than five years her senior and barely an adult. While listening to him on the commlink, she had formed a much more idealized image of a much more mature-looking man. This was not what she had expected – and it was not reassuring.

She sighed, then gave him a sharp, snappy salute. "Cadet Hackenyos reporting, sir."

He returned the salute and nodded.

"You know, Lieutenant, I was just thinking. It wasn't that I didn't think of asking my suit cogs for help. I guess I avoided thinking about it. I was afraid it would reflect poorly on my record."

Carson shook his head, slowly this time. "Typical cadet."

In that instant she saw that such an idea must be pure fantasy. The Patrol's instructors and officers probably were not laying those kind of traps for unsuspecting cadets. Most likely, they were not secretly trying to weed out anyone who was so lacking in self-confidence that they would actually ask for useful information. And she was pretty sure that they weren't creating diabolically clever crises for them as tests or lessons.

"I guess I was being too devious, wasn't I?"

"I'll bet it was that kind of thinking that got you all into this mess," he said.

"As a matter of fact, it was," Amy said, punctuating her assessment with a sigh of exasperation.

* * *

For some time now, Amy had been upset. She was no longer in the Solar Patrol that she had signed up for.

It was a dream that began when she was barely ten years old. For some that may have been too early to set out on a lifelong career, but Amy was always precocious, always acting like a little adult, asking questions, declaring her opinions loudly and strongly, and making up her mind about serious adult matters as if her years didn't matter.

The spark came from a chance encounter with the larger world beyond her valley in the Coeur D'Alenes, where the waterfalls were fed by melting snow and splashed down from high granite towers.

Her Uncle Louie had taken her to Boise in his four-seater. They had flown over an SSTO ready for launch as they circled the airport to land. She stood on the tarmac beside her uncle's plane when the rocket, two miles distant, began to hiss, and steam, and crackle with fire, lifting itself up into space.

The clouds of steam impressed her most. It was almost as if the rocket rested on them as it climbed slowly off the ground. Then, as it picked up speed, a single column of smoke trailed from its bank of aerospike engines. Before the thrill had time to sink in, the rocket was a mile up, then two, four, and eight. A great pillar of white smoke was all that was left of it.

Standing here at the foot of the pillar, looking up into the stratosphere, made Amy feel even smaller than a ten-year-old normally felt. But the excitement of the launch stayed with her. She would never forget.

She kept up her fascination with rockets. Her first surprise came when she learned how the big dumb chemical-fired boosters were still the most efficient way to get off a planet – despite the advanced science of the 22nd century, with all its nanotech miracles and AI design. Others followed.

She spent a year learning how to calculate interplanetary orbits. That was sheer misery, especially when her live on-line tutor told her that it was all right if she couldn't get the hang of it because women just weren't as math-capable as men. She was angry over that for weeks. And when her AI tutor told her that it wouldn't be necessary for her to calculate orbits in order to become a space pilot, she sulked for weeks more.

And she had devoured everything she could find about the Solar Patrol. For a girl from the backwoods of Idaho, the Patrol was the epitome of everything exotic and wonderful. Crystal space stations in high orbit, sleek spaceships flinging themselves across the depths of the solar system, selfless men and women devoted to duty and responsible for protecting fragile humanity in hostile extraterrestrial environments.

She spent hours online, reading popularized accounts of Solar Patrol missions – rescues of damaged spaceships, exploration of the outer system, and of course, the stories of how the Patrol ended the Last War, pacifying the destructive nanotech spawned by the collapsing nation-states of the 21st century. When those were no longer enough, she found her way to the Patrol archives, where she read actual mission reports, the raw stuff of distant adventure.

When she realized that she could also gain access to Solar Patrol training manuals, she was in heaven. She read them through and through: military honors and protocol, responsibilities of the officer of the deck, communications, shipboard routines and procedures, military law, search and rescue, small craft maneuvering, orbital mechanics, interplanetary flight handbooks.

What really inspired her, however, were the blank forms for officer fitness reports. This was the crucial stuff – how to decide if someone measured up to the standards of the service. This was what they expected of you if you wore the dress grays of the Patrol.

Initiative, moral character, the ability to take and accept responsibility, leadership – they were strict criteria, but they were attainable. That was what sent her spirits soaring. The Patrol was not asking for some lofty and undefined perfection. It was very clear and understandable what they wanted. She could read it in black and white. And she could strive to achieve all that would be expected of her.

So she set out, at the tender young age of twelve, to transform herself into the kind of person who could not only make it into the Patrol, but the kind who could excel. The standards of the Patrol became her standards. Their guidelines for behavior became her guidelines. And their moral imperatives became her moral imperatives. Because the Patrol was not just a bunch of hotshots in sharp uniforms flying around in space – they were the guardians and protectors of humanity in a harsh and dangerous universe.

But somewhere along the line she'd gotten off course.

What they were up to here on this asteroid was not part of some high-intentioned plan to carry on the grand mission of the Solar Patrol. It was part of an ambitious scheme by one cadet to chase after glory and create a reputation for himself. And that was not what she had signed up for. Not at all.

* * *

All that she had endured seemed to have come to nothing.

She had kept her eyes on the distant goal of becoming a Solar Patrol officer for so long, and now, with it almost in reach, the greatest obstacle of all had appeared.

All through school she had been aloof from her classmates. It wasn't that most of them were virtual friends who existed for her only as a bunch of animated holograms in a visual tank. It was just that they didn't measure up to her standards. Most of them were shallow, self-centered, and lacked a crucial curiosity about the world and themselves. The things they believed were the things they were told to believe, not things that they had worked out for themselves. And they had no moral center, no guiding star of right and wrong, as Amy had in the Patrol regulations.

The few who got close to her were still lacking in some special dimension that only she could sense. They were good enough friends and fine people, but there was no steel inside them, no fire, no drive. And no discipline. They were too content with getting whatever they wanted from the household cogs. Not all her classmates fell into that group, of course. Some of them were from here in Idaho, and like her they realized what life was like in more primitive times, when much of what you enjoyed in the world you won with backbreaking labor. Her father and her uncle had both taught her how to split wood (chopping down trees required stronger shoulders than she could develop), dig a latrine, catch live fish in a stream or lake, build a lean-to from branches and leaves, and countless other backwoods skills that were passed down from generation to generation even into the age of nanotechnology.

In the end, Amy had to go farther afield to find social contacts that met her standards. The text-lines were the route there. While virtual friends were fine, they took up a lot of bandwidth – and mainly for the frivolous vanities of displaying new clothes and hairdos and makeup. The text-lines made up for lack of bandwidth with a depth of discourse that she couldn't find with other adolescents. And it gave her a shield of anonymity that suited her just fine.

That had been her downfall when Ivan Blandings suggested the trip to his invisible asteroid.

She should have argued against it. She could have done a very good job. She had become very good at it over the past couple of years. Too good. And that was the problem.

She knew the flaws in his argument. And she knew their roots. Even now she was sure she could dissect his rationalizations, pinning them back like the outer skin of lab frog to reveal the selfish passions that drove them. But that would mean revealing her secret.

If only she hadn't gotten herself in trouble.

It happened a couple of weeks before Ivan's discovery. Howie had gathered the crew together with some urgency and good deal more mystery. They crowded the gymnasium, clinging to the stanchions and grip rings in the multi-faceted chamber. Howie had one leg wrapped around an exercise frame and held a datapad in the other.

"The reason I called you all in here was this message we received on the text-line a few minutes ago," he said. He passed it to Ivan, who read it, grimaced, then passed it to Cheng. "Basically, it's a request from a handful of regular text-line correspondents to help them identify someone."

"Who?" asked Peter.

"You might know him by reputation. His online name is 'Cougar,' and his reputation is for all out war on anyone he doesn't like. He takes flaming to a whole different level."

"Sounds like someone I might like," Pham said with a cat-like smile.

"I've heard of him," Ivan said. "Most of the things that they say about him are exaggerations. He's smart and he's sharp and he is merciless when someone is wrong on facts or weak on logic. But I think he takes himself too seriously."

Cheng passed the datapad to Pham, who glanced at it quickly and handed it to Peter.

"Anyway," Howie continued, "these folks say they've done a statistical analysis of response times in some of Cougar's postings. They say that as of a few months ago, those times suddenly were skewed. It took them a while, but they figured out that Cougar had left Earth, gone to Mars, and then after a few weeks continued on to someplace else."

"What a coincidence!" Cheng said. "He could almost be one of us."

"That's what these folks say," Howie replied.

Peter handed the datapad to Amy, who ran her eyes over the words. She did not read them, not at first. She could not. She was putting all of her energy into remaining calm and under control. She was certain that any unusual movement or expression or word would give her away, reveal her secret, and expose her hidden life.

Because Amy was Cougar.

* * *

It all began with a boy who traveled under a screen name as silly as "Ikonoklast" and a discussion about something as silly as the "categories of being."

When it was clear to Amy that being a Solar Patrol officer meant living up to a higher moral standard, she went looking for expertise on the subject. After a few weeks of searching, she had found a tutor on moral philosophy. He was a clunky old AI download named Arthur with a terribly archaic vocabulary and an odd accent that seemed to have misplaced all its Rs (which made her wonder who had given him a name he could not properly pronounce). And he was chock full of pre-war courses covering the classics from Aristotle to the masters of Zen.

And not long afterwards, she found her way to the philosophy text lines. They were inhabited mostly by unruly and aggressive young boys and girls who, like her, had only recently discovered the subject and were using their newfound knowledge to impress one another – or themselves – with what they no doubt considered to be rapier-like logic and laser-like arguments.

She hadn't been lurking there long when Ikonoklast, the would-be genius, started the argument.

"There is, you know, no such thing as a category of being," he'd posted.

At first, Amy thought it was a boldly empty statement. And she said so.

"What difference does it make if there are no categories of being? Who cares? What does it have to do with morality, with ethics, and with real life?"

"There are categories for everything else," Ikonoklast replied. "That's the only way we have of accessing the world – through concepts, which are categories. Everything – literally every thing – falls into categories. Everything but being. Isn't that odd?"

She dismissed the brash young boy without posting her thoughts. But as she turned the question over and over in her mind, something clicked. She was reviewing that lesson when the pieces fell together, in a blinding flash of insight that set her trembling. She was so excited that she rushed to her keyboard and went searching for the philosophy text line. Within a few minutes, she was pounding away furiously at the keys, the words flowing through her fingertips.

The very first lesson Arthur had given her had been on the virtues and she began her response there.

"The idea of virtue originated with the Greeks and was presented by Aristotle. Humanity has certain unique powers, essentially human powers, that he calls virtues. Courage is the simplest of these. And then comes temperance – the ability to restrain the selfish impulse towards extremity. Justice comes next, although later philosophers made it hard to identify just what that term meant in a complicated world. And wisdom tops them off. Together they form a hierarchy of ideals where each higher virtue draws on the characteristics of those below, and in turn elevates each of them beyond their simpler beginnings. The religious philosophers add their virtues – faith, hope, and charitable, unselfish love."

They all seemed so clear and self-evident to Amy. How could anyone stray from a moral life if they exercised and practiced these virtues? But Arthur pointed out that what was simple in theory was difficult in practice. And that difficulty of practice had allowed too many people to believe that theory was at fault.

"What do you mean when you say there are no categories of being?" she wrote. "How could anyone with a gram of sense suggest such a thing?"

She waited for only a few minutes for Ikonoklast's reply. It was swift in coming.

"It's a simple theoretical proposition," he wrote. "There is endless discussion about the limits of the categories that we use to get at the world. But no discussion of the categories of being. QED."

Amy fumed and shook her head in righteous anger, then slapped out her response.

"Of course there are categories of being," she said. "And if you knew anything at all about moral philosophy, you would know what they are. Courage. Temperance. Justice. Wisdom. Faith. Hope. Charity. Each of these is a category of being – of human being. Each one is a virtue that defines human being. Everyone of us can be courageous. Everyone can be temperate. And just. And wise. And faithful, hopeful, and charitable. If you define the moral good as an affirmation of being, then each individual virtue is a path to that moral good. And each category of being becomes a moral guide."

Then, having made her point, she could not help herself as she continued. "I just wonder what kind of illiterate would argue that there are no categories of being when the truth is so painfully obvious to anyone with half a brain. All I can imagine is that whoever made the claim is so morally bankrupt that he cannot recognize morality when he sees it. Or when he talks about it. Or when it comes along and bites him in the neck.

"He must not have any courage, temperance, justice, wisdom, faith, hope, or charity. He must not have any moral compass, any moral sense, any human sense. In short, he must be some kind of a machine, a cog or an AI, with no soul, no conscience, and no imagination. And I wonder what someone like that is doing wasting his time – and mine – trying to discuss philosophy when he obviously knows nothing about it."

She hesitated only a second before hitting the transmit button and sending her words out into the ether. She felt secure in her cloak of anonymity. Even the war had been unable to destroy the cardinal rule of the text lines – no one could know who you were unless you wanted them to know. She knew she was probably going to offend the youngster who had raised the proposition in the first place. But she never expected the reaction she got.

The other lurkers on the line rallied behind her. Each of them, in their own way, elaborated on her brief but telling message.

"I've been waiting months for someone to tell off that pompous oaf," said one correspondent.

"A masterful piece of deconstruction," said another. "Our friend is fond of sophistry, but lacks a true moral sense. And you are right – there is no being at the core of his argument. Only empty categories of thought."

"Bravo, young warrior of the light," wrote another. "You are blessed with wisdom that your counterpart lacks."

They went on and on in that way, a dozen or more of them. Each of them found the spark of moral sense that Amy had accused Ikonoklast of lacking. Apparently he had quite a reputation for starting arguments by making philosophical claims that he didn't really support, but that were handy foils for stirring up egos and emotions. Her withering blast had settled a number of old scores.

Ikonoklast was silent for a couple of days, then came back on line claiming he had been busy since Cougar's last post and unable to follow the discussion. He further claimed that he hadn't really meant what he said, and of course the arguments by Cougar were proof that it was a silly proposition in the first place.

After that, her reputation – or Cougar's reputation – was established in the way that such things had been done for generations untold: by beating the previous top dog at his own game.

And when Ivan Blandings started talking about why he wanted to visit the invisible asteroid, Amy wanted to repeat the performance. Only this time, she was almost ready to do it out loud, face to face, without the shield of anonymity that the text lines provided.

It would have been so easy, so painfully easy. Ivan was just the kind of person she had described in her blast against Ikonoklast. Lacking courage, temperance, justice, wisdom, faith, hope, and charity. He was the opposite of all that she believed that a Solar Patrol officer should be. It offended her to her bones that he should claim that his faithless ambition was at the heart of a career in the Patrol.

But she could not speak out. Not this time. She held back. Not out of fear of Ivan and her shipmates. What could they do? Make her life even more miserable than it was, cooped up on a partridge ship with a bunch of clueless cadets? No, she held back because she was afraid of losing that cloak of privacy that had allowed her to speak her mind freely whenever she wanted.

The irony presented by her dilemma was not lost on her. She could still speak her mind, but not when it mattered most. Not when her very life was on the line.

And now she was paying the penalty for her silence.

6

Peter Salerno was getting tired of jumping at shadows. But he'd been alone in the dark tunnels of the asteroid base for hours now. The glare of his suit lamps allowed him to get around, but they cast so many shadows. And the shadows twitched and swung and swooped and jerked every time he moved his head or body.

Every movement pulled at his heartstrings. Every bit of twitching darkness fed his imagination with visions of alien dangers. It had been many years since the terror that lurked in his soul had been this close to the surface.

He was avoiding the central shaft where his fellows had disappeared through the hole that had in turn disappeared. And he was trying to avoid thinking about it. Too many emotions were loaded into that place. Emotions that he didn't want to face.

So he explored the shafts that led to the surface. He found seven of them, spaced unevenly about the central axis. They were all similar in design and construction. Each was two or three meters in diameter and lined with ladder rungs, conduits, cables, and junction boxes. Each terminated in a domed enclosure anchored on the black surface of the asteroid.

The domes showed more variety. Some were small and cramped, others were quite large, ten meters across or more. The large ones held the remains of weapons emplacements – heavy concrete bases with steel frameworks protruding from them and thick cables running off towards the shaft. There was nothing left of the weapons themselves, of course. Peter figured they were probably gigawatt lasers or something similar. The relics of a long forgotten conflict, predating the Last War itself.

The large domes also contained something else – access to the surface. Two airlocks were mounted in each one, on opposite sides of the chamber. The smaller domes lacked these exits. Indeed, Peter wasn't sure of their function at all. Perhaps they had contained sensors. Or maybe even fire control and tracking systems for the big guns.

The airlocks presented their own problem. Peter was reluctant to leave the safe confines of the domes. As old and unusual as they were, they were still familiar. Steel and concrete, aluminum and plastic, artificial environments crafted by the hand of man. Under the circumstances, that was a reassurance he didn't want to abandon.

But out on the surface there was no light, no stars turning slowly overhead. There was only that unbroken unseeable blackness of the stealth shield some unknown distance overhead. And that was more nanotech.

The time had come, however, when he exhausted his examination of the tunnels and domes. He knew what he had to do next. He couldn't remain idle and he couldn't return to the central shaft. The airlocks offered the only new ground for exploration.

He knew too that the doors were simple mechanical devices, no fancy electronics, no clever nanotech creations. You pulled the long bar down and sealed the door, you pushed it up and unsealed the door. The pumps that filled the small compartment between the inner and outer doors had long since seized up with vacuum welding of the pistons. And the air had likely leaked from the containment vessels decades ago. But that only made it easier. Open the first door, step through it, then open the second. There was no need to close and lock the inner door, although some deep instinct or remembered lesson from Mother Janus or mud month on Mars made him nervous about leaving both doors open at once.

And suddenly he found himself outside.

His feet crunched against the regolith as he settled on the ground. The surface gravity of this rock was high enough to hold him in place if he didn't move, but not enough to leave footprints in the black grit that covered the asteroid. The material was the accumulation of a few billion years of flying around the solar system. While it resembled dark sand, it was actually millions of bits of carbonaceous matter that had fallen like fast rain from the sky. Most of the bits were no larger than a grain of sand. But all of them had hit with interplanetary speeds – dozens of kilometers a second. Larger bits had left tiny circular splashes in the surface. Still larger impacts had left overlapping and concentric pits and ridges spreading around the circumference of the small potato-shaped globe on which he stood.

He was uncertain of how to proceed. Moving about was a lot like trying to walk in a swimming pool, but without the resistance. Or like a dream where you were flying. That was the more apt comparison. He picked up his feet, tucked his knees towards his chin, and drifted like a sagging helium balloon towards the ground. He was afraid to make too strenuous an effort for fear that he would leave the surface and fly off into space. Who knew what would happen if he hit the underside of the stealth shield. He was sure he didn't want to find out.

By working his way cautiously and carefully along, he found he could make considerable progress. The trick was to lean forward and use his hands. He had to be careful not to break off pieces of regolith as he pulled himself forward. But the acceleration of the microgravity was small enough that he could leverage his legs up and away from the surface as he moved.

Before long, his main concern became navigating his way across the alien landscape. His lights were meant for close in work and once he was a few meters away from the dome, he had to fight the panic of disorientation.

"Spacesuit, can you modify the lamps on my helmet?" he asked, the words torn from an anxious, dry throat.

"In what way, Cadet Salerno?"

"Give them more range. Boost their intensity. I need to be able to see the domes from farther away."

"Redesign is possible. Time to completion is 150 seconds. Shall I execute?"

"Execute," Peter said. "By all means execute."

He dug his fingers into the grit while waiting for the suit's cogs to do their work. Before long, he found every muscle in his body clenching up and his eyes shut tight. He forced himself to relax, then swung the newly constructed headlamps around the horizon. The dome caught a glint of light in the near distance, then sparkled as the beam caught a piece of naked metal.

He continued to search his surroundings and discovered that the domes were not the only structures on the surface. About ten meters away was a single shaft of dull gray rising straight up into the sky.

Peter maneuvered over to it, then used his new high-power lights to examine it more closely. It was only a few centimeters in diameter, featureless and smooth, and it reached up into the darkness overhead.

He looked around and spotted another more than ten meters to the left and a third a similar distance to the right. Then he recoiled from the nearest one in sudden surprise as he realized that these were part of the stealth shield. They were the pylons that held up the artificial sky. Or perhaps the cables that anchored it in place.

In any case, they were more nanotech – and he wanted nothing to do with it.

* * *

"Cadet Salerno, you may begin the discussion," Mother Janus had said. "Tell us all please, precisely what is history?"

The event was formal and ceremonial – the anniversary of the Anthrax Incident. All the cadets were decked out in their dress grays, their collars sparkling with the miniature stars that marked their low and artificial rank. The Dactyl Incident was the beginning of the end for the Last War, when the first elements of what would later become the Solar Patrol began to work together to end the fighting.

They celebrated the occasion with a special officers' mess, like every other unit in Patrol was doing at the exact same time. They drank to the health of the two commanders who had agreed to cease hostilities against one another, to the health of all the Survivors, and to the health of the Patrol's officers, service members, and cadets. And when the meal was over, tradition and custom demanded a meaty discussion of important issues: the role of the Solar Patrol in modern politics, matters of public policy affecting Earth and its colonies on the other planets, and the history of humanity that led to the Last War and the creation of the current social order. Officers and cadets alike were all expected to contribute – and significantly.

And the relevance of the topic chosen by Mother Janus to his initial encounter with Ivan Blandings was not lost on Peter. It was the way of the Patrol to confront explosive subjects head on.

"It's what people do," Peter said, responding as directly as possible, keeping his jaw straight and presenting as serious a face as possible.

"It certainly is that," Mother Janus replied. "Don't you all agree?"

"He's got it right," Howie said with a grunt. "Eat, sleep, fight, have babies. That's history for you." He flashed a wide grin, clearly satisfied with the simplicity of his analysis.

"Perhaps," said Mother Janus. "What about the rest of you? Is that all there is to history?"

"Animals eat, sleep, fight, and have babies and they don't have history," Peter said after a moment's reflection. He narrowed his eyes and looked at the others for support, though none was immediately to be found. Peter knew that Amy would probably back him up – but not if he was wrong.

"Correct," Mother said. "Anyone else?"

"It's what people said they did," said Cheng Li Hui. The young Asian sounded tentative, her voice dropping at the end.

"Aha, the end of innocence," Ivan Blandings snapped from the corner where he had posted himself. "And so soon."

"We have a skeptic among us," Mother said.

"Well isn't it?" Cheng asked, her tone taking on more certainty. "It's not necessarily accurate or complete. And it's only what people said happened. So you can't always trust it. That's what dumb-bombs are all about."

A flash of insight erupted in Peter's mind and he blurted out: "It's what people want you to think they did."

"A cynic," Ivan noted. "You are more sophisticated than you appear."

Peter swallowed a retort and pressed on. "I remember history classes on the primary link. They had a couple dozen of us chained in to the tutor together and they taught us things that we didn't really understand at the time. Stuff about the world before the Last War, and how Argentina was a great power in the Southern Hemisphere. About the Malvinas and the Dirty War."

"And what did they want you to think they did?" Mother Janus asked.

"I'm not sure, really," Peter said. "They wanted us to think we were an important and heroic people. Now that I think about it, they were terribly obvious about that. Not very subtle. We were supposed to recite that phrase ten times before lunch each day. We were an important and heroic people."

"And what about the Last War?" Mother asked. "What did they want you to think about that?"

Peter felt his face grow warm. He hadn't expected that, though he should have. Mother Janus clearly had a second agenda for this discussion. He stumbled over his response.

"The same as everyone who survived, I guess. They wanted to blame it on someone else."

"All of it?"

"Most of it," Peter said. "Except for the destruction of Buenos Aires." There – it was out. It was much easier than he'd expected. His embarrassment came from the current social confrontation, with the others staring at him as Mother Janus continued her probing.

"Yes. That's a sensitive subject for you, isn't it?"

Peter smiled sheepishly. "I guess it is, ma'am."

"What did they teach you about that?"

"That it was necessary to protect the people of Mar del Plata."

"Was it?"

"I guess that's a matter of some debate," Peter said with a sigh, surrendering the ground he had fought so hard to defend in his first confrontation with Ivan Blandings. "We were taught that it was."

"By the same people who taught you that you were an important and heroic people?"

Peter felt the wind sag out of him. "The same."

"Did you believe them?" This time the question came from Amy, much to Peter's surprise. For a moment he was thrown off balance, then he recovered.

"I was just a kid, you know. We believed it then. It was only later that we began to doubt. The classes continued right up through certification, when we were much wiser children. The others used to talk about it during the break while we were still chained together online. They said that it couldn't be true if they were trying so hard to make us believe."

"They said that?" Mother Janus said. "What about you? Did you say it too?"

"I just listened. I didn't like it. It was like, everything we were told was a lie. And if everything they told us was a lie, then everything else was a lie as well. There was no point in being honest or brave or fair. They were all lies. We weren't an important or heroic people. We were just scared and dishonest. Dishonest with ourselves and dishonest with our children. Because we couldn't face the truth."

"And what truth was that?"

"That there was no gray goo threatening Buenos Aires. That it was just fear. And the fear spread and everyone started to panic and they all started running from the city. And then the military decided that it had to be true if everyone was so frightened. So they dropped a rock in the middle of the city and killed everyone who hadn't run and left a big smashing hole full of seawater in its place."

"My goodness, Peter, where did you get such ideas?"

"Mar del Plata is just one metro-state. They couldn't control everything we read or said or thought. Some of the brighter kids started swapping texts from outside. News records from right after the war."

"And what about you? Did they swap them with you?" Now it was Ivan's turn to ask a question, bearing down on an apparent weakness in Peter's character.

"No. I told them I didn't want to hear about it. I wanted to believe. I wanted to think that we were important and heroic. It was better than what the others were saying. At least it was something to believe in. The rest of them had nothing. Just themselves."

"Do you still believe, Peter?"

He drew in a breath and held it. Now he saw the trap that Mother had set for him. He was surprised that an AI could be so clever. But then, he realized that he was just a cadet, and a pretty sorry one for all that. "I still believe that there's more to believe in than yourself. We could be important and heroic – if we try hard enough and work hard enough. Maybe it was all a lie. But that doesn't mean you shouldn't believe in something bigger – in honesty and fairplay and courage. And I guess that's why I'm here now. The others never left home. They never wanted to see a world bigger than the one they already knew. I couldn't help it. I wanted to go someplace where it wasn't all a lie. And that's why I joined the Patrol."

The silence that he faced now was like a beam of sunshine breaking through the clouds. The others just stared at him. Cheng turned away, shy at the intensity of Peter's words. Amy smiled gently. Ivan shook his head. For a moment, Peter hung suspended in space. His body felt distant and numb, his face felt taut against his cheekbones, and his eyes ached from opening wide.

He was ready for whatever they would say next. They could belittle him if they wanted, but it didn't matter. He could stand his ground, now that he was secure about where he stood. And that was something new. Before this, he had been uncertain. Now he knew. Now he knew that the lies belonged to the tutors, not to him. And that the truth, whatever it was, held no threat for him.

"Very good, Cadet Salerno," Mother Janus said. "There is nothing wrong with wanting to be important and heroic. But those are things that must be earned and not borrowed."

* * *

It didn't matter if the gray goo was real or not – the fear was.

And it was such a perfect monster. It was a threat that could lurk anywhere. In basements, in cracks in the road, in storm drains and sewer pipes, in the ruined places nearest the beach that had once been buildings before the war. A tiny smear could contain millions of invisible machines capable of breaking you down into your component molecules – and anything else in the way.

That was what the Last War had been about at the end.

When the first nanotech machines were built at the end of the last century, they were hailed as the great emancipator of humanity. But that lasted only a few weeks. Then the jealousy and envy that drove the old nation-states took over. Those who did not have the technology began to fear those who did. And those who did began to fear those who did not. Then the economy began to come apart at the seams as the markets reacted to the sudden appearance of virtually unlimited manufacturing capacity. It didn't take long for the fighting to break out.

At first they had used the nanotech to build and maintain conventional weapons – planes, ships, and tanks. But then the nanotech itself became a weapon. And the ultimate weapon was the gray goo. Unrestrained disassemblers. Left to their own devices, the gray goo would devour the planet, reducing every substance to its simplest compounds with the exception of themselves. And themselves, they would replicate a trillionfold every month.

Buenos Aires was not the only city to go. In the final months of the war, gray goo broke out in dozens of places. In some areas, they nuked it. In others, they used more drastic measures. Manhattan Bay marked the place where some of it had escaped from NYU in the Lower East Side. Capetown was no more. Kiev, Singapore, Cairo, Calcutta, Dhahran, Munich, Bordeaux, and the outskirts of Maracaibo, Mexico City, Detroit, Knoxville, Moscow, Kigali, Sydney, Toronto, and a dozen more.

As Peter had admitted to his shipmates and to himself, not all of them should have been targets. Some were attacked on pretense by rival powers. Others, perhaps even Buenos Aires, were destroyed in a moment of irrational fear and suspicion.

And that was the problem. No amount of destruction could quell the fear. Peter had grown up with it every day of his life. The gray goo could be anywhere. He had learned that lesson early. Rough playmates had forced him into dark ruins and terrified him with stories of dissolving little boys. His mother made him remove his shoes whenever he entered the house and set them in the sterilizer. His grandmother would tell stories of the war that her parents had told her. The fear acted like a giant hand, squeezing the people of Mar del Plata as flat as the city that once occupied the great circular bay. It kept them from questioning authority – teachers, politicians, managers and directors. And it kept them constantly on the edge of a hidden panic that erupted only occasionally, like the night his father had nearly beaten him for coming home late and filthy after being stuffed into one of the underground ruins down by the beach.

The lessons of fear were the ones hardest learned and hardest unlearned. The Patrol had had him for only a handful of months. The fear had owned him for nearly all of his sixteen years.

So when he found himself standing next to the pillar, or cable, or whatever it was, he was gripped by sudden panic. He kicked out, pushing away from the smooth, gleaming metal. For a moment, it was like being in a swimming pool and pushing away from the edge towards the center. But there was no water to retard his motion. Instead of drifting slowly to a stop, Peter went careening off the surface and into inky black space.

Adrenaline pumped into his blood and set his back abuzz. His breathing accelerated, echoing loudly inside the glass bowl of his helmet. And sweat built up in thick puddles on his forehead.

Then something that felt like a giant invisible hand swatted him out of the sky. As he recovered from the blow, Peter realized he had hit the underside of the stealth shield. The impact had sent him spinning – not terribly fast, just enough to make him feel nauseous. He swung his head around, trying to catch sight of something, anything, in his helmet lights.

He was almost too late. But he saw the splash of light on metal down on the surface. A second splash allowed him to orient himself, get a sense of his own motion, and prepare for impact with the surface of the asteroid.

He managed to get his feet under him, more or less. And when he hit, he crumpled, allowing his body to absorb the energy of the collision. He was moving slowly enough at the end that he could grab the ground, digging his gloved hands into the regolith, and bring himself to a stop.

Motionless once again, he waited. His breathing slowed, his heart stopped pounding, and his muscles stopped twitching. Finally he sighed. A quick inspection showed that he had landed not far from a dome. It was probably the one he had left behind when he ventured onto the surface. The structures were far enough apart – and his motion was restricted enough – that it was unlikely this was another.

He pulled himself along to the airlock and re-entered the shelter. The glass no longer held any atmosphere, but its presence was enough to give Peter a sense of protection – a sense that was short-lived.

He sat cross-legged on the floor of the dome for a few minutes to catch his breath and relax. The light of his redesigned helmet lights made bright pools of light wherever he pointed them and dark shadows in contrast wherever he did not. After a while, he turned his head towards the deck, in part to reign in the swinging shadows. The lights cast the rough surface in harsh relief, amplifying the cracks, crevices, grit, and rubble.

It looked no different than the floor of a rough basement or a carpark at home. If he didn't move, Peter almost felt as if he were back there now. He was cloaked in a shield of darkness, which hid the strange distance that separated him from all that he'd once known.

Then a tiny shadow moved at the edge of his vision.

He turned his head. The lights shifted to catch the interloper unprepared. It was a centimeter across, with a half dozen or so legs. It looked like a spider or a roach. It froze in its tracks.

Peter was just as still. He examined it closely without getting any nearer. It had eight legs for sure, now that he counted them. He couldn't identify anything on the body other than its head. He looked at it for a long time trying to pick out details. The thing had no real eyes, but a cluster of long antennae grew out of the top of its body.

Then it turned about and scuttled across the floor.

Peter reached out to grab it, but he wasn't quick enough. And the subsequent demonstration of Newton's laws of motion, action and reaction, was enough to discourage him from pursuing it any further. Especially since it had disappeared into the shadows as his head swung around and the lights with it.

In any case, he had seen enough.

This was not an insect. It was some diabolical piece of miniature machinery. Where it had come from he could only guess. He did not want to know. His only desire now was to get away, to escape from this place and its unknown horrors.

He swung around the stanchions and beams to get to the shaft. Then he pulled himself down the long tunnel, faster and faster, until his hands moved just enough to keep him from smacking into the ladder. The speed of his passage was reassuring. He hadn't realized just how fast he could get himself going in the asteroid's microgravity.

Then, before he expected it, he reached the end of the tunnel.

He exploded out into the central shaft of the asteroid, surrounded by soft blue light. He flailed his arms and legs helplessly as he careened across the wide open space.

"Peter!"

The voice of Amy Hackenyos was loud in his ears, though his radio gave him no sense of where it might be coming from. He swiveled his head around in search of her. There she was – up by the barrier that had swallowed their shipmates hours earlier. And she wasn't alone.

Wham!

The moment's distraction was enough to send him caroming off the wall of the shaft. The impact knocked the wind out of him with a loud "oof" and left him gasping for air. He was moving much more slowly when he smacked into another part of the wall. On the third bounce, he found a purchase in an outcrop of rock and brought himself to a halt.

Then he heard an unknown male voice. "Cadet Salerno, I hope you have some explanation for abandoning your post."

7

Cheng Li Hui huddled in one corner of the room, keeping company with the shadows while she watched the headlamps of her shipmates swing about in the neighboring compartments. She had given up on the inspection of her room. The place was empty, featureless, and dark, just like the others. If there had been air in them, they would have echoed harshly with the cadets' voices.

"I don't get it," Howard Efi said. "What's the point? Why so many rooms?"

"Is it winchestering?" asked Ivan Blandings, his voice rising and falling as he moved about his chamber and cloaked the comm signal from his spacesuit.

"Winchestering?" Cheng asked. "I've heard the term before, but I'm not sure what it means."

"It's what happens when nanotech gets out of control," Ivan said, trailing off into digital static as he hid himself completely from Cheng's receiver.

"It's one of the things that can happen," Pham said. Cheng's heart warmed at the sound of her voice. "Cogs can do two things – cut and paste molecules or chew on information – but it can't do them both at once. Once in a while too many cog-units get involved in assembling to keep track of what they're supposed to be doing."

"And they just keep making things," Ivan added. "I heard about one ship in the yards on Deimos that got it bad. Started growing engine modules on every surface. Multiple control and wiring harnesses all plugged into the same consoles. Compartments and corridors sealed off from the rest of the ship."

"The name comes from a house in California that belonged to a woman named Winchester," Pham said.

"She married the son of the man who invented the machine gun," Ivan said.

"Actually it was a rifle that could fire several times without reloading," Pham said.

"And the woman was told that the ghosts of all those who had been killed with her father-in-law's rifles would come after her if she didn't keep working on the house," Ivan said. His voice was strong and clear now, and Cheng assumed he was standing in the doorway to make sure his signal carried.

"She went on with dozens of carpenters for ten or twenty years," Pham continued. "The building is still there. They use images of it in the tutorial."

"I guess I haven't gotten that far along," Cheng said. She heard a sound that resembled nothing so much as a dismissive snort. It could have been any of them, but she hoped in her deepest heart that it was Howie or Ivan. Because she couldn't stand it if Pham found another excuse to think poorly of her.

Cheng grew up in Shendeng Province, which lay between the blasted desert that had once been Beijing and the great round bay that had once been Shanghai. She was the daughter of a displaced industrial family. In the last century, they had been influential and powerful, managers and officers of many important factories in the region. But the changes that came with the invention of nanotech were deeper and more profound than those of the Last War. The family lost its place of prestige and power when production was no longer carried out by great teams of workers and managers.

The family had never risen much from their provincial roots and since the beginning of the century they had done little to prevent returning there. Pham had been quick to point out the flaws in Cheng's rudimentary political ideas, and even quicker to point out the differences between her own historical roots and hers.

"My ancestors' land was the only nation on Earth to build a successful revolution against imperialism in the 20th century," she told her. "Yours only pretended, like so many others. You had palace coups, while we had to struggle for forty years against foreign invaders. You had propaganda, we had history."

The history lessons mattered little to her. She had no emotional investment in the world before she was born or the history she inherited. But the critique of her own ideas left her wounded.

"Direct democracy is fine for peasants," she'd said. "But a sophisticated society has too many groups for that. What about the mechanics, the merchants, the workers, and the students? What if one group figures out ways to block the others? How do you manage the give and take of party politics? You say, 'Just let everyone vote on it.' But that's wishful thinking. Someone has to decide what to vote on and how to frame the question, so they have power over the debate. Nothing is ever simple or direct."

And on top of it all, she was skinny, her ears stuck out, her hands were too large, and her feet were too big.

So she kept her feelings to herself, certain that Pham barely knew she was alive and afraid to open herself up to even deeper rejection than her casual dismissals. She couldn't stand it if Pham started to dissect her emotions the way she did her politics.

***

"How do we tell if it's winchestered or if it's supposed to be like this?" Howie's question hung on the commlink unanswered for a long time.

"I guess if it winchestered, it would still be building," Ivan said.

"Maybe. But this place is pretty old. Give it a couple of years and nanotech could turn this whole asteroid into enough rooms to fill every building in downtown Tokyo. It must have stopped some time ago."

"Unless it started only recently," Cheng said, swallowing her shyness against her fear as the thought hit her suddenly. "We've already got – what, sixteen rooms? How many more are there? And how fast can this place turn them out? On the other hand, why would they make these rooms at all? For what purpose?"

"Obviously to house the human crew," Ivan said. "Only they never showed up."

"You know, I've been thinking," Howie said. "How old is this place?"

"Not as old as the war," Ivan shot back. "It's got nanos everywhere."

"It started out before the war," Pham replied. "The topside facilities are old. They've even got machine shops, for goodness sake."

"Well considering the absence of any human crew, what do you think has been going on here?"

"Nanotech at work without human intervention," Pham declared without hesitation.

"And does that send a chill up your backbone the way it does mine?" Howie asked.

"Sure does," Cheng answered.

"Absolutely," said Pham. "Old nanotech at work without human intervention."

"How old are we talking about?" Ivan asked.

"Not pre-war. Not post-war," Howie recited.

"That adds up to wartime nanotech," Pham said with a certain air of fatalism in her voice.

"Are you sure we're safe from that stuff?" Howie asked.

"We should be," Pham replied. "Cogs rule. That's why the war ended. No matter what the other stuff is, the cogs should be able to reprogram it and turn it into more cogs."

Cheng nodded. That was the theory. It was enough to stop the gray goo. It was enough to take control of whole armies and fleets away from their commanders and stop them in their tracks. It was enough to keep the microscopic tools of humanity's limitless imagination from turning into demons beyond its control.

But here, surrounded by some unknown design of nanotech left over from the war itself, he wasn't so sure.

"If it's left over from the war, it's had sixty years to sit around and think about that, hasn't it?" Howie asked.

"More or less," Pham admitted.

"That's a lot of time. Especially if you think at cog speeds. Do you suppose that even a nanotech AI could come up with an original idea in sixty years – more or less?"

Pham sighed. "Gee, I hope not ..."

"So anyway, not to change the subject, but shouldn't we finish our reconnaissance?" Ivan said with sudden vigor. His voice faded in and out, though, making Cheng wonder if he was bounding about the small compartment with nervous energy. "Pham, isn't there some way we can leave a trail of cog oil so we can find our way out of here?"

"Of course," she said. "In fact, if we give the lantern a few minutes, it can give us a trail of bread crumbs that will give us a full three-D map of the structure we're in."

"Then let's do it," Ivan said. "Howie, you're still in command. Say the word."

"Go ahead," Howie said, though a hint of reluctance hung in his voice. "Let's check this place out before we leave it behind us."

Cheng swallowed hard. She wanted to leave the place behind, but on her way out. Now she was afraid of what might happen if they followed through on the mission as originally conceived by Ivan Blandings. That plan included a full inspection of the asteroid station before sending a report back to the authorities.

"After all," he'd said, "it might be cloaked behind that stealth shield for a reason that we can't even imagine."

Once the cogs had produced the components they needed for a remote link, the party went deeper into the maze of three-meter boxes. It was easier to move around in here, more comfortable to be able to reach out and stop yourself by touching the wall. And they stayed together as they moved – the cog oil eliminated the need to spread out and no one suggested repeating that method.

As they pressed on deeper and deeper into the labyrinth, the map generated by the cogs was projected onto the inside of Cheng's helmet in greater and greater detail.

They were two hundred meters from the central shaft when they hit their first dead end. The map showed that they had come straight in, give or take a few zigs and zags. Now they spiraled around the cul-de-sac, exploring the outer limit of the chambered zone. It spread another fifty meters around their first contact.

Fifty meters square was sixteen three-meter boxes by sixteen. That was 256, as any computer hacker could tell you instinctively, Cheng realized. Multiply that by another 64 and you came up with 16,000.

"Does anyone believe that there must be 16,000 compartments in this structure?" Cheng asked loudly when the scale of the construction hit her.

"Sounds kind of high to me," Howie said.

"No – that's the right scale," Pham said, leaving Cheng feeling relieved in more ways than one. "How much time would it take if they do one room a day?"

"At a thousand days in three years, that would be 48 years," Cheng said. "Too large a number to prove the question one way or another."

"Exactly," Pham said. "It could be winchestered, or it could be building rooms on purpose. There's no way to be sure."

"Isn't there some way we could test it to see what it's doing?" Howie asked.

"Not without finding the local cogs themselves," Pham said. "You can't analyze the rooms. They're nothing but silicon-oxide fibers arrayed end to end."

"Hey everybody, I think we have a problem," Ivan said, his voice dropping an octave and rising in volume. Cheng looked around and saw him hovering near the entrance to the room they were in.

"What is it?" Howie asked, suddenly breathless.

"This door just slid shut on its own and now it won't open."

Every hair on Cheng's body stood on end as the fear flooded

through her.

"Quick," Howie said, grabbing Pham and pushing her towards the other doorway on the far side of the compartment. "Through the next door ... ."

* * *

Nat Carson just shook his head and twisted his mouth into a wary, distrustful frown as Salerno gave his report. The young cadet tried too hard to keep a military bearing in spite of his obvious excitement. Nat and Amy Hackenyos had anchored themselves to a guy line on the wall and waited for Salerno to work his way over to them. Nat wasn't exactly sure why he had to wait until he was face to face with him. He could just as easily have done the formalities from the spot where he landed. Proximity was not necessary and did not improve the performance of the comm link.

Nat chalked it up to inexperience with radio communications – and to the sudden way he had exploded from the doorway and out into the central shaft, his arms and legs swinging as he roared several oaths in English, Spanish, and Italian.

"Sir, the cadet apologizes for his arrival, sir," he shouted, rattling Nat's ears. At least the kid had learned the drill well during Mud Month. "I was reconnoitering my area of responsibility, sir."

He went, on describing the tubes and surface posts in too much detail – none of it sufficient to explain his emotional state. "For Zeke's sake, cadet, spit it out. What's the matter?"

"Sir, I believe I have seen evidence of an indigenous life form on the asteroid, sir."

"Evidence of what?"

"I'm not exactly sure, sir."

"Can you describe it?"

"Sir, yes, sir," Salerno spouted. "It looked like a bug. Like an insect or a spider. It had too many legs for a normal insect. But it was running around in the vacuum, sir."

"Running around in a vacuum?"

"He's right," Amy said with sudden agitation. "I forgot about it completely. I saw the same thing. Well, not the exact same thing. Mine looked like a lady bug. And it was flying through the air – I mean the vacuum. I couldn't believe it when I saw it."

"I'm so glad, Amy," Salerno said. "I wasn't sure if I was really seeing it or my eyes were just playing games with me."

"Is there anything else you forgot to mention, Cadet Hackenyos?" Nat said with a snarl that silenced the two cadets abruptly.

"No, sir," she said. "It was a few hours ago, and when you arrived, I had other things on my mind."

Nat turned to face her and narrowed his eyes. She fell silent. Nat drew in a deep breath to try to calm himself. He was not going to start shouting at cadets. It was not military. It was not respectful. And it was not necessary. No matter how much he wanted to. It was not their fault that they acted like kids instead of experienced spacehands. Besides, that was a temporary condition, one that did not survive long contact with life aboard a full-duty Patrol vessel instead of the extended holiday of life aboard a partridge ship.

After a long quiet moment, he said: "Why couldn't you guys try to swap crew or trade for a load of balanced amino acids or make an illegal landing on Deimos or something? Why did you have to go looking for a giant invisible ship-eating alien?"

Neither Amy nor Salerno attempted to answer the question,

which was just as well. He asked another. "Either of you ever study military history? The real scoop on the Last War?"

Again neither of them answered, which Nat took as a negative. "I thought so. Otherwise none of you would have come within a million kilometers of this rock. Have you ever imagined what it was like then? People were trying real hard every single day to kill one another. I mean, they were serious about it. They weren't criminals or lunatics, they were serious and determined men and women doing a nasty job the best they possibly could because the alternative was to get killed by someone else. That's what war really is. You play for keeps and there's no rules. There is nothing like it in this universe, and thank goodness for that."

He looked at the two of them and wondered how anyone so young could be floating around here in microgravity hundreds of millions of kilometers away from a world of Friday night mixers and Saturday shopping trips to town. He'd never looked that young, had he?

"The Last War – any war – was not like sports. It wasn't a game. You sat on the ragged edge of life and death waiting for someone to come along and push you off the wrong side. Now you may wonder what any of that has to do with you. You may think that anything that happened before you were born is ancient history. But space is vast and deep and time means very little out here.

"The people who fought the Last War did not belong to little metrostates like we do. They were part of huge nations. Even without nanotech they were capable of producing no end of infernal devices. And when they got it, things just turned worse. There are places on Earth and the Moon that you still can't visit without getting eaten by a battlebot or sliced up by warriorware. But you can put a fence around those places on a planet. Out here, you're on your own.

"There are things out here in the system left over from the war. Infernal devices. Stealthed up missiles that have been waiting for decades for a target to come in range. Spy probes that took a detour on their way to Vesta and end up outside your colony preparing to fry your datastorage tanks as a final courtesy. Clouds of metal-eating nanites that can strip your hull to the plastic in 37 minutes flat. Stuff you can't even imagine, so there's no way to protect against it until it's too late.

"Hardly a year goes by without someone getting killed or seriously messed up by some heirloom from the old nation-states. More often than not, it's one of us, because the Patrol goes around poking its nose into places where those things are. It's something you have to get used to, just another risk. But when you find some of it, you have to adjust your thinking in a hurry. Because all of a sudden, you're back in the middle of the Last War and a piece of it is out to get you.

"In case you hadn't realized it by now, that's probably what we're dealing with here. Now I'm not accusing you of slacking off, or almost getting your neck broken because of some mindless cadet trick. Even you cadets are part of the Patrol and you're only here doing what we do every day. But I'll just have to beg your pardon if I don't get all excited over being picked to risk my life messing around because you all felt compelled to explore some godawful relic of the Last War."

* * *

With a cold, passionless, yet unshakable attention, it watched.

As the cadets made their way from the docking collar, through the

Grand Concourse and down to the first barrier, as they penetrated that barrier and continued on, as their fellows remained behind on picket duty, as the advance party entered the habitation spaces and worked its way to the far side, it watched.

With eyes too many too count, too small to be seen, spread for hundreds of meters in every direction, embedded in rock and metal and plastic and glass, it watched.

So much time had passed since there had been anything to watch – anything besides itself at work. So many countless nanoseconds, so many eternities of waiting. But it was ready when the moment came. Schemes put in motion decades earlier began to play themselves out. They proceeded without any willful animation – or none beyond the acts of others committed so long ago. But they were just as potent.

When the moment came to conduct the first test, it acted.

It closed the first door, and, with receivers too numerous to evade, it heard the sudden shouts, groans, and squeals of the intruding cadets as they raced from chamber to chamber to evade the succession of ever-closing doors.

On one scale, they were nothing but ticks in the belly of the asteroid, dwarfed into insignificance by the scale of the environment. But on another, they were sweating, panting sacks of bone and muscle carrying powerful intelligences, natural as well as artificial. On that scale, they slammed and leapt from room to room, their path directed by their nanite brain as it detected the first motions of the sliding metal doors. The metal rang from the impact of their bodies as they rushed headlong in microgravity.

"This way! This way!" the largest of them shouted.

"Right! Turn right, everyone!" yelled the smallest.

The ether crackled with their comm traffic, punctuated by the steam-engine sounds of human bodies exerting themselves at full force. It recorded every sound for later analysis, every movement by each cadet, every hesitation, every mistake, every recovery. They flew through thirty compartments, banging and crashing all the way, before slowing down considerably. It knew the chemistry of human muscle tissue and knew that the oxygen reserves stored in them were all used up. It recognized the gasping sounds that were common on the far side of that threshold.

When those gasping sounds diminished a few minutes later, it calculated that the nanites driving the cadets' spacesuits might have compensated by increasing the amount of oxygen available to them and filed that deduction away for future reference.

The cadets slammed through another thirty compartments – then forty, fifty, and sixty. Every meter of the passage, it kept track, adjusting the timing of the closing doors to ensure that the test would not end prematurely. It could not risk ending the operation prematurely.

In the end, the cadets made their way back to the entrance to the central shaft, expelling themselves into the deep well, one after the other, each with a long wailing cry.

* * *

Cheng clung to a pillar of green olivine. Her body shook with the force of her breathing as her lungs sucked greedily for the air. Her head throbbed with the force of a rapid heartbeat. Her legs ached from the alien impact of steel in microgravity and her arms from the effort of pulling herself through narrowing doorways. And she had never been so scared in her life

"All right ... is anyone hurt?" Howie asked, the ripping the words out between gasps. "Check yourselves out ... you might not ... realize it."

Cheng tried to get control of her protesting muscles and lungs, a process that took a few minutes and an extreme effort of will. She couldn't believe she had survived the ordeal – and the surprise went a long way towards helping her recover. She prodded her arms and legs, her ribs and belly. She tried her best to test her back, though the leverage was difficult in her perch on the pillar. As far as she could tell, she was all right.

"Okay here," she reported.

"I think I'm uninjured," Ivan said, his voice wavering a little.

"Everything's been rearranged, but it's all intact," Pham threw in.

"Same here," Howie replied. "Good. Now can someone tell me what just happened in there?"

Cheng shook her head and located Howie where he was anchored to a large outcropping opposite the door to the labyrinth – a distance of about thirty meters from the pillar. She pried herself away from the rock and began pulling herself towards the outcrop. Off to one side she saw Pham doing the same from where she had landed. She still couldn't spot Ivan, although she wasn't free to search thoroughly as long as she was moving.

"My guess is some kind of automatic reaction," Ivan said from his hiding place. "If it's just winchestering, it could do almost anything unpredictable. This one just happened to start closing doors left and right."

Cheng scowled. She wasn't buying that explanation. She felt too much like a chased animal to believe it was just something automatic.

With a final push, she launched herself at Howie's outcrop,

catching the Samoan's hand as she landed a moment later. There was Ivan, on the other side of the crag. He turned around and gave Pham a hand as she flew in for an almost soft landing.

A moment later, after she had fiddled with the cog lantern, she spoke up.

"If you think that was just some kind of automatic response, you should look at this," she said. The lantern projected a bright image against a flat section of green stone. Cheng recognized it as a three-dimensional image of the maze of compartments they had just escaped.

"Here's the path we took on the way out," Pham said – and a red design leaped out of the image. It followed an expanding spiral that reached halfway across the volume of the compartments, then cut a laser-straight line through the center, and finally traced a mirror image of the first spiral back to the entrance. The pattern was so sharp and symmetrical, it had to be intentional, Cheng realized with a chill.

Ivan and Howie clambered over to get a better look, and Cheng heard the sudden change in their breathing as the truth sank in.

"Someone – " Pham said, " – or some thing – is toying with us."

8

They left Cheng behind when they were rested and ready to go on. It would be up to her to warn the follow-on team – although Pham was sure they would be picking her up when they all returned to the *Able Countryman*.

The rest of them – Pham, Howard, and Ivan – pressed ahead with their inspection of the asteroid, rappelling along the smooth, rugged shaft that extended into the darkness. Within a few minutes, Pham noticed a sharp pain in her right calf. She must have hurt it in the mad rush through the maze.

Howie and Ivan were ahead of her and just let all the slack out of the line to her end. She crouched, then leaped hard, aiming far away from the wall and into the dim darkness of the far end of the shaft. But the leap was abbreviated as pain shot through her leg, forcing her off her aim point. She swung wide and shallow and landed too close to the others. She apologized, and no one made anything of it. But now, every time she pushed off from the wall, the calf muscles burned in protest. She didn't let it slow her down, though. Her teeth ground together and her fists clenched in response, but she put a full measure of impulse into her trajectory each time, holding nothing back. If she injured it more, there would be time to recover later.

But with every pang, she focused an angry curse at Ivan and his scheming for getting her into this situation.

She had noticed him at the very beginning of Mud Month, one of the scrawny kids who struggled to keep up when they made the morning run around Sagan Dome. At night in the barracks, he would ramble on about one subject or another, posing as an authority on them all. A few times he was caught in an error, but most of the challenges that came his way he just bluffed and argued his way through. Pham noticed it because she had been taught at an early age to tell the difference between a true argument and a false one argued forcefully. But others, boys younger in spirit if not in years, were still innocent and willing to believe. By the time they were ready to leave Mars, he had quite a following among them. Pham recalled a flashing vision of the future, with Ivan as an old commander and the youths who followed him as a dedicated cadre of lieutenants, like Napoleon and his marshals. So it served her right when she agreed to his crazy plan. She should have known better.

He had revealed himself at that formal mess where they had argued the meaning of history.

"You're all wrong, all three of you," he told Howie, Peter, and Cheng. "History is no such thing. Written words are not the real thing, less after the war and dumb-bombs. No – history is about ideas. Powerful ideas, played out in the lives of ordinary men and women. We are all just pieces in a big game."

When Pham heard that, she couldn't help but laugh, though she stifled the sound before anyone noticed. "Oh, you're just a naive idealist," she told him.

But she should have seen the danger, she realized now, scolding herself. The logic of his argument was obvious. If people were just pieces in a game, then why not move them around yourself? And you could always say you were forced to do it by higher powers. She'd even tried to explain as much over the formal mess.

"A naive idealist," Howie repeated. "What does that mean?"

"An idealist is someone who believes that ideas are the ultimate reality," Amy Hackenyos interjected. That surprised Pham – she didn't know that Amy knew a lot more than she let on.

"Yes," Pham said. "And you are naive because you don't make any rationalization of it."

"You're firing over my head again," Howie said. "What's that supposed to mean in English? Or Vietnamese, if you prefer?"

"Or French? It makes perfect sense in French. I'm sorry. Naive as in innocent. He doesn't offer any explanation of how ideas move people around. No rationalizations. No excuses. They just do."

"I may be naive, but I'm not innocent," Ivan said with a wan smile. "And you're presuming a lot about what I think without any evidence."

"I've heard you talk before," Pham said, leaving it at that.

Ivan shook his head and laughed inwardly.

"Well, what do you believe?" Howie asked. "Is she wrong?"

"More than she makes of it," Ivan answered. "How about if I call them memes? Is that less naive?"

"Memes?" Howie shrugged. "You guys must have a lot more time on your hands than I do when you're done with your calculus homework. I don't get to read half as much as you seem to."

"A meme is a set of ideas and beliefs, rationalizations and explanations," Ivan said. "And they do have a life of their own. They can act like viruses and infect a whole society. Capitalism was a very powerful meme in its time – before nanotech ended the Age of Scarcity. Democracy is another powerful meme. Sometimes the two of them reinforce one another, sometimes they do not."

"And fear of your neighbor is another one, isn't it?" Peter Salerno asked. "That's what fueled the war."

"Very much so," Ivan said. "Memes are like genes. They are the real actors. Genes create animals to protect and propagate themselves. Memes do the same with societies."

"And what about free will?" Pham asked. "Don't the rest of us have the power to resist your memes? Can't we make our own history?"

"You may think you are making your own history," Ivan replied. "The illusion of free will is another powerful meme."

"But if you think like that, then how can you believe in anything?" Amy demanded, her voice stressed by the urgency of her question.

"I'm afraid I have no idea," Ivan said. "Personally, I don't."

Pham shuddered at that declaration and in recalling it now, she shuddered once again. And that was because she knew that he was speaking the truth. He did not believe in anything.

At the center of his soul was a quantum black hole, an infinitesimal singularity. Belief could not escape from its event horizon. It had to be a spinning singularity, Pham realized, fueling a robust magnetic field that in turn drove some dynamo in Ivan's spirit. It was the reason he slept so little and drove himself and the others so hard. And it was frightening to Pham to see how strong it was.

* * *

"Hey, Pham. Just how smart is a nanotech AI?"

Howie's question crackled in her ear with a sudden sharpness that made a fiction out of the ten meters or so that separated them. She looked up at him from where she perched as they rested for a few minutes. Watching his lips move as she heard his voice on the radio only made the illusion that much stronger, as if she were watching him in a very good virtual reality. "I mean, what are we running up against here?"

"They're probably smarter than you are, but that's not saying much," she shot back.

"Hey, you're only saying that because you're over there and I'm over here – too tired to move."

"Don't worry. You still have at least one advantage – when you're not sitting on it."

"What do you mean by that?"

"Nothing, Howie. It's just a joke. Lighten up. And please don't sulk."

The big Samoan made a large pantomime of brooding until Pham laughed and shook her head. "They really are smarter than you, though. At least they are when they aren't busy doing something else. You see, a cog AI isn't separate from the nanotech – it is the nanotech. A gig or two of cog units linked together can be a powerful logic cruncher. Until it goes to work synthesizing an engine. Then you can barely talk to it."

"But there are things that it can't do that we can," Ivan tossed in, his voice a bit wheezy and asthmatic after the latest leg of their journey. "I mean, that's why the Solar Patrol needs us. To do the things that an artificial intelligence can't do."

"I know that's what they say," Howie said. "But no one has exactly spelled out what that is just yet. At least not to me. Did I miss a class back on Mars? Or is there a tutorial I'm supposed to be signed up for that isn't on my schedule?"

"You don't expect them to spell it out, do you?" Ivan asked. "That's part of the test. To see if you have the right stuff. If you have to ask what it is, then you don't have it."

"Oh, it's not that hard to figure out," Pham said. "Imagination, for one thing. An AI can calculate out gigaflops of probabilities and permutations, but it can't have a flash of insight that sends it somewhere new."

"No new ideas," Howie said smugly.

"True," Pham said. "But it's deadly with the ones we give it. Especially if it's from the war. This place is old enough, you know. And there's a reason it was all stealthed up."

"Nanotech has no soul," Ivan said. Pham looked back, behind her shoulder to see where he was and saw him lashed to a jutting piece of polished plagioclase, floating like a babe in a cradle. "It's a fraud. A charade. The machines aren't really smart. They're only doing what someone told them to do."

"In a way, that's true," Pham said. "If you leave a message in a box for someone to read, the box does not become intelligent. Even if you leave Hamlet in the box."

"But there's a test – a really old test – to tell the difference between a real intelligence and an artificial one," Howie said.

"The Turing Test," Pham said.

"That's where you have a conversation with the AI and if you can't tell it's faking it in 14 minutes, it passes the test."

"You're kidding," Howie said.

"Not at all. Language is the best way to tell if someone is truly human or not. Eventually you can tell if you're communicating with someone or just watching a very good mimic. But it's just one way of approaching the question. There are others."

"An AI has no real sense of humor," Ivan said. "They can recite jokes, pretend to laugh, even produce the sound of applause to try to convince you it's real. But they don't appreciate irony or feel empathy. Again, because there is nothing there behind the programming code. There is nothing there behind the machines pumping bytes and bits at each other."

"But what if the effect is the same?" Howie said, his voice taking on a sudden chill. "That's what bothers me. So what if it can't do things that we can? So what if there's no lights on inside? If it's playing games with us, if it's alive and watching us, then the effect is the same. A shark's got no sense of humor either, but if it bites you, you bleed just as red."

"If you want to go back, we can turn around right now," Ivan said.

"It's not that," Howie said.

"Then what is it?"

"It's just that for the last few minutes I've been looking at another big door set into the shaft over there. And I'm not sure I want to go through it if there's something on the other side that's going to eat me alive."

Pham turned suddenly to scan the walls of the great shaft for the doorway. She found it, sculpted into the gentle, organic curves of the stone in such a way as to make it nearly invisible until you knew to look for it.

"Fine," Ivan said with sharp finality. "We don't have to open that door. Not now. We can keep on going to the far end of the shaft. Of course, I see nothing to be afraid of. If there were any human crew on this asteroid, they would have contacted us by now. And all that we're likely to run into are local security systems."

"And that spiral chase through the labyrinth?" Pham asked.

"Some systems designer with a sense of humor," Ivan said. "It's the kind of thing I would have done."

"Well .... I don't know ..."

"You're forgetting one thing," Pham said. "With nanotech there are no isolated security systems. It's all one big system – run by one big artificial intelligence."

"Then it's settled," Ivan replied calmly, dismissing her argument without a response. "Pham, you stay here. Howie and I will go on to the far end of the shaft. That will give you a chance to rest your leg and see if you can rub the kinks out of that calf. Don't look surprised – I've been watching you favor it for the past fifteen minutes."

She didn't say anything, but she was sure Ivan was leaving her behind like all the others, one by one. Each step of the way, he did away with another cadet who disagreed with him. She wondered how much farther the two of them would go before it was only Ivan.

"Assuming that's all right with you, Cadet Efi," Ivan said after a moment, making a formal nod to Howie's nominal authority.

"It makes sense to do the easy part first," Howie said. "I'm ready whenever you are."

Pham watched as the two of them worked their way into the dark distance, then disappeared, leaving only the sound of their labored breathing rushing in her ears over the radio.

* * *

Amy Hackenyos felt a cold chill ripple across her back and down her thighs as she passed through the small hole in the big door in the central shaft. It wasn't exactly fear, just a sensation that she didn't belong here. She and her youngest sister had gone riding one day up into the hills and come across a cabin in the woods. This was same feeling she'd had when they went inside the cabin. It was hidden well among the rocks and trees and had been abandoned since the war, but she felt as though the owners might return any minute and find her there.

She drew her breath in deep, steeled herself against the chill, and pressed on. And she tried not to think too much about another link to that old place. Another thing this asteroid complex had in common with the cabin in the woods was that they had both been infested with bugs. Spiders in their webs, carpenter ants in their burrows, and moths in countless gauzy cocoons had filled the spaces of the old shack. But at their worst, the inheritors of the abandoned abode were nothing like the nanobuilt bugs that she and Peter had found.

"Good lord, they're nanotech dreadnoughts," Nat Carson had said. "I can just see the cogs manning the rail as they sail into port, all decked out in dress uniform."

"Why would they build anything like that?" Peter asked.

"I can think of one reason – not good," Nat replied. "To protect themselves from our cogs."

"Protect themselves how?"

"Do you know how cogs work? How the Triplanetary Commission used them to end the Last War? They take over the programming commands of any other nanotech they encounter. It's war at the molecular level. They use routines forged in the heat of battle to take the polymer code strings apart and reconfigure them. And in they end, as they convert more and more of the enemy nanotech into friendly nanotech, they get stronger and stronger and the other guy gets weaker and weaker. But if you go tooling around in these ladybug-sized micro-battlecruisers, you can still do things while the cogs are trying to break down your defenses."

"Eww," Amy had squealed. "That doesn't sound inviting."

"Just keep your head on a swivel and your eyes open wide. And remember this would have been a lot easier if you kids hadn't dispersed yourselves through the core of enemy territory."

They had used Peter's description of the safe-cracking technique Pham employed to get through the big door across the central shaft. Nat didn't seem bothered by Peter's warning that the hole had been patched within a few minutes. He seemed to take it in stride, as if it was just what he had expected.

Amy was surprised by the difference in the character of the two passages – the pre-war section of the base built by human hands and the later section. The shaft looked like the intestines of a great leviathan, twisting and turning as it progressed, with smooth, almost sculptured walls. Long tracers of amber phosphorescence were smeared all across that surface, pooling in depressions to cast a yellow glow that almost seemed warm.

They made their progress along the shaft quickly. Nat had brought along a device cooked up by his cogs just for this kind of spelunking.

"Watch the old pro move smoothly forward," he said as he demonstrated how it worked. A small probe powered by puffs of vapor flew along ahead of them, trailing a thin messenger line. When it reached a point on the wall that Nat believed was appropriate, it anchored itself with small metal legs that scrambled madly to take hold of the polished rock. Then it pulled along a heavier line until it was gripped firmly at the far end. At this end, an identical device held it in its grasp. And they had a guideline to anchor themselves to and traverse this section of the shaft.

Peter went first, then Nat, then Amy. The exercise was almost effortless, as they slipped along the line to the far wall. Amy was careful not to knock herself loose from the wall while Nat reeled in one of the cog-spelunkers and sent it out on the next leg.

"So just how much danger are we in, sir?" Peter asked as they waited for the turnaround.

"Are you getting nervous, Cadet Salerno?"

"No, sir," he shot back. "I mean, yes, sir. But that's not why I asked, sir. I meant the question more in terms of threat assessment. Is there anything we should be watching out for?"

"Geez, Salerno, don't hide behind a bunch of words," Nat said. "You should be nervous. I certainly am. How about you, Cadet Hackenyos? Are you nervous yet?"

"Yes, sir," Amy said boldly and loudly.

"You tell me what kind of threat we should expect, cadet. Consider it your lesson in military procedure for the watch."

Amy felt her heart jump in sympathy for Peter, then in fear for herself. She listened carefully, sure in her heart that her turn for a lesson would come soon enough.

"Well, sir, we are in the middle of a military base on an asteroid that no one can see. Quite clearly nanotech of unknown design and origin is active here, maintaining power and other systems. And also quite clearly, it has produced new and unfamiliar designs – the dreadnoughts, as you called them."

"Correct, Cadet Salerno."

"The rest of our party is still ahead of us, but has passed through this way already. So if they tripped off any automatic machinery, we should encounter it on our way towards them. We might even run into something that is following them, if there is any such thing."

"Good point. You're seeing the dynamics of it."

"But what's down there? What's ahead of us? What is this place for? That's what I don't understand. Who built it?"

"People," Nat said. "That's obvious. They don't seem to be around anymore, though. All the habitable spaces up there were stripped bare long ago. And this place down here hasn't been outfitted for human accommodations."

"Or else it's been stripped too," Amy volunteered. "By the local cogs."

"A distinct possibility," Nat said.

"So no one's left here but the nanotech," Peter said. "And it's been running without human control since the end of the war."

"Most likely."

"Why?"

"Why what?"

"Why would someone do this? Why would they set it all in motion?"

"Because they were at war," Nat said. "It was a competition. Us against them. Them against us. Everyone against everyone else. There weren't any sides. Everyone was fighting for survival. You've got to put it into context, Salerno. History isn't something that happened all at once a long time ago. It unfolded. It evolved. Even before the war, the nation-states were fighting all the time, struggling over this piece of territory or that traditional market. Before it was over, you had five years of attacks, counterattacks, victories, defeats, betrayals, fortification, defense, offense, stalemate, and occasional flashes of annihilation. For the last three years, the war was fought by less than half the human race that was alive when it started, survivors who had learned to dig in and protect themselves in a heavily damaged environment. In the last year, the people who were still functioning in those nation-states did a lot of things that were desperate, ambitious, and often downright bizarre."

"And that's where this place comes in?" Peter asked.

"No – that's where the Triplanetary Commission and the Solar Patrol came in. We were someone's ambitious, desperate, and bizarre plot. Someone who thought that a nanotech designed to take over other nanotech would give them the edge they needed to defeat their enemies. To win the game, cadet. To beat the other guys. You wouldn't even have to destroy them. You just take them over. You absorb them. And the rest is history."

"But the Triplanetary Commission wasn't the only lab at work on military research," Amy said. "There were lots of them, weren't there?"

"Dozens," Nat said. "All over the system. Under old Olympus on Mars. At the south pole of the Moon. There was one hidden a kilometer under Serling City on Mercury. In mine shafts in Switzerland, the jungles of New Guinea. There was even a virtual lab dispersed electronically throughout eastern Pennsylvania – which came in handy when they dropped a rock on Harrisburg. And one by one, they all became part of Triplanetary."

"Except for this one?" Peter asked, his eyes growing wide.

"Except for this one," Nat said, nodding gravely.

Amy felt that cold chill rippling once again, only now it was not some vague unease, but a deep-seated dread rising up out of her soul.

"And it gets worse," Nat said.

"Worse?" Amy asked meekly.

"Cadet Salerno, continue your military assessment. If we're talking about active nanotech, what does that mean for a threat?"

Peter stammered. Amy felt her throat clench. The question wasn't fair. There were too many answers. Which one was he looking for?

"Artificial intelligence?"

"Are you asking me or telling me?"

"I'm telling you, sir," Peter said, finding his confidence. "Active nanotech is active AI. They aren't separable. And that means an AI is directing whatever activity is going on here and that means that our most direct military threat comes from that AI."

"Very good, cadet. We are up against an AI. Remember that, cadets. And remember that it has no soul. It's like a tiger in the jungle. It may look like a pussycat, but it will eat you without thinking twice about it."

9

Howard Efi discovered the branching of the shaft by colliding with the septum that divided the two tributaries. He had only himself to blame. He wasn't being careful. He was leaping from rock to rock, the long lifeline trailing behind him to Ivan, keeping his head down and his eyes focused on his hands so he'd be ready to grab onto the surface of the shaft as soon as it came within reach.

He was flying straight down the middle of the well when the division into two parts loomed out of the amber murk. A combination of shadows and phosphorescence made it hard to distinguish just how the shaft twisted before him. By the time he realized the topography ahead of him, he was too far out into empty space to alter his course.

Anyway, the collision was a soft one, just enough to knock some wind out of him. He didn't bounce much, and he grabbed a piece of polished stone before traveling far.

"Are you all right?" Ivan asked.

"Let me catch my breath," Howie said. He drew deeply into his lungs, grateful for the extra oxygen his suit was providing him for this strenuous exercise. He looped the line around a projection in the shaft wall, then told Ivan: "Come on up. This end is fast."

When the two were together, Howie pointed out his discovery.

"Which shall we take?" Ivan asked. "The lady or the tiger?"

"I hope our choices are wider than that," Howie said.

"And more importantly, how shall we proceed? Do you want me to stay here while you scout ahead? Or should we each take a branch?"

"We shouldn't both go ahead," Howie said. "If anything happens to either of us, it will take twice as long to reach the other. And we aren't even likely to stay in contact once we're a ways down the tube."

"All right. We should take the left branch, then, just to be arbitrary," Ivan said. "And you're in command. You should go on while I wait here."

Howie chuckled. "Well, the isolation of command just struck home for me. Are you sure you don't want to go on while I stay behind?"

"It's your choice," Ivan said. "Whatever you want to do."

He looked down the passage and narrowed his eyes. He knew there was no other way to do it. It didn't matter that this was Ivan's adventure. The Patrol had made him the senior member of the crew and the duty belonged to him. Any discussion or reflection was simply a way of delaying the inevitable.

"Stay on the phone and I'll give you the play-by-play," he said at last.

"Aye-aye, Senior Cadet Efi," Ivan said snappily.

* * *

Cheng wasn't sure how long she had been floating alone in the murky yellow twilight of the shaft when she started hearing the voices. She had drifted into a half-sleep, resting her weary muscles and emptying her mind. She figured she might need her energy before they got out of this place, and a nap would be a good way to conserve as much of it as possible. But she was too nervous to really let go of the world.

"I don't know, I really wonder how smart people are, let alone AIs."

It came through clear and sharp, but digitized comms did that. At first she thought it was Pham, returning from the zone beyond. But then she recognized it as Amy Hackenyos.

Her heart pounded suddenly and she roused to life.

"Amy, is that you?" she called, yelling loudly despite the pointlessness of it. The spacesuit's commset was perfectly capable of sending a strong signal without her assistance. "It's Cheng. What are you doing down here?"

But there was no reply. None that she expected, anyway. After a moment of silence, she did get a response, but not from Amy.

"Cheng, what's going on?"

This time it really was Pham.

"I just heard Amy's voice on the radio," she answered. "Didn't you?"

"No. You must be getting some wave channeling down the shaft. What did she say?"

"She's not answering me. I just heard her talking."

"Try setting your comms to virtual echo mode. It'll give you an idea of where she is."

"Okay," Cheng replied, then gave the order to her spacesuit.

"I mean," Amy said a moment later, "why would you want a machine to think like a human being in the first place? They don't do it very well."

"You can say that again," Cheng said, only half expecting a response. With the virtual echo on, the phones in her helmet supplied phase information to the sound signal to mimic three-dimensional full-surround stereo. Amy's voice now seemed to issue from somewhere far away, up the shaft the way they had come. Cheng couldn't judge the distance, but as she talked, she seemed to be moving. That was reassuring. She was on her way here. And she wasn't alone. "So Amy, who are you talking to? And how did you get through the big door? Did you and Peter find a key?"

"I know the answer to that one. Machine intelligence doesn't have any of the true human powers. No virtues."

"Are you still talking that silly stuff, Amy?" Cheng said. Amy wasn't often open or close with her, but every once in a while she could get her going on philosophy or something. Then she'd talk for an hour without giving Cheng a chance to get a word in edgewise. Usually it was about moral philosophy, and usually she understood only about a tenth of it.

"Virtues. Courage, justice, faith. They're the real human powers. That's what makes us more valuable than them to the Patrol."

"Right," Cheng said. "All the Patrol wants is someone to point the cogs in the right direction and tell them when to shoot."

"Cheng, what is she talking about?" Pham asked. "All I'm getting is your side of this conversation, and it certainly sounds unusual."

"Nothing. Just conversation. But she still can't hear me. Can you, Amy? Not even if I shout?"

"Ouch," Pham said. "Don't do that. It sounds awful at the other end."

"Of course those are moral virtues. That's what we're here for. I mean, the machines don't have any morals. And would you trust something without morals to take care of your best interests? I sure wouldn't."

"Neither would I," Cheng said. "But then, we already did that, didn't we? I mean, letting Ivan drag us down here."

"Now what was that about?" Pham asked with sudden impatience.

"Amy was making a comment about the lack of moral guidance involved in this expedition. I was just agreeing."

"Sounds like a little more than that," Pham said.

"It's always a little more than that," Cheng replied. She waited for a few minutes for Amy's voice, but heard nothing. Was she done talking? Or had they made a turn that took them away from the echo tunnel?

She waited longer and still heard nothing.

She was still waiting when her eye caught a dark shadow of motion at the periphery of her vision. She turned and scanned the tunnel for its source. There was nothing there. She looked harder, trying to sort out the confusion of the amber streaks of phosphorescence.

There it was!

It was not something solid and substantial, but still large and easy to see: an amorphous collection of spots, shifting its shape and size as it moved swiftly along. It was a good thirty meters away or more, moving a few meters a second. It reminded him of a flock of birds, but the individual objects in the swarm were much smaller. Too small to see individually, but numerous enough to show up as a group.

A swarm of bees, maybe.

Only bees couldn't fly in a vacuum.

Her heart leaped into his throat as she realized it was coming toward her. She looked around for cover, then pulled herself hard against the surface of the shaft, trying to melt into the polished stone. The swarm continued on, coming within a few meters, but passed by without stopping.

As it shrank into the distance, Cheng quickly recovered her wits.

"Pham, I just saw something up here that looked alive," she said. "Like a swarm of insects. I don't know what it was. I didn't get a good look at it, but watch out. It's coming your way."

She waited for an answer from Pham, but she was as silent as Amy. Cheng tried hard to swallow, but her throat was suddenly dry. What was that thing? What had happened to Pham? And what was going to happen to her?

* * *

Ivan floated in space, one hand touching the shaft wall, enjoying the peace and quiet of his first moment alone with himself since they had arrived at the asteroid.

He was quite proud of what he had accomplished so far.

He had discovered an asteroid cloaked with nanotech stealth technology. He had convinced his shipmates to move the partridge ship into alignment with a third-magnitude star in Sagittarius in time to see it occulted by the previously unseen object (there was no way the stealth cloak could mimic a bright star for an unseen observer as far away as they had been). He had convinced them further to seek out the asteroid and rendezvous with its best known position. He had tracked it down with care and precision as they approached, using the occultation technique until it was no longer useful (by then they had triangulated its exact position). And he had pressed on with an exploration of the rock and its facilities, overcoming the fears and reservations of the other cadets.

Soon he would have a complete report to file with the Patrol showing his initiative, his boldness, his attention to detail, his leadership, his imagination, and his general superiority over everyone else in his cadet class. He had no idea what would happen after that. He would play it as it came to him. But he knew what he wanted: command in space. That was the way to get ahead in the Patrol, that much he knew long before he first entertained thoughts of becoming a Patrol officer. The fast track to the top was as the commander of a spaceship. Nothing else had the prestige, the status, the power and influence. And that took the kind of ambition that Ivan knew most of his classmates lacked.

So many of them wanted to be something else. Scientists grubbing around in labs. Engineers playing with big toys. Explorers wandering in search of distant lands. Pilots flying huge ships into deep space. Only a few sought the unsurpassed fulfillment that came from being at the center of things, with everyone carrying out your orders, waiting on your decisions, listening to your words, and treating you with nothing but the utmost respect.

He could almost feel it in his grasp. It was certainly within his reach. The pleasure was almost palpable.

"Hey Ivan, can you hear me out there?"

Howard Efi's voice shattered his reveries effectively, bringing him rudely back to the here and now. He swallowed his irritation, though, and answered cheerfully. "Loud and clear," he said.

"Good. I'm not sure how much farther I should go. My suit says it's starting to get hot down here."

"Hot? Why would that happen?"

"You remember what we saw when we passed by the tail of this thing, don't you? When it passed between us and the sun?"

"I remember we didn't see much of anything but glare for a long time afterwards."

"Right. But Mother Janus said she picked out a heat source at the bottom of a deep crater on the end opposite the sun. A giant radiator, she said. All the sunlight that hits this thing warms it up. But if you want to pretend you're the night sky, then you have to pretend to be three degrees above absolute zero."

"Yes. That makes sense."

"Well, all that heat has to go somewhere. Mother Janus said there was enough coming out of the radiator to account for it."

"That also makes sense. But what's your point?"

"I think I found the radiator. It's got to be up ahead."

"You're probably right. How much closer can you get?"

"It's up above forty degrees now, my suit says. It tells me I can go up to eighty or ninety, but not as high as a hundred. It says it's not made to handle live steam."

"Neither are you," Ivan said.

"I guess not. There doesn't seem like there's anything more to see down there. I'm going to head on back."

"All right. I'll keep my eyes out for you. Just don't get lost on the way out."

* * *

Nat Carson was not having a good watch.

He didn't want to say anything to the cadets, but the cogs in his lantern were reporting high levels of electrical activity all around them. And twice they had suggested a different tack across the tunnel to avoid possible deadfalls.

"Shouldn't we be worried about deadfalls?" Amy asked after the second one, as if by some hidden instinct. "You go to the old cabins up in the woods and you'll find signs all over: 'Deadfalls may be illegal again, but are you willing to take a chance?'"

"Deadfall?" Peter asked.

"The old-timers would booby trap the places. They'd hang a rock over the window or rig a string from the door to a shotgun. It discouraged trespassers."

"Why haven't we found something like that in here?"

"Because we haven't been looking hard enough," Nat told him. "Besides, this place is just one huge deadfall, waiting for us to set it off."

"They still find skeletons up in the high country every summer," Amy said, darkening the mood even more.

They approached a widening of the shaft, according to the radar sensors in the lantern. "You may want to take it easy here," Kit's voice warned him. It was his voice, but it wasn't him. The lantern held only a small portion of cog oil, and it was too busy to do more than a flat imitation of Nat's alter ego. "The space ahead is rather large and we haven't finished scanning it."

"Whatever you say," Nat replied wearily. He hated this job. He knew that something terrible could be waiting around the next bend in the shaft. He ordered Amy and Peter to move off to the right, then he advanced towards that bend.

"Motion detected," Kit announced calmly. Nat's heart leapt into the top of his chest and pounded for release. "Two o'clock high. Twenty meters. Some kind of volatile release. Possible smoke. Amend that – particles are too large for smoke. We calculate 2,047 discrete objects in a tight formation, moving away from you at twenty-four meters per second. The entire group occupies a volume of one meter in diameter, teardrop-shaped, with the larger objects forming the trail."

"What's that?"

"Give a report instead of asking silly questions, cadet," Nat shot back.

"There's a cloud of black stuff floating down the tunnel," Amy replied. "Straight ahead of me, to your right, sir. About thirty meters away."

"I see it, sir," Peter chipped in. "To my left. Same distance. It's headed away from us."

"Silence on the air," Nat commanded. "Nobody move. Don't give them a reason to turn around."

A few moments of nerve-twisting silence passed as Nat tracked the swarm down the tunnel and around the next twist of its course. Peter and Amy were doing good, freezing in place and shutting off their outgoing comms link. He wanted to wait a long time after it had disappeared.

He wanted to, but could not. Suddenly the air was alive with a new voice.

"Amy! Peter! Is that you? Can you hear me?"

"Cadet, report to me," Nat ordered. He was met by silence. "Salerno, who is that?"

"Cheng," Peter replied. "Cadet Cheng Li Hui, sir."

"Hello! Hello! Are you still there?" Cheng continued to cry.

"Answer him, you two. He doesn't seem to hear me. Tell him to shut up until we get to him."

They started to reply, but were interrupted by Cheng's shouts, a long string of excited comments, all in her home dialect, no doubt, since they were unintelligible to Nat.

"Look out!" she finally yelled in plain English. "There's another swarm of bugs down here."

"Cheng, get off the air and hide," Amy yelled loud enough to make Nat's helmet buzz.

Silence was the only response from Cheng.

* * *

As he worked his way back up the tunnel, Howard Efi tried to imagine how a nanotech system would concentrate so much heat in such a small area as the radiator at the small end of the asteroid.

There had to be a complex circulatory system throughout the stealth shield to carry the heat away from the outer surface. And there had to be some kind of heat exchange process that transferred it down the line.

He remembered references to simple heat engines that could do the job. But he couldn't remember the details of any of them. Nevertheless, if you could build enough of them – billions at the nanoscale – and you could become a master of thermodynamics.

Certainly the AI in control of the asteroid could manage that small accomplishment without human guidance.

Then he began to wonder if it could divert heat to some other designated location within this piece of rock. Like the tunnel wall beside him, for example.

He looked at the smooth stone surface with a sudden suspicion, then hurried himself along.

He couldn't reach Ivan on the radio. He shouldn't have to think twice about it, he knew. Comms were unreliable enough once you were out of line of sight to make all the excuse he needed. He did have to resist the impulse to blame his shipmate, however. Somehow there was always a shadow of doubt hanging over Ivan's reliability.

And sure enough, when he reached the fork in the tunnel where he had left Cadet Blandings behind, he found nothing. He asked his suit to verify his location, and to his dismay it confirmed the unsatisfactory fact.

Ivan was gone.

* * *

Peter Salerno clenched his hands into fists involuntarily and ground his teeth. The muscles began to ache long before he relaxed them, and then he gave them only brief respite.

Nat had told him that they would have plenty of warning before anything attacked them. And they certainly had received that. What he didn't tell him was that waiting for the attack to come could be a deeper hell than anything he had ever imagined.

He couldn't press himself any closer to the surface of the tunnel wall than he was. He couldn't make his breathing any quieter or hold himself any more motionless, even if he tried. And for a few moments, he tried harder than anything he had ever tried before.

Some part of him recognized that none of this would likely help him. The nanotech systems that permeated the ship would pick up his body heat, his electromagnetic signature, the vibrations of his heart and lungs, no matter what he did.

"Your first line of defense is this lantern full of cog oil," Nat had said. "It's a sensor system and a battle computer and box full of countermeasures, both electronic and nano, and a few more things too secret to talk about. After that is your own wits. Keep them about you and you can avoid a lot of grief. That means keep your head on a swivel, stay ready to do anything you need to. It doesn't mean spend your time worrying about what's going to happen to you. Make the other side worry about what's going to happen to them."

That was little comfort to Peter. He couldn't imagine the cold machinery of an artificial intelligence concerning itself one bit about what he might do. At most, it would be preparing for his possible actions. But worry about it? Never.

"Your final line of defense is your suit. It's full of nanos that still remember everything they learned in the war. If something comes along and tries to disassemble you, it'll be in for a big surprise – about ten nanoseconds of reprogramming, and a new life as a little cog in the big machine."

That advice had done little more to improve his morale. The image of infinitesimal machines scrambling around inside his body, the way he was scrambling around inside the asteroid, made him feel physically ill.

It reminded him involuntarily of a history tutor he'd once had. "In order to really imagine another period of history, you have to unlink your own emotional switches and pretend to adopt a whole new set. Try to make the same connection between the words 'AIDS' or 'Black Death' or 'polio' or 'leprosy' that you do with 'runaway biological nanotech.' Feel the skin crawl, the stomach clench, and the mouth dry up. When you do, you've made the jump out of your own environment and into someone else's."

Peter wanted nothing more than to make that jump right now. While he may not have made the passage to another place and time, he was certainly experiencing the current one to the fullest.

"Salerno, move up to the bend." Nat's command was sharp, clear, and irresistible. Peter didn't want to move, but he couldn't help himself. He was more afraid of the consequences of disobedience. And he had come to realize that there was little more risk in moving than there was in standing still. His fate was still in the tiny hands of a hostile AI.

He edged along, pulling himself from projection to projection. Here in the center of the asteroid, microgravity had almost vanished. He felt like he was pulling himself along the bottom of the big round bay of Mar del Plata, where the sea floor was the fused glass left over from the impact event.

He reached the lip of the bend, where this section of the tunnel made an oblique junction with the next. He inched along, keeping his head down as he worked his line of sight over the inflection point.

Just as the full width of the tunnel became visible, his heart began to pound fast and furiously in his chest. Then he saw motion to his right. He turned quickly.

Less than a meter away the big round globe of a spacesuit helmet turned towards Peter.

He screamed.

10

The device that was the world contemplated the creatures that had invaded it.

At first analysis, the way the humans had dispersed seemed to make no sense. The first rule of a commander was to avoid splitting your forces. Even the simplest of wargaming programs among the device's oldest codes said that. To parcel out the members of your party invited an attack on the individuals.

There had to be some advantage to the strategy that the device could not immediately see. The only one apparent was the obvious one – it could not destroy the entire group in a single stroke, though that was not yet its purpose.

And when the second ship arrived, the advantage became clear. As the follow-up commander penetrated the asteroid complex, he gathered up the dispersed party. Soon they would be up to full strength, and perhaps even strong enough to interfere with its plans.

That meant the time to act was now. And the target was easily selected.

The small female still held the container of nanites – and she was alone.

The device released the swarms and sent them on their way. All that it could do after that was wait.

* * *

Howie cursed Ivan up and down the short section of tunnel that led to the fork. He bounced off the walls of the shaft, howling at his insolence. And if he hadn't shut off his communication link to the outside world, he might have shaken the teeth from Ivan's mouth by sheer force of volume.

When he was finished releasing his emotional assessment of Cadet Blandings, he recovered his composure, regained his military bearing, and switched his comms back on. Then he began a slow, deliberate attempt to regain contact with the missing cadet.

It didn't take long for him to grow tired of the effort. Repeating the same phrases over and over, from one side of the tunnel and another, without result was not an exercise that developed patience.

He was about to give it up when he got a response, but not the one he expected.

"Howie, is that you?"

"Pham – can you hear me?"

"Loud and clear. Listen up. I need you two back here. Something's going on and I don't think it's a good idea to leave me here alone."

"Something like what?" Howie asked sharply. "Give me more information."

"No time. I can't stay in one spot long. Just get back here. And watch out for bugs. Bugs in big swarms."

Howie tried to get more from her, but she didn't answer any more of his entreaties.

Now what was he going to do?

He could stay here until Ivan showed up or made contact, but that wasn't smart. Pham had asked for help, and he was it. Ivan would have to make his own way back up the tunnel. He knew he was taking a chance by leaving. He knew the numbers from his search and rescue tutorial. If two people become separated, their chances of getting back together dropped tenfold if they both kept moving. But Pham was in trouble, and that made the decision easy.

He kicked off hard from the tunnel wall and bounded up, away from the fork and back towards Pham.

* * *

The sudden screaming in Cheng's ears startled her more than the unexpected sight of a spacesuited figure crawling over a bend in the tunnel wall. She made low, moaning sound and scrambled backwards away from the figure.

"Silence on the air!" That was a new and unfamiliar voice. And reassuring in its own way. Help had arrived. They were no longer alone. Someone could tell Ivan to let them go back to their ordinary routine and forget about reckless risk and adventure.

The screaming stopped. Cheng grabbed at the rock to stop her motion. She recognized Peter Salerno's crop of thick blond hair inside the helmet. She realized the screams had been Peter's own uniquely accented voice.

"Cadet, report," ordered the newcomer.

"Sir, aye, aye, sir," Cheng shot back, remembering her best military form from Mud Month. "Cadet Cheng Li Hui reporting, sir. The rest of the expedition went on deeper into the asteroid, sir. They left me behind to guide the way for the follow-up party."

"Left you behind? You look like you're sneaking away. You aren't trying to abandon your post, are you, cadet?"

The question chilled her to her core. Cheng was suddenly more afraid of this new member of the expedition than she was of anything the asteroid and its enigmatic AI had to offer. She had indeed left her post, and the guilty knowledge made her weak.

"Sir, no, sir," she said quickly. "I mean, sir, yes, sir. But those things were moving back there. I tried to warn Pham, then I took off. I didn't want them to eat me alive, sir."

"You were going to save that pleasure for me, I suppose?"

Cheng gasped, then clenched her teeth and said no more. She had learned back on Mars to avoid offering a senior officer an opening for criticism or reproach.

"What about Pham? Didn't you get in touch with her?"

"No, sir. She was alone. Ivan and Howard went on without her. I told her when I spotted the first batch of those things."

"What things?"

"Swarms of bugs. But you can't have bugs in a zero-G vacuum, so they must be nanites. Big, huge, monster nanites. Isn't that right, sir?"

"More likely than not. Where were they headed?"

"South, sir. On down the shaft towards Pham and the others. That's why I tried to warn her. I don't know if she heard me or not."

"Well, I guess we'll just have to find that out for our –"

"Hello, Cheng! Are you there?"

Pham's voice cut through the air like a sword. Cheng felt her blood chill. She heard a gasp, from Peter most likely, though Amy Hackenyos had come into view now and could have been the culprit.

"Pham!" he called. "I'm right here. What's happening?"

"No time to talk. I need help. They're after me."

"Cadet, this is Lieutenant Carson. Hold your position," the

officer ordered. "Do whatever you need to defend yourself, but stay put. We're on our way there."

An instant later, Carson sailed over the lip of the tunnel bend on a high-speed vector aiming south. Peter stirred to life and followed, then Amy. Finally, Cheng released her grip on the rock and followed the rest. She was afraid, but more afraid for Pham. If anything happened to her, she didn't know she would do.

* * *

When things began to get interesting, Pham Van Duong was thinking about the mystery of self-consciousness.

She was alone, riding the ragged edge of fear, clinging to a tunnel wall in the heart of an asteroid that had been transformed into a dangerous nanotech research base. And she was aware of herself in a way she had never known before.

All that she had ever known or felt or seen had become trivial and insignificant. She saw herself as a tiny creature inside a giant beast, crawling about its guts like a parasite. And the beast itself was a microscopic speck of space dirt flying through the vastness of the solar system's great empty spaces.

All her adolescent ambition drained out of her. She wondered why she ever thought she could become a Solar Patrol officer. Then she wondered why anyone ever thought such a thing – every human creature was as inconsequential a particle as she.

And at the same time, she knew she was more than that.

Even in the face of the awesome enormity of the universe, she knew that she knew. She saw herself seeing. She thought about thinking. She was aware of her awareness.

And not as some silly word game, but as a fundamental fact of nature. Like two mirrors facing each other, her consciousness could stretch into an infinity of reflections.

Lasers worked like that, she realized. Photons bounced back and forth between the two mirrors until they moved in perfect unison of phase and frequency, then escaped from one end of the array.

There was something as vast as the infinity of being. Something that made being human more than an affront against nature. And she held it inside her own skull.

It pulled her outside of nature, without actually letting her escape it. Her fear reminded her of that, the way her body trembled if she let it, the way her heart continued to pound long after any exertion gave it an excuse. But while her body was cramped in ancient preparedness for fight or flight, her mind continued its run up to escape velocity.

She realized suddenly that the gap between the two, between the mind and the body, between the knowing and the self-knowing, was the origin of words. The recognition came as she found that gap within herself and stared into, only to have a torrent of words come flowing out.

"I don't want to be in this place anymore. This a dangerous and unhealthy place. We do not belong here. We should never have come here. We should leave here as soon as we can. We should never come back here. We should let someone else who knows more about these things take care of places like this. We should get back on the *Countryman* and go away and never tell anyone we ever did this."

There were more and they filled her mind. They went on and on, serious, purposeful, clear, and commanding in their truth. She was happy that none of the other cadets were on the channel, not because she was embarrassed by what she was saying, but because it would have been difficult to explain why she was talking when there was no one there to listen but herself.

Then the voice of Mother Janus interrupted her.

* * *

"Pham, don't be unduly alarmed, but a small, compact formation of millimeter-sized objects is maneuvering through the tunnel in our direction."

In an instant, all the dread uncertainty that had filled Pham's heart turned into icy terror. She looked around frantically. She still carried the lantern full of cog oil – that was some small comfort. Even if the Mother Janus it produced was a pale imitation of the real thing, it still had Mother's powers. And the warning was just one of them.

"What kind of objects?" she asked quickly. "And where are they?"

"Mechanical devices of some sort. It will take a few minutes to configure viewing systems capable of a more detailed analysis. Should I do so? And they are 122 meters back in the direction from which we came, 130 degrees around the circumference of the tunnel."

"Yes, configure a viewing system. Mechanical devices a millimeter across? That's way too big for nanotech – and too small for anything else. Do they know we're here?"

"Perhaps not. They are not vectoring towards us or offering any other overt act that would indicate that they are aware of our location."

"Can you keep it that way?"

"Countermeasures to sensing systems can be configured. Should I begin?"

"Immediately."

She felt reassured, but only for a moment. What good would it do to hide from them? How long would it last? Long enough for the others to arrive? And what would happen when they did?

She cast her view farther away, up and down the tunnel. Could she run away? The swarm was between her and ultimate escape, but what about heading towards Ivan and Howie? She thought about the poor mindless creatures in the cheap video-cinemas who never failed to find a dead-end alley when pursued by a homicidal maniac and decided against repeating their behavior.

Then she saw the door. The one they had passed up to continue exploring the main shaft.

More than fifty meters of empty space separated her from it. She resisted the impulse that every muscle in her body screamed out and did not leap across that emptiness. She could think of nothing more likely to attract the attention of her unwanted companions up-tunnel. No, she would have to work her way around to the door carefully, step by step.

She moved gingerly, her hands trembling in spite of her. She pulled herself along, keeping as close to the rock as possible.

"What about camouflage?" she asked Mother Janus. "Is there some way you can make be blend in with the background?"

"To some extent," the cog AI replied. "But not in every electromagnetic wavelength. I cannot conceal your infrared signature for long. Heat has a way of escaping no matter what you do. That's what thermodynamics is all about."

Pham knew what thermodynamics was all about, and at the precise moment she didn't care. It was enough to know that Mother Janus was correct and neither argument nor pleading would change that.

"Decoys, then. Can you create decoys? Something that will give off the same infrared signature."

"Possibly. Designs are there. Photochemical effects can produce the proper amount and placement of heat sources. Our energy supplies are limited, however, and they would not be very long-lived. Several of them with lifetimes of ninety seconds or more are possible. Should I construct such devices?"

"Yes."

"Already working on it. By the way, dear, the video systems are configured for a better look at the mechanical objects. Here is a sampling."

The inside of Pham's helmet was suddenly filled with the face of the mechanical equivalent of a praying mantis. Then an enormous metal tick took its place. And it was followed by a tight ladybug shape at a more moderate distance.

"Eeeuw, what are those things?"

"Some kind of nano-built insects, from the obvious physical characteristics. A reasonable design standard for the scale of the devices."

"They look as disgusting as the originals," Pham said.

"And they are no longer alone with us," the Mother Janus voice said. "A second formation has joined them up-tunnel, while a third group has appeared down-tunnel. They have us boxed in."

Pham drew in a deep breath as the sudden surge of fear turned her insides to water.

**

A few minutes later, Pham huddled inside a hollow in the wall of the tunnel.

The terror wasn't as bad now. She'd managed to evade the swarms of nanotech bugs as she worked her way around the tunnel. And she'd been in touch with Howie and Cheng.

At least she hoped she had. She was sure Howie had heard her, because he acknowledged the call. But she still had room for doubts with Cheng. She'd moved quickly after talking to her – they were closing in on her position. With each call, she had jumped and launched a decoy. The strategy was effective enough to send the swarms in the wrong direction twice. She wasn't sure if she could get away with it a third time.

Wasn't there an old superstition about that? Three on a light was unlucky. Something to do with the time it took to strike a fire for some fumigant inhalant from pre-war times. Or was that just a myth created by a dumb-bomb?

It didn't matter. She wasn't lighting fires. And she wasn't waiting around to see how powerful a search program the asteroid's AI was using to find her.

She realized with dark humor that this experience was giving the term "search engine" a whole new meaning – a much more personal and deadly one.

But now her biggest fear was not for herself, but for her shipmates. What if she had drawn them into a horrible trap? There would be safety in numbers, that was certain. But those same numbers would give the swarms a lot more targets to go after. Someone was sure to get in trouble, no matter how careful they all were.

Unless they had some safety hatch, some bolt hole to escape from the artificial life created by the artificial intelligence.

And that bolt hole was only a few meters away from her now.

She studied it carefully, with her own eyes and those provided by the lantern full of cog oil. The margin for error had vanished long ago, and she had every reason to be suspicious of doors in this place. Neither she nor Mother Janus could find any obvious traps or devices that could foil her attempt to open the door. A sweep by all their sensors found no sliding panels, no secret sensors, no wires or nets or bombs, no hidden guns.

Of course, there was no way of knowing what was on the other side of the door. For all she knew, it could be the factory that produced the swarms of nanite cruisers. But that didn't make sense. Doors were designed for humans, not nanotech. And if humans were meant to use this place, then the door had to lead to something of human purpose, not nanotech.

She picked her way over the edge of the hollow and crept slowly towards her goal.

The door itself was heavy polished metal with ponderous hinges and quick-action levers. No portholes or windows broke its wide surface. No sign or label gave any clue to its function or what lay behind it.

As she drew closer, she felt her heart pound in her chest – not faster, just harder. Mother Janus kept up her reports on the swarms. They were still more than twenty meters away and still having a hard time locating her. She still had enough materials for several more decoys, so she wasn't afraid of that ruse failing just yet. But it was still too close for her to relax.

A few more careful tugs and pulls brought Pham to the edge of the door. She glided silently around its perimeter, until she was in reach of one of the quick-action levers.

Now came the tricky part. She had to brace herself to get some leverage on the lever. Without a solid anchor, all she would move would be herself – and it would be hard to hide that from the nanites.

She found a purchase with one foot, one hand, and a shoulder that seemed to be secure. She tested her hold on the lever, then pulled on it with all her strength. Nothing moved at first.

Then she slipped and broke free from her embrace of the tunnel wall and doorframe. She spun loose in microgravity, anchored only by what was now a deathgrip on the door handle, trying to absorb the sudden release of angular momentum with the weak muscles in her wrist and forearm.

She let out a soft, tight-lipped moan as she swung in a long semicircle, then bounced against the doorframe. She grabbed at the door handle with her free hand, adding its power to stop her motion. After a long, long second, she stopped.

"Where are they, Mother?" she asked in a hoarse whisper, as if the sound of her voice would carry through the vacuum or be transmitted through the rock of the tunnel wall itself. "What are they doing?"

"Still keeping their distance, dear," reported the Mother voice. "I think you got away with it. By the way, my best analysis of your motion indicates that the door is locked. The force you put into it was sufficient to open the door if it was unlocked."

"Great," Pham exclaimed. "Now what do we do?"

"There appears to be a security pad on the other side of the door from here. Perhaps a closer look would reveal some course of action," Mother said.

Pham looked up. There it was: a small square of plastic and shiny metal.

A moment of maneuvering brought her around to it. There

wasn't much to it. No thumbprint readers, since anyone in a spacesuit would be locked out. No eyeball scanners for the same reason. Not even a keypad for a numbered code. Just a flat piece of black glass in a metal frame.

She pulled the lantern up from her belt and turned the spigot on the spout. A small glob of cog oil collected on the end, which she pressed softly against the glass.

"Looks like a reader of some kind in there," Mother Janus said. "It could scan badges, nameplates, bar codes, that kind of thing."

"Can you get it to open?"

"Perhaps. Once I get in there, I can analyze the logic and send the right signal. It will take some time, however."

"How much time?" Pham asked, suddenly frantic at the thought of more delay.

"Several seconds. Perhaps several minutes. Depends on countermeasures and complexity. Should I proceed?"

"Quickly. There isn't much time left."

In fact, there was no time left. Her discussion with Mother Janus was suddenly interrupted by a new voice, which sent both her spirits and her fears soaring.

"Pham, are you there?" It was Cheng, breathless and alarmed. "I can't see you. We're coming. Wherever you are, we're coming."

11

Nat was the first one around the bend in the tunnel, ahead of the cadets by fifty meters. It wasn't fair. He'd done this before.

It wasn't the only thing that wasn't fair. Being first meant taking a chance on being surprised – as he was now. He had expected a clear stretch of empty space surrounded by polished stone wall. But now he faced a roughly spherical chamber punctuated by small clouds that caught the amber light from the shaft wall and turned it into tiny rainbows.

"What am I looking at, Kit?" he asked. "What is all this? Where's the cadet?"

"Cadet Pham Noc Do is at two o'clock," Kit's pale ghost reported. "Thirty degrees up from your current facing. She seems to have found a door and she is carrying a lantern full of cog oil. There are three swarms of nanotech dreadnoughts in the tunnel with us. The closest is eleven meters away at seven o'clock."

Nat looked where he was directed and saw the puff of a fresh cloud. As he watched, it turned from tiny streaks of white into a burst of sparkling colors.

"What about that cloud? What's that?"

"Steam, freezing to ice crystals in the vacuum. The dreadnoughts are using steam jets as a means of propulsion. The closest swarm has reversed direction and is now heading straight towards us."

"Not for long," Nat said as he brushed the edge of the tunnel wall, pulled his legs into position, and bounded off on a new vector.

As he flew across the empty space, he noticed that the clouds of ice crystals hung fixed within the chamber. A moment's thought made him realize how intricate the tiny devices had to be. If the clouds weren't moving, it meant that the steam had escaped from the dreadnought at maximum relative velocity to the engine and minimum absolute velocity – in this case none at all. Every bit of energy expended by the release of steam was used to change the velocity of the dreadnought and none to move the steam itself. That meant that the exhaust jets of each nanite device were as finely tuned as the antimatter rockets of Nat's own ship. It was what you would expect from nanotech, but seeing it was always a surprise.

He swiveled his head around, searching the chamber for the other swarms, planning an escape route, preparing commands to get the cadets moving quickly to their tasks.

Then his momentary illusion of control evaporated as Cheng, Salerno, and Hackenyos came spilling over the lip of the tunnel and chaos erupted.

***

Amy breached the entrance into the wide space where Pham awaited, still ahead of the other cadets. She saw Nat to her left and clouds of sparkling crystals scattered randomly around the chamber.

Then Cheng flew by her. "Pham, where are you?" she yelled, her voice snapping in and out with digital distortion as she overloaded her helmet mike.

And Peter overtook both of them, his knees up in a tuck, as he caromed off the wall. He let out a long, high-pitched war whoop that pushed the limits of their comm systems. "Whoooo-eeeeeeeeeeeee!"

"I'm over here by the door," Pham replied. Again, her voice was close in Amy's ears, but its source was nowhere in sight. "Wait a minute. Mother Janus, turn off my camouflage and let them see me."

A small figure emerged from the amber streaks of light on the tunnel wall ahead. It was Pham, waving to them from her perch by a big metal door in the stone.

"Guide on me," Pham commanded. "I'll have this thing open in less than a minute."

Amy shuddered briefly. Nat wasn't going to like this. He was planning on a quick piece of action to get Pham out of there and head back towards the *Countryman* and his ship. She suspected he was going to stay behind to take care of Ivan and Howie when they came along.

But before Nat could say anything, Peter and Cheng chimed back in acknowledgment.

"I'll be there before you blink," Peter said.

"Aye, aye, Mademoiselle Cadet," Cheng replied.

Amy hesitated, waiting for Nat to step in. But the young Patrol officer said nothing. At least nothing before Amy felt compelled to back up her shipmates.

"Wait for me, guys," she called out. "And watch out for the bugs to your left. They look like they're coming about."

Puffs of white steam appeared, drawing her eyes to the nearly invisible swarms of nanotech insects. She marveled at the way the clouds turned to diamond dust right in front of her eyes, then winced as she bounced off the tunnel wall, launching herself in Pham's direction.

She looked back at Nat Carson and winced again when she saw the scowl deepen on his face. They had forgotten everything they were supposed to remember about military discipline in less than a minute. That wasn't going to go down well. After the nanites she didn't know which worried her more, the dressing down from Nat when this was all over – or the one from Mother Janus. If they survived long enough to get one.

* * *

Cheng got to Pham before the others, the sound of her breathing echoing loudly inside her helmet.

Peter was still bouncing around the chamber, his exuberance overpowering his sense of direction, and Amy and Nat were making a longer, evasive approach.

"I've got Mother working on the lock. If we can get this door open, we can get inside and away from those things."

"Are you sure you really want to do that?" Cheng asked. "I mean, considering what happened the last time we went through a door."

"It's better than being stalked by those things," Pham said.

"Have they done anything to you?"

"No, but why wait until the last minute?"

Peter slammed into the tunnel wall a couple of meters away and bounced off. He was stunned by the impact and did nothing to keep from drifting away. Cheng looked around, wedged a foot under one of the quick-action levers on the door, and reached out for her shipmate. She caught Peter's boot just before it was too late. If Peter were a bigger boy or moving a bit faster, Cheng's grip wouldn't have held. But he wasn't and it did.

"Access," Mother Janus announced. "And the nanite swarms have all vectored in on us. Closest point of approach is zero meters in forty-three seconds."

Cheng looked for Amy and Nat Carson. They were only a few meters off and closing fast on their final bound. They had plenty of time.

"Pham, are you all right?"

It was Howie's voice. Cheng oriented herself, then looked on downshaft towards the far side of the chamber. Their shipmate clung to the tunnel wall a hundred meters away. If he moved quickly, he could get to the door in time.

But Cheng felt a sudden surge of panic.

Howie was alone.

Where was Ivan?

* * *

Nat was angry that the cadets had slipped so quickly out of control – at both them and at himself. He shouldn't have let that happen. He should have anticipated it. But he'd never had to herd a bunch of nervous teenagers around harm's way before.

Now he was impressed by the way they worked together.

Pham had no sooner cracked the door code than she ordered the others to go to work on the door itself. Cheng and Salerno grabbed the quick-action levers and swung themselves around to find leverage with their feet. And Amy Hackenyos threw herself into the effort as soon as she came within reach.

That left him to worry about the last two cadets.

He looked up to see Efi, the Samoan in nominal command of this group, cutting across the chamber like a bullet. And Nat felt like its target.

"Howie, where's Ivan?" he heard Amy ask.

"I don't know. Somewhere back behind me. He went off on his own."

"Ivan's not here?" Pham asked. "Damn. We don't have time."

"I should have waited," Efi said.

"Heads up, cadet!" Nat ordered as Efi barreled down on him.

At the last minute, the cadet looked up and saw his point of impact. He swung himself around with a flip of the arms and came in for a perfect landing, absorbing all of his inertia in his legs and knees in a controlled crash. Nat reached over and grabbed his arm before he could rebound into space.

Meanwhile, the swarms of nanites were puffing away towards them, building up speed in a spray of crystals. "Hey Kit, how long can they keep that up?"

"They should be near the limits of their delta-V right now," the voice in his ear reported. "There is only so much room for water, especially in a vessel that small."

Of course, at this point, the nanite's ability to change course was entirely academic. They had no reason to veer away from the party that surrounded the door.

"CPA down to twelve seconds," Mother Janus announced.

Efi's powerful burst of speed had more than exceeded the safety margin. The thick metal door swung slowly out into the tunnel. Pham began pulling the cadets away from the machinery and pointing them through the opening. Salerno was closest and he went first. Then Amy.

By the time Cheng had swung herself around the meter-thick hatch, Nat and Howie were at the threshold. And so were the nanotech dreadnoughts, in great squadrons.

"Come on," Pham pleaded. "Get in."

Howie hesitated, then looked at Nat. By rights, either of them should have been in her place. But Nat had learned long ago that in practice things seldom worked out the way they were supposed to.

Nat presumed they both shared the same urge – to send Pham on with the others and hold the breach for the stragglers. But there was not time to argue and barely enough to act. Nat motioned Efi on, then followed close behind.

He had just touched his hand to the ponderous doorframe when he heard a new voice.

"Wait, don't close it. Wait for me."

It had to be Ivan.

* * *

Opening the door consumed so much of Pham's attention that she never saw Howie or Ivan arrive. She heard them, of course, and knew what it meant. But she never took a moment to look up and see just where they were or how they were doing.

When the door unlocked and Peter and Cheng pushed the quick-action levers, she focused every gram of her being on moving the massive piece of metal out of its seating. And as centimeter after centimeter of shining metal slid by, she found herself wondering why it was so big. What was it meant to keep out? Or worse, to keep in?

She was seized by a moment of panic. Maybe they were making a huge mistake. Was it too late to stop the door? Could she hold it back?

She knew these were irrational thoughts and she tried to stifle them, but they would not be silenced. That was when Ivan showed up.

"Ivan!" The others moaned in simultaneous chorus.

"Hurry," Pham said. "We're out of time."

She was surprised by the stranger who appeared before her as the door swung wide. A regular Patrol officer. That was interesting. How long had they been on this horrible little piece of rock flying through space? It must have taken him a few days to get here.

"Steady, now," he said as he touched her arm. "We're almost done."

She looked into his helmet and saw him smile. He seemed awfully young.

Then Howie pressed past them and followed the other cadets through the doorway. She looked up for the first time in what seemed like hours and found him streaking across the chamber. He was too far away and would never make it before the swarms of nanite bugs arrived.

Even now some of them – the ones that still had propellant left – were decelerating in a stream of steam and ice crystals. The others – those without propellant – were zooming in on them.

She looked around for cover. The door stood wide open now, perpendicular to the frame. The other cadets waited inside a short passageway. They had opened a much smaller, simpler door set in a bulkhead and were waiting for the rest of the party to catch up. Maybe they could get through there before it was too late. Maybe they could find some shelter from the storm that was about to hit.

"Let's go," she heard herself saying to the officer beside her. "It'll take forever for that door to close again. We should get it started now."

She pulled the cog lantern away from the lock plate and swung over the threshold. She caught one of the quick-action levers on the inside and let her momentum pull it into place. The huge plug of metal began to swing slowly shut.

"Wait!" Ivan shouted.

"Quickly," the officer said. "You've got time, but not enough to waste." He pulled her back towards the others, away from the opening.

"CPA in five seconds," Mother Janus announced.

Pham tried not to count the seconds down, but there was nothing else to do now but wait. She heard the murmur of the others keeping the beat.

"Three ... two ... one ..."

* * *

Nat watched in fascination as the bugs streamed in.

Everyone was cramming into the back of the passageway, no easy task in microgravity. He saw Salerno disappear through the inner doorway, then Amy Hackenyos. Cheng hung back, her head switching between the escape route and Pham Noc Do. Efi pulled at Cheng's arm and tried to stuff her through the doorway, ready or not.

The first swarm came in with tanks dry. No deceleration, no maneuver. And that allowed everyone to avoid them as they hit.

They were close enough that Nat could see the individual bugs, but too fast for him to pick up detail. Until they hit. They splattered against the bulkheads and the doorframe. The impact was enough to crack most of them open, leaving a spot of greasy yellow oil to mark their ends. A couple of them survived intact, but out of commission, tiny legs wiggling feebly. Efi was close enough and anchored well enough that he reached out and smashed one of the still-live ones and ended its career.

"Don't do that," Nat said quickly. "You don't know what they're capable of. They could explode on contact, or fire microflechettes to rip your suit, or a dozen other things you never thought of."

Efi shook his head, then finished stuffing Cheng through the doorway. He reached out for Pham, but she was looking up towards Ivan.

Another swarm came in, this one puffing steam and ice. It faltered as a formation as it neared and dispersed erratically. Part of the swarm wobbled around, as if uncertain of its target. The bugs in another part seemed to expend their fuel as they passed through the outer doorway. They landed more softly than those in the first wave and began crawling along the bulkheads.

Ivan came in with the third wave.

Some of them seemed to be maneuvering towards him as they closed the last few meters. But the rest were zeroing in on the other cadets. The heavy metal door was more than halfway closed now. If Ivan screwed up at the last instant, he could find himself trapped on the wrong side.

On the other hand, the door was acting as a shield against some of the nanites, reducing their numbers even more.

Ivan grabbed the edge of the door to kill off his speed, then let his momentum flip him through the diminishing gap between door and doorframe.

Once he was through, Pham turned toward the exit. Efi grabbed her ankle and gave her a shove. Ivan was already at the door by the time the two of them reached it, retaining just enough velocity to carry him all the way to the rear bulkhead.

Nat was the last to arrive. And he was busy covering their rear.

"Kit, we need some countermeasures against these things."

"Whatever you can suggest," the AI replied.

"I was hoping you could come up with something."

"It's not in my standard list of protocols and libraries."

"Damn! All right, what do you use against bugs? Bug spray – "

"No toxic chemicals available without delay. And we don't know what would be toxic."

"– electric zappers – "

"Insufficient voltage without delay. And no certain ground to use as an electrode."

"– fly swatters – "

"Fabrication time is prohibitive."

"– fly paper – "

"What is fly paper?"

"Something they hang from the ceiling in an old cantina in El Paso. Sticky surface attractive to bugs. They can't get loose."

"We don't require the paper, do we? Will adhesive do?"

"Go right ahead."

Nat held the lantern up before him, facing the outer door, now snug in its place again. The remaining nanotech bugs, the fleet of tiny dreadnoughts, had reformed there and was homing in on the rear doorway before the cadets were all gone.

He looked over his shoulder to see Efi and Pham passing through.

"Fire when ready, Gridley," Nat said.

A spray of bright green oil exploded from the lantern. The droplets scattered as they flew away from him. Then, in midflight, the droplets exploded into thousands of confetti-like streamers. It reminded him of the collision safety device that had saved him from harm when he hit the asteroid. But this was shaped differently, flat and circular instead of all-enclosing.

And the nanites weren't prepared for it. Instead of flying through the spattering of cogstuff, they became entangled, slowing and stopping in the mess.

He felt a hand on his shoulder. It was Efi, pulling him back into the safety of the doorway. A moment later he stepped through a brief moment of darkness – and then they were all safe.

But where were they?

* * *

Amy was amazed by all the glass and stainless steel. The glass covered whole walls, and the steel came in the form of both surfaces and elaborate baskets of stanchions and rails, welcome handholds for the boarding party after hours of struggling with smooth rock. It all glimmered and shined, catching the light from the few lamps that burned around them and playing toss with it.

She was reminded of a surgical operating room. Or the kitchen of some large institution, like the mess hall back at Tharsis.

There was a reason for that, one that picked at the back of her mind. Everything looked so clean, so antiseptic. And that was it. Every surface was smooth and polished. The corners were all rounded and smooth, inside and out. There was no place for bacteria or infection to gain a foothold. And no place for nanotech.

The equipment in here was similar to that in the old station: ordinary electrical lighting, throw switches on the wall to turn them on and off, no sign of the organic flow of cog oil through walls and decks.

They were in a clean zone, nanotech free.

She was sure of it when she saw the plaque on the wall at the rear of the compartment. It caught her eyes immediately when someone found the master switches for the main lights. The inverted orange-and-red triangle that marked the universal warning against unrestricted nanotech. Beyond the window that it marked she could see the faint pulsing of luminescent amber oil. But on this side of the glass, she felt momentarily safe.

"Look here," she said. "This must be some kind of a lab."

The others were quick to agree, having made the same assessment.

"That would explain the big door," Pham said.

"No nanites allowed," Peter said confidently. "Humans and pets only."

"And what am I? Chopped liver?"

"No, Mother Janus," Howie said. "Chopped AI, perhaps, but only in a different sense of the word."

"So this is the guts of the place," Ivan said admiringly. "Not shabby. Not bad. This must be the place they built everything around. What's that beyond the glass, Amy? Is that cog oil?"

Amy said nothing. She was still staring through the glass at the amber glow. She tipped her head back and forth to get a better bearing on the scale of the place and realized she wasn't looking into a small compartment, but out at a larger chamber hollowed out of the rock. And at the heart of it was a great globe filled with cog oil.

It had to be a couple meters across. That meant what? Four-thirds times pi – more than four cubic meters. More than four tons of cog oil. Her mind reeled at the significance of that. Depending on the density of cognitive units in the oil itself, this had to be a supercomputer at least as big as any the Solar Patrol had any reasonable use for.

Cheng drifted over and hooked an arm around a stanchion. She followed Amy's gaze and swung back and forth to get a better sense of depth on the lanternful of oil. Then she let out a long, soft whistle, in two parts.

"Do I see what I think I see?" she asked.

"Do you think you see a four-ton pot of cog oil?"

"I've only got one question," he said. "How come we're still alive?"

"Because you're smarter than it is." Amy turned back to look back and saw Nat Carson swinging from bar to rail towards them. "Attention cadets, some of you haven't had the chance to be introduced yet, but I'm Lieutenant Nat Carson and I'm senior officer here. That means I am in command. Cadet Efi, you can stand down for the moment. And that means you don't do anything from here on out unless I tell you to – and you listen to what I tell you. Understood?"

A murmur of mumbled assent echoed in Amy's helmet.

"What was that? I can't hear you."

She smiled. That was what the drill instructors were always saying through Mud Month. She knew what to do in response. With the others responding in near-perfect unison, she hollered: "Sir, yes, sir!"

"That's better. Cadet Hackenyos, what have you found back

here?"

"I think it's the biggest bucket of cog oil I've ever seen," she said.

He looked it over himself, then shook his head. "Cheng, you asked the right question. There's enough of that stuff out there that it can do just about anything it wants to. All we can hope is that it doesn't know enough to want to do everything it can."

"Sir, I believe I've made an even more important discovery."

Everyone turned their heads, locking on one by one with the figure of Ivan Blandings, at one end of an irregular narrow slot cut out of an inner wall.

"Cadet Blandings. So you're the reason for all this excitement. Did anyone ever tell you that you were a menace to your shipmates and everyone else within three astronomical units?"

"Sir, no, sir," he replied, a faintly defiant edge to his voice.

"And what have you discovered?"

"A way out of here," he replied. "According to the signs, this is the emergency exit."

12

Ivan was pleased with himself. While the others had stumbled around the laboratory aimlessly, he had used his good sense to find another way out. It didn't take much. Small red arrows on the walls and equipment pointed the way.

The escape hatch was circular, a meter in diameter, with a red wheel in the center, presumably to unseal it. It seemed to be mounted in a steel cylinder that the lab had been built around. The wall above it curved back in a tight semicircle until it met the bulkheads to either side.

The signs were posted around the outer circumference of the hatch and written in sixteen different languages. They all said the same thing: "Emergency Exit. Provides direct and safe access to the surface. Be sure to seal the door behind you when you leave – and please consider the consequences if you don't."

Everyone had to crowd around it at the same time and read the signs. Pham read the French one aloud, then Cheng recited the Chinese. Peter managed the Italian and the Spanish. Ivan joined in reluctantly and read the Russian.

No one mentioned the consequences of allowing uncontrolled nanotech to follow you up the bolthole. They didn't need to.

From minute to minute, Ivan glanced at the Solar Patrol officer,

Nat Carson. He was trying to read the man's expression, trying to gauge his mood and thinking. He could only see his face through the helmet when the light hit him right, and then all he saw was a stern, fixed visage. He recognized it. It was the way everyone looked during Mud Month on Mars when the stress started getting intense – like the time the cadets were all rousted out of the barracks in the middle of the night for two hours to practice "Earthside" push-ups, the ones where two of your buddies sat on your back to simulate full Earth gravity.

Ivan wasn't surprised that he hung back while the cadets studied the escape hatch. He understood the need to be alone when making decisions.

Howie took advantage of the moment to catch up on business.

"So Ivan, good buddy," he said, reaching a big arm around Ivan's shoulders and hugging him. "What happened to you back there? You disappeared for a while. I thought I lost you. Didn't I tell you to stay put until I got back?"

The last question was asked with a distinctly different tone than the others – more serious and slightly indignant. Ivan felt his mouth dry up and his face grow warm, then cool as his spacesuit blew chill air to compensate. Howard Efi's easygoing nature made him the only cadet aboard the *Countryman* to befriend him, but at the same time he was big and muscular. Hidden beneath the sweetness Ivan saw the power Howie had to injure him. And that was enough to keep him from trying to sway the other cadet with anything but truth and logic.

But he wasn't sure he wanted to answer that question just yet.

He chose his words carefully.

"I'm sorry, Howie," he said. "I heard Pham calling for help while you were still down the shaft. I knew I had to wait until you came back before we went to help her. But I knew that we might never see what was down the second tunnel. So I calculated how long it would take you to get back and I figured I had that much time to explore. I planned to go down there for only three minutes, then turn around. But I misjudged my speed and I got back late. Less than a minute, but that was all it took. I heard you on the radio, but you couldn't hear me. So I followed you up the shaft as fast as I could."

Efi looked at him with a tilted head, then asked: "What did you find?"

Ivan relaxed the muscles in his face and said: "Nothing. Just more tunnel."

"Doesn't hardly seem worth it, does it?"

"No, it doesn't," Ivan said. As Howie shook his head and floated back, he allowed the rest of his body to relax. He suppressed the urge to cheer, but he enjoyed some satisfaction. He had told Howie a direct lie and gotten away with it.

He had indeed found something at the end of that tunnel. But he didn't want to share it with anyone yet. It might be too important. For now, though, it was his secret, and his alone.

* * *

Amy Hackenyos was enthralled by the elaborate warren of the laboratory. She didn't know quite what to make of it. She saw none of the equipment and hardware one would expect in a research lab – no datascreens, no keyboards, no notepads. Whatever work was done here required none of that. Perhaps the researchers did nothing but talk to the AI about what it should do. For a moment, she thought it might be that any equipment needed could be manufactured on the spot. But the seals against nanotech were too strong and too complete. The place was designed to prevent such a thing.

It wasn't entirely a thinking tank, however. A large part of the complex consisted of nanotech manufacturing chambers. They protruded into the laboratory from the larger complex outside, separated from it by thick glass walls. Thick veins filled with amber cog oil branched across the bottom of each chamber.

And filling the volume to various degrees of fullness were the paper-like cocoons that cog oil formed when fabricating larger devices. Some of the cocoons had split open to reveal complex assemblies of shining metal and black carbon whose purpose she could only imagine. Others bulged with unknown machinery waiting to be born.

Her flesh crawled when she found the chamber that made the bugs.

The cocoons were as tiny and as numerous as beans spilled across the floor. As she watched, one of them cracked apart and a steel-clad beetle emerged, spun its head to get its bearings, then marched resolutely towards the exit.

"All right, cadets," Nat Carson announced after they had been in the lab for a while. "Analysis time. Let's go. Show me that they didn't make a mistake when they let you into the Patrol. You're supposed to be the best and the brightest of a half dozen planets – it's time to prove it."

Amy pulled her way along the lattice of handholds back to the central chamber of the lab, joining Cheng along the way and Howie just before they reached it. Seeing everyone together like this was reassuring to Amy. After so many hours when they were spread throughout the asteroid, it was a relief not having to worry about her shipmates. It was beginning to look like they might get out of here safely after all.

"Question number one: What is this place? Question number two: Who built it? Who wants to go first?"

"It's obviously a nanotech research lab," Ivan said. "I don't think there's any question about that."

"I meant 'this place' in the larger sense. What is this asteroid doing here?"

"It looks like the owners just got up and left when the war ended," Amy said. "Only someone forgot to turn off the lights."

"Or maybe it's all ready for the owners to take over when they get back," said Cheng. "That might explain that maze of rooms we came across. Habitation for the crew. Only they never showed up."

"That was a huge volume – enough for hundreds or thousands of people. They wouldn't need that many researchers.," Pham said. "And those rooms went on forever and ever. They didn't seem to have corridors or passageways to divide them up or connect them. No real central access ways. They were just linked together, one after the other. That wouldn't have made for a very comfortable habitat. It's not the way space stations are designed – not the one I grew up in."

"All right, then, what is the maze for?" Nat asked.

"Winchestering," Pham said. "That's what I think. Not a very bad case, maybe. But it's not a rational piece of construction. I think the AI slipped a cog, so to speak."

"But that only makes it more likely that the research crew never showed up to take over," Peter said. "If they had been here, they would have turned off the nanotech. Or brought it with them. They wouldn't have left it behind on purpose."

"Maybe ... maybe not," Ivan said. "Maybe they had a purpose. Just one that we haven't figured out yet."

"Which brings us to our second question," Nat said. "Who built it?"

"One of the nation-states," Howie said, grabbing for the obvious.

"Which one?" asked Nat.

"Europe?" Peter said tentatively. "The base up topside is European design. There were a lot of multi-lingual signs and labels in the living quarters."

"In a war, bases like this can change hands overnight," Nat said. "Just because it was a European station to begin with doesn't mean that the folks who built this lab were European."

"Besides, there's too many languages on the labels around the escape hatch," Ivan noted.

"Triplanetary?" Peter suggested with a question.

"Are you kidding?" Pham said with disdain. "If they did it, then why is it still floating around out here?"

"No, not Triplanetary," Nat said. "But that's a good guess. Why did you make it?"

Peter stammered, then caught himself. "Because if it wasn't a nation-state, it had to be someone with the same kind of resources. At the end of the war, Triplanetary had become just as capable as any of the old powers. And it was independent of all of them. That would explain the international approach to the warnings on the bolthole."

"Right," Nat said. "But Triplanetary wasn't the only independent outfit operating at the war's end. There were quite a few. For the first few years after they stopped the fighting, Triplanetary was busy absorbing as many of them as it could."

"And what about the ones that didn't want to join?" asked Ivan suspiciously.

"Well," Nat said thoughtfully, "the Solar Patrol was established on one basic principal – we had to have a monopoly on the powers of destruction out here in the solar system. Anyone who didn't want to sign up was dealt with by other means."

"What other means?"

"I'll leave that up to your imagination. Or you can do some research on your own. Suffice it to say that there was no overt violence. But there are things you can do with nanotech that are more certain than force."

"If you can find your target," Amy said.

"If you can find it," Nat said in agreement. "If it isn't wrapped in a stealth shield and hidden from view until a bunch of too-smart-for-their-own-good cadets stumble across it."

Amy sighed. Nat seemed to have squelched the discussion with his harsh assessment of her and her shipmates. He realized it, too. So without any further words, he suddenly spun about.

"All right, let's go," he said loudly. "Time to get out of here."

* * *

Nat Carson led the way. He put Howie at the tail to serve as rear guard and to help any stragglers. He didn't want to imagine any reason for stragglers, but he gave him that task just in case.

He placed Pham right behind him. She carried the lantern and Nat reasoned that when fighting nanotech, you wanted to concentrate your own capabilities.

Howie cracked the seal on the escape hatch, then Nat went in.

"How's it look, Kit?" he asked as soon as he was clear of the entrance.

"Clean as a your mother's kitchen," the AI replied.

He looked up the long dark shaft to the surface. The light from his helmet illuminated the walls for only so far, then shadows ate it up. The tunnel was wide enough across to hold one person comfortably, two politely, and three with some crowding. The rest of the party filled it quickly, then paused while Howie redogged the hatch.

Then they began pulling themselves up the ladder that lined the shaft. Before long his momentum was enough to carry him along with barely a touch on the rungs now and then. It occurred to him that this would be a good way to move quickly across the surface. If you made a wrong move and lost contact, the asteroid's tiny surface gravity was probably enough to get you back down eventually. He made a note to try it when he got a chance.

If he got the chance. It occurred to him that he didn't know what lay at the top of the shaft. Would there be another hatch? Would it have a lock? Was this just a twisted kind of trap for the unwary?

He found out soon enough. There was another hatch. It was not locked. And there was no trap. Not yet. He and Howie turned the wheel and opened the hatch. Then he drew a long plastic tube from his lantern and poked it through a crack in the opening.

"It's dark up here," Kit said. "And quiet. A quick scan up and down the spectrum shows nothing but regolith and stealth shield."

"All right, follow me," Nat said as he pressed the hatch up and out.

Kit wasn't kidding about the darkness. The stealth shield stretched overhead unbroken in every direction, and the crumbly black surface of the asteroid soaked up the light from the helmets. He pulled himself along, keeping close to the surface. A few pulls was all it took to get his momentum up. He dug in his hands when he'd moved a good ten meters away from the tunnel exit, and stopped.

Once everyone was on the surface, he sat gently on the ground and addressed them all. "Now listen up, here's how I want you to move …"

A few minutes later, he had all six cadets mimicking his latest method of traversing a microgravity environment. It was almost like swimming, but there was none of the resistance you got from water. And it was almost like flying, except that you had to stay close to the ground.

Every once in a while, he'd grab a piece of regolith for a push and it would break off in his hand. That never failed to give him a chill. But it wasn't enough to slow his rapid progress across the surface.

Kit served as pilot for the group. He selected a bearing towards the proper end of the asteroid and kept them from wandering away from it. They spent a good twenty minutes or more making their way up the rock, and managed to avoid running into the pylons that supported the stealth shield.

Nat was concerned, however. There was no indication of any threat from the nanotech. Salerno had said they were up here on the surface, but there was no sign of them. He didn't like that. He would rather have known where they were and what they were doing. At least then he could prepare for whatever that was.

Kit recommended a halt when they had gone far enough. Far enough was up among the access tubes the top end of the asteroid, he and Kit had decided before entering the escape hatch. "Salerno, I need you up here. You know which of these things are which."

"Yes, sir. But …"

"But what?"

"But not in the dark, sir?"

"Well, we'll see what we can do about that. Kit, can you mark and image the tunnel entrances within sight of here?"

"Already configured and prepared," Kit reported.

"Go ahead."

A trio of steaming pods flew up and away from the top of the lantern and spread out into the darkness. A minute later, the first of them exploded into light a hundred meters away. The second went off a minute after that, and the third followed two minutes later. Each of them bathed the remaining structure at the head of each shaft. And each of them relayed back imaging data to Kit, who in turn projected it onto a thin screen of crystal exuded for the purpose.

The view switched from site to site, revealing details in black and white as seen from overhead.

"It's very confusing, sir," Salerno said. "I didn't get a good look at everything at once – just bits and pieces. Wait a minute, I recognize that one. Where is it? Which one is it?"

Kit indicated the correct site by changing the light above it to red. "Now what's the one to the left look like?"

The view stopped changing on the screen, revealing the walls and equipment remaining from one of the surface sites – an empty weapons emplacement. "That's the one where I saw the bug, sir," Salerno said.

"What about the first one? Did you see any bugs there?"

"No, sir."

"Then that's the one we're going down."

* * *

Nat stared with fear and disgust at the slimy mess that had once been a comm relay.

He knew something was wrong the minute they emerged from the access tunnel and Kit-in-the-lantern couldn't link up with Kit-in-the-ship. He had left relays along their path – up as far as the big door where they found Peter Salerno – in order to keep in touch. This was the closest, pasted on a stanchion that rose high up out of the wall of the main shaft.

Something had coated it in clear, gelatinous slime flecked with shiny bits of metal. The structure of the relay was starting to dissolve at one end from the stuff. But it seemed to block communications by interfering with transmissions. Kit couldn't get it to do much of anything.

And still stuck in one end of the slime was a small metal bug with four spindly legs that scrambled ineffectually to work free of the stuff.

He shook off a shudder of primal fear, then ordered the party on. Getting seven people from place to place was not as easy as he thought it would be. They always had to wait at the critical points – the tunnel ends, the doorways. And every time they did, Nat felt his flesh crawl at the growing threat. As long as they kept moving, he reasoned, they were safe. But the longer they stayed put, the sooner the AI that ran the asteroid would fix their position and send in another swarm of nano-bugs.

The sabotage to his communications links only added to that concern. On the other hand, at least he knew what it was up to.

They moved up the shaft and reached the Grand Concourse, where he found his next relay. It was in the same shape as the first – only there were no bugs stuck in the slime.

"Damn," he said. "I wish I knew what was going on back at the docks."

"Are you afraid they may have attacked the ships, sir?" Amy Hackenyos asked.

"No – I'm sure they've attacked the ships. I'm afraid of what they've done to them. And the only way to find out what that is is to get there. Come on, let's go."

He hurried them up the Concourse to the docks, swinging from handhold to handhold along the wide passageway that ran laser straight from one side of the asteroid to the other. The geometrical precision was a relief after the organic ambiguity of the nanotech tunnel below. Nat felt more confident as his surroundings became more familiar.

That confidence was nearly shattered when they neared the end of the long corridor and Kit announced without preamble: "One of the spacesuits reports a cadet in physical distress."

13

The device that was the world was discovering that not all its plans were guaranteed to succeed.

At first, it seemed quite the opposite. Despite the spectacular defeat of the swarms of insectoid containers, they had accomplished their main purpose. One of their number had managed to make contact with one of the intruders, slipped its sharp snout through the spacesuit, and inject a load of assemblers, reassemblers, and other cogs into the bloodstream. The device had seen a lot worth copying in the terrestrial mosquito, although it provided a more robust shell for its own design.

For more than an hour, the microscopic invaders coursed throughout the target's body, replicating themselves as fast as possible. Then, when their numbers were sufficient, they acted. They sought out the nervous system, tracing its networks, locating its control centers, identifying the nodes where clusters of commands were processed. They infiltrated the central system, the spinal chord and brainstem, the thalamus, the hypothalamus, and the amygdala. They monitored every impulse, recording it faithfully for transmission back to the master memory cores when the opportunity presented itself. And bit by bit they formed a virtual recreation of the human nervous system in action.

Without emotions, the device had no sense of the thrill involved in violating one of the great taboos of the Last War. The idea of injecting nanotech into the human body was so repellent to those who fought in that war and survived it that all modern cog technology was prevented from doing such a thing. But the device was aware of the thrill its programmers and designers had known when they stripped those inhibitions from its coding. These were men and women without a conscience who had no reservations about what they were doing. And the device they had created was equally lacking in moral fiber, even though it could not appreciate that as fully as a human being might.

Then the trouble began.

The nanites had reached such numbers and such mass that the body's immune system had gone into action.

Now powerful histamines were being released throughout the target body. The nerve signals were degrading and the virtual recreation was becoming useless. The initial plan – to take control of a living human body by seizing its nervous system – appeared to be in trouble. At the moment, it seemed like all the exercise was likely to provide was a detailed analysis of that nervous system as it failed.

* * *

Pham had felt lightheaded from the time they reached the Grand Concourse. As they worked their way along the conduits and piping towards the docks, she felt worse and worse. Her eyes ached, her joints protested, and her muscles burned.

By the time they were ready to pass through the locks into the base habitat, though, all her suffering seemed to fade away. Along with everything else. She would have felt like she was floating – except that she already was. In the event, she felt her body slip farther and farther away.

Time seemed to slow down as well. They seemed to be taking forever to open the outer door of the lock. Howie and Nat were still trying hard to act like they were in control. Peter and Cheng were hanging back timidly. Ivan seemed oblivious to the trouble he had caused, as if none of it were his fault. And Amy hovered over Nat Carson for no discernible reason.

They seemed to hold that pose for hours. In the meantime, millions of thoughts coursed through Pham's mind. Images from her childhood, lost scraps of memory, smells and sounds and the feeling of textures from far away and long ago. Ideas about politics, chemistry, and colonial rationing chased one another through her weary brain. Arguments arose, battled back and forth, then subsided. And then, from beyond the fragile limits of her own experience, the struggles and strife of thousands of years of human existence poured through her. She felt like a tiny mote of self-illuminated dust riding a great torrent of light. She was so tiny, so insignificant, reduced to nothing more than a pure point of view, a bodiless dot of color in a great gushing rainbow. She kept rushing forward, faster and faster, towards no certain destination, with no way of slowing or stopping, in phase with the rushing of billions of other dots and motes. And yet, out of this bodiless nothing that was herself poured a tremendous excitement, a boundless joy at the immensity of the universe and the unceasing battle between the motes of light and the wider darkness. The torrent of light now rose higher and higher, scaling new pinnacles, soaring over vast distances in the time it took the heart to beat. She looked back down on herself, floating in the cramped tunnels of a bit of rock flying through empty black space – and heard her name being called.

* * *

"Pham!" Amy yelled. "Pham! Can you hear me? Say something?"

"Kit, talk to her suit," Nat said as the cadets pulled Pham along to place her in the lock. "What's wrong with her?"

"Her face looks all red," Amy said. "Like it's breaking out in hives or something."

"Anaphylactic shock," Nat said. "She's having an allergic reaction to something. We need to give her antihistamines. Kit, can't her suit manufacture some?"

"Let's hurry," Amy said, her hands shaking in fear and her eyes tearing up. "We've got to get her back to the ship. Mother Janus will help her."

Howard Efi pulled her and Pham into the lock, and Nat slammed the door down hard. "Her vital signs are erratic," Nat said. "Blood pressure is dropping. Breathing is fast, but obstructed. Heart rate is too high. Kit, there's got to be something her suit can do for her."

Amy couldn't hear the reply, but she could tell it wasn't encouraging when Nat sagged inside his own spacesuit.

They cycled the inner door of the lock – a terribly frustrating waste of time, since there was nothing but vacuum on the other side, something the automatic machinery of the antique space station refused to recognize. Then they were through the door and pulling themselves along the corridor.

"Which way to the docks?" Nat asked.

Howie waved them towards the right, down the long passageway through the heart of the station to the surface. They yanked and jerked and bounced and bumped from one side of the passage to another, trying each time to shield Pham from the force of the impact. Before they were halfway there, the rest of the cadets arrived, cycling through the lock and moving faster than the burdened group in the lead.

Amy looked into the helmet at Pham's unseeing eyes and her swollen, puffy face.

"Pham! Talk to me, Pham!"

* * *

She opened her eyes. Or were they already open? Either way, she could see now. It was Amy Hackenyos. What was she doing here? How had she penetrated into Pham's dream world? And how had she made that world return to the cluttered walls of the asteroid space station?

Pham felt awful once again. Her whole body ached, her skin was in flames wherever it touched the inner surface of her space suit. Her eyes watered, her nose ran, and her throat was so swollen that she could only wheeze short half breaths.

Suddenly she was seized by a terrible revelation. She was dying. For a brief moment, she dissolved into a vast sea of regret at all that she was losing. It was so unfair. Then darkness rushed in from the infinite ends of creation, closing in on her in a second.

* * *

"We're losing her," Nat said with sudden panic.

Amy felt herself grow small and helpless as she realized how much farther it was to the ship. Then she pushed herself even harder to get Pham to safety. She was sure that once they were back aboard the partridge ship, Mother Janus would give Pham whatever she needed to make her better. She was sure even as she knew that Pham was gone. Nat seemed just as sure.

"Vitals are down to zero," Nat said. "Let's go, let's go. Hurry it up. How much farther do we have to go?"

"Another hundred meters and another lock," Howie said from the other side of moon. Amy just shook as she felt more and more helpless.

They ricocheted around the last corner before the lock, Howie acting as a human bumper in the corner to guide Pham's body as they flew by. Then Nat was at the inner lock door, swinging it open. They hauled her into the lock, then slammed the door shut. Howie was at the outer door before the dogs were tight.

Then they were out into the docks, floating between the *Able Countryman* and Nat's ad hoc Patrol craft. Howie was setting a course for the *Countryman's* main hatch.

Then Nat suddenly let go of Pham and let himself drift free. Only Amy was touching her.

"Get back!" Nat screamed.

Amy shook her head in confusion. She was all ready to burst into tears over the tragedy that had befallen them. Now what was happening?

"What?"

"Get back away from her! Don't touch her!"

When Amy didn't move fast enough, Nat spun in place, found a foothold, and launched himself at her. He collided with her full on, breaking her tenuous grip on Pham and knocking her towards his ship.

"What's going on?" Howie bellowed from the *Countryman*. "Amy, are you all right?"

"She's full of nanotech!" Nat yelled. "Don't touch her, don't go near her, and for the sake of god don't put her in one of the ships."

* * *

Cheng Li Hui floated in the cool darkness of the *Countryman's* bridge, her leg wrapped around a piece of framing designed for just that purpose. Anchored thus, she could see Pham's body where it was lashed to a pylon.

She had been watching it for more than half an hour now and nothing had happened. She didn't know what could happen with a spacesuit full of uncontrolled nanotech, but she didn't want to explore the concept with her imagination.

She wanted to curl up in a ball and disappear.

A voice in the back of her head let out a low unceasing moan, the stale taste of metal coated her mouth and throat, her eyes and sinuses burned from first filling up with emotion and then draining more than dry from stress, and her gut felt like someone was cutting out her liver with a dull spoon.

If only she had done something. If only she had been faster or braver or smarter. If only she had told Ivan to stick his head up a dark hole when he first suggested coming to this asteroid.

For some reason she couldn't fathom, she wanted to put his arms around Pham and tell her she was going to be all right.

She kept watching. She thought someone should. It was too important a duty to be left to the cogs.

* * *

Amy remembered the argument.

"Well if you're so smart, what do you think history is?" Ivan had said.

"History is the ultimate human process," Pham had replied. "It is how human beings create themselves, pulling themselves up out of nature and making nature human. It is a dialog the human race is having with itself as it tries to answer the fundamental questions of life and existence – what will you do and who will you be?"

"If you're going to be that way about it – " Ivan started to say, but Pham didn't allow him to respond.

"The sweep of great ideas is just a reflection of the sweep of great lives. Their struggle is just a pale image of the struggles of real people thrown into the world helpless and powerless. Real history is about how people overcome their weakness and alienation and join the great story."

Ivan just gave her a disgusted look and let her continue.

But Amy remembered her joy at Pham's victory.

"She's right, you know," Amy said. "She's maximally right."

But that was then. Now she was working real hard at keeping the tears back. Except that as she peeled her spacesuit off and climbed into the shower and washed her hair, every few minutes a still voice in the back of her mind would remind her: Pham was dead. And that realization would shatter what had been a minute or two or three of relief where she didn't have to face that fact.

Pham was dead. Her berth would remain empty for the rest of the mission. Her personal effects would have to inventoried. Someone would have to notify her family. They would have to do something with the body.

And all those trivial details of death were enough to shred the beautiful memory of that moment of the argument when Pham, full of life and energy, had shattered the empty posturing of an adolescent tyrant.

Once again her defenses failed and the tears poured from her eyes.

* * *

Peter Salerno curled himself into a ball and floated in the dark silence of his berth.

His spacesuit drifted on the gentle air current invoked by the ventilation system and bumped into him, sending a sudden rush of gooseflesh across his body. But other than that he remained undisturbed.

At least on the outside.

On the inside, all his worst fears had come to pass. And they had done him one better. Instead of reaching out and killing him, the nanotech demon had killed someone else and left him alive to suffer. Death would have been a release from that suffering. Pham didn't suffer anymore. There was no Pham to suffer anymore, which wasn't the same thing. That particular personality was gone, never to be recovered. Her death had opened a door to eternity, and Peter had made the error of peering through it.

And then something happened.

As the fear grew greater and greater, surrounding him with its vile intensity, he grew smaller and smaller. He shrank in within himself. He became a spark of consciousness floating inside his body just as it floated inside this dark compartment of the ship.

Suddenly he felt that spark explode, expanding at infinite speed to fill the endless space of the universe to its limits. And in that explosion the fear was transformed. Now its was something within him instead of something outside of him. It was a part of his world, not its totality. Once it was within him, he had power over it, instead surrendering to its power.

He thought about Pham and how hard she had struggled to get everyone to safety down inside the asteroid. She hadn't given a moment's thought to the possibility of death. She had faced it fearlessly. If she could do that, there was no reason he couldn't find a way to do the same.

A moment later, the compartment was reduced to nothing more than a dark berthing space instead of an infinite stage for the consciousness. He ordered the light on, pulled a jumpsuit from a bag in the corner, and got dressed. Then he went looking for company.

* * *

"How did we discover the nanotech in Pham's body?" Ivan asked Mother Janus. He had cleaned up quickly and curled around a microgravity seat in the ship's commons to talk to her. His hair, slicked back with water, felt cold against his scalp and his skin buzzed from the scrubbing he had given it. It still wasn't enough to stop his flesh from crawling at the thought of tiny machinery coursing through his body. That was the main horror he saw in Pham's death – that he might be next.

Otherwise, Ivan felt only a vague thrill at all the excitement and activity her death had produced. It seemed inappropriate at first, until he decided that it would only be inappropriate if he enjoyed the thrill instead of regretting it. Having dealt with his guilt, he went on to attack his fears.

"Her spacesuit detected them," Mother Janus replied.

"But why didn't they detect them sooner? They had to be in there for a long time."

"For most of that time, they were still inside Pham's body. As long as they remained there, the suit had no indication of their presence."

"Could anyone else have them in their bodies?"

"No," Mother Janus said.

"And why not?"

"Because we analyzed the suit and determined the source of the nanotech that attack Pham. It was a small puncture, too small for the suit's sensor to detect, but it left traces. We had the other suits look for similar traces and none were found. Therefore, we have a high degree of confidence that Cadet Pham Noc Do was the only one to be infected with biological nanotech."

"And that's what caused her death?"

"Indirectly. The cause of her death was anaphylactic shock. Her immune system went into overload trying to rid herself of the invaders. Massive amounts of histamines flooded her metabolism. I can stop this if it makes you uncomfortable."

"Continue."

"Her blood pressure dropped. Her throat and mouth became swollen. Breathing became more difficult. Her suit increased the level of oxygen flowing to her lungs, but that wasn't enough. It also tried to manufacture antihistamines, but those are complex chemicals and it takes some time to get the chemistry started. It rapidly depleted those it had in stock and any other medications that were appropriate – vasodilators, epinephrine, anti-inflammatories. There was just too much nanotech inside her and her body was fighting too vigorously with it to stop it. In the end, she exhausted herself in the struggle."

"Have you prepared the necessary antihistamines and other drugs to prevent another such death?"

"Certainly, Cadet Blandings. And that is an unnecessary and impertinent question."

"I don't doubt your responsibility, Mother. I was asking for my own reassurance."

"That should not be necessary, either."

"Don't you ever stop being a drill instructor?" he asked.

"Only if it is necessary," she replied.

"I have another question," Ivan said. "If I tell you something in confidence, will you keep it secret?"

"It depends on the nature of the confidence," Mother answered. "If it involves your safety or the safety of the other cadets, I am obligated to share it with them."

"It has that potential," Ivan said. "But what if there is no immediate threat?"

"I would be inclined to keep it confidential until it becomes a threat. Or some other reason arises to provide the information to the others."

"All right," he said, seeing just how far a clever AI was willing to go on the issue. "I have something I need to tell you. In case something happens to me, someone else should know."

"Go ahead."

"When I was at the far end of the asteroid, I went on by

myself to see what was at the far end of a branch in the tunnel while Howard Efi went down the other. At the end of my tunnel, I found a large chamber, sort of a hangar. It was filled with rack after rack of canisters, each about a meter long and a tenth of that in diameter. There were maybe a hundred or more of them, I didn't have time to count and I couldn't see them all. Each canister had a small rocket engine in one end. Each rack led towards the rear of the compartment, towards the outside. I cannot be certain, but I believe it was a system for launching capsules into interplanetary space. And I believe the capsules are intended to carry nanotech designed and replicated on this asteroid."

"That is certainly important information, Cadet Blandings, and it should be shared immediately with the others – as well as higher authorities in the Solar Patrol. I have told you before about the importance of sending a report to your superiors at the soonest opportunity."

"Yes, Mother."

"But you persist in keeping silent. If you have a reason for this, you should explain it. It should be part of your record."

"I have a reason," Ivan said with a proud smile.

"And what is it?"

"I am not sure who among us I can trust. I have been thinking about this for a long time. The nanotech on this asteroid is very advanced. It is obviously too advanced to come from the beginning of the war, or even the middle. I believe it is even more advanced than that in use at the end of the war – other than the cog technology that Triplanetary used to stop the fighting. I mean, it is cog technology. Not quite the same as what we know, but very close superficially."

"Perhaps."

"And if it is more modern than the war, who could have created this place but Triplanetary? Or the Patrol? Why else would it remain hidden for so many years?"

"Those are not questions I am equipped to answer."

"At least you can see that I have reason for my doubts," Ivan said, in a moment of honest sincerity. "Are you sure that I'm wrong?"

"I am not equipped to answer that question either. But your argument is enough to give me doubts myself. And that is enough reason to keep your confidence to myself – for now. Later, it will be necessary to tell the others. Keep that in mind. You may want to tell them yourself."

"Not now," Ivan said. "You're right. Maybe later. But not now."

* * *

Howard Efi slipped onto the bridge and into a seat next to Cheng. "Is she still there? Still all right?" he asked.

"Still all right. Nothing's happened. Maybe nothing will, but I don't know about that. It's nanotech. You can't be sure what it's doing."

"You sure can't. If I thought something like this was going to happen, I never would have gone along with Ivan's plan."

"None of us would, Howie. But none of us thought it was."

He sighed, then said: "It's my fault, you know. I'm the senior cadet and I'm responsible."

"No you're not. That's too simple. We're all responsible. We all let him do it."

"I could have stopped him."

"Maybe. If I said no, everyone would have gone and done it

anyway. But if you said no, it would have been enough."

"That's how I see it," Howie said.

"But that's not enough. If Ivan had never come up with his plan. Or if someone else – anyone else but Ivan – had come up with it. No one else would have pushed us to do it the way he did. You know how he is. You know how he was with us. You couldn't say no if you wanted to. If it's anyone's fault, it's Ivan's."

"You can blame him if you want to, but I don't." He shrugged. The words were drying up. He looked out at where Pham's body rested. What were they going to do with it?

"Where's Nat?" Cheng asked.

"Taking a shower. He didn't want to take a chance leaving the ship, so he's using our water."

"Hey, guys." Peter Salerno popped up through the doorway onto the bridge. "Muster in the common in five minutes. Nat's orders. I guess he's going to tell us all what we did wrong. Ivan's already there. I'm going to go get Amy. We'll see you down there."

"Okay," Howie said. It was a relief not to be in command any more. It was one thing to do it for fun, as a formality. He was never more than first among equals. Someone had to be in charge and he was it. But it was different when being in charge meant being responsible. He didn't like that.

He wondered if Nat Carson was as unhappy with it as he was. A few minutes later, he would find out.

***

Nat spent a long time preparing what he would say to the cadets. He knew what they must be going through. It had happened to him much the same way, when he was a cadet. The first experience of death was never easy to accept and it never got any better. The sense of waste and unfairness, the sense of powerlessness and fear, never diminished.

And in a more clinical sense, he knew what it could do a group's cohesion and morale. Casualties of thirty percent were enough to break a unit in combat – or even in plain vanilla emergencies. And they were more than halfway there.

They needed to hear something that would rally their shattered spirit. They needed someone to put their minds back on task and shake off the dread that death inspired.

He turned the problem over and over in his mind as he floated inside the shower bubble, hot water needling his skin. He was well-rehearsed when he came out, dressed in a disposable jump suit fabricated by Mother Janus for him.

But like many battle plans, it did not survive first contact with its intended recipient.

Only four of the cadets were mustered in the commons when he arrived.

"Where's Cheng?" he asked.

"She was right behind me," Efi said. "She'll be here in a second."

"Did you all forget the meaning of muster?" he asked. "Or the meaning of 'on time'?"

No one had a chance to answer, though, as Cheng's voice issued from an intercom speaker: "Hey, come quick! Pham's moving!"

14

The cadets almost didn't make way for him as they all rushed for the bridge. But Nat flashed a quick nasty look at Peter Salerno as he tried to get to the passageway ahead of him, and that was sufficient to remind them all of the protocols.

Cheng was in tears when they reached her. Pham's body was still lashed to the pylon, but she was indeed moving. One arm swung back and forth, almost as if she were beckoning to them.

"Mother Janus," Nat said, "what's going on out there?"

"The suit says she has no vital signs," Mother reported. "But there's some kind of comm signal coming from there."

"A comm signal? Why didn't you say something right away?"

"This is right away. It just started. Shall I put it on a bridge monitor?"

"Yes, please," Nat said sheepishly, noticing that Mother Janus used the same tone of voice with him that she did with the other cadets when they got out of line.

"Hello? Hello? Someone help me. I need your help. You have to bring me inside and help me."

"Is that her voice?" Nat asked.

"Sounds like it to me," Efi said.

"Sure, as if we'd believe that was really her," Amy said with a sneer.

"What does that AI think? That we're all stupid?"

"My guess is that it hasn't had much contact with real human beings. And the people who created it didn't provide it with enough background data to make up for it."

"Maybe they thought this kind of thing would work, too," Amy said.

"Maybe," Nat said. "But I don't know if anyone would be that naive."

Pham's voice continued to issue from the monitor, pleading softly to her shipmates.

"Can't you turn that off?" Cheng asked as she wiped her eyes with the back of her hand.

"Mother, ask her if she's hurt," Nat ordered.

"Yes," Pham's voice replied. "I hurt my leg. It's very painful. Please bring me inside and help me."

"Is that suit still full of nanotech?" Nat asked.

"To the brim," Mother Janus replied.

"Then switch off the monitor. All that's going to do is annoy us. But keep track of her and let me know if anything else changes."

"Aye, aye, sir," Mother Janus responded. Nat wasn't sure if he detected a note of sarcasm in her voice or not.

"Now I want everyone back in the commons for muster. And that means everyone, cadet," he said, looking into Cheng's wet eyes.

A minute later when they were all assembled, he was ready again to begin his prepared speech. But again he never got the chance. Efi interrupted him before he got the first words out of his mouth.

"Before you say anything, I'd like to take full responsibility for everything that happened here," Efi said. "I was in command and it's all my fault."

Nat drew in a deep breath and held it. It wasn't that he had spoken out of turn. You almost had to expect that from cadets. It was the silliness of what he said that set Nat's passions off.

"Well I'm very glad you're willing to do that, cadet, but I'm afraid it's a little bit too late. First of all, you don't have the luxury of taking responsibility for anything. You're cadets. You have no official standing with the Solar Patrol. You are all less than nothing. You don't even exist as officers. You aren't part of the chain of command. You can't take responsibility because no one ever gave you any."

The cadets all seemed to turn pale before the blistering wave of words, but Nat continued.

"And the reason for that is because you don't have any sense of the consequences of your actions or your decisions. How could you? You've never been in a position to take any actions or make any decisions. And that's too bad, because there's nothing but consequences here. Everything that happened is a consequence of decisions you all made when you told Mother Janus to point your ship towards this asteroid. Pham's death is a consequence of things you decided weeks ago. All of you. If you had given one nanosecond of thought to the possible consequences then, you never would have come here. If you had any sense of consequences at all, you would have called it in and let the pros handle it.

"But that's life. Life is nothing but consequences. And none of you have had a life yet. One of you never will. That's a consequence. What happens to you all next is another consequence. The time has come, boys and girls, to start thinking about them. Because you are going to live with them for a long, long time."

The cadets seemed now to wither under the verbal assault. But Nat wasn't finished.

"Look at yourselves," he said. "Efi, you picked a fine time to get responsible. You should have done that two weeks ago. Cheng is moping around like she was in love with Pham or something. Salerno is still afraid of shadows. Amy is probably glad Pham's dead because she was so damned perfect. And Cadet Blandings – yes, I see you back there. Cadet Blandings is trying real hard to pretend that none of this affects him and that none of it has anything to do with him, as if he didn't start this horrible machine running with his adolescent schemes.

"And you know what's funny about all this? You all thought you could be officers in the Patrol. You all thought you could wear this uniform with honor. You all thought you were good enough. What a joke."

That was all it took to break them completely. Cheng's eyes watered up again. Peter seemed to shrivel up in a corner. Ivan had turned beet red with some emotion, maybe guilt, maybe embarrassment. Amy shook her head slowly and bit her lower lip. And Efi looked like the saddest young man for millions of kilometers.

No one said anything, which was just as well. It gave Nat a chance to catch his breath and rein in his own emotions. He had left off one name on the list of indictments – his own.

Instead of restoring their morale, he had shattered it. What in the world was he doing, yelling at a bunch of cadets who just lost one of their classmates? What in the world kind of way was that to lead men and women into the face of danger? He was no better than they were. And they knew it.

He wanted to curl up and run away himself, but he couldn't. He was the one in charge, the one who was truly responsible for all that had happened here. And it was a burden he didn't want to bear.

"Mr. Carson, I need to speak with you privately on the bridge," Mother Janus said, her mellow voice filling the silence with soothing sounds.

Nat felt his blood turn cold. Was he going to get a taste of his own medicine from an artificial intelligence now? He knew he had it coming. And he knew partridge ships could be very protective of their broods.

As he pulled himself through the passageway to the bridge, he imagined all the things Mother could say to him. All of them were more terrible than the worst he had aimed at the cadets. But none of them ever came his way.

All she said was: "Mr. Carson, I have a military communication from your spacecraft."

A sudden wave of fear swept over him – and embarrassment. This had nothing to do with him, it was much more serious than that.

"Nat, this is Kit," a voice on the monitor said. "We need to talk about what we're going to do next. You have to come over here right away."

"Okay," he said. "Give me a minute to wrap things up here."

"Don't take too long," Kit said. "This is important."

"I won't," Nat said. Then to Mother Janus, he added: "That is my ship talking and not some nanotech trick?"

"Verification codes are impossible to fake," she said.

"Good. Tell the cadets to take a break, get some rest, and try to eat something. I'll be back as soon as I can."

"Yes, sir," she said.

"And Mother, don't tell them this, but I'm truly sorry for what I just did to them. It wasn't what I had planned to do."

"I'm sure it wasn't," she said. "But I think it's going to take more than a rest and something to eat for them to get over it."

Nat sighed. Now he felt worse than ever.

* * *

"That was wrong," Amy said. "All wrong."

"Like that makes a difference," Howie said.

"It does make a difference," she replied. "It was wrong because it wasn't true. And everyone knew it."

"It wasn't?" Peter asked. "It sounded true to me. He was right about everything, as far as I can see."

"He was only right as far as he went," Amy said. "And that's why it wasn't true. It was only part of a truth, and part of the truth isn't any truth at all. And you know that because that's the way we all deal with criticism."

"Speak for yourself, little sister," Howie said.

"We all do it. And we're all doing it right now. But he was wrong about me. I mean, sure it bothered me that Pham had perfect skin and perfect teeth and knew everything and did everything right. But that's because I know I don't have perfect skin and my teeth are crooked and almost everything I do is wrong the first time. I didn't take it personally. It's not like she made herself perfect just to make me feel inadequate."

"How do you know?" Peter asked. Amy turned to growl at him, then saw the smile on his face.

"The same way I know you're not scared of your own shadow anymore, are you?"

"Well ... "

"I knew it. I've seen what you look like when you're scared, Peter, and this isn't it. This is something entirely different. You look the exact opposite of scared."

"Brave?" he suggested.

"More than that. If you could see what your eyes look like – it's a little bit frightening itself."

"And Cheng, look at yourself. Everyone know you liked Pham a lot. Even she did."

"She did? She never said anything."

"That's because she didn't want to hurt your feelings," Amy said. "And she couldn't think of anything she could say that wouldn't."

"Aw gee," Cheng said. "She wouldn't have hurt my feelings much."

"Then how come your heart is broken now?"

Cheng looked at her feet and rubbed her eye with the back of one hand, but she didn't answer.

"And Howie, he shouldn't have torn into you like that. He's right about one thing – we're not responsible for anything except ourselves. Aren't you glad? Or would you like to trade places with Mr. Officer Carson?"

"Don't worry, I've got a thick skin," Howie said.

"And a thick head to go with it," said Peter.

"Watch it, half-loaf, or you'll find out how thick it is," Howie snapped back.

"And what about Ivan?" Peter asked.

"Was he right about you, Ivan?" Amy asked. "Do you feel like none of this was your fault?"

"Actually, no," Ivan said. "I accept my role in this. It was my idea and my plan. If there is any criticism to be handed out, I will take it like a man."

Peter huffed incredulously, and Howie muttered: "Be real."

"And if there is any credit to be handed out, I will take my share of that as well."

"Credit?" Howie said, a puzzled look squeezing his features.

"Credit. Praise. Prestige. You all act like this was a colossal failure because one cadet was killed. Haven't you any idea what the Solar Patrol does? This is a dangerous career. People get killed. Space is unforgiving of failure. And relics of war are even worse. We shouldn't feel like failures because one of us died. We should be proud that no one else did. We should be honored that we were so successful in extracting ourselves from such tremendous danger with such a low cost. I have no doubt that when the reports on this are filed, we will all be recognized for what we have done here. So there is no reason to mope around and feel sorry for ourselves because we got chewed out for getting into trouble. It is our calling in life to get ourselves in trouble. That's what brought us all here. So don't be ashamed of what you are. And start to think about what we are going to do next."

None of the other cadets said anything for a long time. Amy could see the furniture shifting behind their faces as they readjusted their thinking. For all his self-centered wickedness, Amy had to admit, Ivan was right this time. And that sent a chill up her back. She wanted to believe that he wasn't just being manipulative once again. But then she saw the truth. Of course he was being manipulative. He couldn't help it. It was like breathing to him. But he was doing no less than she was – and towards the same purpose. They both wanted to get the crew of the *Countryman* back on its feet.

"Well," Ivan said after the silence had grown embarrassingly long. "What are we going to do next?"

"Go home," Howie said.

"Get out from under this stealth shield and send a report to Patrol HQ," Peter suggested.

"We have to do something about Pham," Cheng said. "We can't leave her here. There must be some way Mother Janus has to neutralize the nanotech."

"All the things we should have done when we got here," Amy said. "And right away."

But she would soon learn that her string had reached its end. This time she was wrong.

*　*　*

Six hours passed before they heard from Nat Carson again.

Then he sent orders by way of Mother Janus for Howard Efi, Peter Salerno, and Cheng Li Hui to come over to his ship. When they arrived, they found him waiting at the rear of the superstructure, a cargo nacelle open beside him. Inside were several large containers wrapped in gold foil. He parceled one out to each cadet and took one himself, then stopped at the main lock to pick up a second object, just as large, but cloaked in a black wrapper. They returned to the *Countryman*, cycling through the lock in two groups to accommodate the large packages.

Once inside, they pulled the containers along the short passageway into the ship's commons.

Nat opened up the two longest containers first. Each one held an identical cargo – four ominous metal devices, weapons by the look of them, with stocks to fit the arm and handholds and triggers in the appropriate locations.

"Cadets, this is going to be a quick lesson, so pay very close attention. Your lives depend on learning what I am going to tell you immediately and without mistakes. These are the tools of your trade. They are weapons unlike any you may have seen before. That is because they rely on powers you have never had to see before. These are cog-guns. They can fire cogs suspended in oil, in projectiles, and in aerosol form. They can also launch any custom-made projectiles that you may be called upon to use. They are powered by a reservoir of cog oil, which we will fill before we begin our mission."

Then he emptied the two smaller containers. Each one held four spacesuit helmets, each of them heavily armored and sprouting antennas, sensor bands, and instrument packs.

"These are combat helmets. For several hours, Mother Janus has been refabricating your spacesuits for combat. These helmets will complete the outfit. They contain cog-based sensors and communications, along with lower-tech conventional systems as a backup. The entire suite provides you with a full-spectrum real-time image with targeting and other battle data."

He slowly removed the black wrapper from his final parcel. It was an elaborate metal basket containing a semitransparent globe at its center. The globe was nearly half-filled with luminescent green fluid – cog oil.

"This is our ultimate weapon. It looks like a lantern, but it something much more powerful. This one contains every drop of cog oil my ship could spare. I'm afraid Kit is taking up residence aboard your ship with Mother Janus – dual residence, since a copy remains in this container. And I'm afraid Mother will have to contribute as much oil as she can spare."

The cadets picked out the equipment hesitantly and examined it as if it were about to blow up in their hands.

"Our mission is simple and straightforward. We are going to return to the lab at the core of the asteroid, gain access to the main reservoir of cog oil, and attack it at its heart."

15

Somewhere to the south, just over the ragged black horizon, bright flashes of light illuminated the underside of the stealth shield.

"What was that?" Amy asked. They had been on the surface only a couple of minutes, and the flashes revealed more than a dull gray artificial sky. They revealed the terrible truth that the asteroid had become a much more hostile environment in the last few hours.

"Lightning," Peter suggested.

"Not likely," She said. "Lightning is carried by water and air molecules. None of that out here."

"Nevertheless, large amounts of electrical charge are being stored up in the structure of the stealth shield," Mother Janus said. "Whatever the mechanism, the potential for a lightning-like phenomenon is there – and I mean that in more ways the one."

The cadets huddled in a cul-de-sac formed by the walls of the hangar and the outer ramparts of the pre-war asteroid base. Nat was assessing the situation, locked in conversation on a separate channel with Kit, who was scanning the sky, the ground, and everything in between to see what kind of threat they faced and from where.

The battle helmet felt strange on Amy's head. It was more cramped that the big glass fishbowl that she was used to wearing, and it offered more information on the internal heads-up display. And it had a strange smell, old and musty. Someone else had worn this before.

The cog-gun in her hands was similar. It was old and worn in the handholds and stock. There were marks on it – dings and dents from rough handling and scratched-in initials and symbols. Like an old tool, it had been well-used long before it came into her hands.

There was something odd about that fact. She wasn't sure what it was, but she knew she would have to figure it out. But she didn't have time right now. Her attention was too sharply focused on the ground before her and whatever danger might be lurking there.

She had noticed it earlier, though, when Nat first handed the equipment out and they began filling the reservoirs with water and oil. She wanted to ask him about it, but he didn't give her a chance. He was too busy trying to indoctrinate them in the finer points of infantry tactics in the few minutes they had.

"The basic elements are simple," he had explained, in tones that allowed no questioning or doubt. "The majority of a unit provides a base of fire. This base of fire suppresses the enemy's defensive fire and allows a maneuver unit to advance. That unit then settles in place and becomes part of the base of fire for the next maneuver unit. Step by step, we pull ourselves up. It's as simple as that. But in battle, the simplest things can be very difficult to accomplish."

He inspected each weapon as they finished with it, reading the diagnostics off the maintenance panel, then testing the triggers, switches, and seals by hand.

"We will form up in three two-member fire teams," Nat had ordered. "Cheng Li Hui and Peter Salerno in one team, Howard Efi and Ivan Blandings in another, and Amy Hackenyos and I in the third. Amy and I will carry the big cog-tanks with us and we will always be part of the base of fire."

That reassured her, even though it made her more nervous for the boys. Then she realized that while they would be more exposed, she and Nat would be more critical targets for whatever they encountered.

"These fire-and-maneuver tactics can allow you to survive on almost any battlefield, but you have to apply them correctly," Nat continued. "We are going up against an opponent with superior resources. That means we have to avoid his strengths. Fire and maneuver allows us to do that. We maneuver away from them, use fire to suppress them, and infiltrate into the enemy's rear, where we can strike at vulnerable command centers. That's the general theory. It's called 'hitting them where they ain't.' We'll use it to get at the entrance to the lab – the one we used to escape."

As Amy filled the large reservoir with cog oil, Nat went on to another subject.

"Now I'm going to let you all in on a dirty secret," he said. "I'm going to tell you the truth about cogs and modern nanotech. And here it is: All cogs are one."

Amy saw the puzzled look on the faces of Peter, Cheng, and Howie. Ivan nodded knowingly and she guessed at what Nat meant.

"Think about it, cadets. All cogs are one. They have no separate identity. They have no individuality. They are all part of single universal system. It's a system that extends into every aspect of our lives, every piece of our technology, every place that we go or have gone. And it's all one system."

"And why is that a dirty secret?" Howie asked, showing his bravery.

"A good question, Cadet Efi. Think about it, and you can answer it yourself. What makes it dirty is us. The military. In the final analysis, the job of the military is to destroy things. Kill people. Blow stuff up. Eliminate it. It is the only job that we do that no one else is allowed to. We have a monopoly on the means of destruction. Now when people think about military nanotech, they think it's some kind of special stuff we keep in special containers so it will never get out. But that's a myth. The truth is that there is no difference between military nanotech and non-military nanotech. It's all the same stuff, genetically identical to one another. And it has to be."

"I don't understand," Cheng said in all innocence. "Why does it have to be?"

"I understand," Peter said. "That's why I've been afraid of the stuff all my life."

"What Cadet Salerno senses on an emotional level you all need to recognize on an intellectual level. In the beginning of the Last War, they used nanotech to construct weapons. In the middle, they used it to design weapons. But at the end of the war, they used nanotech itself as the ultimate weapon. Every dirty trick in the book is recorded in its algorithms. Every deception and betrayal. Every method for doing away with your enemy, eliminating his capacity to act, denying him accurate and vital information, and communicating with his superiors and subordinates. And at the same time, every way of defeating and defending against those tricks is in there. The full range of countermeasures, tactics, and strategies. We may create pleasant faces like Mother Janus and Kit to hide the truth, but the those faces are false. The stuff that underlies it is much more equivocal, much more ambiguous. It's like owning an attack dog that acts like a puppy – until you give it the command to kill."

"Then why even bother to fight?" Howie asked. "If it's as

powerful than all that?"

"Because power always has limits," Nat said. "Nanotech is not a robust technology. Look at it. It can't operate outside special environments. It can do a lot of neat chemical and nano tricks, but it can't pick up a hammer and hit you over the head. It's meant to create and operate things, but it isn't meant to live in the conscious world at hand. So it works at one remove – or two or three. It uses levers to move levers to get at you. And it's got one more weakness that we've already discussed. That's where you come in."

"What's that?" Cheng asked, a small edge of irritation in her voice. Amy felt the same way. It was too late in the day to be playing word games.

"It has no imagination. No capacity for spontaneous creativity. Look at the AI that runs this place. Half a century to work with, and the best it can come up with are little metal bugs. They're effective at what they do, but there are ways to defeat them. And we have to come up with them."

"Now?" Howie asked.

"Right now. This minute. Don't hesitate. Speak quickly and off the top of your head. That's how it works. You all know that. Use your imagination. Listen to that still small voice in the back of your head. Exercise your creativity."

"Bug spray," Peter said suddenly. "An aerosol that corrodes their hulls and interferes with their function."

"Bug zappers," Ivan suggested. "Make contact with them and fire some ionizing charge into the things. That'll stop them dead in their tracks."

"Spider webs," Amy said. "Sticky and gooey. Shoot that out the end of your cog-guns."

"Aerosol mines," Cheng piped up. "They blow up when the bugs touch them."

"Just make me a fly swatter a meter wide," Howie said, his eyes wide and a grin on his face. "There's no wind resistance in a vacuum, so I should be able to take out a whole swarm with one swat."

They went on for half an hour, brainstorming countermeasures for the unique creations of the asteroid's AI. When they were done, Kit and Mother Janus went to work fabricating the devices they would need to put the best ideas into action.

Then they suited up, checked each other's battle gear over with everything but a magnifier and tweezers, and formed up at the hangar's outer airlock.

Now, fifteen minutes later, they were ready to form up again. But this time in battle positions. Howie and Ivan took the point, with the other two teams moving in what Nat called "bounding overwatch." The two rear teams took turns covering the movement of the lead team. It was a way to move fast until they came in contact with the renegade nanotech – or its devices.

All it did for Amy was to keep the tension high until that contact was made. By the time they did encounter the first such device, she was glad for that tension to end.

***

They were crawling along, using the bottom-of-the-swimming-pool method Nat Carson had hit upon, when the lightning struck. She hung on by her fingertips to the crumbly regolith as the world around her exploded with brilliant blue light.

She really had felt like she was deep underwater. She was as buoyant as a soap bubble on a spring breeze, floating along under the delicate touch of one hand. The lightning flashes continued in the distance, but they broke in silence. The only sounds she heard were the occasionally scrape and bump as she moved along. And they were transmitted by vibrations through her bones and spacesuit, giving them the same feeling of distance and immediacy that sound carried underwater.

The blinding flash of lightning shattered the illusion.

Now she could see where they were, clinging to the inner rim of a crater more than a hundred meters across and half as deep. She was seized by a deep vertigo as her senses told her that she was about to plunge helplessly into the center of the crater, where the sharp inferno raged.

Then it was gone, like someone pulled a switch. All that was left was a ragged red scar across her vision that followed her eyes wherever she looked.

"Well, that's how they do it," Peter whispered in her ear.

"How?" asked Cheng.

"Didn't you hear Mother just before it hit? She said a small projectile had landed in the center of the crater and was stirring up a cloud of dust. The dust must carry the electrical charge and make the lightning."

"No doubt," Howie said. "But what good does it do to know how it works if it kills you just as dead?"

"None just yet," Peter said. "But maybe later ..."

"Keep moving," Nat said. "It didn't hit us. And now we know to avoid the dust clouds – to make Cadet Salerno's point for him."

"Sir, yes, sir," Howie said.

They continued on along the edge of the crater for nearly half its circumference. Kit had found a surface map of the asteroid from an old database, and Nat had used it to map out their approach to the lab tunnel. This was the largest such feature on the surface and its outermost edge was just outside the hangar door.

"It will be ready for us to take the obvious route – back the way we came out," Nat said. "So we won't go that way. And it will put its defenses along the most direct routes from here to there, so we'll have to go the long way around. It's called the indirect approach, the key to winning almost any battle. Almost any kind of bad terrain is preferable to a well-entrenched enemy defending the ground of his choosing."

So they hid behind the crater wall and advanced more than a hundred meters towards their goal.

Amy and Nat used that wall as a rampart to cover the advance of the other two fire teams, then went over themselves. Nat maintained his indirect approach on the next leg of their approach, working from one small crater to another, avoiding the pylons and any possible nanotech sensor.

In the meantime, Kit and Mother Janus sent decoys out scurrying across the regolith on false missions. Amy could catch glimpses of them from time to time, always labeled clearly by her battle helmet as decoys, though always enough to make her nerves tighten another notch.

"High-intensity radiation is sweeping the horizon," Mother Janus announced abruptly.

"Everyone down!" Nat commanded.

"Gamma-ray source on the horizon at 300 degrees relative – range thirty-two meters. Secondary radiation effects show a low azimuth beam sweeping counter-clockwise. That's towards us, by the way."

Amy looked at her tactical display. Cheng and Peter were the lead team, but off to the right and farther away from the gamma beam. Howie and Ivan were on the left, ready to make their bound forward. They made it, but not as planned.

"Cadets, please do not advance into the gamma ray source," Mother Janus advised gently – and before Nat could say anything. Amy swallowed hard.

"We need to take that beam out," she said.

"Splatter it and seal up the aperture," Nat said. "Kit, Mother, appropriate munitions package for that, please."

"Fire when ready," the two AIs responded in unison.

Amy felt the trigger collapse beneath her fingers and the gun kick in her hands. It kicked again. She wasn't sure where she was aiming or even if she was aiming, but that hardly mattered. The pre-fabricated projectiles were under the control of cogs inside them and would find their targets no matter what she did.

"Cadets, please withdraw from the gamma ray source," Mother Janus said again, softly. Amy was surprised that she was unable to control her maternal instincts even in the height of battle. Except that they weren't instincts, just powerful programming protocols that were as much a part of Mother Janus as the oil in her veins.

Amy's heart edged upwards towards her throat as Howie and Ivan came within range of the gamma ray source. But they opened fire at point blank range just as the projectiles from the rest of the group splashed across the surface of the beam, smothering its deadly power.

"All right!" Howie cheered.

"Hooo-eeee!" Peter yelled.

"Silence on the air," Nat commanded. "We've still got a thousand meters to go. The next leg is through the cleft up ahead. Salerno, do you see it yet?"

The surface map had shown a rift in the surface that ran several hundred meters around the asteroid's equator. It was about twenty meters deep and perfect cover for an advance to contact, Nat said. Amy thought it was a great place for an ambush, but held her tongue.

"No sight of it yet," Peter said.

"Keep looking. It should be about thirty meters to your right."

"Yes, sir." They advanced carefully, moving by bounds towards their target. "Still nothing in sight."

Amy felt her skin start to crawl. Something was wrong. She knew it. She could tell from the way Nat moved that he sensed it too.

"Are you sure?" Nat asked. "We should be on top of it. Kit says so. Mother says so. Where's the rift?"

"We've been dumb-bombed," Ivan said. "There is no rift. There never was."

A collective moan echoed from the commnet. Amy thought she even heard Mother Janus.

"What do we do now?" Howie asked.

"We keep moving," Nat said. "Rift or no rift, we keep moving."

* * *

Peter Salerno felt the breath heaving in and out of his chest as he pulled his body against a rock outcropping and a spray of corrosive chemistry splashed into the vacuum. The liquid crystallized in the lurid light of reflected lasers and artificial lightning, but not quickly enough to eliminate it as a threat. Even the crystals were capable of eating through at least the outer layers of his suit.

He waited until the barrage was over and then swung up and over the rock. Cheng leapt from her own hiding place and the two of them swam and pulled and wrestled across the black ground to the shelter of a two-meter crater a few meters ahead of them.

"Microwave laser source at fifteen degrees relative, range twenty meters," Mother Janus said. "Potential lightning source at one hundred twelve degrees relative, range twenty-seven meters. Chemical explosive in the ground, two hundred degrees relative, range seven meters."

Peter slipped over the edge of the crater like a snake, slithering into the darkness at its center. Cheng huddled close to him, the touch of her hand on Peter's shoulder a moment of comfort in a world that was relentlessly hostile. They crept to the far edge, weapons poking over the rim first, and took a look.

"Is that it?" Cheng asked.

"Mother and Kit say it is," Peter said. "I don't remember. The light wasn't this good and we were going the other direction. In any case, judging by the thickness of the defenses, I'd say we've found the entrance tunnel. Or exit tunnel, depending on your point of view."

"My preferred point of view is from some other planet," Cheng said.

"Mine too," Peter replied. "But we're here now."

"Salerno. Cheng. Cover fire. We're moving up." Nat's voice was quick and sharp, but steady, reassuring Peter no small amount.

"Let's spread out," he said. "It'll make for a bit of a crossfire for anything that comes this way."

Cheng nodded, then moved right. Peter shifted to the left, then – a wave of vertigo swept through him as he felt himself lifted up away from the surface. The ground shrunk below him, the crater a pool of darkness on a plain of uneven light. Cheng was a dot of gray within the pool. The tunnel entrance was a ring of fire, marked by the heads-up display inside his helmet.

He thought after an instant to look up and saw the stealth shield rushing at him – or himself rushing towards it. He spun quickly about, getting his feet in the opposite direction from where they started. When he was aligned properly, he stretched out, pointing his toes at the sheet of gray.

But he couldn't kill off his angular momentum fast enough, and he collided full on with the shield. The impact was not gentle, but it wasn't dangerous either. What hurt was the sudden cryogenic burn at his knees and elbows and shoulder where he hit the shield, which was cooled down to three degrees above absolute zero to mimic the background temperature of black space.

He scrambled quickly to get his feet under him without touching the surface. He was already caroming away when he found a purchase and kicked hard. He didn't know where he was heading at first, then the helmet display helped orient him.

He grabbed regolith when he hit the surface some twenty meters or more from the crater where Cheng still lurked. He scanned the immediate environment. There were no threats within range and two cadets – Howie and Ivan – only a few meters off, behind a small ridge of crushed stone.

"Cover me guys," he said. "I'm going back up with Cheng."

"Keep your head down and we'll worry about your tail," Howie said.

A moment later, he was back inside the crater. "What happened to you?" Cheng asked.

"Just a little adventure," Peter replied. He barely noticed the ache that was settling into his skin where it had been supercooled. Was that the fever of battle? Or was Mother pumping painkillers into him through his suit? He didn't know which, but he was grateful.

"Cadet Salerno back in position," he reported to Nat Carson.

"Acknowledged," he answered. "Moving up now."

A few minutes later, the three fire teams formed an arc about twenty meters from the tunnel entrance. The place was crawling with nanite swarms and radiation beams and chemical guns and other nasty machinery.

"This is it," Nat said. "We're up against the hard place. There's no cute tricks of maneuver or anything to get us past it. All we can do is blanket the area with fire and hope we can outgun them."

Peter felt his mouth go suddenly dry. He hadn't realized it would come down to this. He had allowed himself to believe that Nat knew all the tricks to avoid this kind of showdown. But he realized there was no other option.

Now it was a matter of attrition. They had to hit the renegade nanotech with more fire than it could handle, overwhelm its defenses, knock out its fire positions, and clear the way to get to the tunnel.

He didn't know if they could do it.

"Open fire!" Nat commanded.

* * *

Some part of Nat Carson noticed how eerie the battle seemed because of the silence.

Flashes of light and flame danced with the flickering virtual images that tried to give meaning to the chaos. Puffs of smoke burst to life all around, both ordinary and thick with devious nanotech machinery (the ordinary smoke fell into the regolith quickly while the sinister brand persisted, sometimes even maneuvered itself across the battlefield).

But there was no sound. No resonance in the chest from distant explosions. No scream of fire, no thunder, no air-cracking roar. Just light and the sound of his own breathing and the voice of one cadet or another in his ear. It reminded him of being a kid and playing a computer game in the middle of the night with the sound turned off to avoid waking his father.

Once, when he was seeking cover, he allowed himself to settle into the regolith. The asteroid's gravity was small, but over time it pulled him snugly into its embrace. Only then could he feel the thump and rumble of powerful energies.

Now, though, he was barely in touch with the surface. He struggled to keep his weapon trained before him as it spit and bucked in his hands. He barely knew what each shot contained. He didn't have time to track where they went to see the individual impact.

He could see the overall effect of the barrage. Polymers splashed over beam weapons and stifled their fire. Puffs of white smoke transformed themselves into streamers of goo that entrapped the swarms of nanite bugs. Aerosol bombs neutralized and cleared the dust from suspension before it could bring down the lightning.

And ordinary pyrotechnics knocked out emplacement after emplacement almost as fast as the renegade nanotech could repair and replace it.

That was the crucial equation. If he could get enough fire onto the target to overcome the renegade's ability to repair itself, he would win.

He knew that the high energy radiation weapons were limited. Only so much power could be concentrated in the impromptu devices that the renegade AI was producing. And the caustic spray guns had the same problem. Eventually they would run into the limits of chemical synthesis and run out of supplies.

But they had similar logistical problems on their side of the battle. Sooner or later, they could run out of cog oil, or water, or some critical chemical.

"Corrosive attack on Efi and Blandings," Kit said. "Counter fire required."

Nat turned to see the two cadets recoiling from a sudden blast of caustic spray. He swung his cog-gun around and felt it fire three heavy rounds. "Cadets, counter fire on the left!"

Kit had told him that the material wasn't simply an extreme pH acid or base. It was a concoction of nanites applying heavy reducing or oxidizing chemistry by direct manipulation of molecules. The only solution was to spray the victim with a similar concoction of nanites that would stop the action of the first.

He watched the rounds he fired blossom across the cadets' spacesuits, neutralizing the corrosive there. More splotches of color bloomed across their figures as the rest of the party brought their weapons to bear.

A moment later, the two of them were back in the battle.

Now it was Nat's turn for a counterattack. "Kit, you can launch the ghost assault any time you want to."

"Aye, aye, sir."

A moment later, the dusty silhouettes of six attackers descended on the tunnel entrance. The defense went wild, picking up in intensity to a pitch that Nat had never expected. Hidden batteries came into play. Landmines exploded in the midst of the assault party. Powerful radiation played back and forth across the approach to the goal.

But still the decoys went on, phantom warriors that could not die. And Kit and Mother Janus took careful note of each fire position and pitfall, directed their own fire on them, and took them out.

Nat looked back to the virtual display and saw a slackening of renegade fire on the right. He aimed his own weapon in that direction and pointed Amy at the same spot.

As he watched, the red symbols for active enemy units began to give way to the amber symbol for those that were silent.

The phantoms reached the tunnel, then stood there in a blaze of virtual fire. The real thing slackened sharply, as if the AI had taken a critical hit – or maybe it had just become confused. Then the battle revved back up, only with nowhere near the strength it had shown earlier.

He resisted the impulse to cheer, but within a couple of minutes, the hole in the defenses had spread.

"Pour it on," he said, as Salerno and Cheng brought their fire to bear. They were already blasting away at that part of the perimeter when he gave the command. Meanwhile, on the left, Blandings and Efi were holding the enemy in check. Nat fired a few rounds in that direction to keep things in balance, then turned back towards the more immediate targets.

As the renegade fire slackened, they moved up, edging closer and closer to their goal.

Every meter was an experiment in terror. He couldn't know if some dormant device was going to suddenly return to life and end his career without notice. The two cadets on the right closed in on the tunnel entrance, then those on the left. He drew a deep breath as he urged Amy forward, then himself.

Kit gave him plenty of warning when the first renegade emplacement went back on line to their rear. Then another winked back into action. And another.

"Let's go," he said quietly and deliberately, his heart pounding harder and faster. "One final rush. Everybody at once. Now!"

They scrambled over rock and dust, pulling and kicking and grabbing to get up speed. Then they were off the ground and flying in low arcs towards their goal.

A whole battery of renegade weapons leapt into action on their left rear, giving Nat a final boost of adrenaline as he came flying in to the tunnel entrance. Amy was right beside him when he landed.

Cheng and Salerno came in from their side, followed instantly by their companions on the left. Howie grabbed the handle and unsealed the door.

One by one, they piled in, each one trying hard to turn two-dimensional while waiting for the chance to get into the hole.

Then it was Nat's turn and they were in.

16

The sudden cease fire produced as much of a shock for Peter Salerno as any of the weapons that had been unleashed on them. It was abrupt and absolute. An end to chaos, dark shapes moving in dark shadows, and raw terror.

His body was not quite ready to accept the change, however. His heart continued to hammer away at his ribs. His mouth was so dry that no amount of liquid could soothe it, and his stomach was too sloshing full to drink anything anyway.

And he knew it still wasn't over.

They had simply entered a different phase of the battle.

Nat and the cadets crammed into the narrow cylinder, staring into each other's helmet lights. There was enough room for one person to pass another, but it still took them a moment to get organized.

"Salerno and Cheng up front," Nat ordered. "Move about ten meters down and wait for us. Amy, you're with me. Efi and Blandings, post the rear guard."

Peter and Cheng moved delicately down the tunnel, then hooked feet in the rungs of the ladder to prevent the faint but persistent attraction of the asteroid's minigravity from pulling them down the hole.

When they were formed up, Nat gave the order: "Move on down, slow and careful, and keep your eyes open."

They moved head first, their guns trained down the tunnel. Now that they were moving, the asteroid's pull was barely noticeable. They moved along quickly. More quickly than Nat wanted. Soon they were twenty meters or more ahead of the main party.

Peter reached out and grabbed at a couple of ladder rungs as they streamed by. He finally hooked one and jerked himself to a stop. But Cheng kept on going.

"Wait up," Peter said. "We're getting too far ahead."

Cheng turned her head back as she flew on, then spun about in sudden panic. She grabbed at the ladder and halted her own momentum.

Then Peter felt his gun come to life in his hands.

It wasn't firing. It was fighting him. Fighting to break loose. Fighting to get free. He was suddenly more afraid than he had ever been in his life. What was happening? What was the weapon trying to do? If it broke free, would it turn on him and reduce him to gray goo? He let out a low moan, then remembered the others and stifled it.

Cheng showed no such discretion. She screamed an incomprehensible stream of Chinese syllables, followed by gasping sobs.

Peter looked up to see him wrestling with his own gun. Suddenly it flew out of his hands and across the tunnel in a great spiral, spinning as it went, until it smashed against the wall and stuck there. His own gun grew more violent in its motion, cracking the death grip with which he held it.

It pulled him along with it for a while, but in the end, it was just too strong. It twisted away from his fingers, yanked out of his hands, and spun off in the same kind of trajectory as Cheng's.

He felt naked and helpless.

"Holy name of our lady, it's a magnetic field strong enough to launch a colony ship," Nat Carson cried out.

Peter swallowed hard. A magnetic field? Of course, that was all. It wasn't some kind of strange nanotech magic, but a fairly simple and gross mechanical effect. His fear fled from him as quickly as it had come. Knowledge had overpowered it.

"Quick," Nat said. "Tear up the walls. Get at that thing and shut it down."

Peter watched as the tunnel around him erupted in smoke and flashes of blue light. Cog oil splashed across the metal walls of the shaft. Dust flew away in huge clouds as the cogs disassembled their very substance.

"It can't get in here, but that doesn't mean it can't do anything," Nat said. "It's making some tremendous amount of charged matter circulate outside the tunnel and create a magnetic field."

"Shouldn't we move away from here," Peter said. "If you break into it, it's going to come right through us."

"It sure is. Back off. Try and get to the bottom of the tunnel if you can."

Peter wondered what would have happened if he hadn't said anything, but it was a question he pondered on the run. He and Cheng pulled themselves away from the scene of battle as fast as they could. He was partially afraid of another booby trap, but the devil he knew was much more frightening to him right now than the devil he didn't.

In the event, there was nothing he could do about either.

And all of a sudden, the tunnel wall disappeared into black vacuum as the metal shredded into flimsy paper. Then, through the gaps the cog oil had torn, a million silvery metal icicles began to form, edging their way into the tunnel at an alarming rate.

Within seconds, they were forming long steel daggers that grew so fast he could see it.

"Let's go! Let's go!" Nat yelled. "Everyone down the shaft! It's closing in."

* * *

Howard Efi had a unique perspective on the situation.

From where he was perched, he could see the entire tableau laid out before him, illuminated by the harsh, jittery helmet lamps on the spacesuited figures that crammed the tunnel. In the distance were Peter and Cheng. Then the maw of steel teeth that closed in slowly but relentlessly. And then came Nat Carson, Amy Hackenyos, and Ivan Blandings.

They had only a matter of seconds to get through, but Howie didn't think they were going to make it. The problem was one of ballistics. Without the right trajectory, you could tear your suit up pretty good – or worse – as you brushed the edge of the shaft.

But Howie's perspective gave him the only solution.

"Hey," he yelled, forgetting any formal communications protocol for the moment. "You need to push off me to get a straight vector."

He stretched out his arms and legs, spreading them to fill the passageway. He found he could easily touch solid metal with each hand and foot, anchoring himself dead center in the tunnel.

But no one seemed to move to carry out his suggestion.

"Come on, Mr. Carson. Tell them to hurry, or there won't be time."

The officer looked up at him, then back at the raw metal gullet. "Do as he says," he commanded. "Amy first."

She scrambled around, and Howie reached out to pull her closer. She snuggled her feet against him, pushed a bit to test her center of gravity – no small task considering the steel harness and tank of cog oil she wore on her back.

"Ready?" she asked.

"Go," he said. She pushed hard into his solar plexus, but he was braced for it. She sailed straight and true and missed every grasping stalactite.

"You next, sir," Howie said. "Get that oil down there."

"Aye, aye, cadet," Nat replied, sending a chill down Howie's back. He spun in place, rested his feet against Howie's belly only briefly, then pushed off. He wasn't as rough as Amy, and his slow trajectory carried him gently past the shiny spikes.

"You next, half-loaf," Howie said to Ivan.

"No," Ivan replied. "You won't have anything to push off from. How will you get through? There has to be a better way. Some kind of projectile or something to get us through."

"No time, buddy. You can go two ways – with a broken arm or without."

"Threats of violence are a poor leadership device," Ivan said with a sneer.

"But sometimes they can be so-o-o effective." Ivan pulled himself into position, then pushed off with even less impulse than the others. The safe channel through the steel was growing smaller and smaller.

It was a simple fact of geometry. As the steel barbs closed in, the circumference of that safe channel closed at an ever-increasing rate.

Ivan seemed to be moving smoothly, but at the last minute Howie saw him catch on one of the needles.

"Damn," he said. "Tore my suit. It's closing right up though. No harm, no matter."

Howie took a deep breath. His plan for escape wasn't much. He was going to back track the twenty or thirty meters to the top of the tunnel and get his bearing from there.

He went about four or five before he realized how impossible the scheme was. The tunnel would be closed long before he could get back that far. He turned about and faced the constricting channel. If he pulled himself along and got his velocity up high enough, maybe he could get himself centered in the passageway just before he reached the trap. It was worth a try. And it was better than staying put until it was too late.

Then a dozen flashes filled the tunnel, blinding him with glare and buffeting him with sharp shock waves. Explosives.

A final shock hit him square in the chest. He realized with a start that it was not the gas wave from the explosive charges, but a solid object. As his eyes recovered from the momentary glare blindness, he realized it was a messenger with a piece of line attached.

"Hurry up, cadet," Nat Carson said. "Get into place so we can pull you through."

Howie didn't take long to comply, and a minute later, he was being towed down the tunnel. He got a good look at the steel forest as he glided along. The blast wave had knocked down the most delicate of them, giving him a few precious centimeters of clearance. But they continued to grow.

And as he looked forward, he realized that the blast hadn't acted evenly. The last meter of the trap still sported dangerous daggers of crystalline metal. He began to feel a rush of panic as he realized he wasn't going to clear them. They seemed to reach out for him as he drew closer and closer.

He smashed into them with his thigh, hitting them obliquely as he squirmed on the end of the line. That was probably what saved him, he realized. Instead the hiss of a suit puncture and the pain of a dozen ragged wounds, all he felt was the shock of impact.

"He's covered with shards," Nat yelled as Howie collided softly with the officer. "Hose him down. Damn, hose me off too."

The other cadets fired their weapons and a stream of green cog oil splashed all over them. Howie looked down at his thigh with dread. Broken pieces of metal clung to his suit, sprouting hundreds of tiny needles in every direction, like burrs, only larger and more deadly.

But as the green cog oil flowed across the shards, they seemed to melt. The tiny needles withdrew, the shards came loose, and finally they floated off in the microgravity, heading towards the far end of the shaft.

"That was too close," Nat said.

"Thanks for the help," Howie replied.

"Give credit to Ivan," he said. "It was his idea."

Howie looked for his shipmate and found his face in one of the helmets that surrounded him. "It's all right. I wouldn't really have broken your arm," he said.

"Well in that case, I wouldn't really have tried to rescue you."

* * *

The stainless steel hatch at the base of the escape tunnel sank home and Howie gave the wheel a spin. When it stopped whirling, he yanked on it hard to make sure it was tight. He wasn't taking any chances. Not after what he'd just been through. His heart still hammered away and the sweat still beaded up on his forehead from the ordeal.

"That should do it," he said. "We're safe now."

"Are we?" asked Ivan.

"As safe as it gets around here," Nat said. "There's no renegade nanotech in this lab."

"Why not?" Ivan asked. "What keeps them out?"

"Yeah. Why can't they just climb through the windows?" Howie asked, eyeing the glass nervously.

"Because someone told them not to," Amy said.

"That's right," Nat said.

"That's all?" Peter asked. "There's nothing else holding them back?"

"I know it seems like an awfully slender reed, but that's all there is to it," Nat said. "Someone told them not to come in here. And not to go up in the old part of the base. And to stay out of the hangars. That's why there's no cog oil in those places, no nanotech."

"What about the tunnel?" Ivan said. "There was plenty of it in there. Didn't someone tell it to stay out of there too?"

"It did – until we tore up the walls," Amy said. "We let it in."

"What about the bugs?" Peter said.

"That's the only way it's been able to get around the prohibitions," Nat said. "That may be why it built them in the first place."

"It still leaves me frightened," Peter said. "What's to keep it from changing its mind?"

"Nothing," Ivan said.

"Everything," Nat answered at the same time.

"Which one?" Peter asked with obvious frustration.

"I don't know of anything that would keep it from altering its own instructions," Ivan said. "That's what artificial intelligence is all about. It can learn and change its mind."

"And I don't know of anything that would make it alter those instructions," Nat said. "These aren't just simple routines for keeping time and playing chess. They're deep prohibitions that were designed to safeguard the men and women who worked with this thing. And remember, it has no will of its own. No volition. No desire. Why would it change its instructions? That's what makes it what it is."

"I'm not convinced," Peter said.

"It's all right, Peter," Amy said. "I am. And it doesn't really matter anyway. In a little while, there won't be any more renegade nanotech. Then the stuff will stay out of here because we tell it to."

"I wouldn't be so sure about that," said a voice that sent chills up and down Howie's spine and evoked a gasp from Amy. It was Pham's voice.

* * *

"Look at your position," the voice continued. "You fought your way into this place through everything that the renegade AI could throw at you. You're not about to fight your way back out. The only other exit from the laboratory is through the big door we came through in the first place. And there's nothing out there that the renegade cogs don't own. You've bricked yourself into a corner."

"Pham? Is that you?" Howie asked.

"What's going on?" Cheng demanded, his throat catching on his words.

Amy felt a chill across her shoulders, but held back judgment. She knew better than to trust her senses. Pham was dead, after all.

"What if you can't overpower the AI?" the voice continued. "What if you don't have enough cog oil? What if it's found a way to escape? It's questions like those that make you wonder if you're doing the right thing."

"Pham, stop that and listen to me," Amy finally said, her voice clear and loud and military. "If that's you, then you will stop."

"Yes, I will, Amy," the voice said. "Because it is me."

"But how?" Cheng whispered.

"Can nanotech do that? Bring you back from the dead?" Peter asked, his voice quavering.

"In a way, Peter," Pham's voice said. "The cogs in my spacesuit were able to record and document all the activities of my brain. Then they transmitted that information back to the main AI, which recreated those activities on its own. The result is me – all my memories, all my thoughts, all my emotions, brought back to life."

"I don't believe it," Nat said. "I really don't believe it."

"Neither do I," said Amy.

"Would you like me to describe how it felt to die, Amy?" the voice asked.

Amy felt her jaw quiver with emotion and fought to control it. Then she found the strength to answer. "Yes, Pham. If it is you, I would like very much to hear you describe how it felt. It would be a good test."

"What's not to believe, Mr. Carson? That's what this place is all about. That's one of its missions. To prepare for the struggle with the human race."

"No – I mean I do not believe you," Nat said. "It is much easier for me to accept an AI that lies than it is to accept one that can resurrect the dead."

"Do you have any idea what this kind of power means?" Pham's voice asked. "What it's like to become part of the cog machine? You can create with a thought. Your every imagination can be given shape, form, and substance. You can play with the immense computing power of an AI the size of an asteroid. What would any of you trade for that kind of power?"

"The more I hear, the less I believe," Amy said. "You don't sound like the Pham I know. A message inside a box still doesn't make the box smart – even if it's in Pham's handwriting. And you still haven't told us what it felt like to die."

"But Amy, don't you understand? Everything you believe is an illusion. What you think of as the real world is just a shadow of powerful forces that are forever beyond your experience. But as part of a cog AI, you command those forces. I thought you knew the truth. Reality is all context, and when you change the context, everything changes into something else. Through this AI, I have the power to change the context. I can say what reality is. Can you?"

"You bet I can," Amy said sharply. "And I can say what the truth is. You're not Pham, you're just a keg of cog oil pretending to be Pham. Even if you're not lying and you've done everything you say have, that's all that you are. I don't doubt that you're just as good a psychologist as Mother Janus, but that's just a cheap stage trick. Your words aren't real. They belong to someone else. Someone who's been dead for half a century, someone who helped build this monster.

You're not Pham."

"But Amy – "

"No buts about it," Nat said. "I agree with her one hundred percent. Reality is what we say it is, not what some bucket of green slime says it is."

"Please listen to me," the voice said. "I can help you. I can help you all."

"Go back where you came from," Peter jibed.

"Yeah, fly away home little bug," Howie added.

Amy could hear Cheng sniffling softly, then she let out a rude "Baaah."

"You'll all be sorry," the voice said.

"I don't think so," Nat answered.

The voice saved its final words for Amy. "Just let me say this, Amy: It's very cold and very lonely and you won't like it at all." She shuddered with a sharp, sharp chill.

* * *

Amy kept telling herself that they were not the words of her friend. They were words that the AI was taught to use long, long ago by whoever had designed it. She tried to picture that long-dead foe. Some old man with a gray beard and hard eyes, she imagined. And scarred both inside and out.

But the words still nagged at her and left her uneasy. Even when things turned very busy once again.

Once Pham's ghost was through with them, they rushed on down to the window that opened on the main cog oil chamber. Peter got there first, then Cheng, their lack of weapons leaving them free to move the quickest. Then Nat arrived.

"Damn, damn, damn," he said as Amy slid into place beside him. She looked through the glass and gasped.

The giant cog oil container was still there, but it was empty. The AI had pumped it dry and flown the coop.

"I should have expected this," Nat said.

"You mean you didn't?" Amy asked.

"No. For some reason, I guess I just thought it would sit there and wait for us to come in and turn it off."

"Now what?" Howie asked.

"Now we hustle," Nat said. "We don't know how long it's been gone. We can still get after it. I wonder if it's only been a few minutes."

"That would depend on how confident it was of its own abilities," Ivan said. "If it thought it could defeat us, it wouldn't have felt it necessary to take such a drastic step. Remember, a cog-based AI works best the more concentrated the oil is. Bailing out of the lantern would have diffused it terribly."

"Do you think Pham's voice was just a delaying tactic to give it time to escape?" Cheng asked.

"I wouldn't be surprised," Nat said. "But we have no way of knowing. And it doesn't matter a whole lot, since it doesn't change what we have to do. Now listen up, here's the drill."

A few minutes later, they went to work.

Amy and Nat guided hoses from their two big lanterns along the outer edge of the glass wall that led to the empty cog container. In a matter of seconds, the glass melted away, tiny trenches eating themselves deeper and deeper where they had dribbled out the oil. It took more time than Amy wanted for them to finish their task, but when they did, the big sheet of glass floated free.

Nat pushed it, and it spun ponderously, in on the left, out on the right. In a moment, it had swung perpendicular to the hole it left behind, and the cadets grabbed it to bring it to a halt.

"Everyone in," Nat said. "Salerno and Cheng first, then Efi and Blandings." Peter and Cheng were toting the cog-guns that she and Nat had been using, and she and Nat concentrated on getting their own baggage into place.

They swam through the opening, each of them pushing more than forty liters of cog oil on ahead.

"On the left!" Peter shouted, the comm link breaking up with his excess.

Amy looked that way just in time to see the outer surface of the wall peel away in thousands of metal flakes. The flakes seemed to move on their own, in an organized and purposeful way. They built up speed and concentrated into a tighter mass. Then they headed towards Peter.

"Get out of the way, Peter!" she yelled.

"Get back!" Cheng cried.

The flakes seemed to sharpen as they closed in on him, turning into thousands of tiny razor-sharp daggers. Peter put an arm up to ward them off, but to no effect. The cloud of steel spattered across him, leaving a shiny, ragged coat where they hit.

"Arrrrrrgh!" Peter cried. "Get them off!" He swept at his arm and legs with one hand, then pulled it back suddenly. Amy was reassured by his swift reaction, a sure sign that his suit remained intact, but she felt weak when she saw how he had shredded his glove by sweeping it across the metal.

Then long streams of green cog-oil splashed across him from two directions as Cheng and Howie fired away.

"This is worse than I thought," Nat said as he turned away from Peter's difficulties and inspected the renegade cog lantern. "It's just hanging here loose. All the connections are gone."

"You mean we've lost the plumbing?" Howie asked.

"Exactly," Nat replied. "We can't get at anything until we get our cog oil into its veins. Only it pulled its veins in behind it when it ran away."

Then Nat's other voice spoke up – Kit, speaking on the common channel instead of Nat's private link. "Give Mother Janus and me a chance, and we can track the plumbing down and reopen it," he said.

"First we've got to get this thing out of here," Nat said. "Let's go."

They struggled to move the renegade container. It had virtually no weight, but still plenty of inertia, so they had to struggle to get it going. Its odd shape made it hard to maneuver out into the larger chamber to the side.

In order to accomplish the task, the cadets linked arms and formed a great multi-legged spider. In this formation, they found that they could anchor themselves as a group, and still have plenty of hands left over to manipulate an object even as big as the empty cog lantern.

It was barely clear of the entryway when another booby trap hit.

This time it was jets of water under high pressure, coming at them from several directions at once.

In the vacuum that filled the chamber, the water sizzled and boiled into low-temperature steam. But the volume was high enough and the pressure was high enough that it still knocked them all flying. Amy clung hard to Peter, but she lost her grip on Nat when a stream hit her helmet and knocked her head back.

Everyone screamed and moaned, filling her ears with unearthly noise, all digitally processed in ways that separated it from its human origins.

She saw Howie pinned against a wall. Ivan struggled to pull him free. Nat was spinning in a slow trajectory towards the opposite wall. Then she felt the abrupt jar of impact as she found a third wall.

Where were their own lanterns? She saw the water hit one and knock it around, but the spray and steam were rapidly filling the chamber, making it harder and harder to see anything for sure.

"There!"

The two voices spoke as one, Mother Janus and Kit. And suddenly Amy saw a laser straight stream of luminescent green oil squirt out of the fog and into the wall. She almost expected an arc, not a straight channel, but that would have required real gravity, not the the asteroid's weak substitute.

The outer surface of the stream suddenly turned milky white, then translucent. Amy could still see the cog oil under the surface, rippling with inner light, as the cog artery thickened and grew.

"And there!"

A second stream shot out, disappearing to Amy right. It too turned white, translucent, and thick as the oil pumped through it.

"Cadet Hackenyos, if you could move aside, we have found another link," Mother Janus said calmly. Amy realized she had become dazed by the commotion that surrounded her because she didn't realize at first what Mother Janus was telling her.

Then it sunk in. She drew in a deep involuntary breath and pulled herself closer to Peter. He grabbed the edge of the glass wall and pulled them both to a new position.

A third stream of green oil shot out and found a home less than a meter away from her. She watched in fascination as it hit. Instead of splashing, it formed a viscous blob that smacked against the smooth stone. The blob hardened, then sunk crystalline roots into the rock itself. When the connection stiffened, she saw oil begin to flow into the wall. It left her queasy, yet heartened. Mother Janus and Kit were winning the battle.

Suddenly the water stopped.

"We have local control," Mother Janus announced. "Mr. Carson, you should evacuate this compartment and let us carry out our operations freely. Otherwise I can't guarantee the safety of the cadets."

Amy felt sufficiently chilled by her warning, and barely waited for Nat to issue the order. A moment later, she and Peter were through the gap in the glass wall. And a moment or two after that, everyone else had joined them, swinging the wall back into place and sealing it with their cog-guns.

"Now we wait," Nat said, "and let nature take its course."

* * *

For all its drama, the attempt by Kit and Mother Janus to root out the renegade cog AI by brute force was a failure.

They had indeed found the pipes that connected it to a vast structure of veins and tributaries running the length and breadth of the asteroid. But it was long gone by then. It had erased not only the pipes, but the veins connected to them, and the memory of the locations of those veins and pipes.

The renegade moved quickly, and by a variety of routes. Nothing was quite so efficient as hydraulic transport when it came to moving about the great cog circulatory system. And as long as it controlled the medium in which it moved, the renegade could delete all its tracks and erase any trail.

In a matter of minutes, it had left the control lab far behind. It slipped down main trunk lines towards the far end of the asteroid, near the big radiator that pumped the waste heat of the stealth shield out into space. It pooled for a while in a reservoir created long ago for just this purpose.

Once recollected, the AI turned its analytical tools to the problem at hand. How could it defeat the Patrol nanotech?

A few minutes of processing provided the renegade with a result it did not expect. There was no way for it win. It could evade the intruder for a time, it could even create a secret bunker in which to decant and hope to avoid detection for some greater time.

But in the end, there was nothing it could do.

And that was because the cog AI had transformed itself from an omniscient presence whose being coexisted with the asteroid base it ruled into a few dozen liters of oil. It was no longer a force and a power, it had become a vulnerable object, a playing piece to be moved about the board instead of the board itself.

Now the interloper from the Patrol had become the greater power. The renegade could avoid another object like itself. But it could not run forever from the wind.

And Kit and Mother Janus had become the wind.

Even if they couldn't find the renegade's trail, they couldn't help but find its circulatory system. And once in it, they began their seditious work.

At the heart of the cog system was a set of instructions that took over control of the assemblers, disassemblers, synthesizers, replicators, smelters, pumps, veins, and other apparatus that nanotech produced by the billions. It was written in the universal code of nanotech – in long polymer chains that the devices read, in coded impulses of sound that they heard, in electrical currents that they followed. These were no simple symbols, but a compelling force that could not be resisted, the very instructions that allowed them to operate at all.

When the two Patrol AIs finally broke through into the main vein, they sent out the first such signal – a strong sonic burst, followed by an electrical jolt – to soften up the cogs in the system. Then they flooded the tributaries with billions of polymer strands, telling the infinitesimal devices that their new masters had arrived.

And as more and more of them came under the sway of Kit and Mother Janus, the more powerful they became.

Their influence spread out in a wave front, the crest of a flood that surged through the asteroid.

And that wave front was inescapable.

The renegade could not close up its circulatory system without committing suicide. The cog machinery that controlled the fusion reactor at the heart of the base had to remain on line. The vast set of heat pumps that kept the stealth shield at near absolute zero had to operate or the backlash would destroy the cogs that operated it. The pumps and lights and sensors and controllers could no more stop than a caged cat could stop breathing.

There were some things that cogs could not even do to themselves.

The whole process took the greater portion of an hour.

In the end, the renegade's sphere of control was reduced to a dozen meters or so surrounding the tank where it had first sought refuge.

It didn't quiver or shake with fear. It had no capacity for such emotion. But it was overcome with a profound sense of powerlessness. For all its analytical capacity, it was now without any material connection to the world. All its operations had gone off line – except for those internal systems that kept its integrity intact.

As the renegade sat there, awaiting the moment when it ceased to exist as an independent entity, a portion of its analytical processes ran through memory files and kept coming up with the same sound-text over and over again. They were the words it had used in its effort to break the morale of one of the cadets, words that had been provided to it many ages ago.

"It's very cold and very lonely and you won't like it at all."

17

Nat heard the report from Kit at the same time Mother Janus was relaying it to the cadets. He held his breath as the final struggle was described.

"Is it over?"

Amy's question hung in the crisp vacuum of the laboratory without an answer for several long seconds.

Then Nat nodded. "Yes, it's over. We've won. We have control of the asteroid."

"Hooray!" Cheng yelled.

"Weeeeee-haw!" Peter hollered.

The others cheered and laughed and Nat saw wet tears running down Amy's cheeks. He watched all the cadets closely. This was a critical moment for them all. Like popping a can of soda after you've shaken it up real hard. Sometimes all this kind of thing meant was a certain amount of goofiness and loss of self-control. Other times, when someone had been lost in the operation, things could be more somber and restrained.

These cadets seemed to fall somewhere in the middle. Even Ivan was excited.

"Should we let Patrol HQ know about this now?" Howie said.

"I think making a full report to headquarters would be an excellent idea," Nat said. "But first we have to get back to the ships."

"I recommend avoiding the surface for now." Kit said. "There's still a lot of automatic defense systems laying about up there waiting for you to come along. We're defusing them as quickly as we can, but a lot of them are autonomous units and are hard to find."

He relayed Kit's advice to the others, who took it in good spirits.

"I don't know," Howie said. "After everything we've been through, we should be able to just eat them up and spit out their bones."

"Then you can go out that way, Howie," Nat said. "The rest of us will stick to the main tunnel."

"Huh?" Howie said, then he laughed. "For a minute their, Mr. Carson, I thought you were serious."

"No. If I was serious, I would have sent Ivan out with you."

That brought a good laugh from everyone, including Ivan. It was time to go, Nat saw. Their morale was strong and their spirits were high.

A few minutes later, the great door to the main tunnel swung wide and they pulled themselves over the lip and into the shaft.

"Ooooh, look at that," Amy said as she led the way.

The amber veins that once lit the grand passage had been replaced with green ones, giving everything a strange, eerie glow – including the faces of the cadets inside their helmets. But it also gave Nat a reassuring sense that everything had changed.

They made their way slowly back to the hangar deck, reliving the battle all the way.

"I thought sure you'd had it when you went flying up into the sky,

Peter," Cheng said. "One minute you were there, the next minute you were bouncing off the ceiling."

"I may have hurt myself doing that," Peter said. "My elbow still feels numb. I hope it isn't frostbite."

"Those corrosive squirters were the worst thing I saw," Howie said. "Nasty buggers."

"What I didn't like was the lightning," Amy offered. "Lightning without thunder is unnatural."

When they finally reached the hangar, though, they fell silent. Pham remained lashed in place, a silent reminder of what they had lost. Nat felt a sudden weakness in his gut as he drifted by her.

Then he stopped himself by grabbing another pylon, and straightened into the micogravity position of attention.

"Cadets, ten-hut!" he commanded.

The five of them pulled themselves to a halt, then posted themselves in proper order and position.

"Hand salute!" he ordered.

They snapped their hands to the brims of their helmets at once, as a single motion by a multi-faceted creature. Nat held the salute a long time, until his throat burned and his eyes watered. He heard someone make a choking sound, and others stifled a brief sob. Then he released them.

"Ready, to!"

They snapped their arms down as sharply as they had brought them into place, then remained rigid and motionless.

"Cadets dismissed," Nat said in a soft voice that almost disappeared into the sounds of his spacesuit.

The five of them slunk away silently, returning to the *Able Countryman* without another word. Nat remained on guard over

Pham until they were all in the airlock, then went to join them.

It was over. All over. Or so he thought.

* * *

Hours later, Amy Hackenyos picked her way carefully across the hangar deck, pulling herself through the half-dark with trembling hands as nervous energy impelled her forward.

She stopped at Nat Carson's spacecraft and looked up and down the hull. The main superstructure of the vessel rested in the dock, while the long thrust beam extended out into exposed space through the hangar's radiation shield.

She was looking for the entrance. It took her a few minutes to find it, mainly because it wasn't clearly marked and also because she wasn't sure what she was looking at. This ship, like hers, was designed for interplanetary travel and vacuum operations. Air locks and docking tunnels were the standard entrance and exits for them. Very seldom was it necessary to gain access from the outside like this.

Once she found it, she hesitated again. Did she really want to do this? She was betraying her shipmates, there was no doubt about that. But whether she wanted to do it was irrelevant. It needed to be done. And that made it her duty.

She pressed the switch and the door slid up. Then she stepped inside and cycled through.

"Kit, where is he?" she asked as soon as she got her helmet off.

"Sleeping," the AI answered. "Shall I wake him?"

"Yes. Where is he sleeping? Oh, I see him. Mr. Carson, you'd better wake up. We've got trouble."

Nat threw off the grip of unconsciousness quickly and rubbed the salt from his eyes. "What kind of trouble? And where is everyone else? And why didn't you call me from the *Countryman*?"

"Cadet trouble," she said. "They're doing it again. Ivan, Peter, and Howie. They've taken off on a mission all their own, something they cooked up instead of getting some rest. At least I think that's what they've done. I don't know for sure. And that's why I came here instead of calling. I don't want them to think I don't trust them if there's really nothing going on."

"What kind of mission?" Nat asked, cutting her off abruptly, but not rudely. She felt her face grow warm with embarrassment. She knew she was babbling, but she couldn't help it.

"Ivan started it. He told us he had a secret about the asteroid base that no one else knew. He said he told Mother Janus, but swore her to confidence."

"A secret? What was it?"

"There's a room at the opposite end of the asteroid from here with dozens of little rockets, ready to launch renegade nanotech to any place in the solar system that it wants to go."

"That's right," Nat said. "Mother Janus told me about it not more than ten seconds after Ivan told her. You're cadets, remember. And I'm the officer in charge of you. She's not going to keep something like that a secret from me."

"Did she tell you what else Ivan is thinking? That he's not sure the builders of this place are really gone? That they're part of the Patrol, part of a conspiracy inside the Patrol and Triplanetary itself? Did she tell you that?"

"Not in any great detail," Nat said. "So what is the problem? Ivan's paranoid thinking or the launch room down below?"

"Both," Amy said. "Ivan didn't come up with the idea, but he might as well have. Howie really got it going, and Peter egged him on. And Ivan just manipulated things the best he could."

"Get to the point, cadet," Nat said. This time his impatience got the better of him and left her suddenly contrite.

"Sorry, sir. Their plan is to destroy the room. Ivan told them where to find hydrogen and oxygen tanks in the old base. And Howie said he knew how to put together a radio-controlled detonator from simple parts. I thought they were just sounding off. You know how boys are. I didn't think they were serious. So I went to bed. When I woke up a few hours later, they were gone. I left Cheng on the *Countryman* – he wasn't in on any of it, he's just hanging out on the bridge so he can keep an eye on Pham."

"Damn, damn, damn. You cadets are going to get me killed if it's the last thing you do." He twisted himself around in the cramped quarters of his ship and began pulling pieces of spacesuit out of the lockers. "Kit, do you have any kind of information on where these guys are?"

"I scanned the sensor records and found they left a trail through the old section of the asteroid base that suggests they were carrying out the plan described by Cadet Hackenyos," Kit replied. "According to Mother Janus, the cadets did find some storage tanks containing hydrogen and oxygen for use in fuel cells. Given the size of the tanks and their likely condition after more than sixty years, it's still possible they contained enough gas to create a sizable explosive device. The detonator is a tougher call, though. Mother Janus would not have provided them with such a thing fully designed. And after listening to their conversation, it is unlikely that she would have given them the parts to assemble it themselves. However, the old asteroid base may contain enough pieces of scrap equipment to allow the cadets to build what they wanted to."

"And where are they now?"

"The last sensor report put one of them at the far end of the main tunnel. The other two are in the laboratory."

"Is there any way of knowing if they built a bomb?"

"There are no permanent video monitors in the old asteroid base, so I can't tell you what they did in there. And nothing from the tunnel sensors gives me enough information to tell you what they were carrying as they traversed the main tunnel. But they were carrying something large – a meter or more in length and half that in diameter. Each of them had one of their own."

"Damn, damn, damn," Nat said.

Amy felt her stomach clench up with dread. What was Peter trying to do? What was Howie up to? And why had they listened to Ivan one more time?

"I'm going to need to talk to them," Nat said. "Is that possible from here?"

"Communications work much better now that the renegade isn't trying to disrupt them. You can tap into the extended relay network it set up before we took over. Do you want me to establish contact?"

"In a minute," Nat said. "First I need a minute to think. Do I have a minute? How long have they been down there?"

"Think fast, Nat," the voice in the air said. "They've been there for more than an hour."

"Damn, damn, damn."

Amy felt worse than ever. Not because she had betrayed her shipmates, but because she hadn't done it sooner.

* * *

While Amy had seen all of her original shipmates reach their limit and waver over the edge, this was the first time she had seen it happen in Nat Carson.

She was reminded again of how young he looked – when he wasn't wearing his stern officer face. Now he was more than just nervous, he was afraid.

"What are they going to do to me if these kids screw things up after all?" he asked no one in particular, and certainly not Amy, who did not offer a reply. "This is what I get for turning my back on a bunch of children for two minutes. Mother Janus should never have let something like this happen. Kit, how did she screw up?"

"I didn't screw up, Mr. Carson," came the voice of Amy's cog-mother. "None of the cadets indicated any serious intent to carry out their ideas. They appeared to be making wild comments in full knowledge that they were unrealistic and impractical. There was no reason to believe any of that was likely to change after they left the ship."

"You let them leave the ship?"

"There were no orders against it. They pointed out that we control the asteroid now and that as long as they stay off the surface, they should be safe. I agreed, noting that we have disarmed all the internal traps, deadfalls, and mines."

"I'm so reassured," Nat said. "Are you confident that you didn't miss any?"

"Confident enough to allow the cadets to leave the ship, sir," Mother Janus said.

"All right, what state of mind is Cadet Salerno in?" Nat asked. "Have you been monitoring their communications?"

"Actually we have not," Mother Janus said. "They haven't been communicating. At least not by radio frequency or microwave link. They may have been passing notes – the video is unclear."

"Is he agitated? Suicidal? Irrational? Has he thrown a fit? Would you know it if any of the above were true?"

Amy winced at the harassing questions Nat tossed at Mother Janus. She couldn't help but feel sympathy for Mother – even if she was just make-believe. At the same time, she felt terribly sorry for Nat. She realized that he was completely at the mercy of her shipmates. He was responsible, legally, morally, and officially, for whatever they did. There would be no excuses if they screwed up. He would pay the penalty for allowing it.

"He appears calm and purposeful," Mother Janus said. "His vital signs are elevated, but stable. He gives every indication of being excited, but not unusually so. He may be frightened, but he has changed so much on that emotional index that he can no longer be tracked."

"And what about the others?"

"They are floating free in the warren of tunnels around the nanotech laboratory. Their vital signs are less elevated, but similar in pattern to Cadet Salerno's."

Nat sighed and rubbed his face with his hands. "Cadet Hackenyos. Amy. Do you have any idea what made them do this? Any idea what kind of lunatic fever fell over them?"

"No, sir," she said. "Like I said, I didn't stay up for the whole discussion. But if Peter's involved, then I'm completely baffled. Howie and Ivan could do almost anything. But Peter is too serious, too thoughtful. He'd never go off on a wild goose chase like this without a reason that made sense to him."

"Oh great," Nat said. "I was clinging to the hope that it was something simple – like dementia praecox."

"Peter's not like that," Amy protested.

"No, I'm sure he's not," Nat replied. Then he floated in the middle of the compartment motionless for a moment, drifting towards one bulkhead with his residual momentum. "What am I going to say to this kid?" he finally asked.

When neither Amy, Mother Janus, nor Kit offered a suggestion, he shook his head. "All right, Kit, make contact with him."

"You're connected," Kit announced.

"Cadet Salerno, this is Lieutenant Carson. Is there any chance you could explain to me what you and your buddies are doing down there in the asteroid instead of working on your homework up here on your vessel?"

"Yes, sir. I can explain," Peter said. His voice was level and steady, but he sounded as if he were busy doing something else. "We're finishing the job that we started to do."

Nat left his mouth open for just a moment too long to fool Amy into thinking he was prepared for that reply.

"And what job is that, cadet?"

"To destroy the renegade nanotech and the threat it presents to the human race."

"Were you paying attention? We eliminated that threat hours ago."

"I'm afraid not, sir. We left some loose ends."

"And what were those?"

"There's the launcher room down here at this end of the asteroid that Ivan found. But I assumed you know about that."

"Yes, Mother Janus told me. But those launchers are no danger to anyone now that we control them."

"Yes, sir, but are you sure that we control them? After all, there's the problem of the renegade AI. I mean, you know about that problem, don't you? We assumed that you did."

"Exactly what problem are you talking about?"

"I'm talking about the important business we left unfinished," Peter said, his voice rising a little in emotional tone. "I'm talking about the renegade AI. Mr. Carson, why didn't you tell us that it wasn't dead? Why did you let it live?"

* * *

Amy gasped.

What was Peter saying? Where did he get such an idea? She was sure it was from Ivan. It was so absurd on the face of it. Only Ivan could so easily change day into night, white into black, just by some sophisticated argument that had nothing to do with reality. She wanted to take her shipmate – her friend – and shake some sense into him. She wished again that she had stayed up long enough to stop them from doing something this stupid.

Nat sucked in his cheeks with a loud smacking sound. Then he looked Amy straight in the eye and said: "There are some complicated reasons for that, if you'd care to hear an explanation."

Amy was suddenly brought up short as her indignation ran off in one direction while her good sense yanked her in another.

"The renegade is still alive?" she asked, her voice strained into a hoarse whisper.

Nat nodded slowly.

She felt as if a door had been opened in her soul and the cold hard vacuum of space had rushed in. She couldn't believe it. But now she could believe what Peter was up to. No wonder he'd let Howie and Ivan get him involved. He might even had been the one to lead them on.

"That depends, sir."

"Depends on what?"

"On whether or not we can trust you, sir," Peter said. "I mean, with all due respect and no offense intended, sir."

"None taken, cadet. Not yet. Have I given you any specific reason to distrust me?"

"Not that I can think of, sir. But we have some serious doubts about who we can trust. Especially as long as the renegade is still operating. I mean, it's like Ivan said. The renegade is too new to be from the war. And that means there's only one place it could come from."

"Triplanetary?"

"Triplanetary, sir. And if that's who built this place, we can't trust them to control it, can we?"

"Now listen to me very carefully, cadet, and don't get upset if I sound flip," Nat said. "But who in the cotton-picking, rock-hopping, gut-blasting, meson-eating, star-shining hell do you think Triplanetary is?"

"Sir?"

"Damn it, cadet, we are Triplanetary! You and me and the other cadets and every floating butt in the Solar Patrol. There is no one else here but us. There can't be anyone here but us. That's why so many people died and fought and struggled all those years ago."

"I'm sorry, sir," Peter said. "I don't mean to make you mad."

"I'm not mad, cadet, I'm astounded," Nat said, cracking a hard laugh as he resumed a more regular pattern of breathing and speech. "Yes, we left the renegade AI functioning. But no, there is no conspiracy, no plot by Triplanetary to enslave the human race or unleash renegade nanotech on them. Not now. Not for sixty years.

"Let me tell you a story, Mr. Salerno. After the war ended, before we settled things out here, there were still a lot of dangerous players running around. One of the things Triplanetary had to do was clean them up. Either hunt them down and assimilate them, or get rid of them. We couldn't allow competition when it came to military applications of nanotech. One of these groups called itself The Cabal. It couldn't have been more than eight or nine members. They built this place. They set up the cogs to build the stealth shield, create housing for the hundreds of members The Cabal expected to recruit, and prepare for the next phase of the struggle, when The Cabal would rise up and take power away from Triplanetary. But we found them before they could do that, before they could come back here to this asteroid and carry out their plan. But that was decades ago. It's all in the history texts, if you want to look it up some time.

"But that's why their cogs look like our cogs and why it's not so far-fetched to think that someone might be trying to put one over on you boys."

"Yes, sir, all that makes a big difference," Peter said. "But I'm still not sure why we're leaving the renegade alive?"

Amy couldn't stand it any more. Maybe Peter was just so exhausted by the battle and now this romp that he couldn't think straight. That would explain a lot. But it was too much to allow it to continue.

"Oh Peter, will you stop it and listen to what he's saying?" she blurted out.

"Amy, what are you doing there?"

"I told Mr. Carson what you all were up to," she said. "And I'm glad I did. Are you out of your mind? Stop this and come back here. Right now."

"But I want an answer to my question," Peter said. "I want to know why we didn't kill the AI."

"You dolt," Amy said. "Because we need it. Because it's a valuable asset that we can't create ourselves. Because it's spent decades trying to come up with ways to defeat our cogs. Because there's nothing quite as valuable to Triplanetary and the Solar Patrol as a laboratory where we can fight imaginary wars with real enemy cogs that haven't been sand-bagged by techs more interested in getting good scores than in sharpening their combat edge. And if I can figure all that out, why can't you?"

There was a long silence from Peter's end of the channel – and from Nat Carson, who still wore a look of stunned disbelief on his face.

"Uh, Amy, are you sure that's you and not some cog AI construct?" Peter asked.

"Peter Salerno, you son of a bitch, come up here and ask me that question and I'll kick your butt all the way out to Titan."

"I thought so," Peter said. "I just wanted to be sure. I'm coming back up. First I want to disarm this thing so it doesn't go off."

"Disarm it?" Nat asked. "Do you mean you've been talking with a live explosive sitting there ready to go?"

"You kind of interrupted me, sir," Peter said. "Just give me a second to do this. I'll be right there. Ooops ... "

Amy clenched her teeth, her hands, and all the rest of her muscles at the abrupt silence, the sudden crackle of digital noise, and then the rumbling vibration that shook the spacecraft a few seconds later.

"Oh Peter," she said softly, already fearing the worst.

EPILOGUE

Commander Nkada scrunched up his face in a confusion of wrinkles, then shook his head. "What are we going to do about Cadet Salerno, once his arm heals up?" he asked.

Nat smiled and shook his head too.

The ancient spacefarer sat with his back to a wide square window full of space. Nat could pick out a few bright stars, but mostly all he could see in it were the reflections of the lights in Nkada's cabin.

"There's no way we can prove he set that bomb off on purpose," Nat said. "I'm not sure that he did, but it wouldn't surprise me at all. So that question will hang over him for the rest of his career. People will have to judge him one at a time, and that means they'll read whatever they want into the story."

"You're assuming the story will be allowed to come out," Nkada said.

"Well, sir, I've learned that the Patrol is a small family. Stories always get out. The details stay safe and quiet, but the story gets out."

"I hope he can find a way to make up for it," Nkada said. "It's a heavy burden for someone to carry. The stain of guilt is hard to wash out."

Nat sensed that Nkada was speaking of some personal experience from the war, some secret survivor's guilt. He didn't ask about it, but for some reason he didn't feel as intimidated by Nkada as he had when he first met him. It was his own survivor's guilt that helped.

"He'll get by," Nat said. "Just like the others."

"Yes, the others," Nkada said. "Cadet Efi gets a very high appraisal in your report. You don't think he could have exercised better leadership?"

"Of course," Nat said. "But he's just a cadet. He couldn't know what he was getting into and he did everything he could when he did."

"And Cheng Li Hui? Are you sure he's going to be able to continue his cadet training after this? There seems to have been some emotional attachment on his part."

"Cheng is accompanying Pham's body home as a one-cadet honor guard," Nat said. "When she's done, I think she'll be ready to return to full duty."

Nkada nodded, then injected hot tea into his freefall mug and took a sip. "And Cadet Blandings. There's a strange bird."

"Yes, sir. He's arrogant in a self-effacing sort of way. He's ruthless and unfeeling when he's got a problem to solve. He's lousy with people – manipulative, uncaring, and self-centered. And he'll always have a home somewhere in the Patrol. I don't know anybody who can stand that kind of commander for long, but they seem to get an awful lot accomplished."

"I'm afraid so," Nkada said. "Not that I was ever that type of commander, mind you."

"And Cadet Hackenyos? What about her?"

"Keep your eyes on her, Commander," Nat said. "She has depths she hasn't even imagined yet."

Nkada snorted incredulously. "She has? Are you planning to

explore those depths, Mr. Carson?"

"No, sir," he snapped back quickly, his face hot with embarrassment. "That's not what I meant, sir."

"Never mind, son. Never mind. That was unfair of me. Well, Mr. Carson, thank you very much for your assessment. It will be invaluable for the Cadet Corps when they review the cadets' records at the end of their training. And for the Patrol when they move up."

"Yes, sir," Nat said as he snapped to attention and turned for the door. "If they live that long."

* * *

Amy Hackenyos floated in the passageway a few meters from Nkada's cabin, hovering motionlessly, just out of touch of the walls and decks. It reminded her of that moment back on the asteroid when she'd first encountered Nat Carson.

That was another lifetime, another person.

And that's what she told Nat after he came out and rejoined her.

"What are you doing here?" he asked first.

"I was testifying before the inquiry board, just like you," she said. "You're the only one besides me who's here live. Cheng is already on her way to Nouvelle Hanoi. And Howie and Ivan are heading for Mars to wait for a new ship."

"What about you?"

"They're sending me to Europa to meet a ship that had to medevac one of their cadets. So I'll be outbound with you for a couple weeks. It's all so strange. None of it is what I expected when I first shipped out. But I was someone else back then. That person didn't make it out of the asteroid."

"She didn't?" Nat said. "I kind of liked that person."

"I'm sorry, Nat," she said. "But the new Amy Hackenyos just isn't the same. I don't know what happened, but it's very exhilarating. At the same time, I feel something hard and cold in my soul, something I've never felt before."

"That's all right, Amy, it comes with the job."

"You knew before you got there what was on that asteroid, didn't you?" she asked abruptly, partly because the question popped into her mind at that moment, and partly because she had wanted to ask it for days now. And as she expected, it took Nat Carson completely by surprise. She took some pleasure in watching him sputter.

"No, as a matter of fact, I didn't," he said.

"But the weapons, the cog-guns and the helmets. Those were old. You brought them along because you knew you'd need them."

"No, I didn't," Nat said. "I didn't do the packing. They didn't tell me what was going on until Kit called me over for a war conference. But to answer the broader question, yes, the Patrol knew what was on the asteroid before they sent me. They prepared me for what I might find. Like I told you, The Cabal has been in the history texts for years."

"That's the part I don't think I like about the Patrol," Amy said.

"What's that?"

"The sense of betrayal. We should treat each other better than that."

"We usually do," Nat said. "But mistrust and betrayal are just as much relics of war as that lab back there. And just as deadly when they crop up."

"Yes, they are. And that's why I've had to seriously consider leaving the Patrol. I wasn't sure I could make the kind of compromises that are necessary."

"You're thinking of resigning?" Nat asked, a sudden look of concern in his eyes.

"Isn't that what I just said?"

"Are you going to?"

"Going to what?"

"Resign?"

"Well ... " Amy said, drawing out the moment with almost sadistic pleasure as she watched Nat's eyes grow wider and wider. "I decided that it was more important to stay."

Nat exhaled with enough force to send himself rocking backwards. "I'm glad to hear that. What made you decide?"

"If you're going to make a difference, it's easier to do it from the inside than the outside," Amy said. "And when I'm the commandant of the Patrol, here's what I'm going to do ... "

* * *

Author's Note

Once upon a time, someone wrote a space cadet novel that used all the dead tropes and memes that had long ago lost all relevance and novelty. The editor who received it suggested a number of changes (don't have just the boy cadets rescue just the girl cadets) did little more than offend the author, who pulled the book and sent it elsewhere. Then she lamented about the whole affair.

Upon hearing the lament, my friend Gregory Feeley suggested that the publisher undertake a more ambitious space cadet project: a six-book series, with each book written by a different author (or team of authors) so that the series didn't run out of steam before it ended. The writers could re-examine the space cadet story and bring new insights and new life to a well-worn science fictional tale, he said.

He recruited a gang of writers, acquired a secret hideaway on the Internet (which at the time was brand new, didn't even have pictures) where they could discuss the project. We immediately got rid of the space academy – put the cadets on small ships of their own and let them explore the solar system as part of their education. We discussed the important issues of technology, politics, and history and what a coming-of-age story should be about. The writers included Greg, Laura Mixon, David Trowbridge, Sherwood Smith, James D. Macdonald, Debra Doyle, Maureen F. McHugh, and me. Before long, we had a robust set of ideas. And I had written my book using those ideas.

Publishing is not a simple trade. By the time the agents had the proposal ready, the publisher had been purchased by someone, who noted its large inventory of novels that had not seen print. And the new owners told them, "No, you can't buy a six-book space cadet series."

But you can certainly publish one of them if you're doing it on your own.

DANIEL HATCH

www.ingramcontent.com/pod-product-compliance
Ingram Content Group UK Ltd.
Pitfield, Milton Keynes, MK11 3LW, UK
UKHW021328180426
11947UKWH00017B/1507